The Wine of Violence

The Wine of Violence

JAMES MORROW

Holt, Rinehart and Winston • New York

Published by Holt, Rinehart and Winston,
383 Madison Avenue, New York, New York 10017.
Published simultaneously in Canada by Holt, Rinehart
and Winston of Canada, Limited.

Library of Congress Cataloging in Publication Data
Morrow, James.
The wine of violence.
I. Title.
PS3563.0876W5   813'.54   81-1153
ISBN 0-03-059051-5   AACR2

First Edition

Designer: Amy Hill
Printed in the United States of America
10 9 8 7 6 5 4 3 2 1

Acknowledgments

My gratitude goes to those friends who commented on this novel in its various stages of repair. Some of their names are Linda Barnes, Jean Kilbourne, Lee Richmond, Robert Cohan, Robert Stewart, William Filippone, and Jean Morrow. I am also thankful for the contributions of my editor, Donald Hutter; my agent, Patricia Berens; and my mother, Emily Morrow.

to R.J. Develin, my Uncle Ralph

In the seventh century, the Toltecs, an agricultural people, moved from northern Mexico down into the vicinity of Mexico City. In all of history, there was never a people more civilized or humane. According to the old histories, the Toltecs went to war with wooden swords—so that they would not kill their enemies.

—The Book of Lists

For they sleep not, except they have done mischief; and their sleep is taken away, unless they cause some to fall.

For they eat the bread of wickedness, and drink the wine of violence.

—Proverbs 4:16–17

The Wine of Violence

There was a time, believe it or not, when human beings did each other harm. In the chaotic ages preceding the Stromboli Solution, torture, rape, war, and murder happened almost daily. Violence reigned like a soulless despot. Self-defense was a growth industry.

Scholars today agree that, of all the pre-Stromboli schemes for conquering aggression, only one merits preservation in our collective memory.

This is the story of Quetzalia.

ONE

The Atheist

1

NOTHING IN FRANCIS LOSTWAX'S past experience had prepared him for the sudden disappearance of his native planet.

He was an ardent disciple of natural law. When Francis dropped a fresh ripe mamula, he believed it would fall downward and in no other direction. When he collected a newborn gorgathon from its nest and took it to the laboratory, every particle of his faith told him the mother would follow with rage and stabbing mandibles.

It happened at noon, Nearth Equatorial Time, during the final fifty million kilometers of their return from Arete. He was sitting in his cabin, feeling all plump and dozy after a heavy lunch. Before his eyes, the bland chunks of the Malnovian Asteroid Belt floated like croutons. Boring, he thought. Boring as spacefood. He dialed his holovision monitor into the close-up mode, bypassing the belt. There, that's much better—home.

Viewed from space, Nearth's smooth cyan clouds made her Queen of the Solar System. One would never guess that their undersides were dingy and stinking. The planet approached at velocity-factor one: as per the flight plan, they would get there by coasting, having consumed the last of their fuel yesterday. Leaning forward, Francis punched his cushion till it got fat, then repositioned it under his rump and sat down in front of the monitor, ready to indulge a fine homesickness.

Now he saw it, now he didn't. Nearth was gone. In her place loomed an endless gloating night.

The terror that came cut him loose from everything. He was as lost as his planet. "Good God!" he said out loud, though the truth was he believed in no gods, good or otherwise.

Quivering, Francis sprang from the cushion and dragged his steel boots through the phony magnetic gravity. A back tubeway brought him to *Darwin*'s control deck, where, centerstage, Burne Newman fidgeted near one face of the main monitor. The Malnovian Asteroid Belt orbited as if nothing had happened.

Under less awful circumstances Francis loved watching the great cubic monitor, with its stirring displays of imprisoned suns. *Darwin*'s was a Sozyo Model 3560, which meant the holojector was mounted in the ceiling instead of the floor or wall. Sozyo made 4-D equipment. The image had height, width, depth, and a fourth D that eluded precise definition. It was called Presence. Somehow, you *felt* that the subject was there in the room with you. You could seemingly walk up to it, savor its fragrance, finger its texture, rub a few eons' grime off its contours. Francis felt the Malnovian Belt's Presence, and he reeled with total loathing.

Burne snorted, acknowledging that Francis, too, had Presence. Good old Burne. Smooth, nervy Burne. *Burne* would explain all of this.

Francis clunked forward. The floor of the control deck was a huge disk, immaculately metallic. "There's been a war!" he croaked. "Nearth has disintegrated!"

Burne regarded him with half-closed eyes. Saying nothing, he went to close-up, got a jolt. Nearth was just as gone, the starless night just as endless, as in Francis's cabin.

But Burne's voice was resonant with calm. "Hell—something's blocking our view, that's all." He reversed the zoom. Slowly the night congealed into a single object, a black globe that made a hole in the sky. It floated in moonless silence. "God's magic mousetrap!"

"What is it?" asked Francis. He exhaled in gratitude: it wasn't the end of the world.

"Carlotta!" Burne whistled in delight. "Carlotta the ghost!" He socked a relay on the intercom panel, sending his voice to a dozen places at once. "Kappie! Luther! Fire up your monitors and zoom! Go to two thousand millimeters and you'll see pretty Carlotta like she's never been seen before!"

Francis knew about Carlotta. For years, several of the more dissident astronomy journals had been lending their support to theories of an uncharted body somewhere in the Malnovian Belt—an Atlantis among asteroids, too small to disturb its neighbors and too large to be uninteresting. But so far only one telescope-bespectacled scientist had ever reported seeing the thing with her own three eyes. This was Dr. Carlotta V. Quippet. In a convulsion of vanity, Dr. Carlotta V. Quippet had named it after herself.

She couldn't decide whether to call her discovery a planet, a planetoid, an asteroid, an escaped moon, or a stable comet. Francis called it trouble. "We're not going to *collide*, are we?"

"We'll graze it." Burne sidled toward the nearest computer terminal with annoying nonchalance. For the last six days, their L-17 had spewed out plastic rectangles stamped with a cybernetic subtongue few could fathom. He grabbed the stack and shuffled. "Which is to say we'll miss the troposphere by fifty kilometers."

"Better tell them to get their hens off the roof," said Francis, grinning. But he was not happy. He wanted Nearth, not this dismal world that hovered before his eyes like a scoop of poison ice cream.

The far wall undid itself and Kappie McKack appeared, working her way across the flypaper floor with an ease Francis envied. She was a tall woman, bright and sly, with crisp features on a thin face. Francis enjoyed her young voice.

"Didn't anybody get the *coordinates*? Don't you dwart-ches think of *anything*?" Kappie flipped through the print-outs, took the electrostylus from her mouth (there was always an electrostylus in her mouth), and recorded Carlotta's location on a scrap of flimsy. "We've got to publish this—become famous. We should contact Nearth *right now!*"

"You'll never get a message through all that radiation," said Burne, eyelids on a snide descent.

Kappie gave him a let's-try-anyway look and sprinted, slow-motion, to the keyboard. XM-2 TO DR. ALBERT THORNE, she typed, GALILEO INSTITUTE, PLANET NEARTH.

XM-2 was the name of their scientific party: X for exploratory, M for mission, and 2 because the first time they'd gone to Arete they hadn't come back dead. The name was a lie: Francis had about as much desire to *explore* the solar system as he did to eat glass. He was a biologist, an insect authority (Ph.D. dissertation: *Gall Midge Ecological Strategies*), not an adventurer. The gratifying thing about insects was that you could study them indoors.

A plastic rectangle shot up like toast, and Kappie caught it in midair. "TRANSMISSION TO PLANET NEARTH SCATTERED BY MALNOVIAN BELT RADIATION," she quoted merrily. "I *told* you it wouldn't work." Turning to avoid Burne's eyelids, she studied the gypsy planet. "It's just like all the disreputable theories say, isn't it? A dark cloudcover, soaking up the sun—the perfect camouflage. But now your secret is out, Carlotta."

Eyes flashing, Kappie began improvising myths. Here, she explained, lived the Marduks, a lost race that spoke in music and thought in smells. This was the legendary Garden Planet, teeming with a fabulous herb that, ingested, enabled you to reverse the one decision in your life you most regretted.

"If only our main engines were fueled, Carlotta, we'd land on you and *find out!*"

Land—the thought made Francis flinch. Watching the homely little planet, he tried mightily to feel all the marvelous, exciting things Kappie felt. He knew he had a romantic bone, but right now it refused to sing. Disgusted, he hobbled to the edge of the monitor, found the switch, nudged it. Carlotta and the rest of the universe vaporized, clearing the way for Francis's reflection: nascent potbelly, elfin face, small thirty-seven-year-old eyes, curly hair.

"I'm worried." There was a new voice on deck. Two generations ahead of his shipmates, Luther Gorst was aging well. He slogged to the terminal without breaking stride, and his breathing did not accelerate. "That damn asteroid may capture us."

Burne explained that they would clear Carlotta by over fifty kilometers, "just enough to get some terrific snapshots."

"Even a *hundred* kilometers won't necessarily keep her gravity at bay." Luther was doing his listen-to-me-I'm-old bit. "If we're sucked to the surface you'll *really* get some terrific snapshots." Snatching a mamula-shaped mug, he lifted it toward *Darwin*'s coffee urn, a squat device anachronistically overgrown with nineteenth-century filigree.

"Unlikely," said Burne. "It's a puny body, like Dr. Lostwax. You saw it."

Francis laughed without enjoyment.

"I also saw an atmosphere." Luther poured coffee. "What do you think holds those clouds in place, rubber cement? I tell you, this object is *dense*. Probably some sort of esoteric fusion at the core."

Burne massaged his beard. "God's holy fastball! Carlotta spends her days turning gold into lead! Let's just hope that gravity isn't as heavy as it used to be. . . ."

Francis could feel his intestines kinking.

TWO STANDARD DAYS LATER it became excruciatingly clear that gravity was as heavy as it used to be. "We're pinned, gentlemen," Kappie moaned. "Pinned like one of Francis's moths."

Luther switched on the retros, the only engines that were still fueled, and the computerized alchemy began. Cesium vapor poofed into ions. Speed braked, fall broken, *Darwin* started to orbit Carlotta fewer than ninety minutes before the fibrous atmosphere would have reduced them to lumps of ash.

The retros were banked, the monitors were revived, and the scientists milled lethargically around the control deck, each mired in a private gloom.

Eventually Luther said, "*Think* of something, Burne. Get us free. You've pulled bigger rabbits out of smaller hats."

"*I* have a suggestion," Francis offered in the frail voice of a patient asking a neurosurgeon to go for a hopeless tumor. "We've still got cesium vapor in the retros, right? If we fired those engines, and then gave them some moral support from the chemthruster, we might be able to bust out of here."

Despite his best efforts, condescension crept into Burne's reply. "Yes, we *could* do that. But how do you propose we steer afterwards? You want to stand on the hull and blow on the solar panels?" He began to circle the monitor, occasionally extending his palm and binding it to the glass with static electricity. On the screen, Carlotta's equator rolled by, sheathed in seamless fog. "Besides, we need the chemthruster for the landing."

"The landing?" Francis knotted up. "*What* landing?"

"Friends, I've concluded that our best move is to decelerate again, touch down, and pray for good news—cesium and oxygen and fresh fruit and friendly natives."

"But you've never *been* there."

"The alternative, as I see it, is extreme and painful hunger. I've been *there*."

Francis had known all along that Burne would end up managing this crisis. Burne was tough. Burne practiced archeology, the most inconvenient of the sciences. He slept under stars and got local inhabitants to do things they'd rather not. Once when Burne was looking for shards of civilization on an icy outer moon, the life-sustaining thermal-pump at his chin froze inside his normally impervious pressure suit. Resourceful Burne bit through his own tongue, spat warm blood upon the motor, and got it working again. Still in his early thirties, the man already had a modest reputation as the sort of interplanetary soldier of fortune whose life would one day be turned into a stupendously inaccurate kinepic.

Luther, by contrast, was an introvert, a crusty eccentric who in the name of sociological research had once tried getting a government grant to become a hermit. Now past seventy, the self-contained chemist asked little of the world beyond silence and matter. If all the human race were to blow away one afternoon, Luther would go study some exotic crystal and flourish; if all the exotic crystals were to blow away one afternoon, Luther would die of loneliness.

Kappie, the group's prodigy-in-residence, had turned twenty-three last week. Her calling was anthropology, an ambition that, like Burne's, carried her to inhospitable outreaches and taught her to take the dark side of nature in stride. In one year alone, Kappie had published three papers, two textbooks, and *The Kindred Beast*, a work of pop anthropology she was beginning to regret.

Francis, for his part, had managed to work up a pornographic crush on Kappie during the second half of the voyage.

Within the hour Burne began a photography project, launching dozens of transmitter cameras that, before succumbing to friction, provided massive visual evidence of vegetation and animal migrations. (Oh, God, let the beasts be edible!) But the corker came when Luther read the first spectroprints and noticed sparse but indisputable deposits of pollucite, a cesium-rich mineral. (Cesium!) Francis cheered, and his innards unwound.

Sensorprobes, leaping from *Darwin*'s sides at the flick of a relay, beamed back further reasons for calling the planet benign. Carlotta's temperatures, air pressures, radiation levels, and water supplies were all sympathetic to human survival. Its bacteria were garden-variety and loath to enter into pathogenic relationships with higher organisms.

A few minutes after *Darwin* started its third sweep around Carlotta, the scientists saw the clouds yield to a ragged hole nearly a thousand kilometers across. The landscape below was a patchwork of ice, snow, and frozen earth. It all looked blessedly solid. Slats of emerald sun broke from the west, spanned the hole, vanished. Down there it was morning.

Burne lunged for the chemthruster controls. Above his head, a dozen scopes glowed with flat and open terrain, a pilot's dream. "To your cabins, chums!" he said. "We're going sight-seeing."

As FRANCIS PLODDED down the tubeway, the idea of being marooned on Carlotta brought tears, hot tears cooled only slightly by his admission that home was not a place where he had known great happiness.

Like everyone else's forefathers and foremothers, Francis's forefathers and foremothers had come to Planet Nearth on the great space ark *Eden Two*. It was the major adventure of the twenty-first century, a chance to bury the calamity that was Earth and begin afresh. Everybody wanted to go.

The goal was an elderly star, UW Canis Majoris, so named because it rounded out a constellation that, viewed from Earth, looked to generous imaginations like a Great Dog. The best evidence said UWCM had many satellites, at least one of which could abide *Homo sapiens*, and it was agreed that, once reached, this promised planet would receive the unimaginative name of New Earth. By the time *Eden Two* got there, etymology and lazy tongues had collapsed New Earth into Nearth.

The voyagers, like the destination, were picked for tolerance. No one could sign up who was convinced that his age, gender, race, or scheme for salvation had anything to recommend it over anyone else's age, gender, race, or scheme for salvation. The precaution paid off. While *Eden Two* sought its sun, benevolence ruled within. Passengers who believed in rationality and social planning were actively forgiving of those who believed in seances and ESP; passengers who believed in seances and ESP were boundlessly eager to learn from those who believed in Boyle's law and the Doppler effect. Pairing across racial lines progressed reliably—from the acceptable to the faddish to the invisibly commonplace—until, six generations later, everyone had turned the color of coffee with two creams.

When Nearth had been found and tamed, though, a different ethic emerged, a fact skirted over in the history books but taught to Francis by his anarchist, misfit father. As opposed to *Eden Two*, with its highly rationed resources, the new homeland bulged with the sort of free-for-the-grabbing bounty that invites greed, envy, exploitation, profiteering, and politics.

People found ever more ingenious ways to hate each other. If the venerable irritants of gender and nationality no longer worked, very well, now they'd have segregation by temperament. On one side of civilization stood the Affectives—romantics who declined to distinguish intuition from truth. Their foes were the Rationalists—guardians of intellect, debunkers of illusion, bursters of bubbles. When the Rationalists held political office, enormous sums were spent on industry and technology, and the orphanage down the street went without a new wing. When the Affectives held political office, everyone went out on the lawn and talked to

God, and the orphanage down the street went without a new wing. "Smugness kills all utopias," Francis's father used to tell his son.

Like other monuments to science, the Galileo Institute naturally found itself in the Rationalist camp, though many members labored to demonstrate an appreciation for art and, by extension, a distaste for things worldly. Kappie was planning a novel. Francis had published a paper called "The Spirituality of Beanlice." Luther owned a harp.

Fewer than five years following the inauguration of Nearth, a teen-age girl was lynched for saying something funny to the leader of a superior-consciousness cult. Shortly thereafter, the planet's very first jail went up. Its bars were of a new metal called crysanium, mined in unconscionable misery and sold at unprecedented profit.

In June of 2283, the Nearth Police Academy graduated its first class of willing young law enforcers. They stuffed their bandoliers with artificial-yeast bullets and protected the right of scabs to work the crysanium mines. When a yeastbullet found flesh it began to expand, crushing the recipient from the inside out.

In Francis's opinion, home also had some things to write home about. All was not thievery and unrest. Throughout its troubles, Nearth maintained a nutty, deuces-wild diversity that afforded everyone an equal opportunity to waste his time.

The proper word was Fudge.

Nearth had roller coasters, pool halls, comic strips, trading cards, tap dancing, 3-D kinepix, stand-up comedians, terribly convincing toys, happy surprises in the mail, candy that tasted great but didn't hurt you, sports played with balls, and Halloween.

Nearth was unlovable, for it was not of a piece, but it was thoroughly likable, for it had Fudge.

Fudge was what Francis would miss most if Carlotta the Ghost Planet proved a prison. Fudge and bugs and—

"STRAP DOWN, CHUMS!"

Burne's voice broke uninvited into the middle of Francis's musings. Realizing that he was in his cabin, Francis moved to the reentry chair, secured his stomach with nyoplene bands, and, by way of keeping Carlotta off his mind, fixed on immediate details. Anatomical drawings of insects crept up the walls, and he had positioned his bunk by the porthole, thus guaranteeing that night, the crystalline night of outer space, would always be the last thing he saw before falling asleep. The reentry chair, unfortunately, faced away from the porthole, so he was now forced to rely on his monitor to tell him where they were. By its account *Darwin* was slicing through an ugly yellow stratosphere. He braced himself for the landing and prayed to the gods he didn't believe in that his booty from the voyage, the *Cortexclavus areteus* specimen, would not perish.

Battered and old, *Darwin* was nonetheless a reliable spaceship, with a comforting sort of clunkiness that the drawing-board people had through resolution and humorlessness managed to breed out of the line's subsequent generations. Guided by a gentle pilot, *Darwin* would always land on its feet. Burne is an *especially* gentle pilot, Francis kept telling himself. Burne can land a crate of eggs on a sea of boiling cheese and not make a single omelet.

The specimen in jeopardy was a beetle, the first living insect ever found on Arete, so beautiful it made Francis hum. Francis fully expected the beetle to bring him fame, fortune, or some mingling of the two. He named it Ollie.

From Kappie and Burne's pedestrian perspective, of course, the trip's achievement was not Ollie but their close-up analysis of Arete's indigenous population, the third sentient species found thus far in the solar system. The Aretians were not human. Burne surmised they were descended from the small-brained groundslugs of the Jemdetian age. They locomoted by wiggling, and their bodies glistened with slime. They had a culture.

Burne studied the Aretians' history while Kappie studied their habits. The scientists took back with them five masks, nine knives, one spear, twenty vases, seven fossil skulls, and three gods. They left nothing. Luther, meanwhile, chipped away at the planet's stony skin. He filled the specimen room with rocks and soil samples, carefully labeling each by hand. Luther's printing was so neat it made people angry.

Bumps shook Francis out of his prayers. They were regular, careful, subtle bumps. Burne had brought the ship down well.

Francis freed himself, noting with enormous delight that the magnets were dead. Dancing briefly, luxuriating in the natural gravity, he started to peel off his pressure suit.

At the open door Luther knocked, then sauntered in as if he hadn't. He carried an unlit pipe and a black-and-white photograph, and he couldn't decide which hand should hold which. "Everything's aces in the specimen room," he said grandly.

"I hope that includes Ollie."

"He looked healthy to me, son."

Francis breathed easy. Good old Burne. "How about it, Luther? Are we going to have trouble refueling?"

"It's chancy." The chemist's left hand swapped pipe for photograph. "To tell you the truth, I could *use* a big challenge in my life right now."

"Gorst, you bastard, don't you *dare* enjoy this."

Francis grabbed the photograph. A framework of some kind, badly blurred, was all he could discern. It looked like a bedspring, and he told Luther so.

"Most of the optical shots were nothing, but then this came through on the last transmission. The camera-to-subject distance was three kilometers, which would make your bedspring about the size of the Galileo Institute."

"Which would make it not a bedspring."

"I think it's a rib cage."

"What the hell kind of animal has a rib cage the size of the Galileo Institute?"

"A very *memorable* animal, son."

Francis whisked his finger around the circumference of the porthole. "Luther," he said, "I want to go home."

2

WHEN FRANCIS LOSTWAX was eight years old, he had his first experience with violence. Occasioning the event was a splendid and locally famous collection of insects that young Francis had caught by his own cunning and mounted in a glass cigar box. Children, being close to the ground, have a special rapport with insects.

Now this particular collection was coveted by one Robert Poogley, a corrupt child whose various villainies were abetted by a pair of eyes unfailing in their innocence and a pair of parents unshakable in their opinion that Sonny Bob could do no wrong. Robert Poogley had a tubby body, cloudy yellow hair, and thirty-one badly maintained teeth, including two fighting canines he had once tried to file into points. Francis always thought of Robert Poogley as a personified fart.

One day during recess Robert Poogley waylaid Francis in the woods behind the school and requested the box of insects. If Francis showed up tomorrow without it, Robert Poogley would instruct his German shepherd, Ratdog Snarler, to visit Francis's home for the purpose of removing Francis's throat. The next morning a cowering Francis placed the box in his briefcase and went to school, where during topology class he struck up a conversation with Judy Shout and learned to his everlasting relief that Ratdog Snarler's ferocity was a fiction. If you showed Ratdog Snarler a hologram of a cat, he would turn tail and run. If you cornered Ratdog Snarler in the bathroom and switched on a noisy laser toothbrush, he would evacuate his bowels on the linoleum.

At recess Robert Poogley maneuvered Francis and his briefcase to the swampy side of the woods. The night before, it had rained, and the muck was particularly soft and thick, like the surface of a lavishly frosted cake. "They in there?" Robert Poogley asked, pointing to the briefcase with one hand and seizing Francis's collar with the other.

Francis surprised himself by getting angry. "Take your abortion tongs off me, you big fart."

"You want me to bring my *dog* over tonight, is that it, Lostwax?"

"You can't con me, Poogley. Judy Shout says your dog loses fights with crippled hamsters."

At this Robert Poogley became irrational. He hurled Francis to the ground and tried uprooting his hair. Then, as if plugging leaks, Robert Poogley began to stuff vile guck into Francis's ears and nose. Francis lay embedded in the swamp, howling pitifully, as Robert Poogley rose and located the briefcase. He yanked it open, seized the cigar box, and was the first child in from recess.

Robert Poogley, insect pirate, grew into a successful holographer with a mustache. His portraits of unspeakably sweet children were displayed in Nearth banks. The portraits fooled everyone but Francis, who looked beyond their iridescent expressions and saw the lust for other people's moths.

Francis had by now decided that violence was natural and instinctive to the human species. At the time of the insect robbery, however, he had merely decided that violence was an extremely uncomplicated way to get what you wanted.

The world's odd tolerance of fighting cropped up again and again in Francis's studies of history, particularly ancient history. On Earth, where his remotest forebears lived, a person could be indisputably responsible for the deaths of thousands and still go down in the history books as some sort of great hero. This was before Francis understood the biological inevitability of violence, so he was bewildered. Why, he wanted to know, were the names of Samson, Napoleon, Joan of Arc, Ulysses S. Grant, and Julius Caesar not obscenities, spoken after dark in whispers of revulsion and shame? The same teachers who couldn't bring themselves to say *shitbrain* or *ortwaddle* openly discussed Alexander the Great.

He never found anyone who had the answer. Until he got to Planet Carlotta, he never even found anyone who had the question.

FRANCIS ENTERED BIOLOGY not because of his insects but because of his father. A Gammaday afternoon found the two of them walking the family dog, a tense collie named Alice. The boy noticed that Alice would not urinate on a tree or lamppost until she had sniffed first. Urine was something Francis thought about a lot in those days, for he had recently been diagnosed as diabetic. The word *diabetes* fascinated young Francis. It sounded to him less like a disease than the name of some magical planet in another galaxy.

"Why does she sniff first, Dad?"

"Dogs don't urinate unless they know that another dog has already been there," his father said, stabbing at an explanation. He was a good-hearted man whose blankest expression looked like a smile.

"But what about the very first dog in the world," Francis asked, "the one who came before all the other dogs on Earth? What did *he* do? How was *he* ever able to pee?"

"You ask the right questions, Francis. That's the mark of a scientist. Why not become a scientist?"

"Okay," said Francis. He never did find out about the very first dog in the world.

NEARTH CONTINUED TO CIRCLE its sun, measuring out the years, and the blessings of adulthood fell upon Francis.

Now he could: stay up late, spoil his appetite, spill his milk, bolt his food, lose his socks, not look it up, dislike his relatives, and wax nostalgic. He became an entomologist.

A part-time teaching position at the Galileo Institute gave Francis a reliable income and enough hours in his day to pursue a pet notion, the spirituality of beanlice. But he was never assigned to lecture in the great amphitheater, which had a computerized atmosphere and oak bookshelves containing simulated first editions of *On the Origin of Species* and Newton's *Principia*. Francis was a mere permanent visiting professor, and he was told to take a conventional room with too many windows and like it. He was also given an office, the size of which in his estimation hovered between a large birdhouse and a small tree fort.

In Entomology 101 Francis lectured about the indigenous insects of Nearth, notably the snow beetle, the harlot fly, the swamp aphid, and the gorgathon, which was not really an insect for the same fussy reasons that a spider was not one either. He lectured about the insects imported on *Eden Two*, ants and bees and a thousand other kinds, including species made extinct by flaws in the ark's ecology: *Mantis religiosa*, which, like humans, had managed to accommodate preying and praying, and *Photuris pennsylvanica*, whose luminosity now seemed as fanciful as the unicorn's horn. He even lectured about the beetles that could conceivably inhabit Planets Verne and Arete and Kritonia, though none had been discovered yet.

Francis's most tantalizing student was Luli Verdegast. While the class gazed through the surfeit of windows, Francis gazed at Luli. She was the prettiest creature he had ever seen outside of his moths.

Luli was at the institute to become a psychologist, was broadening herself by learning about bugs. Francis started accompanying Luli to dinner, and one night, after drinking a whole half-bottle of wine, he asked her to marry him. Luli, who knew Francis had atypical integrity and terrific curly hair, agreed.

It was not a marriage to buy shares in. Luli turned out to be uncompromising and brilliant. She could prosecute honey before a jury of bears and win. Francis, who was intelligent and dedicated but not brilliant, soon became an object of Luli's scorn. They quarreled as a matter of routine, with Francis always at a loss for words of the mordant sort Luli was forever finding.

In physical pursuits Luli was considerably less passionate. Her idea of a good time in bed was breakfast. Nevertheless, shortly after their first anniversary they found themselves in possession of a pregnancy, which Francis named Bugs, followed by a child, whom Luli named Barry.

Francis loved Barry's freckled face and odd little cartoon-character voice. He took Barry to the kinepix, played backgammon whenever Barry asked, and bought Barry treats, such as a wonderful android rabbit. Barry thought his daddy was the greatest thing going.

When Barry was seven, a message reached the Galileo Institute that Francis Lostwax's son was lying unconscious in the emergency room of Qualamy Hospital. Francis left Entomology 101 in the middle of a sentence.

A nurse led him down a sullen corridor to the end room. The room was dark. Drapes hung like wet hair across the windows. Barry was in bed, soundless and still, so encumbered with tubes and wires he looked like a marionette.

"Barry, this is your father!"

"Ssshhhhh," said the nurse. She had a dopey, uncomplicated face, the kind people draw inside circles.

Francis became livid. "Are you afraid I might wake him up? Barry! It's Daddy!" Barry did not wake up.

A brisk, stumpy woman entered, identified herself as Dr. Alexander, and, declaring Barry mildly comatose, asked for Francis's own medical history. Francis explained that he was a childhood diabetic.

Medical science on Nearth had evolved to a point where diabetes, if found in time, no longer debilitated. You merely had an artificial pancreas implanted in tandem with your real one, after which you took bimonthly injections of supplementary insulin. While Francis never fully adjusted to the idea of puncturing himself, his affliction rarely disrupted his thoughts. Now, without warning, foiled by the plastic behind Francis's navel, the disease was avenging itself through Francis's genes.

Dr. Alexander snapped up the nearest videophone transmitter and ordered a supply of crystalline insulin sent to the room. She informed the dopey-faced nurse precisely how much to give the boy, forty units, then bustled out the door. When the insulin came, the nurse methodically filled the syringe from the U500 bottle.

"You're giving him too much!" Francis protested.

As if Francis had said nothing, were not there, the nurse pinched the skin on Barry's arm, drew back the plunger, and, ascertaining that she had not hit a vein, delivered the overdose. Thirty minutes after the injection, the boy had traveled all the way from manageable diabetic coma to profound and tremorous insulin shock. Compensatory glucose was pumped into Barry, but the convulsions did not subside. Within two hours he was dead.

A shrill whimper leaped from Francis's innermost place. He was aware of bringing his fists down on the nurse, pounding her through his tears. A robust orderly entered the room, separated the shaken bodies, and held Francis flopping against the wall while the nurse made a wise exit. When Dr. Alexander arrived, she covered Barry's body with a sheet that smelled like cheese.

Thus ended Francis Lostwax's second experience with violence.

For five days Francis did not report to the Galileo Institute. He stayed in a broken chair, swallowed corrosive quantities of gin, and fingered books without reading them. There are widows, widowers, and orphans, but there is no word for a father who has lost a son. Some things, he decided, are not fit for words.

The funeral done, the android rabbit burned, the storybooks and little clothes given away, he was finally ready to start forgetting. Should I sue the nurse? The thought clawed at him repeatedly, but eventually he decided he must put this impossible death as far from his external experience as possible. As for his marriage, Francis and Luli both realized there was no grace in keeping the poor benighted thing in one piece. Within the month they were rid of each other.

Francis resolved to lose himself in scholarship. He wrote his paper, "The Spirituality of Beanlice," for the prestigious *Journal of Evolution*. The prestigious *Journal of Evolution* turned it down flat. Then a minor-league periodical called *Bestiary* accepted it for their winter issue. They sent him a check for twenty dancs, and he spent it at the circus.

Francis used beanlice as a metaphor for *Phthiraptera* in general. Chemically, beanlice posed few puzzles. They were a rational arrangement of molecules. But how, Francis asked his colleagues, could you account for the *will* of the beanlouse, its spooky ability to go on eating, breathing, moving, and churning out further beanlice when it didn't possess enough physical substance to choke a swamp aphid? How could so much behavior be squeezed into so small a space? He hoped that his paper would open new vistas in biology, but he knew that it would not.

The day the winter issue of *Bestiary* appeared on the stands, Francis walked through four kilometers of snow and bought eight copies. He took one copy, cut out the title page of his article, and framed it. He hung the display over the bookshelf in his apartment. Nobody ever noticed it.

TRUE TO FRANCIS'S FAITH in natural law, Nearth reached the frigid farpoint of its orbit, rounded the corner, and pushed

on toward perihelion and warm, sunny weather. One especially photogenic day he was sitting in his compacted office,
wondering whether he would ever become a full professor, when a secretary whose name he couldn't remember
peeked in to say that a videophone call awaited him down
the hall. Francis's office did not come with a videophone; at
times he was surprised that his office came with a floor.

Burne Newman of the institute's archeology department
was calling to say that he had pried a larcenous amount of
money from the government, a grant for a scientific expedition to Arete. Kappie McKack, the *enfant terrible* of
anthropology, and Luther Gorst, the *vieillard terrible* of
chemistry, had already signed up. Would Francis like to
join them, look for bugs, and become famous?

It took Francis ten seconds to realize that his personal
terror of space travel was vastly overshadowed by his professional itch to be the first entomologist to luck into insect
life on Arete. "Save me a seat," he said.

The trip was a mammoth and costly failure. Kappie and
Burne found no natives to study, Luther found no crystals
of note, and Francis found only that spacefood was at best
boring and at worst constipating.

When Burne attempted to return the remaining funds,
two thousand dancs, he was told to go away please. It would
cost the government more time, more trouble, and ulti-
mately more money to take back the surplus than to pretend that Burne had managed to unload the entire grant
somewhere in the economy. Kappie suggested a two-thou-
sand-danc night on the town, but to the others this smacked
of squander.

Then Luther received a belated Poelsig Award for doing
something about the weather. Pooled with the unspent two
thousand, it was enough to put the group in business again.

This time they landed in the eerie north, where the cra-
ters spawned by errant asteroids, twenty pocks in the
planet's face, had by dint of underground rivers and Are-

tian rains begun evolving into lakes. Reaching the first lake, Luther availed himself of scuba gear, plunged into the dark waters, and emerged with a meteorite of collector's-item caliber. Two lakes later, Kappie and Burne found a fishnet, then a canoe, then a native Aretian. Jealous, Francis decided he would spend the next day in the likely marsh that adjoined the Aretian village, and he wouldn't come out until he'd found something with six legs, three body sections, and the soul of a beanlouse.

UW Canis Majoris nuzzled the horizon as Francis put on his nyoplene boots, shouldered his pack, and tiptoed out of *Darwin*. After two soggy hours, he seriously considered changing professions. If he were a botanist, for example, he would have reasons to delight in this marsh—in its portly trees, its migrating vines, and its bizarre shrubs that showed every evidence of reproducing by coitus and liking it. Then he saw an unusually solid patch of mire spreading among monster ferns. There, in the knife-cold Aretian morning, with dirt on his hands and triumph on his mind, Francis turned over the right rock.

The moment he saw that proboscis, he knew he had discovered a new genus. His specimen must be called *Cortexclavus areteus*, the Corkscrew of Arete.

The corkscrew beetle's proboscis was a spiraled, rotary tool that it used to bore through tree trunks and boulders. If you took the corkscrew beetle in your hand, it would penetrate your palm like a crucifixion nail. If you put the corkscrew beetle in a wooden cage, it would saw away the lid. Big as a beet, green as the sun, the creature sat smugly in the shadow of the overturned rock, confident that its thick shell, unappetizing midgut, and deadly nose would forever deliver it from natural enemies.

A sudden inspiration sent Francis scrambling through his pack. He found the kit by which he kept his diabetes in check, opened it, and carefully set the insulin flask and the two five-cc, crysanium-needled syringes on the ground.

Maneuvering *Cortexclavus areteus* into the empty box, he counted to three and shut the lid. Furious, the beetle rushed forward, proboscis whirling, then tumbled back in defeat: like the needles it contained, the box was made of pure crysanium.

Walking back to *Darwin*, Francis began composing the lead paragraph of his paper on the corkscrew beetle. Will the *Journal of Evolution* publish it? Publish it, hell, they'll make me an editor. And the Poelsig Award in entomology is sewn up, unless some dwartch at Sarl Lab discovers what makes gorgathons weep. As for the Galileo Institute, I'll settle for nothing less than the Atwill Chair.

True: such optimism was uncharacteristic, yet Francis could foresee no disaster capable of keeping him from these assorted gains.

The day they blasted off from Arete and set their course for home, he finished his *Cortexclavus* paper, sneaking in lots of points about the spirituality of beanlice. At two minutes before midnight, Nearth Equatorial Time, Francis turned thirty-seven. He still had all his hair.

3

FRANCIS PEERED OUT of the hatchway and gulped down a healthy helping of troposphere. After three months of canned air, the real thing tasted like honey. Smiling upward, he noted with pleasure that Carlotta's sky was no longer a dead-liver yellow, but a warm, melodious gold.

Burne had brought them well beyond the ice, within spitting distance of the equator. Spitting, however, was not advised. They were in the kind of dry, sandy country where spit ranks next to blood.

Straight ahead, east, the sand rose and fell like convolutions on a cerebrum. Animals with outsized rib cages were nowhere to be seen. But Kappie was. She bounded among the dunes like a puppy. If Carlotta's northern hemisphere contained a fossil, Kappie would surely find it before the day was out.

Francis thought he would like to join her, perhaps using the opportunity to hint of his crush. But it was time to feed the corkscrew beetle. His affection for Ollie, thank God, was unencumbered by lust.

Entering the specimen room, dashing to the vitreousteel cage, he saw that *Cortexclavus areteus* was its usual grumpy, gorgeous self. He had been giving it live verneworms whenever it scuttled a certain way, pairing each tidbit with a bright light aimed directly into the left compound eye. After three lessons, all he had to do was strike a match and Ollie, a fast learner as well as an insatiable carnivore, would start tap dancing.

Francis harbored no illusions about the cognitive powers of insects. Their intelligence, he knew, was amazing, profound, sinister—and startlingly narrow. Like all beetles, *Cortexclavus areteus* was locked into an evolutionary niche. Its drilling behavior provided one clear demonstration. A surface creature, it lived and hunted in open air. Whenever it encountered a tree or boulder, it simply swirled its proboscis and scuttled forward until the obstacle was traversed. Above ground, this was a useful and straightforward way of operating. But, as Francis put it in his paper, "plant a *Cortexclavus areteus* six feet under, and you will see how single-minded Nature can be." The beetle, of course, would just keep drilling, kilometer after kilometer, halfway around the globe if necessary, until the earth sloped down and set it free, assuming that exhaustion did not kill it first.

Francis struck a match, and *Cortexclavus* danced for its supper.

ON THE FLOOR of the control deck, Burne and Luther had assembled a dozen spectroprints into a huge jigsawed picture of Carlotta, and when Francis arrived both scientists were creeping around like babies, pens and protractors in hand, drawing lines.

"Any luck?" Francis asked.

Burne swirled his extended index finger near the center of an outer photograph, then pressed it down suddenly as if snuffing a gnat. "We're here." The finger was aloft again, spiraling east across thirteen hundred kilometers. "The closest pollucite is here." The finger came down, another gnat gone. "And in between is . . . well, you've seen the view."

Francis walked to the edge of the map. "That's what this planet has to offer? Sand?"

Burne nodded. "Enough to fill every catbox on Nearth for the next million years."

"Oh, there's more than sand," said Luther. "The pollucite is in a jungle. Then there's *this* thing." His unlit pipe traced a warm aberration that snaked along the jungle's western edge.

"A river?" asked Francis.

"Yes, but an uncommon river, hot and pulsing, like some transcontinental blood vessel."

Rhetoric made Francis itch. "How long before the ore's in hand?"

"Three days by magnecar should get us to the river," said Burne. "We put on the pontoons, float the car across, then forty-eight hours of plowing through the jungle and we're at the edge of the vein. And, of course, it's a round trip."

"Oh." Francis's mood hit bottom. Ten days!

Francis detested the magnecar. The magnecar reciprocated. Whenever he drove down Nearth byways looking for insects, the spiteful invention invariably snapped a tread or cracked a chip, and he had to waste the rest of the afternoon reading a repair manual written in some cretinous rendition of English. Francis would have preferred spending ten days deveining shrimp.

"And once we've got the mineral on board?" he asked.

"If I had a real lab," replied Luther, "I could remove the cesium in two hours. In *Darwin*'s lab . . . hydrochloric acid as the extracting agent . . . two days."

"Does it matter if—?" Francis stopped when Kappie ran through the doorway, panting and thrilled.

"Look!" In her hands she cradled a face. Not a live face, but the grim, toothy framework of a face.

"God's sacred tax return!" said Burne. "The engines aren't even cool and McKack here thinks she has to go find a fossil skull."

Haughtily, Kappie cleared her throat. "Burne, dear, look closer. This is no fossil. We've got natives." She held it out like a gift.

The fact of the skull was less troubling than its condition. There was no cap to the thing, only a ratty rim, crudely scalloped by human purpose and human tool. Francis, Luther, and Burne shuddered in unison.

"A head is typically pried open for one reason," said Kappie softly. "To get at—"

"I saw no neurosurgery clinics on the horizon," said Burne.

"Which forces us to assume that the brain was used as . . . nourishment." She passed her discovery to Burne. "These interior scars lend weight."

"Yes," he said. "And look at the *foramen magnum*. This species walks upright."

"Stop being so goddam deductive!" Kappie blurted. "Don't you recognize a male adult *human* when you see one?"

Francis accidentally bit his tongue, and his eyes teared up. "Folks, I was wondering, do you think maybe I could stay on board?"

"I'll vote against you on that, Lostwax," said Burne. "This skull is lousy news, and we'd better start thinking of ourselves as a small army. I have a feeling we'll be killing cannibals before the week is out."

"I can't kill," said Francis. "Not me. It's against my nature."

"The bumblebee can't fly," noted Luther. "It's against his nature. He's too heavy for his wing size."

"You needn't tell *me*."

"Then how does he stay in the air?"

Francis pondered a moment, then smiled weakly. "The fact is not widely known, but bumblebees possess a tenacious faith in miracles."

THEY WOULD HAVE BEEN off first thing in the morning, only Kappie and Burne got to scrapping. The early sun was flowing through the porthole of Francis's cabin, spotlighting his stomach, when two voices—loud but not screeching, razzing but not ridiculing—reached his ears. "You're out of your *skull!*" "You're not being a *scientist!*" He blinked himself awake, just as Kappie and Burne broke in.

"Hi, Lostwax, friend, how did you sleep?" asked Burne.

"Don't soften him up," said Kappie. "Francis, dear, we want you to settle an argument."

"How did I *sleep*? How do you *think* I sleep in cannibal country?"

"Burne insists we should travel light," Kappie continued. "Nothing but food, a proximascope, his yeastgun. Now, my idea is, hell, we're the first scientists here. We can't betray the cause of knowledge just because we might lose a day or two. We should take cameras, soil-test kits, wistar rods, shovels. We're standing on the greatest find since . . . since *Cortexclavus areteus.*" She smiled coyly.

This hit home. "What does Luther say?"

"He's on my side."

Francis thought: Come on, Lostwax, don't be Burne's puppet. Besides, Kappie has breasts. "I guess I'm on your side, too."

Throwing up his hands in mock despair, Burne marched out of the cabin.

Kappie shot a pleased look at Francis. "If we could fit Burne's mouth over the accelerator grids," she said, "we'd have enough exhaust to leave here and tour the rest of the Milky Way."

By midday they had detached the magnecar, jammed it with the necessities of science and outdoor living, and locked up the ship. Each explorer carried a personal copy of the key, a bumpy cylinder threaded onto a thong and slung around the neck. Francis was also careful to bring the two most important objects in his life: his insulin kit and his corkscrew beetle.

When everybody was stuffed inside, Kappie, in the front seat, typed the proper latitude and longitude into the microputer. The magnecar got the message, spinning itself twenty degrees and ka-thunking away at an unimpressive velocity. Looking toward the back of the viewbubble, Francis endured neck cramps long enough to see *Darwin* become a tiny metal seashell on an endless beach.

Within an hour the monotonous dunes yielded to the kind of titanic chiseled rocks that invite one to see things. The magnecar zagged past forms that were to Francis morgs—the great spuming seabeasts of Planet Kritonia. Later they came upon a wall of upright screws, as if a colony of giant *Cortexclavus areteuses* was about to surface. This time Luther insisted not only on taking a photograph, but on putting Francis in it.

"Why do I have to be *in* it?"

"For scale," Luther explained, lining up the shot. "And don't stare into the lens. It looks gauche." Francis was happy to oblige. He wanted to keep an eye out for cannibals with giant rib cages.

Before they left the screwrocks, Luther chipped a dozen samples into a plastic bag. Wandering again, Kappie returned with a bleached relic. The second skull differed from the first in that it was young and female. It resembled the first in that it had no cranium.

With daylight's departure they stopped in a canyon and made camp. Burne brought out a luminon and placed it in the middle of things. "These are pure gems," he said. "One flick of the switch and we'll be dining by a light to rival the sun's." He flicked the switch, and there was a faint mechanical cough—no light.

"Must be an eclipse," Kappie said, no sarcasm in her tone because the words were enough. Burne snarled.

That night they dined by firelight. The main course was boiled beans from Nearth and three-eyed fish from Arete. Carlotta's bounteous oxygen inspired the flame to a soaring blue fountain, superior to luminons in every way.

A wind came, nibbling at noses and earlobes. The scientists sought their sleeping bags and installed them close to the fire. For Kappie the occasion required horror stories told in strangled whispers. Francis fell asleep in the middle of a werewolf attack.

THE NIGHT LEFT DEW and took his fear—some of it, anyway. He awoke feeling strangely adventurous. Wiggling out of his sleeping bag, knocking away the sand deposited in his hair by the nightwind, he resolved to work up a spectacular appetite for breakfast. He said to himself: I'm more like Burne than I thought.

When he got to where the canyon turned a corner, he met a wonder and stood blinking. He was fewer than ten meters from the ruins of an immense spaceship.

"Burne! Kappie! Luther!" His friends were soon there. For a full minute amazement locked them into a tight band of passive onlookers. Slowly Kappie ventured forward until she could touch metal.

There wasn't much left. Cabins, computers, greenhouses, stockyards, field generators, hull plates, reactors, holojectors—all, Francis surmised, had been pelted to nothing by the diligence of wind. Only the superstructure remained, rearing up from the sand like the ribs of some blessedly extinct behemoth, its every bone picked clean of carrion by a flock of steel condors. Ribs! Smiling hugely, Francis turned to Luther.

"That's one mystery solved. Now we know about your blurry close-up."

"Two mysteries solved," said Luther. "Whoever flew this thing must have had a skull in his head."

"Let's go for three mysteries," Kappie added. "This is not just *any* ship. Fill in the blanks, gentlemen. We are first witnesses to the fate of *Eden Three!*"

Francis retreated into the library of his memory, walked through stacks he had not visited in years, and selected a dusty schoolbook called *Ancient History: Grade Seven.* Turning to the chapter about the twenty-first century, the age of the space arks, he recalled the whole story.

The whole story was that not one but two arks were built for the Canis Major adventure. *Eden Two* reached Nearth on schedule, and *Eden Three* was never heard from again. Presumably the twin was obliterated by a meteor shower, ingested by a black hole, diverted from lofty purpose by internal war—any of the numerous logical Armageddons that had made the founding fathers insist on redundant arks in the first place. Who would have guessed that, just around the solar corner, Nearthlings had whole batches of slightly-off-course relatives?

Burne and Kappie, having entered the wreck, were huddled in interdisciplinary conference. Archeology and anthropology squared off, met, reached consensus.

"The first thing to notice," Kappie began, "is the lack of structural damage to the hull girders. This suggests that the vessel was landed by rational minds. We may therefore assume human civilization came to Carlotta in pretty much the same condition it came to Nearth."

"But then Nature got the upper hand," said Burne. "The harshness of the planet, the maddening sand, the ice, all kept the pilgrims from constructing the sort of high culture we have on Nearth."

"*What* high culture?" asked Francis. The high culture of Nearth consisted of one olfactory-comicbook stand, two Uncle Andrew's Liver-on-a-Stick franchises, three Mother's Mocha Milkshake bars, and four hornopornovision theaters on each and every corner.

Burne ignored the question. "The years dragged on, generation following generation, and the human race dissolved into its earliest, animal ways. The people here, when we meet them, will be outright savages—no table manners or indoor plumbing."

"Behold the wages of atavism," Kappie declared, pulling a ravaged skull from her pack. "Dog-eat-dog."

Francis felt nauseated. Until now, he had seen Kappie's

finds as badly mistreated cousins. Could it be that within these bony walls no symphony had ever rung? No proof of Euclid's? No dirty joke?

Luther rapped a girder with his pipe. "Your theory has a rather sorry hole in it, Burne. Among us chemists there's an old saying: Matter can be neither created nor . . . I forget the rest. And yet this thing is missing nearly all its vital parts. There's only the merest hint of the quadrillion devices it needed to sail across the light-years, stay on course, and keep everybody amused for two centuries."

"Erosion?" asked Francis.

"What kind of erosion can clean out a space ark as neatly as an Aretian can clean out a three-eyed fish, yet leave the girders barely bruised?"

"The girders are made of steel," Burne explained.

"So are hull plates, ion chambers, you name it. No, I propose that some well-formed intelligence has carefully and systematically looted this ship." He yanked a panel from the remains of an airlock. "Look at this."

Burne conceded that it had been cut away by neither savage whim nor random sand. "My answer is simply that the devolution process did not begin immediately. After they landed, our would-be ancestors found reasons to cart everything away."

Luther lifted a finger toward the horizon. "Yes, but *where* did they cart it? Does a more livable country lie out there somewhere? A civilization?"

Civilization! To Francis the word was sweet. It rang of deliverance.

"Those are cute questions," said Burne, "but if we meet any natives this week, you can be the one who starts talking religious philosophy and Schillachi equations with them." He flashed his yeastgun. "I'll be betting *this* is the language they understand."

A SCANT TWO KILOMETERS past the canyon, an oasis pushed out of the desert like a huge spreading plant. No mere anomaly in the sand, this was a world unto itself, a dense network of pools, waterfalls, boulders, stalks, vines, fruit, and flowers. Collectively each blossom's sex organs looked like, and were the size of, a human face.

Entry was along paths whose weaving randomness suggested that their makers had followed no plans, only instinct and thirst. The learned citizens of Luther's more livable country apparently did not come here.

The scientists parked the magnecar under a huge fibrous leaf that could probably have supported its weight, then followed the handiest path to a lagoon. Waiting for Luther, the others snapped pictures and sniffed the thick, steamed-vegetable air. "This one reminds me of an awful boy I knew once," said Francis, commenting on a nearby configuration of stamens and pistils. "Robert Poogley."

Luther arrived and stabbed the bright water with a wistar rod, perusing the lights, meters, and litmus plates on its bulbous top. The rod said the water was not water, but a greasy Carlottan facsimile of water. Francis condescended to let it kill his thirst.

His romantic bone began to sing. Here he was, Dr. Francis Lostwax, the soon-to-be-great entomologist, trapped on a secret planet, exploring a fabulous garden, questing a forgotten civilization. Inspired, he walked alone to a paradisiacal spot where a small gamboling stream dropped like a toy waterfall over the edge of a cuboidal boulder. Surrounding the cuboid were occasional clumps of tufted organic parasols, the scene's one prosaic feature. Under the largest clump Francis, drained, flopped down. The parasols blocked the blistering star.

Doubtless these are trees, Francis thought, much as the Yorkshire terrier is doubtless a dog, however lean the glory it brings to the name. Francis was a collie man. He liked their smiles.

LATER, THE WORLD BEGAN to scream. Dazed, afraid, Francis groped his way upright. Then, from above, the horror came.

Like wormy fruit, in clusters of three and four, the dark shrieking shapes quit the trees.

Stone ax in hand, a gap-toothed bipedal thing rushed up. Francis felt a stunning thwack on his left shoulder. Miraculously the bone held. But a second blow, straight on the mouth, brought blood.

Steadying himself on the cuboid, Francis faced the savages. There were over two dozen, all looking broken and pain-wracked and only nominally human, like gorillas who as babies had been swaddled in barbed wire. Their eyeballs were yellow with disease, their hair was matted with nameless ooze, and from their putrid lips saliva rolled uncontrollably.

Somehow Francis cut through his confusion, his pain, and got to the path. Parasols flew by as he dashed from pool to pool, desperate to solve the maze. Finally the Poogley blossom was before him, marking the way to the desert. As he reached the magnecar, he looked ahead and saw, approaching, two welcome faces, Burne's wrenched with fury, Luther's with the pain of overworked lungs. Fifty savages followed in a vicious pack.

"Lostwax, the micromputer!" Burne's voice stuttered between panic and resolve.

Obeying, Francis ripped back the viewbubble and dived in. He pushed the right keys. His friends arrived, and Burne guided Luther into the back seat.

"Where's Kappie?" Burne demanded.

Francis was about to moan that he didn't know, when, thirty meters away, something leaped out of the oasis. "Behind you!"

Kappie emerged only slightly closer to the tribe than to the magnecar, but the margin proved fatal. In seconds she was overtaken and encircled. Realizing that she had only two choices—helpless screams or rational arguments—she struck a pose that said: I am not about to let five years of costly instruction in the virtues of cultural relativism fly suddenly to hell. "Stop!" The savages did not stop. "We're all the same kind!"

They were at her throat.

"Have you forgotten *everything*? We're all the—" Suddenly she could no longer talk but only gargle blood.

Burne had aimed the yeastgun carefully, but when he hit the relay there was just a dull electronic whimper.

"Get in here!" yelled Luther. "You can't save her!"

Burne jammed the failed weapon into his belt. Returning to the magnecar, he ordered Francis out of the driver's seat, then secured the viewbubble. The savages did not follow. Kappie's corpse commanded their total notice.

Francis strained to witness what he did not want to see. He fought to ignore what he made himself know. One savage was kneeling, using his tool, entering her forehead.

Even as the magnecar sped away, Francis could see them scooping out morsels of cortex, chunks of medulla, bits of cerebellum—the whole wondrous engine of Kappie's once formidable mind. The blood in his mouth now mingled with gushing vomit.

Thus ended Francis Lostwax's third experience with violence.

THE TRIBES WERE SOON OUTDISTANCED, the oasis was soon gone, and the rest of the day brought nothing but passing sand and hot, crawling anguish. Luther banished his camera to the magnecar's storage compartment, and he collected no more rocks. Burne started leaving his yeastgun in careless places. Francis stopped using words.

They parked long before the sun went down, knowing it would take hours to camouflage the magnecar and dig themselves under the dunes. Once holed up, each man warmed a meal with the inconspicuous heat of a kelvinsleeve, eating right out of the can, burying the evidence half a meter deep. They took scheduled turns watching for savages, and unscheduled turns weeping.

The loss of Kappie was like a surprise yeastbullet in the leg. The full pain does not hit right away. At first you say: Is this all there is? Then you burst open.

This death, Francis decided, must not be *allowed* to happen. Barry gone . . . now Kappie. His life couldn't lose two major characters. Only the extras, at most the supporting players, were supposed to die.

By midnight, Francis had been hit full, had rallied, and was thinking. He had so much lost thought to regain he couldn't sleep. It was Burne's watch.

"Burne?"

A grunt from the west, then a low, "Yeah, Lostwax?"

"I can't sleep."

"Is it your lip still? I could try a stitch."

"No, it's fine, provided I don't smile, something I'm not planning to do for three years." He crept out of his hole. Burne sat with glittering pieces of yeastgun spiraling around him like the suns of Andromeda. Before the night was over he would have fixed the weapon and gone on to outwit the finicky luminon.

"Move slowly," Burne cautioned. "Keep your voice down."

"Burne, is it sensible to keep chasing after cesium?"

"A goal will keep us sane."

"Suppose we returned to the ship? We could make a wide circle around the oasis, then wait inside until Carlotta brought us within transmitting distance."

"You're talking half a standard year, Lostwax! What do we eat? Sand? And getting past the tribes won't be as easy as you think. For all we know they've found *Darwin* by now."

"They'd stray that far from home?"

"For a predator the distance isn't great. They could reach it in one day—less. And you might recall that the first skull was practically on our doorstep." Burne pointed to a sad western star. "No, the next time I move in that direction, it will be with an *army*."

"You're counting on Luther's civilization?"

"What *else* can we count on?"

Francis annihilated the star by easing it into his retinal blindspot. Yes, dammit, Burne is right. For the moment we must leave the tribes to their lush nation, leave them sleeping on high, defecating on flowers, feeding on fruit and each other's thoughts. For the moment we must run.

THE RIVER WAS WIDE and deep. Like a mirror, it looked from some angles dark, from others silvery. The dark moments were impossibly dark, dark as the inside of a sin. The silvery moments suggested eels made of mercury. They were fast, dazzling, metallic moments, and they caused you to notice that a low electric hum snapped across the surface.

Was it a geological accident? Or a human canal, the enterprise of *Eden Three* engineers? Most puzzling of all, why did a mammoth stone wall rise from the far bank? None of the three scientists who walked the river's edge cared just yet to guess.

Francis got down on all fours, leaned over the bank, and prepared his nostrils for a dung beetle's socks. But the river's smell was far more pleasurable, like the various aromas spouted by one's own body.

"Bad?" asked Burne.

"Merely unsubtle."

The river was pungent and thick. It was a Mother's Mocha Milkshake compounded of polluted milk, depraved sugar, degenerate solids, and evil fats.

"A moat that only a chemist could love," Luther concluded. He inserted the wistar rod, noting how its colors shifted and its meters twitched. "Well, it sure as hell isn't water, and the wand asks us to believe that the genetic materials and amino acids are biologically integrated."

Francis dropped his jaw. "You mean this broth is alive?"

"I will merely say that it has too much silver halide to be organic and too much tissue to be anything else. Imagine a substance that is neither animate nor inanimate. It can grow, like a crystal, and reproduce, like a cow. Now imagine somebody *melted* it—"

"Luther!" Burne was pointing to the wistar rod. All eyes shot toward it. The middle was now a stump. The bottom, gone. Chewed off by the hungry moat.

Luther performed one last test. He took out a crysanium pipe and sacrificed it to science. "There are three more in my pack," he explained.

The pipe floated with the current, dissolving like brain in a cannibal's maw.

The river was malignant and vile. Why, then, did Francis permit himself to be fascinated by it? Why was its wickedness so alluring? "If I jump in," he said to Luther, "will you give my bones to the institute?"

Their attentions went to the wall. At thirty meters, it was as high as the great screwrocks. Hidden from view, the thickness was impossible to gauge, but intuition said, Think grand, grand enough to play blasterball and land space arks.

The wall was everything the river was not. It was beautiful, gray, and still. Its massive interlocking stones had been set by a master's hand, every joint clean, unshowing, and tooled to last forever.

One thing was certain. The wall had not been built by savages.

4

DR. TEZ YON, whose race had built the wall, was looking for an herb. The sun, once called UW Canis Majoris, now Iztac, daubed its light on the plump leaves and knobby bark, reaching even the ground, a latticework of naked roots. A good time to be in the forest, she thought, remembering her last herb hunt, two epochs ago, when Iztac was visibly closer and her skin had blistered like an aging fresco.

Tez did not normally bother to distinguish Iztac the ball of gas from Iztac the idea of enlightenment, nor Iztac the idea of enlightenment from Iztac the god. Thus ran the antidichotomy bias of Quetzalian philosophy. Quetzalian philosophy was simultaneously a religion—Zolmec—and a science—biophotonics. Nobody had ever heard of biophotonics until Tez's childhood heroine, Dr. Janet Vij, invented it. Dr. Janet Vij said things like this: "It is far more arrogant to profess intuitive knowledge of the sacred than scientific knowledge of the tangible."

Zolmec admitted that some dichotomies were inevitable, even useful. Quality versus quantity. Having your teeth fall out versus not having your teeth fall out.

Nevertheless, Zolmec held the neat schisms of primitive days—art/logic, mind/brain, spirit/flesh—accountable for all sorts of ignorance, most notably the idea that the physical world was something to be transcended. After all, had not Tez's Earthling ancestors smuggled their measuring devices unnoticed into the atom itself, cleaving quark from quark and ferreting out the Divine Ulticle? Had they not proved the mystical quality of matter and healed forever the rift between science and spirituality? Zolmec issued few taboos, but one of them, surely, was The Putting of Things into Pigeonholes.

Today, for the first time in memory, the pigeonhole taboo was causing Tez pain. Dr. Mool is a dogmatist, she thought. Yet in calling him that, I am doubtless dropping him into a pigeonhole, so that for me he stops being wholly human. Yet without that pigeonhole, dogmatist, I can't even picture the oily bastard in my mind.

The forest was thinning now. Trees became bushes. Bushes, grass. Her shy mount, Mixtla, found the footing suddenly to its liking and so bore its mistress with a happy bounce. Mixtla was a lipoca, the six-legged species that the Quetzalians had years ago domesticated from the wild huanocez. The lipoca looked like a child's drawing of a horse.

Dr. Mool is deft, Tez told herself, respected throughout the entire Hospital of Chimec. Dr. Mool is wise, she told herself, and his wisdom says that coyo root, once boiled into serum, will revive my father and restore his health.

Dr. Mool is wrong, she told herself.

Under Mixtla's hooves, soft humus melted into softer sand. As Mool had predicted, the border between forest and desert bloomed with coyo flowers, their fleshy petals feasting on the noon sun. Tez dismounted.

Why was Mool so willing to stake her father's life on a notorious herb like coyo? How could he be sure that the warnings so decisively lettered into a dozen antique texts— forecasts of dire side effects, including profound coma— amounted to little more than myth? It was not a question of regressive old ideas versus enlightened new ideas, but of reasonable caution versus arrogant caprice.

She remembered disclosing her doubts to Mool on the

front steps of the Hospital of Chimec. As usual, he answered not the question he was asked, but the question he felt like answering. "Left to orthodox treatments," said Mool in his growly-bear voice, "your father may never regain certain motor functions. Left to my approach, given what I have learned about the proper administration of coyo—you've read my acclaimed studies of dosage schedules and keyta counteraction in chactols and chitzals—given what I have learned, your father will dance out of here." Keyta was a nerve-growth culture that commonly snapped people out of profound comas.

"The combination has never been tried on a human subject," said Tez, kicking one of the stone jaguar-heads that hedged the steps. "I think you are too quick to ignore the possibility of cure through neurogestalting."

"And I think *you* are too quick to ignore who is the chief surgeon at this hospital and who the resident." End of debate.

Teot Yon was a victim of his profession, stonecutter. When not engaged in the universal Quetzalian pursuits of tea, chess, and incessant conversation, he had worked the eastern quarries, splitting and shaping the mammoth blocks that constituted the city of Aca. It was an honored trade. Stonecutters enjoyed the prestige of clergy. They also got maimed.

To dislodge a block, the cutters perforated its contours, filling the deep holes with water. When the water froze, a simple matter of inserting an icestick, the stone split. The sport of cutters was to stand on the block until a KRAACK was heard, then jump off.

Ten days ago a block holding Teot Yon had split with freakish silence. His fall damaged his spinal cord. It ripped one of his kidneys. He came to the Hospital of Chimec paralyzed and afraid.

An odd coincidence: the same sorts of icesticks used at the quarries were also used at the Hospital of Chimec, to freeze brain tissue and prevent its hemorrhaging during surgery.

On her knees, Tez clasped the stem of a large coyo and pulled until the root dangled freely. It was studded with short, pulpy shoots. Nesting the herb among the folds of her robe, she felt like a snake: a venomous snake equipped with a toxin it didn't particularly want to use.

But she would use it. She would bow to Mool's deftness. To Mool's wisdom. To Mool's reputation.

But she would not bow to Mool's unholy certainty.

For a grown-up, Tez Yon was notably new-looking, remarkably vigorous, and unrepentantly playful. Since age five she had regularly staged marionette shows, a hobby she betrayed no sign of forsaking even now, at age thirty. *Walk Naked in the Rain* was the title of her most recent production. It was not for children.

Her frame was diminutive, as though a full-scale human had been magically reduced ten percent, all proportions intact. Her face suggested something far tougher than flesh. It was not molded but carved out, carefully, chip by chip. The resulting hard angles and sudden turns avoided austerity through a supple mouth. It smirked constantly, as if in on some joke that eluded her other features.

Besides puppets, Tez enjoyed wine, theory of any kind, and playing gobletball on Tolcaday afternoons. She was by some standards slovenly, failing to see any virtue in made beds, since, as she put it, you are either asleep or somewhere else. On her birthdays she was sad. This tradition traced to earliest childhood, when she had constantly misinterpreted her birthday parties to mean that she was dying. Why *else* would the world be going to such exorbitant lengths to cheer her up?

Science was her first love. Long after the preschool years, she aspired to know the why of everything. Why babies had a Babinski reflex, and why the reflex disappeared. Why people licked their upper lips when concentrating, and why there was humor. Tez wanted to understand light. She wanted to solve mud, decipher rocks, and unlock grass.

As an adolescent, Tez had come close to disproving the Darwinian theory of inheritance, a doctrine that traced clear back to her ancestors' Earthian days. Darwinists viewed evolution as an immense poker game in which Nature never left the table. This tenacity on Nature's part apparently owed to the occasional big pots (the eye, the gill, the thumb, the wing), which presumably compensated for such painful losses as brontosaurus and Neanderthal man, and for such tainted winnings as predation and cancer.

By contrast, the beaten theory, Lamarckism, also imported from the old planet, saw evolution as willful improvement. Tez liked this. It had heart.

Her heretical experiments involved the chactol, a native fish that, through a combination of extraordinary parenting and unbridled luck, she had bred in her basement to the tune of eleven generations. Chactols had no eyes. As cave dwellers, they didn't need them. She reared her chactols amid odorless food and omnipresent enemies, an environment that made eyes desirable. In her maiden attempt at surgery, she gave the first generation narrow incisions where sighted fish had eyes. The incisions went clear to the brain. Scar tissue closed them.

Tez performed the same operation on the second generation, then on the third, then on the fourth. By the fifth generation, the incisions were closed not by scars but by corneas. Finally: a tenth generation, and the only word for the healed wounds was *eyes*.

She stopped making incisions. The eleventh generation was born with eyes.

Medical school forced Tez to interrupt her work. When she came home for Legend Eve, she was devastated to find her specimens dead, their inherited eyes reduced to an amorphous putrescence. She vowed to repeat her experiments one day. If the Hospital of Chimec ever opened a research wing, as Dr. Zoco continually claimed it would, she intended to hang up her scalpel, tell Mool what she thought of him, and set biology on its ear.

AAARRRRRRRRNNNNNNNNNNNN. What was that?

Tez faced the forest. Everything was as usual: chunks of sun, fluttering leaves, slithering vines. In the distance a stone aqueduct sat high and silent while, farther still, the Library of Iztac and the Hospital of Chimec thrust their temples above the treetops.

She turned, stared across a kilometer of wasteland, and fixed on the wall, which at this distance, in this sun, seemed little more than a long mound of sand, hardly the impregnable rampart it was supposed to be. As she walked forward, the noise seemed to grow.

No question now. It came from behind the wall, presumably from the writhing hot dunes on the far bank of the river made of hate. Were the neurovores, the awesome devourers of central nervous systems, up to something?

The mildest recollection, the smallest mention, the puniest thought of neurovores was enough to rattle any Quetzalian to the bone. In Tez's mind a doctor rushed up. "I'm sorry to tell you, my dear, but you have a tumor. You're doomed." *That* was how she felt.

Although only a dozen living Quetzalians had ever seen a tribe, neurovore phobia stood palpable in the soul of every citizen. Even today, unimaginative fathers and mothers were known to inspire discipline by announcing that the Brain Eaters, you see, have a taste for ungrateful little girls, and the Brain Eaters, I fear, come in the night and steal away boys who won't consume vegetables, and the Brain Eaters, it is known, offer irresistible quantities of gold to parents who want to rid themselves of lippy progeny.

When these same children turned thirteen, they were told the facts of life. Not the sexual facts, which were mastered at four along with compound fractions and Latin, but the hereditary facts. Truth to tell, the neurovores were not some irrelevant aberration, a remote species with nothing to say to the human race. Truth to tell, neurovores and Quetzalians traced to the same genetic stock.

Tez shook. She would prefer being close kin to a carcinogenic virus.

Pure logic, of course, assured everyone that between the rapacious contents of the moat and the unscalable heights of the wall, their civilization would never be breached by Brain Eaters. But pure logic broke and ran, soiling its pants all the way, at the idea of even one neurovore, through some trick of Nature or turn of luck, finding itself inside Quetzalia. The conservative estimate, happily, was that the neurovores would not achieve a culture capable of bridges and ladders for at least eighty generations. By then it would be somebody else's problem.

And yet the noise persisted, ominous and insectile. Returning to the forest's edge, Tez paused under a tree and plucked a red, squooshy relative of the Earthian apple, forgotten dabbling of some selective breeding hobbyist. Afraid that in her nervousness she would choke, she gave the fruit to her lipoca, which dined eagerly and listened with politeness to words it couldn't comprehend.

"Mixtla, my friend," the words went, "what an exquisitely stupid beast you are. I can say you have the mental powers of broccoli, and you don't even care. And yet, somewhere deep within that delightfully absurd little brain of yours, you are hearing that sound, and, and"—here she began stuttering—"you sense that it signals a change for us all."

Aaarrrrrrrnnnnnnnnnnn. "You know what I think, Mixtla?" Fear ground her flippancy to a grotesque whisper. "I think we've been invaded from outer space."

5

AAARRRRRRRRNNNNNNNNNNN. They were submerged in dirt. Down, down the magnecar plunged. Theirs was a stop-start, back-forth sort of progress. The huge drill choked noisily on Carlotta's crust.

Francis, of all people, had initiated the journey by musing absentmindedly that if no way existed to cross over the moat, then they must cross *under* it. Burne added a practical touch by recalling that the magnecar's snout accepted a miraculous perforated bit that gulped down earth, chewing it, compacting it, and spewing it out with such velocity that the hole was transformed into a rigid tunnel. He had used the attachment only once before, to bore through a Giant Tree of Kritonia; given a sufficient portion of eternity, the diameter of a Kritonian tree reached two kilometers.

Francis loathed the journey only slightly more than he thought he would. He felt entombed. He sat facing the rear of the car, Ollie's vitreousteel cage cradled between his knees.

"Don't doze off," Burne told him. "They might try to follow us down."

"And what if they *do*?"

"Don't keep it a secret."

Lunchtime arrived, and from his pack Francis rummaged a dried Aretian fish. It tasted like aspirin. He pushed the more unsavory parts between the bars that roofed the vitreousteel cage. Before applying its mandibles, *Cortex-*

clavus inspected the fish by walking on it. The insect could smell with its feet. Francis remembered telling his ex-wife Luli about this common talent of insects, and Luli, who was not really listening, said, "I once put *my* foot in something that sure smelled." Francis felt that in many ways this exchange summarized their relationship.

The car continued to lurch and burrow, its drill shrieking like a tortured animal. Francis watched the cylindrical wake and imagined he was a germ sitting in the anus of a corkscrew beetle. After an hour's travel, the control panel announced that they were twelve meters down, presumably below the riverbed.

Burne rushed the news into the micropputer. "The river's edge is only a meter away," he concluded, "if the Pythagorean theorem has anything to say about it."

Under orders from the micropputer, the magnecar ate its way into a new course, parallel with the planet's surface, and jumped forward. "Ten decimeters," said Burne. "Nine . . . eight . . . seven . . ."

But Francis's mind was not on the metric system. It was on dying horribly. If the car were too high it would drill into the bed, and the river would gush upon them. Their chances would be those of sherbet on the sun.

"Three . . . two . . ."

"This is it," whispered Luther.

"One."

Francis gulped. Luther spat. The earth held.

New troubles arose. The dirt, wet with the river's exotic seepage, clung to the bit, filling the threads. The bit became smooth and impotent, its sound a blend of gargling and birdsong.

Burne killed the drill motor, threw it suddenly into reverse. He backed up the magnecar. Clots of mud took to the air and splattered the front of the viewbubble.

Burne pushed the drill's forward lever and drove mole-blind into the mud. The bit penetrated ten centimeters and clogged.

Each man took a sweating, swearing turn at the controls. Luther got the car to go two meters per hour. Francis, exhibiting a talent he didn't know he had, boosted their speed to three.

When at last they reached the far side of the moat, Luther's wristmeter disclosed that they had drilled all afternoon and well past sunset. They could no more see the galaxy's stars above than the planet's leaden core below, yet their knowledge of the night was throbbingly real. Each man winced with fatigue

"Let's assume our wall is thirty meters thick." Burne twiddled the machscope controls. "Right, Luther?"

"Fifty to be safe."

"This toy will tell us for sure."

The machscope blinked on, its needle revolving in silent circles. Burne pressed a button inscribed with the numeral 12, and a listless electric sound bleeped out whenever the needle passed the twenty-meter mark. The sound meant: solid stone twelve meters above.

Progress came easily now. The earth was firm, and their speed increased. Three meters bounced by. Six. Nine. The machscope began to pulsate. Bright, dim. Bright, dim. A sound like a happy piccolo filled the magnecar. The sound meant: open air twelve meters above.

Burne glanced at the odometer. They had traveled under nine and a half meters of foundation. "Narrower than we thought, but reasonable." He brushed the keyboard and the microputer started them on a severely angled ascent.

Thrown against the rear of the viewbubble, Francis steadied the vitreousteel cage and told Ollie not to worry. Forty minutes later, the bit broke the surface and the magnecar shot out of the hole, righting itself on solid ground.

They had tunneled into a starless room of glass.

"GOD'S MAGIC MOUSETRAP!" said Burne when everybody was out of the muck-encrusted car. Luther activated a luminon, spilling light in all directions.

The room was not large—almost any eighty-thousand-dancs-a-year vice-president back on Nearth had an office that dwarfed it—but its featureless vacancy made it seem ample. Austere taste had furnished the place. Before the Nearthlings arrived, there was nothing in it. No window, chair, couch, bed, rug, door, baseboard, fissure, or mousehole. No dust. The four identical walls were as smooth and dark as frozen beanlouse-blood. The high ceiling, also smooth and dark, capped the room like the lid of a specimen jar. The floor was dirt.

Luther walked to the south wall and touched the surface tentatively. "Transpervium," came the verdict, "probably from *Eden Three*."

Transpervium, an obsolete synthetic, had at one time been used for the portholes of spaceships. It could withstand meteor showers, intense radiation, laser beams, and almost anything else you cared to throw at it. From one side transpervium was dull as lead, from the other it was just like a window. The dull side mockingly faced the scientists. Whatever wonders lay beyond, they would remain tonight unseen.

Francis did not like the room. Its sterile symmetry chilled him; its infinite opacity made him feel he was inside a blind man's eye. As far as he could tell, the room's only virtue was that it was not the magnecar.

He looked at the magnecar. At least it had aspects: lights, treads, a viewbubble, and, of course, the drill, jutting like a nipple designed to suckle some gross war machine. A pit yawned where the magnecar had blundered into the room, halfway between the south wall and the center of the floor.

Holding Ollie's cage tight, Francis kicked the nearest surface. "I don't suppose transpervium ever cracks," he said wearily.

"Easier to carve marble with your teeth," Luther replied.

Burne beamed a wicked smile at Francis. "Of course, maybe a *Cortexclavus* could chew through it. Shall we test his nose against transpervium?"

Francis pulled the cage hard against his stomach. "Don't think of such things. You could *damage* him."

As an alternative, Burne drew out his yeastgun and fired point-blank at the north wall. Like a harlot fly encountering a viewbubble, the bullet splashed helplessly.

"So we go down to riverbed level and we keep on going," said Luther automatically. "We dig far, really far, and we don't end up in any more goddam crystal outhouses."

Burne said, "Let me remind us that we're all about to fall down. I vote we make camp here, nab a good night's sleep—"

"First we'd better fix *that*." Luther was pointing to the ruptured floor. "The savages haven't the manners to let us sleep."

There was much huffing and sweating until at last the magnecar blocked the hole. If the room smelled like a stink bug's armpit, Francis did not mind. For the first time in days, he felt that being eaten was unlikely.

DINNER WAS CONCISE: dried fruit, dried fish, freeze-dried coffee. Only fifteen words were spoken during the entire meal. Francis said, "Do you suppose somebody built this room?" and Burne replied, "Do you suppose God can do long division?"

As if to persuade himself that he was in some snug bedchamber on Nearth and not some barren crypt on Carlotta, each man methodically smoothed his sleeping bag into a corner and piled his belongings—electrostylus, wristmeter, carrybelt—on the tidy surface of an imagined night table. Burne reduced the luminon to a whisper of light. In minutes the organic drone of snores echoed off transpervium walls.

Francis's snores were not among them. He thought: Why can't I sleep?

Apparently his body was in one of those moods. It demonstrated how wide awake it was by opening its eyes to their fullest. An hour snored by. The corkscrew beetle scuttled in its cage.

Bits of Francis's life jumped in and out of his mind. Losing his insect collection, losing his son. Finding *Cortexclavus*, finding he had diabetes. Pretty Darlene Spinnet, who taught biochemistry down the hall. Pretty Kappie McKack, who got her head sucked out. Francis ┆ his life was a kinepic edited by someone who ┆ what he was making as long as he got the splic ┆

Why can't I sleep? He rolled over and faced ┆ car, blinking until its dim bulk came into foc ┆ denly he knew.

Someone had entered the room.

Francis felt his stomach unhook itself and ┆ ward. His impulse was to shout and wake hi ┆ something held him back. Mysteriously, the ┆ as quickly as it had come. He said to himself: ┆ more like Burne than I thought.

The stranger was no savage, but a timewor ┆ robes. He sat on a stool. Tall and serene, with ┆ beard that came to a perfect point, he seem ┆ Francis and the magnecar, so attentive was ┆ ment of his hands. Slowly, precisely, wit ┆ slender fingers and a tongue that curled fir ┆ upper lip, the man fashioned an intricate coc ┆ hide, and strips of supple wood.

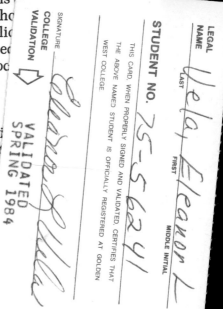

Francis knew at once that the cocoon served no practical purpose; it existed only to fascinate. Its geometric loveliness recalled his favorite insect masterworks: the wing of the whiskey moth, the web of the gorgathon, the nest of the swamp aphid.

Am I dreaming?

Given the feebleness of the luminon, the sculptor was weirdly bright. He pulsated. He bled sheets of mist, as if compounded of dry ice. The atmosphere thickened with a smell like burning hair.

By the west wall a second materialization occurred. This time it was a red-haired boy, all freckles and spunk, dressed only in white linen trousers. The stick in his hand propelled a wooden hoop. He played madly, blind to all but his amusement. Reaching the magnecar, he passed through it like a bird through fog.

The scene sprouted details. Beneath the sculptor's stool a grassy hill grew, ringed by flowers and washed in sun. Where the boy had been, a second artist, a watercolorist, manifested himself.

Boy in tow, the hoop rolled on, right up to the sculptor. It struck the cocoon squarely, snapping a guyline and bouncing away. Francis heard a froglike gasp.

The hoop's surprise turn shocked the boy into reality. He fought against the momentum of his legs. His runaway body fell forward. Briefly the air crackled with a sound like hot popping sap, and the cocoon lay flat, a ruin of splintered wood and tangled wool.

The sculptor approached, as if to help the boy up. Astonishment and chagrin reddened the boy's face. His freckles disappeared.

Francis fully expected the sculptor to be forgiving. Artists naturally distinguish between the careless and the carefree. But the sculptor was not forgiving, and he made no such distinction. Instead, he methodically placed a boot on the boy's mouth.

He used the other boot to kick in every one of the boy's ribs.

Francis was too stunned to move or cry out. Even on Carlotta such an atrocity seemed impossible.

As soon as the boy was dead, everything stopped moving. Flowers no longer bent with the breeze, grass ceased to shiver, the painter froze. The sculptor had become a statue of cruelty, its visage baked into a hideous laugh, its foot planted in the boy's bloody side.

A grotesque tarnish grew like moss upon the statue. The

scene began to melt. Soon a patchwork of black puddles stood in its place—puddles that moved, amoebalike, looking for each other.

One puddle passed under the magnecar and poured itself into the tunnel. The others managed to collect in the center of the room. They fused like droplets of mercury, becoming a pond. Slowly, the pond that had been a murder oozed through the dirt floor and vanished.

Much to his surprise, Francis found that he could now sleep.

6

THE NEXT MORNING they discovered that Francis's dream had eaten through the treads of the magnecar.

"There!" he said, pointing to the raw ends of macroplastic. "This *proves* I didn't just imagine it!"

"I'm afraid it proves nothing of the sort," Burne replied. He kneeled by the car, saw that the metal underbelly was still in one piece.

"But it was so *real!*"

"My guess is that some moat fluid percolated in here last night and got to the treads. We're lucky it didn't get to *us*."

"Better count your toes," said Luther.

Burne yanked a shard of tread away. "We've lost a dozen at least. Too many to improvise our way around."

"Not without a vulcantorch." Luther crouched next to Burne with droop-mouthed intensity.

"Looks like a tight seal," said Burne. He rocked the car but failed to move it even one millimeter. "So whoever was here last night—assuming Dr. Lostwax really did see people, which I doubt profoundly—they sure as hell didn't enter through the tunnel."

Luther rose and drummed the west wall, listening for secret doors. "What do you mean *real*, son? You mean like a play?"

"Yes," said Francis. "Or a kinepic."

"Kinepix aren't real."

"This one was."

"Why didn't you wake us?"

"I don't know. None of it seemed threatening."

"You mean it was like a dream?"

"No."

"Then what was it like?"

"Like—a hallucination."

Luther grew sarcastic. "Let me get this right. *Like* a kinepic, *not* like a dream, *like* a hallucination—"

Francis saw that his case was weak. "All right, I'll drop it. What now?"

"First we admit that our magnecar is at present both a cripple and a burden," Burne began, puffing up. "Then we leave the thing where it is and proceed on foot."

"Proceed where?"

"We could try digging out with my shovel. But we don't know how deep the transpervium is set, and there's no guarantee we won't find ourselves in an adjoining room. I propose we get back outside before something happens to block our way."

"Then what?"

"Follow the wall."

Luther took out his favorite pipe and hung it in his mouth. "I've been thinking about that wall. It looked solid—well maintained—so I'd say the civilization that built it is still around."

"They don't like the savages any better than we do," said Burne. "They never invite them over."

"So maybe if we move along it, we'll spot a repair crew," said Francis. The plan sounded promising even to him.

Breakfast was fried Aretian reptile eggs that had evidently been fertilized. Beautifully embryonic turtles and lizards stared plaintively from Francis's plate. He ate them with his eyes averted. On Nearth, animals were served only in the form of bland, unaccusing components. You never had to swallow life whole.

Burne ordered an inventory. The men broke up their camps and cleaned out the magnecar. Sleeping bags, pillows, clothes, kelvinsleeves, frying pans, knives, forks, spoons, canteens, canned food, dried food, rock samples, soil-test kits, wistar rods, proximascopes, cameras, compasses, and luminons spread from glass wall to glass wall.

Two piles were started: Take With, Leave Here. As Burne explained, "The less we carry, the faster we move. The faster we move, the sooner we can put that wall between us and the savages."

Approaching the Take With pile, a canteen of fine Kritonian coffee in his hand, Francis had sudden visions of a soup tureen. His cerebrum floated among vegetables. He laid the fine Kritonian coffee on the Leave Here pile.

A few minutes later, Luther began negotiating with Burne and Francis to get one of his best rock samples—it was small and light—into the Take With pile. He won.

Certain items were too sacred for either pile. Burne's yeastgun stayed in his belt, Francis's insulin kit stayed in his jacket, Luther's favorite pipe stayed in his mouth. The purpose of each device, Francis realized, was to deliver something to the interior of the human body. He had never seen anyone die from yeastbullets or tobacco smoke, two notorious killers. His son had died from insulin, a life-sustaining miracle.

Before Francis's helpless eyes, Burne casually lifted the last item, Ollie's cage, and placed it atop the Leave Here pile.

"Done," said Burne. "Let's get packed."

Francis's lower lip moved up and down like a guppy's. "B-B-Burne! You *can't*!"

"Dammit, Lostwax, that cage weighs almost as much as *I* do."

"He's the first one ever found!"

"It would take up a third of your pack!"

"He'll starve!"

"Leave it some tunafish. It doesn't even need a can opener."

"We don't know that we're ever coming back. I'd sooner let him go."

"Let it go." Burne liked Francis, even liked *Cortexclavus*, but *somebody* had to take charge of this ragtag army.

"This isn't his planet, Burne. He wouldn't fit in. He'd die *slowly*. And besides, goddam it, I *deserve* that Poelsig Award."

Burne tugged his beard until it hurt. Usually decisions came more easily. Logic said abandon the damn bug, but Francis's distress was touching. We need a *logical* reason to take it, he decided.

"All right, Lostwax, you win. We can't have you so dithered that you slow us down, and we certainly can't have you sneaking away in the middle of the night to retrieve the thing."

Happiness beamed from Francis's teeth and eyes. "I'd have done it, too," he fibbed. "I'd have sneaked off."

"One stipulation. The bug travels in *my* pack. If the savages start chasing us, we throw our packs in the moat and take off. It's the only way we'll outrun them."

Francis nodded. "And you can't imagine me throwing *Cortexclavus* in the moat?"

"Easier to imagine the savages writing an opera."

GETTING THE DAMN MAGNECAR off the hole was appreciably easier than getting it on. It was lighter, the men were rested and full of eggs, and they needed to budge it no more than the broadest pair of shoulders, Burne's.

The scientists jostled each other into bulky packs. Luminons were distributed. They hung snugly around necks, clacked dully against *Darwin* keys. Burne descended the dirt slopes with the oblivious abandon of a ten-year-old entering a swimming hole, Luther with the tight-lipped concentration of a competitive diver making his final attempt to stay in the running, and Francis with the wincing disgust of a captured spy being thrown into a vat of shit.

I've got to distract myself, Francis thought as, grimy hand over grimy hand, he eased his way along the plunging tunnel, forcing his palms deep into its walls lest his legs race uncontrollably. Like a lead plumb his luminon dangled in short precise arcs. At least it was staying lit. At least something was going right.

He fixed his mind on kinepix. A year ago he had attended a thirty-hour marathon of bawdy historical spectacles. By the seventeenth hour he lay slumped in his chair like a forgotten raincoat. Voluptuous women grinned above a sea of dark, silhouetted heads belonging to connoisseurs of bawdy historical spectacles. Had he struggled to raise himself a few centimeters, he could have seen nipples. It wasn't worth it.

The floor stopped falling, but his spirits did not. He knew the riverbed came now, with its unpredictable acid. Yes, it was clearly the moat that had dissolved the magnecar treads. But could ordinary percolation account for its sudden, aggressive appearance?

Certainly last night's murder was not a dream. Francis knew dreams. A mirage? Mirages were nebulous. Francis had seen freckles and a crisp white beard.

The river was passed without mishap, and soon a distant puddle of sunlight beckoned. Choking on apprehension, the men climbed the rising tunnel. When at last Francis broke into the dazzling day, he remembered what it was like to leave the historical-spectacle marathon: for a moment, fantasy and truth had switched places, so that the people on the sunlit streets seemed to be playing out some insipid crowd scene while reality lay abandoned in the dark theater at his back.

No savages were waiting.

"If you were a civilization," asked Burne, "where would you put down roots? At the mouth of your river?"

"At the source," said Luther. "Get your goods to market fast."

They turned and marched south, against the current. UW

Canis Majoris soon had them sweating by the liter. To their left, the vagrant, tread-eating fluid hummed and shimmered and refused to divulge its secrets. Beyond, the wall crept by in a silent procession of stones, not once leaving its guardian moat or spicing its perfection with corner, turret, tower, or gate.

Pack straps began to chew Francis's shoulders, and the luminon bounced against his sternum, raising a welt. Sand got everywhere, or seemed to: boots, pants, jacket, hair, fingernails, armpits, earfolds. It got inside the sockets of his eyes.

For all this, he was feeling better. His romantic bone was singing. He saw himself as a character in one of the bawdy historical spectacles, a swarthy chieftain leading a desert attack. This isn't so bad, he told himself. Throw yourself into it.

He looked over his shoulder, saw the comforting right-angle protuberances of Ollie's cage as it rode up and down in Burne's pack. Just then, everything seemed right.

By early afternoon UW Canis Majoris, having parboiled its little planet, now proceeded to cook the thing for real. Francis and Luther went goofy with the heat. They fell in behind Burne, advancing only through mindless mimicry. When Burne paused, the zombies paused. When Burne shifted his pack, the zombies shifted their packs.

Francis studied the silver-black river, trying to snap himself out of his trance. Talk might help. "There's something about that thing," he said, pointing. "I don't mean the shine or smell or even the unhealthy effect on wistar rods. There's something else."

"What?"

"The . . . holiness."

Luther did not reply. A long silence settled like night upon the men, and they trudged on.

FINALLY, AFTER THIRTY KILOMETERS of monotony, Burne saw that, not far ahead, the wall presented its first turn of the day. The river arced gracefully around, passing from view. Did the long-awaited gate lie beyond?

"Look!"

Burne had stopped walking. The minute they realized this, Francis and Luther fizzled to a halt. "Salvation," said Burne, "may be just around the—"

The thought went no further. Burne's jaw kept moving, but the words stayed inside. Pulling out his proximascope, he trained it on the wall.

On the wall was life. Human life, civilized life, life that in all likelihood sprang from the children of the children of *Eden Three.*

Francis took the proximascope, saw the life: a man and his son and daughter, all astride a peculiar six-legged animal that looked like a child's drawing of a horse. The girl was a plucky pre-teen with tawny skin and sensuous black hair. Bedecked in glasses, her younger brother seemed studious, perhaps even a trifle world-weary, like a child prodigy who had composed one too many sonatas. As for the father, he had evidently bequeathed so much amiable enthusiasm to his daughter and so much brooding thoughtfulness to his son that there was little left for him besides a beefy build and a boringly honest face.

All three citizens disported themselves with the carefree air of a family out for a holiday. It was clear that in riding the wall they had no real goal beyond the trustworthy pleasures of wall riding.

"Look at their *robes!*" yelled Frances, handing the proximascope to Luther. "Just like the one in my dream!"

"Are they the same people?" asked Luther.

"No. But it's all one culture, that's obvious. So it *wasn't* a dream!"

"He doesn't *look* like the sort who goes around kicking children's ribs in."

"Neither did that sculptor."

THE FATHER SAW the scientists, and the shock nearly un-horsed him. He snatched the reins from his daughter, drawing them tight until the lipoca's pea-brain made the correct translation: stop.

The children were more curious than fearful. They had always wanted to see what these mythical Brain Eaters looked like. "Where are their *teeth*, Father?" asked the boy.

"Those aren't neurovores. I don't know *what* they are."

"I'll bet they're from another planet!" said the girl.

Pasting a huge phony smile on his face, Burne shouted "Peace!" and stretched both his palms up high, as if waiting to catch a trapeze. Francis and Luther, still under exhaustion's spell, did likewise. The Nearthlings believed themselves the very picture of goodwill.

To the girl the Nearthlings were the very picture of saphood. "Why do they grin like that?" she whispered. "Are people from other planets ninnies?"

Her father's only response was to mutter, "God of the brain, they speak English!" after which he made a megaphone with his hands. "My name is Zamanta!" he cried. "Our planet is Luta, our country Quetzalia! Where do you live?"

Francis decided to play a role in this historic contact. "Fourth from the sun," he said triumphantly, but then his stomach sank. Did he get it right? Lapus, Verne, Kritonia, Nearth, Carlotta (what had Zamanta called it—Luta?), Arete . . . yes, fourth.

"They're human," Zamanta whispered to his daughter.

"I'm disappointed," said the girl, reporting her feelings matter-of-factly. "I was hoping for a tentacle or something."

Matter-of-fact was not Zamanta's mood. Cautiously he broadcast another question into the desert. "What do you eat?"

"Nothing but vegetables!" said Francis with bizarre conviction.

"We hate the savages, too!" Luther added.

Zamanta's sigh was a fountain of gratitude.

The scientists' minds were ticking in unison. Here was a chance to get *Darwin* back! Burne pictured himself at the head of a vast Quetzalian army, trumpets blaring, banners puffed with Lutan breeze, saddlebags jammed with pollucite ore. The army charges the oasis, obliterating the savages in a matter of hours.

Francis leaped even further into the future. He could see the Poelsig Award on the mantelpiece in his office—a big office right next to the great amphitheater, where he lectured only if he felt like it, because now his real work was research.

Francis's ambitions were interrupted by a sudden shout, its content so jolting that Luther dropped the proximascope.

"Neurovores!"

Half a kilometer to the right the sand swirled and boiled. Fifty savages charged over the dunes, the air above their heads abloom with a forest of spearshafts.

"This way!" Zamanta screamed, his arm erect, his hand extended and palpitating. "Run!" Dismounting, father and children broke for the corner of the wall. The scientists felt no shame in following their panicked example. The Brain Eaters were minutes away.

Oh, how I hate thee, Planet Luta, Francis thought as he ran. Why don't you just kill us and get it over with? The sand came up hard against his feet, with thuds that rang grittily inside his head.

The bend in the river took forever to arrive. Rounding it, the men at last saw their hopes fulfilled by a pair of pyramidal towers that slanted down to within a meter of the moat. Between the towers a massive drawbridge, polished-oak-and-iron-bolt triumph of Quetzalian art, stood poised for rescue. It began to descend, a great clamouring portcullis crawling up behind it like a metal spider.

A ghastly awareness grew in Francis: Luther had fallen behind. Francis stopped, and he turned. And he saw.

Finally, fully, Luther's age worked its betrayal. He stumbled, colliding with the soft sand. The neurovores fell upon him.

"Burne!" Francis thought his larynx would pop out. "Burne, the gun!" But Burne, far ahead, ears dulled by his own footfalls, did not respond.

The neurovores feasted greedily, quickly. They raised high Luther's violated body and tossed it like garbage into the moat.

Francis stood and wailed. "You'll all die for this!"

By now Burne had paused, observed, reacted. Drawn too late, the yeastgun flashed impotently in his hand. "The bridge, Lostwax!"

The cries cut through to Francis's genes, igniting the ancient need to save oneself first and mourn the dead second. He took off.

Perfect timing. The moment the bridge smacked the river's far bank, Burne was ready to cross. He had reached the middle of the moat when Francis's foot touched wood.

Like a sprung trap the bridge leaped up, drawn by woven cables. Francis tumbled forward, smashing into Burne and knocking him down. Neither minded; they were falling to sanctuary.

Sprawled in the arching gateway, Francis cranked his head forward and saw that two fearsomely armed neurovores—one male, one female—had together gained the far bank, jumped for the edge of the rising bridge, grabbed it, pulled themselves athwart. He saw that the monsters would now be fated with one of several deaths. They would either tumble forward, hitting the hinge of the bridge with concussive force, or they would tumble backward, dissolving in the moat, or they would stay put, getting mashed between the edge of the bridge and the ponderous stone lintel that jutted from the wall, crowning the portcullis.

But neurovores, Francis guessed, do not leave their evolution to natural selection. They *act*, quickly, with ferret guile and monkey moves. Jump, said their primal minds, their springwound muscles. Jump for the top of the wall.

The neurovores shot skyward, disappearing behind the lintel.

Francis and Burne staggered through the gateway and collapsed in weary heaps. The bridge was fully upright now, shutting out the desert and its horrors. Burne unstrapped his pack, eyed it dully. He had completely forgotten about throwing it into the moat.

Their rescuer, the gatekeeper, approached timidly. He was a frail man, middle-aged, with bounteous gray hair and a face that looked partially deflated. He had raised the bridge and its companion portcullis only with help from an elaborate arrangement of windlasses, pulleys, weights, and cords.

"Praised be Iztac," he said in a creaky voice. "I thought for certain you were doomed."

"Let me try to thank you," said Francis, his panting head supported by his pack.

"You've lost a friend," said the gatekeeper.

Burne gagged. "It happened, didn't it?" Slowly he pulled himself upright, brushing sand from his jacket with one hand, gripping his yeastgun with the other.

"We owe you our lives," Francis mumbled, blowing tears off his cheeks. He kept thinking how Luther would never discover what was in the moat.

"I only did the *moral* thing. After all, you are civilized."

Francis sensed traces of a question in the gatekeeper's voice. "Yes," he croaked, "we are civilized." The relief on the gatekeeper's face: Francis had seen it only minutes before, on the man who called himself Zamanta.

"Forgive my piety," said the gatekeeper, "but in Quetzalia we try to—" His gaze drifted aimlessly to the wall. "No!"

Never before had Francis heard such a No!, this No! that went beyond any kind of personal anguish—even the kind he was feeling about Luther—to say that all hope and light were now ripped from the world. He looked up, saw a stone stairway leading from the ground to the summit, and brought his popping eyes to rest on the two neurovores who had jumped. They were shambling toward the children.

Seeing an escape, Zamanta's daughter ran for the stairway. Neurovore breath warmed her neck. She had descended ten steps when her pursuer, the male, drove his spear forward, catching her sash, hooking her like a fish. He yanked her back for the kill.

Overhead, the female lunged cruelly for Zamanta's son. She shook her spear, raising her ax high. The boy did not cry out.

Francis lay staring in boggled disbelief. The incredible thing was not the ruthlessness of the neurovores, nor even the courage of their prey. The incredible thing was that Zamanta made no move to help his children. He simply stood, white with horror, wet with tears: a man watching his house burn down.

There was a noise like raw meat hitting hot metal. A bright gold bead divided the air and flawlessly found its target. The female neurovore staggered backward, a purple hole growing in her neck. Her weapons fell, clattering on the stones.

Seconds later, the neurovore's throat burst open like a ripe tomato left in the sun.

Blood rained copiously on the boy. Roaring in pain, the monster fell backward toward the river. The splash of the corpse was deep-voiced and conclusive.

The gatekeeper shivered with amazement. "You said you were civilized!" he shouted. "I don't believe what I see!"

"Stay around and you'll see it again," said Burne quietly. He did not lower the yeastgun, but merely pivoted until the second neurovore, the male, entered its sights. Coolly Burne squeezed the trigger . . . to no effect. VVVSSSSS came the dull electronic whimper, the same kind that had attended Kappie's slaughter. "Dammit to hell!"

The male bristled, all senses on the alert. He tore his spear from the girl's sash, raised it aloft, and dashed to the bottom of the stairs. His other hand wielded an ax, a beveled granite brute, and this he used first, swinging it in crazed circles, launching it with a numbing shriek. Burne felt the air part by his cheek. The ax plowed into the sand, a meter from where Francis rested wild-eyed against his pack.

The girl ascended the stairs and joined her gory brother. Zamanta scooped them up. Trembling, he held them tight.

The monster drew back his spear, aimed it for Burne's brain. Nearthling eyes and neurovore eyes met, locked gazes, mingled enmities. Burne's attacker had horrid nostrils, deep and gaping like bullet holes. Not far below, a stinking mouth displayed broken teeth, bloody gums, abundant drool, and a saw-edged tongue.

Burne dove for the spongy ground. The spearhead whistled past the nape of his neck, its shaft glancing off his shoulder. Slowed, the spear stayed in flight. Francis saw it coming, could not evade it.

A sharp nut-cracking sound told Francis the spear had hit—had entered—his cranium. The pain was immediate but not extreme. Fear pressed intolerably upon his heart.

He slumped over, and the spear dislodged itself. Wetness rushed down his temples. Gazing across the sandy field, he saw that the neurovore had broken into a run and was heading south, straight for where the forest was thickest.

And then the sun vanished.

7

A DISORGANIZED GALAXY. A pounding soreness. Slowly the jots of light threw themselves into focus, became a face. Francis blinked twice. The face was male, human, non-neurovorean, old. Its features were craggy and pitted, a bombed landscape.

"Welcome to the Hospital of Chimec," said the face. Its owner crouched over Francis like a winter coat, frayed and protective. "I am Tixo Mool, in charge of your case."

"Chimec?" moaned Francis. "I thought I was *dead*." Somebody had been playing blasterball with his head. "No, it doesn't smell right. Death should smell like formaldehyde. And there shouldn't be any hunger. I'm hungry."

"I hope so. You've been unconscious for two days."

Francis coughed and rolled over, crisp linen slipping noiselessly across his skin. He found himself looking through an open window into labyrinthian gardens. Breezes drifted down blossomed footpaths, swirled around marble benches holding convalescents. Here and there, brilliant white arm-slings flapped like flags of surrender.

"Luther lost his brain, didn't he?" asked Francis. "The neurovores took it."

Mool bit his lip, grumbled. He proffered a mug filled with something hot and pungent. "Drink this."

"Soup?"

"Cuiclo tea. Finish it up. Leave only a tear's worth."

"*How* much?"

"We always leave a tear's worth." Mool's voice assumed a quoting tone. "Never forget the tears of war-bereaved parents."

Francis, trusting, took the mug and drank deeply. The tea was sour, chalky, and altogether awful.

"It's an acquired taste," Mool said in answer to Francis's grimace.

"I hope I never do."

"You're not drinking it for pleasure. It will blot out your pain."

"Burne's brain wasn't eaten," said Francis dully, as if this were a common expression.

"No."

"Where is he?"

"In the southern jungles somewhere, on a—how shall I put it?—a mission of mercy. He's going to track down that male neurovore for us, the one that came over the wall, and he's going to . . . kill it." His voice skipped on "kill."

"The neurovore has a good lead, doesn't he?"

"Yes, regrettably. You won't see your friend for at least three opochs."

"Opochs?" Francis slurped his tea.

"Our calendar is flawless. Twenty-five hours to the day, twenty-five days to the opoch, twenty-five opochs to the year. But the runners will tell us where he is."

"Oh," said Francis feebly. Blood-borne, the tea was in his brain now. Why the hell did they send *Burne* to do it? "Runners?"

"Yes. Does that sound crude to you? Well, the truth is that Quetzalia has no mass communication. But don't let our apparent backwardness cast a shadow on this afternoon's ablation. It won't hurt."

"Ablation?"

"On Earth they were called operations. Ablation is better. We're going to *ablate* the stone in your head."

"But the spear fell out!"

"A chip stayed behind, poised above your laughter site. Odd as it sounds, you're in danger of losing your ability to laugh."

Francis shrugged. "The way my life is going, I won't be needing it." He knew from his biology training that the laughter site existed. It was discovered by an Earthling surgeon named Richard Hassler in a year named A.D. 1955.

"This ablation is quite necessary. The laughter site is in the thalamus."

Francis walked his fingers up the side of his head. They ascended his jaw, traversed his ear, forded a wet bandage covering the spear hole, and eventually touched smooth, drum-tight flesh, whereupon he realized he was bald as a clam. "You're not going in through the wound?"

"Think of the chip as a trapped miner. You don't necessarily open up the old shaft to reach him. Often it's best to dig a new one."

"Just remember that this time it's the *mine* that's alive and the miner who's made of rock." Francis elevated himself slightly, as if trying to see nipples at a kinepic marathon. "Burne had a live insect specimen in his pack, a *Cortexclavus areteus.* It must be fed."

"All the curiosities Dr. Newman brought into Quetzalia—the nontechnological curiosities—were taken to the Library of Iztac. I think he had a dried fish and a rock sample. Your bug must be there too. I'll see to its needs."

Francis didn't understand what "nontechnological" was doing in that reply, but he was infinitely relieved to hear of Ollie's apparent rescue.

Mool began to indulge his habit of answering unasked questions. "You're lucky they brought you here and not to one of Nazra's bureaucrats. Nazra governs out of Aca, but he's got a bunch of toadies—a *swamp* of toadies, does that amuse you?—here in Tepec." Mool snickered. "I said, *does that amuse you?*"

"I don't laugh these days," Francis replied. "It's the rock in my brain."

"Neither do Nazra's bureaucrats. Yesterday they barged in, clung to me like burrs. 'The hemorrhaging has stopped,' they said. 'Don't do the ablation yet. First find out his intentions.' Two hours later Nazra sends word down, tells us your coming is a *religious* matter, and so the bureaucrats move out and the goddam clergy moves in, and they, too, want to know your 'intentions.' But then the high priestess herself shows up, and she says, 'I'll get them off your back, just save this man's life, it's the *moral* course.' "

Stepping toward the open window, Mool inflated himself with morning air. "That's enough about you. Let me tell you about me. I'm sixty-three years old and hearty as a Cuz year-rounder. I have a son who . . ."

Without particularly meaning to, Francis let Mool's words blur into meaningless vocables. He found himself staring across the room at a tall and uncompromisingly avant-garde oil painting. When he tuned in again, he heard, "If you *yourself* find me authoritarian, don't fret, for the actual ministration of your case is the responsibility of our best resident, Dr. Tez Yon, who is both modest and competent, and whose sunshine youthfulness I envy."

By now Mool had left the window, was grasping a leather thong that dangled from one side of the oil painting. When he yanked the thong, the painting pivoted on its opposite edge, proving itself to be a door. "One more thing. I'm afraid I must ask for your machines."

"My what?"

"Did you bring anything technological into Quetzalia?"

"There was a luminon around my neck. My pack contains an electrostylus, a kelvinsleeve, things like that."

"They must all be taken to the Temple of Tolca and burned. This is required."

Despite his numbness, a sudden unease shot through Francis. Who are these people? Romantics who believe machines breed godless rationality? Terrible news, if it's true. They won't want to help us get *Darwin* back.

"You've banned all machines from Quetzalia?"

"The word is *forbidden*," Mool replied. "In Quetzalia machines are forbidden."

"Did Burne play along?"

"His wristmeter, luminon, and yeastgun are nothing but ashes and molten blobs."

"Even his gun?"

"Dr. Newman is an archeologist. He knows that playing along, as you put it, is a reliable way to ingratiate yourself with the natives. Will you, too, indulge us on this point?"

"How can Burne kill the neurovore? You've disarmed him!"

Mool grunted. "He said that if a neurovore didn't need a yeastgun, then he didn't either."

"Melt the luminon, the kelvinsleeve, everything. But there's a metal box in my jacket—it contains an insulin flask and two hypodermic syringes."

"We know about diabetes, Dr. Lostwax."

"My health is not touched. Nearth has the plastic pancreas now."

"*Quetzalia* has the cure now, and I don't use the word lightly. Until you take the cure, we'll grant you your syringes. But don't show them around." Mool crossed the threshold.

"A detail," Francis called after him. "That kelvinsleeve won't melt. It's crysanium."

"Then we'll dissolve it in noctus."

"In what?"

"Noctus fills the river."

"The river that follows the wall?"

"Yes, the river made of hate."

"But what *is* noctus? What does it consist of?"

"It consists of hate," said Mool with a narrow smile, and briskly he closed the door.

THE CUICLO TEA not only freed Francis of his pain, it made him deliciously drowsy, so that when the two adolescent orderlies came they had to shake him six times before his eyes opened. Together they lifted Francis, deposited him on a wheeled table, and pushed him into a glassy corridor muted by pale afternoon sunlight.

Frescoes of astonishing impact glided by, not one of them bowing to the unimaginative, noncommittal style with which Nearthlings felt obligated to embalm their institutions. There were sagas full of hairbreadth escapes from monsters and cataclysms, fantasies featuring ghosts and potions, and sexual transactions stimulating enough to rehabilitate a eunuch.

There were moments of comedic truth so self-evident that Francis found himself giggling.

If the corridor could have doubled as a small art museum, the operating room could have doubled as a gigantic funnel. The orderlies wheeled Francis through an archway into the broad circular spout. Its center was a padded table, onto which he soon found himself painstakingly transferred. A nearby cart bristled with surgical instruments. Above, fanning outward and sloping upward, rows of seats held a scant dozen medical students. They hunched forward expectantly, and their smooth startling youthfulness made Francis feel extinct. Higher still, sunlight spread across a glass ceiling and rolled into the funnel's mouth.

On the circumference of the spout, every sixty degrees, a floor lamp flared merrily, its wick soggy with perfumed oil. Between the lamps hung tall and uncompromisingly avant-garde oil paintings. One painting pivoted forward, revealing a small woman and two men, one rangy, the other a gnome. The orderlies took the cue and backed away.

WITH COLOSSAL RELUCTANCE Tez Yon entered the operating theater, stewing in her hatred of the coming job. If I succeed, she thought, Mool gives the glory to "my crack surgical team," by which he means himself. But if the Nearthling dies on the table, all the blame falls on me, and everybody goes around shedding big juicy tears—crocodile tears, since nobody *wants* him to live.

The sight of the helpless patient ended her bout of self-pity. She realized that her nurses had already started circumscribing his cranium with kuskdye, daubing his scalp with the local anesthetic called lethewort, and wrapping his arm with tendrils from a kardiovine, that wondrous plant whose color shifts warned of dangerous fluctuations in blood pressure. She reached the table, seized her scalpel, and held it like a dart. Addressing her audience, she jabbed repeatedly in the direction of Francis's brain.

"As you have all heard, Dr. Lostwax comes from Iztac Four, the original destination of *Eden Two* and our own *Eden Three*. He calls his planet Nearth. He is an entomologist. For our purposes, he is not an extraterrestrial but a human, not a Nearthling but a Quetzalian. The fact of his coming is not widely known beyond this hospital, and I am told that Governor Nazra and Vaxcala Coatl want it to stay that way. I realize that it is taxing to imagine a governor and a high priestess agreeing on *anything*, but for now we must keep this man's identity a secret." There was laughter. "If you have questions . . ."

A diffident hand went up. "May I ask the patient something?" The hand belonged to a sad-eyed young man.

As Tez approached, Francis saw a face that, by virtue of its size, might be called "cute," yet "cute" was wholly unjust to her rubbery mouth, her genius eyes, her opulent terra-cotta hair. Mool had mentioned that Francis would find Tez competent and young. He had neglected to mention that Francis would fall in love with her at first sight.

"Will you answer a question?" Tez asked.

"All right," said Francis, reveling in her husky voice. Just then he would have agreed to any Tez Yon proposal short of a suicide pact.

"Do you practice the rites of Zolmec?" asked the sad-eyed man.

"Most of us are not religious," Francis replied.

"What keeps you from hurting each other?"

Francis gave a recumbent shrug. "Nearthlings hurt each other all the time."

"That's what I thought," the man said with a smugness that was somehow not annoying.

Tez circled the table, glancing every which way like an actor counting the house. She stopped directly behind Francis's naked scalp. The house was silent.

"Since there are no further questions, we'll start digging."

The gnome sifted through the implements, found a small flute, and moved to the end of the table. Framed by Francis's feet, he arched his fingers, blew gently. The melody was weird. Meanwhile, unseen, unfelt, Tez and the rangy one bent over Francis's head, plying their trade.

"Does it trouble you that we don't wear surgical masks?" Tez asked. "The fact is, Luta's microorganisms are nonpathogenic to a fault."

"Our sensorprobes said as much. Tell me about the music. Is it for my benefit?"

"Mine. Are you enjoying it?"

"I'd give *anything* to play like that." It was a silly remark, but he treasured the whole idea of talking with this particular Quetzalian.

"I'd give the wart on my right arm." Tez's lowered tones did not reach the gallery. "My flutist is hardly a master by Quetzalian standards."

"It's not the sort of tune people play on Nearth."

"I'd like to hear Nearth music sometime."

"If Burne and I get our ship back, I'll lend you our bachbox."

"Yes, except that machines are forbidden here. By the way, we've cut through your scalp, doctor: skin, muscle, periosteum, galea, everything. I can see skull."

How strange, Francis thought. I'm not afraid. "Is there much blood?"

"Enough to drown a rat, but my assistant is ladling on the proper coagulants and clipping the right vessels. Don't worry, we know what we're doing."

"I trust you instinctively."

There was a sudden grinding screech.

"What's that?" His trust was beginning to evaporate.

"Metal on bone."

"It's horrible."

"This is a craniotomy, Dr. Lostwax. We're not popping pimples. First come the burr holes, right? Then we connect them with a saw. It's not unlike the way my father gets blocks out of the eastern quarries."

"Let's discuss something else Why are machines forbidden?"

"They are forbidden by Tolca, our god of peace."

"I see," he said with manifest lack of enthusiasm. Francis had always been ecumenical in his atheism. He was as prepared to disbelieve in this Tolca character as he was to disbelieve in Yahweh, Jesus, Buddha, Vishnu, or any of the other words for what his father used to call "forcing yourself to misperceive the obvious."

"You should understand," said Tez, sensing his objection, "that the gods of Zolmec are not gossamer promises of the kind who, as the historians tell it, enjoyed enormous popularity on Earth." The screeching stopped. "They don't refuse to show themselves. They're down here, among us, in forms so tangible you could stub your toe. This knife . . ."

She dangled her scalpel before her patient's eyes. Its obsidian blade glistened with fresh Francis Lostwax blood. Its handle swirled with delicately carved birds and fish. "This knife is not a knife, it's the power and beauty of intellect. Scientists and artists designed it in partnership, so it would cut artfully into tissue, lay bare exquisite truths about spirit. The final fact, doctor, is that Quetzalia's gods are not divinities at all, but whatever unguessed potentialities we find inside ourselves. What else is *worth* worshiping?"

"I don't know what you're talking about," said Francis evenly.

"Your cranium is off."

"I'm frightened."

"You had cuiclo this morning. If you feel yourself getting sleepy, don't fight it. Just fall away and dream."

"I wish this *planet* were a dream."

"Have you ever seen a living human brain, Dr. Lostwax, all throbbing and coral with blood?"

Francis thought for a moment. Kappie's brain was killed by the time it surfaced. "No."

"Dr. Zoco says that learning about human brains from gray pickled specimens is like learning about human beings from corpses."

"Try to leave everything just as you found it."

Tez laughed aloud, pondered silently. Our Nearthling seems rational enough. Yet his friend was able to murder. The human race may not sort neatly into Quetzalians and monsters after all.

Again she played to the gallery. "As you can see: a modified radical scalp-incision, a transcephalic bone-door, and the great god cortex is before us. Now, the first danger is herniation when we open the dura. The second, of course, is functional deficit. To avoid the first danger, a standard number-two sterolthorn is pushed between the hemispheres, four millimeters short . . . of . . . the . . . corpus callosum. To . . . avoid . . . the . . . . second . . . . . danger . . . . . . it . . . . is . . . . necessary . . . . to . . ."

For Francis the husky voice was softening, fading, was gone. Before drifting to sleep, he realized that the elegant woman presently working miracles inside his brain was going to be impossible to get out of his mind.

8

EVERY SO OFTEN you encounter an animal that does not know what it is.

Such specimens are wholly unlike the cat, who is an expert at being a cat, or the cod, who partakes authoritatively of codness, or even the unassuming earthworm, who at some level beyond our untuned perceptions understands what is expected of it. Planet Luta held cats, cod, and earthworms, descendents of *Eden Three*, and it also held a homegrown beast called the chitzal, a mammalian furball on reptilian feet, with two ordinary eyes plus a third that evolution, in a moment of frivolity, had located on a stalk atop the chitzal's head, an all-seeing lollipop.

The chitzal did not know what it was. Surprisingly, the chitzal served a purpose.

Benched in the gardens immediately outside his hospital room, Francis stared toward the nearest tree and with growing aggravation beheld an adult male chitzal. It hung upside down by its claws, contemplating Francis with its lollipop. It breathed, blinked, and did nothing else discernible. If only it would *behave* in some way, Francis thought, I could be loyal to my calling and take notes. If only it wouldn't just *hang* there like a wasp's nest.

Five days had passed since his operation, five afternoons in the gardens, and Francis was numb with boredom. For all I know, his brooding went, Luta is bursting with undiscovered insects, gorgathon offshoots, perhaps, who came here inside meteorites and to this day retain their species's uncanny ability to shed tears at the death of a near relation. Yet here I sit, immobile lest my head fall off.

The one sunny moment of each afternoon occurred when Tez Yon made her rounds. She supervised his recuperation with an ardor that extended noticeably beyond duty. She brought gifts. Do I attract her because I am extraterrestrial, Francis wondered, or is there a more auspicious explanation?

Whatever fascination Tez felt, she suspected that it owed less to Lostwax the individual than to a kind of anthropological curiosity—do spacemen make good lovers? She was skeptical. Not that she thought romance and copulation weren't first-rate. But no manfriend had ever absorbed her quite so much as a tantalizingly half-true article in the *Chimec Hospital Journal*. Tepecans were so fashionably open about their private hours, perversions included, that affairs paled rapidly. She had heard that things were more lewd in Aca, that they had something called the telepathic orgasm. Doubtful. Still, to love the only Nearthling in town was a novelty that might endure.

Yesterday Tez's gift had been an assortment of solitaire strategy games that divided rather hopelessly into those Francis found boneheadedly easy and those he found grotesquely opaque. The day before that she had brought a basket of opos, a corpulent domestic fruit, its skin scaly, its pulp succulent. The day before that she had brought a hand-lettered copy of the national epic, *The Divine Cocoon*. Francis read how the human race was first a worm choking on the filth of a contaminated planet, then a pupa metamorphosing in a space ark, then a butterfly flourishing in a utopia. Poetry was not a usual pleasure for Francis, but he loved every word.

The day before that Tez had awakened Francis in his room. "Promise me you won't cough," she said, "and I'll give you two pieces of good news."

"I won't cough."

"It increases the intracranial pressure. Would you like to hear about your ablation first, or your beetle?"

"My beetle."

"Mool sent me to the Library of Iztac, and everybody agreed that your friend Newman took it with him on his neurovore hunt. Nobody knows why."

But Francis did, or thought so. "Good old Burne, he figured I might be too sick to care for Ollie." Then he added, in his mind: And he also figured these quirky Quetzalians might throw it away. "Tell me about my ablation."

"The chip is gone. Your thalamus is saved."

"I won't have to give up laughter?"

"No," said Tez, "but you'll have to give up freedom for a while—five days." She brushed him gently on the instep and pointed to the open window. "Our gardens are therapeutic."

"You're a genius."

"Merely an apprentice genius. The great god Mool gets all the credit around here."

"I don't like him either."

"Mool was raised by a wire mother. But it's not his manner that galls me. It's the way he's treating my father."

"I would suspect Mool treats everybody badly."

"*Medical* treatment." Tez found herself telling about Teot Yon's accident, about her conflict with Mool over the safety of coyo root as a therapy.

Francis strained to say the right thing. "I'm afraid herbology is out of my line."

"I think it's out of Mool's line, too. At least you're *listening*."

The subject needed changing. "How did my mind appear, deep down? I must admit, I feel slightly raped."

Tez brightened. "Clinical neurology is intimate, I suppose, but hardly carnal. Everybody's brain looks pretty much the same."

"Did you try any of that cortex-stimulation business? You know, pressing the soft spots so I experience my past and talk about it?"

"But of *course*," Tez joked. "I know all your deepest secrets now. I know about those overdue library books, and the lady plumber with the trick knee. By the way, that cuff link you lost six years ago is on the washstand."

"May I get up?" asked Francis.

"Slowly."

Sliding out of bed, Francis realized that someone had dressed him in Quetzalian robes. He approached the painting that was a door. Before his eyes, millions of brush-thrusts congealed into mind-reeling designs.

"How nice of you," he said aloud, "to decorate my room with so skillful a representation of my recent life."

By "recent" he meant the last eight days, which had surely featured more improbabilities than all the Francis Lostwax life that had gone before. Last year at this time his principal worries were whether to drop by that cathouse down the block and whether to spend forty-five dancs on reprints of "The Spirituality of Beanlice." Kid stuff, compared with watching two friends get eaten, having the top of your head sawed off, and falling in love with an extraterrestrial. It baffled him that he was still sane, baffled him even more that he felt entirely ready for further excitements.

Tez pulled a mirror from her robe and thrust it before Francis. He saw that, right above his original wound, his head had been spliced together like two pieces of kinepic film. The seam, a tacky yellow goo, ringed his scalp like a hatband. He fingered it.

"Gently," she cautioned.

"No stitches?"

"Murm is better. Your incision will not heal in the conventional sense. It will *solidify*, like paraffin."

"Murm." Francis sang the word.

"It's the miraculous stomach-lining of an otherwise useless animal called the chitzal. Nourishes your scalp just like blood, keeps your dura irrigated, and needs replenishing only once a year."

"You mean the suture extends under the *bone*?"

Tez nodded. "Don't worry, your skullcap and dura are permanently separated. If a lover pulls your hair too hard, your brain might get exposed, but there'll be no ruptured arteries."

Francis gasped. Is this science? he wondered. Then what do they do around here for witchcraft?

"You implied that my hair will grow back."

"Thicker than ever, and just when you're sick of seeing that ugly scar every time you shave."

Tez grasped the door thong, then stopped, turned, her smile failing to mask her blush. "I know this experience has been completely outrageous, but someday, Francis Lost-wax, you may find uses for your chitzal scar that you never dared *dream* about."

She was gone before Francis could even ask

THAT AFTERNOON, Tolcaday by what Mool had called "our flawless calendar," Tez brought neither mirrors, epics, opos, nor games, but a beefy man familiar to Francis. It was Zamanta, the one whose children Burne had saved from unequivocal death at the paws of neurovores. Zamanta's wife, frail in build but assertive in carriage, with wild eyes and chaotic yellow hair, stood smiling by his side.

"We had to express our gratitude," said Zamanta, "Momictla and I."

"It's really Burne you should go see," said Francis. "Not that I don't applaud what he did." He felt no geniality toward this man who had almost sacrificed two children without a fight.

"*We* don't applaud what he did," said Zamanta. "Only the result."

"Yes, well, *I* don't consider myself violent either, but

given the chance I'd disembowel all those savages. They slaughtered two of my"—he was going to say "colleagues," felt a sudden hollowness in his soul—"best friends."

"You think I'm a coward, don't you?" asked Zamanta.

Saying nothing, Francis stared toward the great step-pyramid that was the Hospital of Chimec. Faced with solid gold, a sunstruck temple blinked down from the summit.

Momictla touched Tez's sleeve. "He's cured, isn't he?"

Tez nodded. "We discharge him tomorrow."

"Oh, I'm fine," Francis injected phlegmatically. All around, postoperative patients sought out each other for talk, games, commiseration. No doubt they would flock over in a minute should someone give the word that Francis was the famous visitor from outer space.

"Remember," said Momictla, "any favor we can ever do for you—just ask."

"I'll remember." His voice was still dead. Not far away, a spry child with a bandage over one eye was making life miserable for the local chitzal. She chased it down a tree, across a footbridge, around a bench. The chitzal ran like a cheesy broken toy. Francis smiled inside. It was high time somebody told a chitzal there was more to life than wasp's-nest imitations.

Zamanta said, "We understand you brought a rare and beautiful insect into our country."

Suddenly Francis realized he was smiling—beaming—outside as well as in. Coward or not, Zamanta knew how to win you over. "It's a *Cortexclavus areteus*," said Francis. "The larval form is probably a—"

What he noticed was enough to distract him even from thoughts of Ollie. The one-eyed girl and her quarry were on a collision course for a well-advanced chess game. The chitzal tilted the table, the girl finished the job. Castled kings, pushed pawns, and a dozen other tactics took to the air like startled pigeons as the girl toppled unharmed into the grass.

White had been a muscular teen-age boy with a linen bandage around his forehead. Black had been a plump middle-aged woman with one arm in a sling. On both faces shock faded into a blank serenity that admitted of no obvious interpretation. Already Black had started for the sprawled girl. White was rising.

Francis quaked. The crime in the glass room flooded back with chill clarity.

"What's the matter?" asked Momictla.

"They're going to *kill* her," he said hoarsely, leaping off his bench.

But Black was asking, "Are you all right, friend?"

"I ruined your game," the girl replied, contrite but not gushy. Black's good hand grasped the girl's extended one, and the latter regained her feet.

"That's no problem," said White, arriving. "I was losing."

"I'm not usually clumsy. It's this silly eye-patch."

White picked a leaf out of the girl's hair. "You were just having fun."

"I've never been enthralled by the Nimzo-Indian defense"—Black winked at her partner—"even though I had a clear mate in seventeen moves."

"I'll help you set up," said the girl, extracting Black's queen from the grass. The three of them hunted amiably for the remaining pieces.

That was it. End of episode. Curtain. No blood, no drubbings, not even a raised voice.

"You really thought they would kill her?" asked Tez.

"Before we realized that Quetzalia had a drawbridge, my friends and I tunneled under your wall. We ended up in a transpervium room."

Tez tensed, not quite perceptibly. Francis explained that he had witnessed a murder whose inspiration was scarcely more goading than a ruined chess game.

"Everyone here seems so kind—even pacifistic." He shot

an involuntary and awkward glance at Zamanta. "Yet I saw it." In the background, Black and White were telling the girl about the merits of Pawn to King Four. The chitzal was back in its tree. "Unless, of course, it was a dream."

Anxious glances rebounded among Tez, Zamanta, Momictla.

"I'd better let my other patients know I'm still sawing bones," said Tez. She turned, and the glowing Temple of Chimec bronzed her face. "Good-bye, Francis Lostwax. Let's keep in touch."

"I'll keep in touch with you if you'll keep in touch with me." He liked talking about touch with her. "But what about my dream?"

"I suppose . . . I suppose it was only a dream."

FRANCIS AWOKE the next morning to find his bed encircled by five overweight men who called themselves priests of the Temple of Iztac and no doubt were. The most forceful among them, also the fattest, gave his name, Mouzon Thu. Mouzon was homely, all bubbled by warts, with an incongruously musical voice.

"Please get dressed, doctor," he sang. "Vaxcala Coatl expects a visit."

Francis said, "And I suppose it would be lousy interplanetary diplomacy to keep the high priestess waiting."

They escorted him through the ascending corridors, into the brilliant air, down the proliferous exterior steps of the hospital. A wagon waited at the bottom, its lipoca pawing and snorting. One priest, a swarthy adolescent, moved up front to steer, and the other joined their catch, their prize Nearthling, in the back. The wagon clattered off across a broad and dustless plaza. Narrowing, the plaza became a causeway threading drinkable lagoons together.

"That's the place," said Mouzon.

"The Library of Iztac, god of the sun," added a priest whose face was mainly beard.

Pointing fingers led Francis's eyes to a great pyramid, twin to the Hospital of Chimec. The steep-sided giants, masterworks of sun-dried brick, faced each other across five kilometers of causeway. Lesser pyramids and low stone buildings intervened, casting their reflections into lustrous waters.

"You can see her temple on top," the bearded priest continued.

"No shortage of divinities around here," Francis observed.

"We have three," said Mouzon frostily. "Iztac, god of the sun. Chimec, god of the human brain. Tolca, god of peace."

Francis touched his chitzal scar. "Temple of Iztac . . . Temple of Chimec . . . so where is the Temple of Tolca?"

Mouzon smiled haughtily. "The Temple of Tolca is all around us."

Once inside the building, the party divided. Three priests lingered in a friendly sunlit anteroom while Mouzon, Francis, and the swarthy driver entered a passageway that eventually deposited them in the central nave, a vast and resonant belly. Francis felt like a swallowed Aretian fish. The woman seated in the farthest corner seemed swallowed too, but swallowed so long ago that she had adapted and was thriving.

Vaxcala Coatl thrived amid smoking incense and dripping tallow. She sat on a sensuous red divan. The crowded shelves at her back held mechanical bric-a-brac and beautifully bound sacred writings. Francis noticed a telescope, a microscope, and a soldering iron. He scanned the titles, some familiar, most not. *The Rig Veda, The Gospels, The Iliad, The Divine Cocoon, Complete Writings of Janet Vij, Biophotonics, Basic Wiring.* . . .

Vaxcala was tall, brittle, with a swan's neck and bottomless eyes. Her scrawny face, its nose so thin you could open letters with it, seemed little more than a painted skull. Her fingers, long and powerful, were always working, like the legs of an overturned beetle. There was no telling her age. Somewhere between forty and forty thousand.

"So we meet at last," said Vaxcala in a voice redolent of antique china.

"We?"

"Nearth and Quetzalia." She gestured to a plush pile of lipoca wool, and Francis snuggled himself down. "When did our common ancestors last walk Planet Earth together?"

"Centuries by *any* calendar. I understand from Dr. Mool that yours is perfect."

"Yes. . . . Of course, *everything* Mool concerns himself with is perfect, or he wouldn't concern himself with it. When he picks his nose, rare coins fall out. Would you like some tea?"

"Your planet makes the worst tea in the galaxy," said Francis, good-humoredly. He liked this Vaxcala.

"Oh, you've been swilling that slug-drug they peddle at the hospital. Cast your lot with sacred herbs."

Francis kneaded his scar, nodded.

"Mouzon, would you mind?" Whether Mouzon minded or not, he transcended his bulk and zipped out of the nave.

"I hope you realize that your coming creates difficulties," said Vaxcala. "To be frank, nobody quite knows what to do with you, especially our governor. The whole affair is in my skinny lap."

"Help us fight our way back to *Darwin,* and we'll be off your planet"—Francis snapped his fingers—"like that."

Vaxcala appeared to be experiencing a bad odor. "You're proposing a war, is that it?"

"If we raised a large enough army, only the neurovores would die."

"You don't understand. The neurovores, whatever their depravities, are human."

"You're right, Vaxcala. I *don't* understand."

"Having conferred at tedious length with other Zolmec clergy, Dr. Lostwax, I have decided to tell you something about our race. Something you would have learned eventually from observation or loose tongues."

"Or Burne Newman?"

Vaxcala's thin mouth became a perfect crescent. "Then you've already guessed?"

"It has something to do with why Burne must kill your neurovore for you, and why that man Zamanta couldn't defend his children."

"I'm *still* against telling him," the swarthy priest interjected, grunting for good measure.

"Shut up," said Vaxcala, as winningly as a human can say those words. "The plain truth, Francis, is that Quetzalia is a country without violence. Since the building of the wall, no deathblow has ever been dealt here."

The priest decided to make the best of his defeat. "Flogging is a fiction," he chanted loftily, "assassination a legend, kidnapping a myth, torture a vanished nightmare."

At this point Mouzon, carrying a full tea tray, bustled into the nave and continued the litany. "Thieves are unknown, warriors unnamed, rapists unthinkable."

"We are without prisons, penalties, weapons, or revenge," said the swarthy priest.

Francis poured tea and sipped. The dark drink quickened his wits as surely as anything Nearth called coffee. "But do you merely inhibit aggression, or are you actually *incapable* of it?"

"After two hundred years of Zolmec," said Vaxcala, *"incapable* is the word. So whether you know it or not, you and Burne come to Quetzalia as walking bombs, thus far unexploded. The neurovore who got in comes as something even worse."

A spiky despair swept over Francis. His hopes of a *Cortexclavus* triumph back on Nearth were starting to look dim. If only Burne were here. Burne would talk them out of this nonsense. "I have trouble believing a religion can be so effective."

"Until now Zolmec has indeed been effective. There are

liabilities, of course. Stability breeds boredom. We have a radical faction, the Antistasists, who want change of some kind. They haven't decided *what* kind yet, and I'm not looking forward to the day they do. But the worst of it is our pathetic vulnerability."

Francis gave a knowing smirk.

Vaxcala rotated the teapot by its spout, eventually took the handle and poured. "We are guilty," she said. "Guilty of assuming that our wall, if not our moat, if not our planet's invisibility, would shelter us forever."

"Let me assure you that Burne and I have no intentions here beyond getting home. Our arrival was a total mishap."

"Yes, but once you return to Nearth the word is out. How long before another spaceship comes, and then another? Quetzalia is not without its tempting resources, and our capital, as you know, can be successfully invaded by an unarmed kindergarten."

"You'll just have to trust us."

"True," said Vaxcala without spirit.

"If you won't kill neurovores for us, at least help us find fuel. Do you know what pollucite is?"

"A rare mineral. Find the high-grade stuff and you can count on thirty-six percent cesium oxide. It's the cesium you want, correct? Your ship has ion drive?"

"The southern jungles are studded with granite pegmatites," Mouzon volunteered, "and that could very well mean pollucite. We could also try the Ripsaw Mountains."

"So, you traffic in science as well as faith," said Francis.

"What makes you think Zolmec has anything to do with *faith*?" asked Vaxcala. Rising, she approached the shelves and gently swatted the telescope. It rolled into her arms. "This is here for repair. Upstairs we have an astronomical observatory."

Francis was impressed. On Nearth, astronomy had always been religion's least favorite brand of knowledge. But it would be a mistake to let Vaxcala win a point now. "Looks like a machine to me. Aren't you afraid of contamination?"

"The clergy is allowed to touch *anything*." She returned the heavy cylinder to its shelf. "We'll organize a pollucite expedition the minute you give the order."

Francis was about as good at giving orders as he was at giving milk. "Thank you. I think we'll wait until Burne gets back." He pursed his lips, siphoned tea.

"Meanwhile, we intend to make your stay here something out of a travel folder. You'll get a private lipoca, a private fortune, a private house—Olo, the seminar center."

"Not *entirely* private," said Mouzon, unfurling a calendar. "There's an herb conference next opoch."

Vaxcala frowned. "Unfortunate. You'll hear motherweed-talk far into the night. I'll ask them to stay out of your hair."

Francis patted his embryonic curls. "Am I free to come and go?"

"Yes, but try to pass yourself off as a native. Quetzalians are prejudiced against non-Quetzalians. You can't blame us. Burne Newman kills. Maybe you do too."

"No."

"There is one restriction. I must ask you not to attend any Zolmec rites. Stay away from the Temple of Tolca. The presence of a nonbeliever could prove damaging."

"Suppose I get curious?"

"You already are."

"You can't keep me out."

"True," said Vaxcala with an unnerving grin.

Francis shrugged elaborately. "I never went to church on Nearth," he said. "I've got no reason to start now."

THE OLO SEMINAR CENTER was a stark villa faced with stucco and beset by vines. Through some inconceivable gymnastics a housepainter had gotten behind the vines to whitewash every surface. Cheerful patches of sun god greeted Francis whenever he came home.

Three dozen rooms hemmed an ample courtyard paved with plaster and sliced by rivers of flowers. The indoor swimming pool adjoining Francis's bedroom prompted him to suppose that his corkscrew beetle liked to swim, its nose serving as a propeller. He would have to test this hypothesis on their reunion.

Learning to ride a lipoca is not difficult if one is willing to spend some time on the ground. Francis, being an entomologist, was willing. The day he conquered the beast he went into Tepec, touring incognito as Vaxcala had instructed.

The Quetzalian genius for building was everywhere on view. Fountains fed by masonry aqueducts sprouted where Nearthlings would have put videophone poles. Brimming agricultural terraces sloped down step by step to artificial lakes. Flawless causeways and sleek irrigation canals raced each other to the horizon. Green parks and yellow gardens made a lush chessboard when seen from the Library of Iztac.

"Library" was putting it mildly. The sprawling pyramid accommodated museums, lecture halls, classrooms, laboratories, stores, and restaurants. And, of course, books. Not only the entire *Eden Three* collection, but thousands of original Quetzalian manuscripts, hand-lettered, from plays to monographs, epic poems to cookbooks, arranged not by subject matter but by presumed degree of truth, so that a novel of psychological validity and a treatise on topology might be stacked together a half-hour's walk from a trendy set of instant and absolute solutions to life's mysteries.

From every library window Tepec looked good: tidy, purposeful, vast. Francis favored the east vista, not only because it included the verdant settings of the divine star for which the building was named, but also because it included the Hospital of Chimec. He hypnotized himself with the view, aching to master his bashfulness and pay Dr. Tez Yon a visit.

His library trips became daily, and each time Francis made a point of noticing Zolmec's influence on average citizens. The faith was kept subtly. Children roughed and tumbled like children, but they did not kick, spit, or bite. Parents suffered the normal ordeals, cajoling and fussing all the way, but they never spanked. Athletes aimed for self-selected goals, not the humiliation of opponents. Even when it came to team sports, such as gobletball and flipflop, Francis saw no sympathy for the gore 'em, gash 'em, geld 'em mentality of the Nearth equivalents.

And yet there was that murder, a boy slaughtered in a glass room. The memory visited Francis with cruel constancy.

A WEEK AFTER HE HAD MOVED to the seminar center, Francis rode beyond Tepec's western edge, all the way to the great unmortared wall. He followed it for hours, trying to convince himself he was looking for insects. But in time he knew what he wanted. In his mind he could picture it, adjacent to the wall, sitting surrealistically on the sand like a huge videophone booth.

Not until Iztac was low in the sky, balanced atop her own distant temple, did Francis admit defeat. He was exhausted, saddlesore, and ready to believe that not only the murder but the glass room itself was a ghost born of his grief over Kappie McKack. Then something happened.

The best way home took Francis through the suburban settlement called Motec. Local pride jelled around a park, a handsome expanse of bulbous trees and flat-topped hills.

On one particular hill, artists had collected; they daubed pigments, practiced pirouettes, wrote verse, and spun wondrous cocoons from yarn, hide, and strips of supple wood.

On one particular artist, a dense white beard came to a perfect point.

Francis stifled a yawp. Cautiously he approached the elderly child killer. "Hello."

The killer cocked his head, smiled pleasantly. "Good evening."

"Nice design. I think my eyes are in love."

"This?" The old man plucked his cocoon like a lute. "It's not going right, but I appreciate your praise. I don't get comments as a rule, fewer than you'd think. People are shy."

"Or jealous?"

"You're not from around here, are you? I know everybody who comes to the park."

"No, I'm not from around here." Francis chuckled to himself.

"If you're lost, I could draw you a very artistic map."

I might have guessed, Francis thought. On the surface he's eager to please, underneath he's ready to strike. "Art is a blessing, isn't it?" I need proof. "I mean, without it we'd all be *athletes* or something." Suddenly the proper plan came. "I'm not just being friendly. I'd like to buy it."

The sculptor glowed like a new luminon. "Wonderful! Can you afford eight cortas?"

"I'd like to buy it so I can take it home and *wreck* it. I want to smash the thing until there's nothing left but sawdust. *That* would make you mad."

"Probably," said the sculptor, apparently more confused than resentful.

"You'd want to drop by my house and beat me up."

A counterfeit smile crossed the sculptor's face. "Are you from Aca? There must be some sort of humor going around that hasn't caught on here yet."

"And then you'd kick my ribs in until I was *dead*."

"I've never hurt anyone in my life," the sculptor pouted.

Will nothing jog his memory? wondered Francis. He's repressed the whole thing? "You're a liar! I *saw* you."

The reply was firm. "I don't lie."

"You're a bastard liar with a whore for a wife, and this hideous sculpture looks like something a *neurovore* would make!"

"Are you feeling ill?" The sculptor's voice rang with irritatingly authentic compassion.

In a sudden spasm, Francis leaned forward and yanked a crucial guyline from its moorings, so that the cocoon toppled over. He swung his feet away from the lipoca's flanks, ready to jab its kidneys as soon as the sculptor advanced.

But the sculptor just stood there.

Francis gulped, his heart socking his rib cage. "Maybe I *am* ill," he muttered, and the sculptor nodded. Reluctantly Francis urged his lipoca into the dusk.

The sculptor had unnerved Francis, more than if he'd attacked him with an ax. On the one hand, the man was evidently as sweet and moral as Quetzalians were supposed to be. And yet his anger had once expressed itself so powerfully that the treads of a magnecar were turned to oatmeal.

He knew the feeling was capricious and impermanent, but right then Francis decided that if he could just reconcile these two facts, he wouldn't care if he never saw home again.

9

"HELLO, DR. LOSTWAX. Want to go on a picnic?"

Francis glanced up from his breakfast, a lumpy amalgam of whole grains, fresh opos, and milk. Lipocas, as it happened, supplemented their horsey virtues with all the best features of cows.

"Tez! How enchanting to see you!" Syrup dripped slowly off his words.

The doorway framed her. "I'm on a self-declared holiday," she explained, her tongue tucked fetchingly into the corner of her mouth. She licked a morning sunbeam.

"A picnic is exactly what I want to go on, Dr. Yon." That blue robe was perfect. He had never before seen her in anything but drab medical gray.

"It's a movable feast," she said, gesturing toward Olo's courtyard. Mixtla, her lipoca, was hitched to a wagon overflowing with the raw materials of a picnic: cheese, bread, meat, fruit, wine.

"Want some breakfast?" he asked.

"Not *too* much," said Tez, smiling, stepping forward. "That cereal looks overnourishing."

Francis clanked around the kitchen. "There's no second bowl," he concluded, mildly panicked.

"Do you have a second *spoon*?"

"Yes."

Together they ate cereal from the same bowl. The sensation was wonderful and obscene.

Tez explained that she had taken the day off to celebrate
the seeming victory of coyo root over her father's paralysis.
Two afternoons ago Teot Yon had hobbled unaided from his
room to the gardens and back again.

"And the side effects?" asked Francis.

"Too early to tell. Mool says I shouldn't worry."

A silence came, making Francis twitchy. On Nearth such
silences were not permitted. Tez, contented, ate cereal.
Thin white dribbles rolled from each corner of her mouth.
She looked like a milk vampire.

"What is Vaxcala like?" she said at last. "I've never
met her."

"An intellectual witch," Francis replied.

"Is that good?"

"Oh, I thought she was fine. She told me about your
nonviolence."

"It's all true." Balancing her chair on a rear leg, Tez
pivoted away from the breakfast table until she could see
the next room, a tapestried parlor in need of furniture.
"I've never been at Olo before," she explained.

"It's strange to *me*, too." A silly thing to say, he decided.

"It looks large and fascinating."

"Too many rooms."

Tez swung toward the doorway, studied Iztac. "We must
drive northeast on Aspiration Road, toward Aca. My brother
is debating in the Vij Arena."

"About what?"

"I don't know, but after you've followed his arguments
around you'll be plenty hungry for this picnic of ours."

As they settled into the wagon, Francis realized that he
should have invited Tez on a tour of Olo. He blenched.

Aspiration Road had the texture of decayed teeth. "It
used to be the second worst road in Quetzalia," Tez explained as they jerked along, "until they repaired it. Now
it's the *worst* road in Quetzalia."

The passing scenery was a different matter. Trees of a
hundred shapes and colors grew side by side in a peaceable

vegetable kingdom. Clouds glided by like majestic airships. Voluptuous hills showed waving grass and nesting birds.

"So, Francis Lostwax, what do you think of our little civilization?"

"Not bad. For Utopia."

"We're hardly *that*. The winters are god-awful. The government's in hock to the merchants. The economy is a lot of paper backed by a few crummy thermalstones. And last year the crops went to hell."

"Was there starvation?"

"No. Dwarf's foot has kept the population in check: an herb."

"It prevents ovulation?"

"No, the overwhelming majority of the Quetzalians who take it don't ovulate. But it does knock down their sperm counts."

Francis reddened eyes, fixed on the lipoca's silly kidney-shaped ears. Tez came to his rescue by changing the subject.

"Now, I must admit those *hills* are fairly utopian. Do you have splendid hills on Nearth?"

"Yes," said Francis gloomily, "but they're all under the ocean."

A QUETZALIAN DEBATE, Francis learned, resembles nothing so much as a sleazy circus act sponsored by a disreputable philosophy department. There were no podiums, nothing so refined. The opponents stood inside a pit. They stood inside adjacent circles, the better to run around in, carrying on.

By evoking her brother's name, Tez obtained two enviable seats near the blue circle. Francis eased into a swiveling lipocawool cushion. Behind him, granite tiers carried rows of spectators aloft. The Janet Vij Memorial Arena stood at capacity.

The walls of the pit were broken on the north and south by ponderous iron doors. Francis wondered aloud if one of them would eventually swing open, thus giving a hungry lion access to the loser.

"You guessed it," Tez replied. "Only we use rabbits. It's slower that way."

Francis thought: At least they have a sense of humor about this pacifism business. At least they don't take it too far.

The sign on the north door said, HUACA YON VERSUS QUILO LOIR.

Huaca was rubber-boned, aristocratic, with crystalline eyes and a scar-thin beard running ear to ear. He did not walk into the blue ring, he undulated into it, like protoplasm.

As Quilo stepped toward the red ring, Francis experienced dismal memories of his ex-wife Luli. Quilo was trim, peppery, presumably a champion arguer. Her young features, though less conventionally beautiful than Luli's, made you look again. She was moon-faced, soggy-eyed, sensual.

"She's an Antistasist," Tez whispered, leaning on Francis in a way that made him sad when she stopped. "A radical."

He replied, "If she wins, does the government topple?"

"Nobody *wins*, Francis."

As far as Francis could fathom, the topic of the debate was the supposed rift between creativity and reason. Is art mainly emotional, irrational, and beyond words, intellect mainly cold-blooded, logical, and prolix?

Yes, said Quilo Loir.

No, said Huaca Yon.

Quilo came out swinging. She promised to cite neurological evidence. Francis was impressed. If you want to wow a crowd, cite neurological evidence.

Her neurological evidence turned out to be the old chestnut about the right cerebral hemisphere thinking pictorially and musically, the left thinking verbally. Cleave the hemispheres along the corpus callosum—the ancient "split-brain" experiment—and you have isolated two different kinds of intelligence, one artistic, one rational.

The crowd went wild.

Huaca oozed into action. He spouted words as a Kritonian morg spouts water, torrentially and inexorably. At first his line of reasoning seemed circuitous beyond salvation, but if you listened closely you realized that the half-formed proof he left stranded three corollaries from the main point was eventually rescued and nurtured to maturity by that *reductio ad absurdum* he picked up on his way back from the tangent. Huaca argued that human brains hold many species of intelligence, not just two, and that Quilo was courting the kind of pigeonhole mentality Zolmec warned against.

The crowd was on its feet, cheering.

The really weird part, Francis felt, was Quilo's reaction. She conceded Huaca's superior position with ease, grace, and something Francis was inclined to call enthusiasm. Crisscrossing her circle, smiling hugely, she would nod, chortle, and say things like "Good point!" and "You've got me there!"

The intermission was barely under way when the south door smacked the wall, dislodging mortar. A young man, shiny with sweat, breath gone, lurched into the center of the pit. Tez pinched Francis. "Runner."

"The news is good!" the runner shouted. "The toll of the Brain Eater did not exceed one today, a farmer in Oaxa." He added that fewer than twenty kilometers separated Burne and the juggernaut.

Murmurs of gratitude wafted through the crowd. Francis experienced alternating relief and guilt. It was good to know that his friend was thus far safe, good to imagine that, if Burne's mission succeeded, the Quetzalians might be so thankful they would put away their scruples and aid in the recapture of *Darwin*. And yet . . .

He leaned against Tez, doing his best to mimic the sly way she had earlier leaned on him. "Of course, if it weren't for us," he whispered, "you wouldn't have a neurovore in your lap to begin with."

"I'm glad you admit it," Tez replied crisply. She led him back to the lipoca wagon, where they spent the intermission not resisting the temptation to start their picnic early. Francis ate an opo.

Tez said, "You know Burne. Will he stamp out this plague?"

"I suspect that Burne Newman can do anything he decides to do."

"Huaca Yon versus Quilo Loir" raged on for another hour, and the hot, lazy sun made Francis lose interest, then consciousness. Every ten minutes he startled himself by waking up, always just in time to witness Huaca's chess-knight mind zagging quirkily forward.

"If it were a black cat I'd dye it *pink*, and then you'd see it was just like any *other* kind of cat!"

To which Quilo replied, "I still maintain *The Divine Cocoon* creates an *ipso facto* inaccurate world in which there is no epic poem called *The Divine Cocoon!*"

Eventually the show ended with Huaca telling a joke, risqué by Quetzalian mores, about an Earthling convict who led so many brilliant prison breaks that when he was finally released they honored him by retiring his number. The debaters smiled and bowed amid a standing ovation.

"Very stimulating," said Francis over the din, with a yawn more honest than his words.

Tez ignored him, hurled a "Congratulations!" into the pit.

The familiar voice caused Huaca to break through a circle of admirers. His fragile eyes looked up, scanned the disbanding crowd, alighted on Tez. "Sister! How *beguiling!*" He wriggled across the pit. "Who's your friend?"

"You'll never guess."

"Good afternoon," said Francis stiffly.

"Are you from the mountains?" asked Huaca. "You're soft for a Cuz year-rounder."

"Farther than that," said Francis.

"What's farther than that?"

Tez cut in: "Ask me about Father, Huaca."

"I was going to."

"He's still alive, no thanks to your flawless record of absence from his bedside."

"I've been busy. Training for a debate takes time."

"So does dying."

"He's not *terminal*, Tez. Yesterday I saw Mool. Father can walk."

"He walked *once*. And the side effects haven't hit yet."

"Keep me posted," said Huaca laconically.

"Maybe you'd like to set a date for the funeral now, so there won't be any conflicts."

"Let's be *fair*, Tez."

"I'll be fair if you'll visit Father."

Huaca extended his thumb, rammed it into his sternum. "I promise. Promise, promise, promise. Good-bye, sister." He started toward his fan club. "And good-bye to *you*, spaceman," he said in a loud whisper. "I mean, who else could you be?"

"I THOUGHT YOU WERE MORE OPTIMISTIC about your father," said Francis as the Janet Vij Memorial Arena shrank to a dark mass on the horizon.

"I am optimistic," said Tez. "But I need to keep my brother on his toes. I need to *humanize* him." By Tez's account, Huaca wanted a world where everybody was a disembodied brain floating like a kite through the ether, debating telepathically, spinal cord dangling for a tail. "Instead he was born into Quetzalia, where people have relationships and *obligations*."

"He *is* a good debater."

"Oh, Huaca's an authentic genius, no doubt about it. But totally constipated when it comes to small kindnesses, simple favors. He's never allowed himself a trivial moment in his life."

"I've always regretted not having a brother. Maybe I shouldn't."

"For me it's always been like having pubic hair. You have it, but what the hell is it for?"

Now silence came, and again Francis squirmed. The road got better, became concrete, while the surrounding grassland worsened, grew bald and patchy with sand. Finally he thought of something to say.

"Are we near an ocean?"

Tez was playing cat's cradle with the reins. "Yes. Aca survives on fishing. I have a beach picnic in mind."

Now there was nothing but sand, then a marsh, then the ocean itself, an endless glassy line, unexpectedly orange. Francis squinted north, studied the distant silhouettes where marsh and ocean joined. A range of pyramids, bleary and flat in the late sun, proclaimed a great city.

"By the way," said Tez cheerily, "why don't we agree that at some point this afternoon we'll have sexual intercourse?"

Yeastbullets could not have disorganized Francis's stomach more completely. He laughed a foolish, stuttering laugh.

"I thought if we settled the issue now," Tez continued, "we'd save a lot of uncertainty and fuss."

"Fine," Francis gulped. He'd say one thing for these Quetzalians, they knew how to get to a point. "What about . . . ?" He raced blindly through the word. "Pregnancy?"

"Dwarf's foot is part of today's picnic."

"It won't make me infertile?"

"Francis, if we can give you a detachable cranium, we can certainly restock your semen."

Crashing symphonically, orange waves intruded on their conversation. It was a wonderfully hideous ocean. Tez directed the wagon south, where boulders subdivided the beach. Soon they found full rockbound seclusion, and Tez tethered the lipoca to a piece of driftwood that looked like a loon. They ate cheese, fruit, and contraceptive sandwiches. They collaborated on an entire bottle of wine. Not once during the picnic did Francis find himself bemoaning the outrages of Luta or the uncertainty of his fate; he was happy. Several kilometers offshore, a trawler slogged across orange sherbet.

They chatted idly about the Quetzalian fishing industry, and then Tez removed all her clothes.

Francis was shocked when he saw people without their glasses on. A missing wig stunned him. Nakedness overwhelmed him.

He needed Tez's assistance getting his robe off.

Francis wondered if he looked as inharmonious to Tez as she did to him. Her body didn't go with her face. Not yet, anyway. Eventually it would. It had the same qualities: inevitability, urgency, sculptedness. It had small but emphatic breasts, a concave navel, a straight stomach.

Tez did not find Francis's nakedness especially intriguing. She had already imagined it accurately. In Quetzalia, bare flesh conveyed no automatic eroticism. Penises were flooded, frigidities thawed, through touching.

Tez touched.

Sex was not Francis's forte, but he did his best. Tez copulated energetically, forthrightly. Quetzalian pacifism and human passivity were evidently two different things.

Iztac departed, off to light the sea. Francis started a driftwood fire, so romantic it was laughable. The day's wine worked its blunting way, and he lay down for a nap.

Tez fed leftovers to Mixtla. She joined Francis by the fire. They nuzzled like newborn puppies. They slept.

Stars flecked the sky when Francis awoke. The sleeper at his side beckoned. He touched the moving stomach, the breathing breasts, the bumper-crop hair.

He touched something waxy and strange.

Slowly Francis rolled the curls back from Tez's forehead. The thing he'd felt was visible now, lit by starshine. A yellow band ringed Tez's scalp. A chitzal scar.

Should he ask about it? No, it might pain her to discuss an imperfection. Yet he couldn't forget it, couldn't deny his urge to force a seashell into the murm, pull back her cranium, and see his lover in a nakedness beyond flesh.

Tez shuddered, opened her smiling eyes. "Hello," she said huskily.

Francis kneeled over her like a sorcerer performing a levitation. "On your planet, how do you tell somebody that you love her?"

"It's very complicated. You say, 'I love you,' and then you stand back and see what happens."

"I love you, Dr. Tez Yon." Her clever surgeon's hand rose out of nowhere. Fingertips trickled like rain down Francis's face. "And do *you* love *me*?" he asked.

The yes that came from her mouth startled Tez no less than it did Francis. Suddenly she knew that in his guileless bumbling, his selfless uncertainty, this Nearthling was the sort of person she'd been wanting. He did not represent the final end of a quest so much as a validation that quests are always worth undertaking, because life and goodness spring up unexpectedly.

Francis gave a whoop. Tez propped herself against his body. He licked the tip of her nose. She spiraled his curls around her finger.

"Let's look for constellations," said Tez. She told Francis how Janet's Dragon, Lamux's Teapot, The Cracked Mirror, and The Queen of Seasons had all ended up in the sky. She traced them with her index finger. Francis enjoyed this game. It was the most imagining he'd ever done with his eyes open.

"And now we must invent our own," said Tez.

"Why?"

"It's something Quetzalian lovers do. You want to be a Quetzalian lover, don't you?"

"All right, I see one. Next to Janet's Dragon there's a woman bending over a triangle."

"It's not a triangle, it's a marvelous toy. A sailboat."

"And she's the life in all toys," said Francis. "She makes them real."

"We'll call her The Toy Queen," said Tez. "Our own constellation."

Before making love again, they found themselves on one last search. No words passed between them. Intuitively each knew the object sought.

"There it is," said Francis.

"Where?"

"Between UWCM-2 and The Cracked Mirror."

"Yes. I see it."

The star was small, feeble, a redundancy among countless redundancies. But finding it mattered at this particular moment. It was their shared heritage, their common seed, their bond across the light-years.

They remembered that its name was Sol.

TWO

The Agnostic

10

IN THE CLEARING the predator paused, awaiting the star-shine. This was the leaden hour, the time between the passing of the sun and the inauguration of the night. It was the hour for the predator to rest his flesh, to gather his energies, and to picture his quarry at hand.

There were other predators in the jungle, but none like this one. This predator hunted his own kind. He could kill within his species.

A fallen log, grooved and mossy, caught Burne Newman's eye, became in his mind a chair. When he attempted to use it as such, it promptly disintegrated. Insects no longer inhabited the log, but before vacating they had mined and farmed it until there was more air than wood.

Burne did not bother rising, but merely shifted his rump from the splinter pile to a fern patch. His every tendon taunted him with an ache. This chase had been exhausting, nauseating, a depraved rendition of connect-the-dots: his prey was zigzagging, leaving its mark, a debrained body, at the turns: each gamekeeper's hut, each hermit's treehouse, each firemoss cutter's cottage where the neurovore stopped became a scene of unresisted murder, thirteen to date. Connect-the-deaths.

Luta was not the first planet where Burne had been called upon to kill. After graduating from high school he served a hitch in Nearth's police force and saw action during a strike at the Donaldson Crysanium Mine. The miners, Affectives forever, expected retirement benefits from their Rationalist employer, John Donaldson. Mr. Donaldson went home, did the arithmetic, and called out the police because it was cheaper.

The strikers, who had enthusiasm, attacked the police, who had yeastguns. The enthusiasm made martyrs; the guns, holes. A courageous young woman got a hole from Burne the second before she would have furrowed his face with a hoe.

Burne did not mind killing courageous young women in self-defense, or even risking his life in a vicious skirmish, but he minded terribly being on the wrong side. The next day he resigned from the Rationalist Party and asked his captain for a desk job. He spent the remainder of his hitch sorting obfuscations into file folders.

With the present task, though, Burne knew he was on the right side. The Zolmec priests had confessed their race's devotion to nonviolence by way of convincing him to hunt the neurovore, and, while he couldn't bring himself to believe that Quetzalian pacifism was total, he was nonetheless forced to admit that the father at the drawbridge had behaved with a restraint bordering on the supernatural.

His debates with jungle residents also failed to disclose hypocrisies. "What would you do if you came home tomorrow and found somebody raping your sister?" he remembered asking a firemoss cutter, a high-cheeked woman who was a dead ringer for Nefertiti Jones, the kinepic star. It was a question commonly posed to those who refused to enter the Nearth police force on grounds of conscience. Induction officers were unadmiring of such claims. Willing young people should feel *lucky* to serve their planet, and unwilling young people *deserved* to serve their planet.

"I'd tell him to stop raping my sister," the Nefertiti Jones lookalike replied.

"That's all?"

"That's all—since raping my sister is *already* something he wouldn't be doing. You're in Quetzalia."

"Suppose everyone here thought as you do?" Burne asked. "Wouldn't your enemies run you over?"

"Everyone here *does* think as I do," replied Nefertiti Jones's double, "and consequently I have no enemies."

BEFORE BEDDING DOWN, Burne had instructed his subconscious to refuse him a full night's sleep, to in fact wake him after three hours. He sensed the Brain Eater's proximity, could practically inhale its miasmic breath. Far better to lose sleep than time. If he kept going all night, he would catch his prey at dawn.

He was lucky. The nocturnal sky bloomed clear and cloudless, permitting the Milky Way to pour down and silver the trees. Forty days ago these stars became his sole beacon when the jungle had clotted to an impassable tangle, and the lipoca and its provisions, oil lantern included, had to be abandoned. Burne carried only a pack filled with selected essentials, such as food, matches, and a method for killing neurovores.

Awakening on schedule, he shouldered his pack and entered the jungle with a final-seconds, score-tied queasiness. He had not gained twenty meters before a sphere of light bobbed in the far darkness, denoting either a gigantic relative of the mythical firefly or a human with a lantern. "Who are you?" he shouted.

The quiet presence approached. It was a human with a lantern.

"Runner!" said a reedy voice. By the glass-mantled flame she looked meager, spectral, a will-o'-the-wisp. Her handsome young face and pliant limbs made Burne nostalgic for Nearthian holovision. He had seen such provocative prettiness a thousand times before, in close-up, telling him to employ the correct deodorant, purchase the proper magnecar, and get himself a screw.

Entering the lantern glow, Burne divulged that he was the famous extraterrestrial. "Ticoma Tepan" came the response. He expected that Ticoma would follow the custom of previous runners, pestering him for news, then racing off for Aca or Tepec. But her intention, he learned, was to stay with him for the next eight hours, nine hours—however long it took to get the Brain Eater at bay.

"It won't be easy keeping up with me," he warned. "The neurovore doesn't stick to the trails."

Ticoma replied, simply, "I'll keep up with you."

Keeping up was not the question. The runner soon forged ahead, her lantern becoming Burne's guide.

Ticoma had grown up in Oaxa, the northernmost jungle town, where children could make a tidy income catching chitzals and selling them to the hospitals for their murm. She had learned her jungle's every stump and trail. She understood its moods, anticipated its transmogrifications, mourned its losses, fertilized its floor with her urine.

Now her talents rushed back, and she found herself spotting neurovore toemarks with the same inexhaustible acuity she had once used to track the gawky furballs. Burne shivered with admiration. By midnight he badly wanted to sleep with her.

A cacophony blurted from the darkness. Somewhere in front of Ticoma, an orchestra of aliens, each from a different world, was tuning up. "What's that?" Burne called.

"Big Ghost Bayou. Don't wander off."

With the constancy of a shadow, Burne followed Ticoma as she tightrope-walked fallen branches and jumped astutely from stump to rock to root to stump. All around, smooth trees squatted on their exposed roots like teeth atop gum disease. Acrid moss, hanging everywhere, evoked from Burne unfavorable comparisons with the underbelly of a wet dog. And weaving it all together: a treacherous porridge of water, mud, silt, sand, where floated countless logs crowded with warbling reptiles, their beautiful eyes, embedded with luminous bacteria, swirling around the travelers like a galaxy of double stars.

By dawn the swamp was blessedly behind them. Better yet, the neurovore's trail became synonymous with a sleek, human-built road. Compared with the previous night of swatting away vines and negotiating gunk, this present journey seemed effortless, fun. Burne took advantage of his renewal by running.

As he drew up next to his scout, a small pond, clear as a mirror, swung into view, and Ticoma suggested a rest. They collapsed gratefully, awakening their sluggish faces with water. Ticoma smiled toward Iztac, addressed it playfully. "No more need of your little brother." She brought the oil lantern toward her face, peeled back the globe, blew. Gray fingers of smoke curled upward from the wick. Burne followed Ticoma as she rose and pressed on toward the lantern's sibling, awesome and ascending.

THE NEUROVORE'S LATEST ZAG, launched in a straight line with the dead pointing finger of its latest victim, a male hermit with big hands, pulpy lips, and, now, a gutted head, had by the evidence of bloody footprints brought the beast off the road and into a vast orchard, source of that exquisite native fruit, the opo. Seeing the corpse, Ticoma nearly vomited. Burne urged her away, onto the orchard's grassy floor. They paused by the first tree, taking its fruit, sucking hard until the sweet opoblood trickled into their throats.

Everywhere they turned, straight-cut corridors formed by rows of opotrees sat mute and still while the opos brazenly proceeded to subvert the rationality of it all by dropping themselves thrumpt-thrumpt at random spots and times. Burne gazed down a corridor, walked, gazed down a corridor, walked, gazed . . .

The jolt was total, penetrating, marrow-scorching. From the dim but undeniable distance came a salivating exception to the rule of peace and quiet and thrumpting opos, its eyes flaring, its beard snot-matted. It opened its mouth, and all the toilets of hell flushed at once.

Was it sight, sound, or odor that told the neurovore of an enemy's approach? Whichever, it now presumed to run, to charge, left paw tight on a tool designed for unlocking skulls. Burne, who had tracked and killed giant bonetoads on Lapus, wrestled and walloped huge bladderbugs on Verne, had never before faced such a quarry, this hunted which sought in mindless fury to prove itself a hunter. He would prove it wrong.

In a single jerk Burne removed his pack and swung it onto the grass. Pushing food and matches aside, he seized his weapon. Armed, ready, and trembling only slightly, he anchored himself next to his inherently defenseless, strangely unpanicked Quetzalian ally.

"I've never seen one before," said Ticoma grimly, setting down her lantern.

The Brain Eater halted a meter shy of the secret weapon. Burne's fingers spanned the lid of the vitreousteel cage, pulled it back. The Brain Eater cocked its head, eyes spurting hate, lips parting to display a broken battlement.

Burne pushed the cage toward the neurovore, gave the freed prisoner a nudge. In a hop invented by its remote *Coleoptera* ancestors, the corkscrew beetle took to the air. It landed where Burne had aimed it, on the neurovore's round, hairy stomach. Nose spinning, it proceeded to behave as a corkscrew beetle behaves. It drilled.

There were cries, cries of fear and incipient agony, so shrill they seemed to gouge pits in the air. What followed was ghastlier yet, and when it was done the neurovore's insides poured through a three-centimeter hole. The monster lay oozing and gurgling and dying, and then oozing and quiet and dead.

"God of the brain!" Ticoma's face was solid sweat.

They stared at the mess, relieved and revolted, burdened by neither time nor thought.

Finally, Burne said, "Help me get the damn bug or Lost-wax will throw six fits."

Together they kneeled, rolled the body over, their teeth clenched, their nostrils awry, as if they were handling the equivalent in excrement. The insect was just now surfacing through the lower back. Burne dropped the cage, rattling it until *Cortexclavus* tumbled forward, trapped. He rose and pushed the cage deep into the pack, getting the assassin out of his dazed sight if not out of his stunned mind.

Ticoma also rose but did not take her eyes from the butchered neurovore. "It will be difficult to mourn this one," she said.

"Don't go," Burne barked, as if she'd said she would.

"Well, Dr. Newman, my true wish is to stay here and light a candle to you, but the sooner I run this good news to Tepec—"

"What do you mean, 'mourn'?"

She weaved her hand through the air above the corpse. "We must acknowledge the death of this human," she said, voice fluttering.

"You're joking." He studied her eyes. They were excellent crystals milky with tears. Tears! Incredible! And no less pretty for it.

He brushed her cheek. "Come here." But she stayed weeping by the corpse. "Come *here*, runner, and help me cool down." He stroked her arm repeatedly, making sure his fingers snagged the robe until at last it rolled from her shoulder.

A hazy fear spread through Ticoma. "You expect copulation, is that it? Three opochs ago I got *married*, Dr. Newman."

"I deserve this," Burne said, kicking the dead thing. "But for me your husband's brain might be sitting in that heap's gizzard, getting turned into—" No, this approach is wrong, he thought. I don't want her *upset*.

"There's no way I can stop you. Do you enjoy taking candy from babies?"

"Babies," Burne repeated dully. "It's my style to insist on things, Ticoma, not beg for them." He turned his ardor to the other shoulder and, by unclothing it, sent the whole robe gliding like an opoleaf to the orchard floor.

Ticoma made no countermove. Burne smiled. A breeze brought goosebumps to her breasts and thighs. How far can these people be pushed? As far as I want? His curiosity was as burning as his penis.

"Dr. Newman, this is absurd," she quavered. "In a few days you'll be a national hero. Women will throw themselves in front of your oncoming genitals."

"I know. But you're here *now*." The helplessness of Ticoma, her native incapacity to break away and the certain consummation this foretold, aroused in Burne alternating lust and pity. With lust on top, he thought slyly, removing his robe.

"It's settled then?"

"Don't be frightened," said Burne.

"Where there's inevitability there's no fear." Her voice was toneless.

"Excellent," said Burne. Then he added, "On Nearth we have *emotions*."

"God of the brain!" Ticoma snapped back. "You think because violence is dead here then so is caring? You think I won't experience total disgust?"

"I think you won't."

"Smug parasite! You'll find me unresisting. Don't misinterpret. It's pseudo-willingness. It's just to minimize pain."

He embraced her limp nakedness, brought it to the grass. I must plant her gently, he thought—a city dweller planting his rooftop garden. But no measure of gentleness could redeem his pleasure or change its name.

Afterward they had nothing to say to each other. Why should I be ashamed? Burne thought as Ticoma lost flaccidity, got nimbly to her feet. I didn't hurt her, didn't rip her. There was a snubbing, almost mortifying arrogance in the way she didn't bother to reclothe herself. She picked her robe off the ground, tossed it smoothly over her shoulder, and, grabbing her lantern, strode naked across the grass.

At the orchard's edge she stopped, spoke without deigning to face her tormentor. "There is no revenge in Quetzalia," she said through vibrating teeth. "But we *do* have the Temple of Tolca." She started forward, and the jungle bore her away, an insolent Eve refusing to bemoan her exile.

As he got dressed, a thick gloom settled over Burne. Shouldering his pack, he retraced Ticoma's footprints in the grass. He foamed with self-hatred. At first he decided he hated himself for feeling nothing, not a twinge of guilt, over murdering the neurovore, who by Quetzalian criteria was a human being. Next he decided he hated himself for allowing such cataclysmic guilt to accrue to his recent, silly, harmless discharge of semen.

Eventually he realized that he hated himself for having raped Ticoma.

After an hour's hike his depression vanished, not because his opinion of himself improved but because the unexpected appearance of granite pegmatites crowded all other events from his mind. Pollucite! he thought, dropping to his knees. The crystals were isometric, cubic, colorless; they contained conchoidal fractures.

Certain now, he seized a pegmatite, hefted it in his palm. He made a solemn vow. Somehow, some way, he would get this rock back to *Darwin*. He would make the Quetzalians renounce their creampuff ways. He would make them fight neurovores.

Having finished his vow, Burne put the fuel to his lips and kissed it.

11

WHAT MORE could a human want? Francis Lostwax boasted classy food on his plate, an expensive roof over his head, and now a requited love in his life. Tez's decision to live at Olo was quick and immutable, despite romantic entanglements, one of whom, an entanglement named Ixan Tolu, was grimly serious about the joy Tez brought him and on learning of her move took to saying things like, "If there were a harmless way to do it, I'd kill myself." But Tez refused to feel guilty. She knew where her fascination lay. Ixan Tolu was vain and ordinary, whereas Francis Lostwax was diffident and from another planet.

Quetzalia even satiated Francis's scholastic appetites. He owed this last comfort to a man he hated named Loloc Haz, Tez's collaborator on marionette plays. Loloc, a bachelor, showed every evidence of being a rival. He was obnoxiously handsome, having no doubt willed himself that way for the purpose of baiting Francis. It didn't help that Loloc and Tez were working on a sex comedy, *Planet of the Interchangeable Genitalia*.

But as days went by and the puppeteers continued to stay a chaste distance from each other, Francis realized that he liked his rival immensely. One wouldn't know it from his hobbies, but Loloc was a thoroughgoing intellectual, a heavyweight in the Iztac Library's biology department. Between rehearsals, he and Francis talked insects. Luta had only a few of its own, all of them fully studied and quite dull, but enough of Earth's more provocative species had survived the *Eden Three* voyage to keep the discipline alive. It was a treat to be arguing about parthenogenetic progenesis again, and prothoracic glands and morphs and molts.

Loloc invited Francis to offer an entomology course, and the initial lecture was so successful that the library president cut the Nearthling in on a mammoth publishing project: a natural-history encyclopedia whose authors would be profusely paid by the government. Francis responded with a quartet of articles, not because he wanted more cortas but because a world finally wanted his ideas. He wrote about *Siteroptes graminum* reproduction, gall-midge ecological strategies, the *Cortexclavus areteus*, and the spirituality of beanlice.

Crowning it all was the curing of Francis's diabetes. The weekend of the herb conference he lay snoozing and reading in his bedroom, the one place where he was unlikely to encounter another lecture on arteriosclerosis or side-conversation about leukemia. These sorcerers reveled in pathology; the most cheerful thing they ever discussed was gastric ulcers.

Tez entered, propelling a bald man toward the bed. "This is Dr. Murari," she explained. Like everybody else in the room, Murari had a chitzal scar around his head, but Francis did not have time to marvel at the coincidence. The doctor plunked a bottle of green pills onto the mattress.

"Every hour on the hour," he said brightly, "until you're at the bottom."

"What for?" asked Francis.

"Your pancreas."

"My plastic one?"

"Your real one."

Francis picked up the pills and rattled them. They were colorful and egg-shaped, like jellybeans.

"The pills will work." There was no Moolian arrogance in Murari's voice, only a bland professionalism.

The pills worked. Within twenty-five hours Francis's

blood passed every excess-sugar test known to science. The thought of retiring his needles unleashed a happiness that hung around for days. Tez said that he must now permit Vaxcala to burn the vile devices in the Temple of Tolca, but Francis argued that this gesture would all but guarantee a relapse. He placed his insulin kit in the drawer with his socks and forgot about it.

EXACTLY FORTY DAYS after *Darwin* landed on Luta, it flashed upon Francis that he never wanted to leave. He was sitting in the courtyard gardens, sipping herbwine and waiting for Tez to get home, and he said to himself, Whatever the distinctions between this planet and the Kingdom of Heaven, they are too fine to matter.

TWO DAYS LATER he began to miss rye bread. The Kingdom of Heaven had no rye bread.

The day after that he found himself longing for bawdy historical-spectacle marathons. He grew misty-eyed thinking of Mother's Mocha Milkshakes. Before long he would have killed to see the Galileo Institute, with its glossy plastic grass, so orderly, and his cozy little office, everything just where he wanted it, all the books that had shaped him showing their spines to the world.

Nearth's natural beauties were long since plowed under, but the civilization that grew on their graves boasted its own romance. Francis wanted to sit with Jack August in The Brief Candle, his favorite bar, and solve the world's miseries over beer as live jazz sinuated through the cigarette smoke and the whopping generalizations. He wanted to go to a Halloween party and get scared.

Tez nursed Francis's nostalgia not by making logical appeals to Quetzalia's virtues but by letting the disease run its course. Her mere presence caused well-being.

To see a sample of Tez's handwriting lying around was to feel a flush of serenity. To watch her button a fuzzy coat or snuggle a silly wool cap over her forehead before she went

into the end-of-summer air was to know total contentment.
The things she fingered became talismans. Her marionettes
were enchanted, as were her comb and her hourglass and
whatever book she had borrowed from the Library of Iztac.

Words flowed between them with perfect ease, particularly when the topic was science. They talked about the
astrophysics of the Malnovian Belt, the ecology of Planet
Kritonia, and the medical traditions of Quetzalia. Francis
learned that whereas Nearth treatments were largely al-
lopathic, confronting the disorder with its natural enemies,
the Chimec Hospital practiced homeopathy, dispensing
toxic herbs that produced symptoms in well people and
wellness in people who already had the symptoms. Small
doses were the key.

At the Galileo Institute, such clinical research would
have been scorned in favor of the laboratory. Germs bred
and studied and diddled with in isolation were fine, but
as soon as they contaminated themselves by infecting a
human they ceased to be of interest. In Francis's view
there was ultimate gold in this commitment to impractical
knowledge, to theories that had no responsibilities other
than to be true. On good days the new ideas inched human
intellect toward the grand understandings that were science's pride and joy. They let you see far more than God's
answers. They took you into God's private study and
showed you his scratch pad.

Tez concurred. Ever since adolescence she had understood the lure of pure research. Her account of growing
chactol eyes in direct defiance of Darwinism left Francis
gasping. "These experiments must be repeated!" he declared, though it turned out that he was not the man for the
job. He failed to deliver even one generation that was still
alive by morning.

HIS HOMESICKNESS CURED, Francis could finally see Quetzalia for what it really was, neither prison house nor
Shangri-La, but an imperfect earth inherited by a diverse

meek. Tez enjoyed showing the place off. Together they visited a restaurant that specialized in food with tentacles, a gallery that featured pornographic upholstery, a high school that arranged for sex-tortured adolescents to lose their virginities under controlled conditions, and a theater that ran episodes of an interminable chapterplay called *Vicarious*.

Vicarious proved a lowlight. Patronizing the theater capriciously, Francis and Tez caught *Vicarious Seventeen*, *Vicarious Twenty*, and *Vicarious Twenty-six*, all of which concerned a large Quetzalian family's heroic attempts to build a footbridge between Luta and the next asteroid over, a project that was apparently taken up by each successive generation. The trick, Tez explained, was to identify not so much with particular characters as with the family itself, so that, after twenty or so episodes, you'd begin to feel like an immortal presence, ceaselessly reincarnated as the plot plowed its way through births and deaths, lives and loves, wars and peaces, dark ages and new days. Francis spent the first half of *Vicarious Twenty-six* loudly voicing his opinion that they would never get their goddam bridge built, after which he fell asleep.

Puppet shows proved more his speed. When *Planet of the Interchangeable Genitalia* opened in a minuscule cabaret beneath an obscure corridor of the Library of Iztac, Francis's only loudly voiced opinion was his laughter. Afterward, he took Tez to the restaurant that specialized in tentacles. There was a violinist; they ordered cuttlefish.

Playing with a tentacle, Francis asked why Quetzalian pacifism did not prevent the slaughter of animals.

"I have no good answer." In fact, Tez explained, the topic of Huaca's next debate was "Resolved: Quetzalians Should Be Vegetarians."

"Which side will he take?"

"He's not sure. He's trying to decide whether anything matters to vegetables."

"Things matter to beetles," said Francis. "I'm sure of it."

Tez said nothing, pantomimed a kiss. It was his gentle foolishness she most cherished. Quetzalians were raised to say the worst of all *Eden Two* descendants: barbarous, insensitive, bereft of Zolmec. But across the table sat this terrific living contradiction.

Tez always had warm feelings about contradictions. It was the scientist in her.

THROUGHOUT THE LOVERS' TRAVELS, one face of Quetzalia— the Temple of Tolca—had remained conspicuously unseen. When the opoch turned and Tez went to her Zolmec service and came back all rosy, Francis realized he was afflicted with what his father used to term "an erection of the curiosity organ." Four times he asked to join the next rites, and always Tez chose to endorse Vaxcala's ban.

The words did not vary.

"I'd like to go with you," Francis would say.

"Nearthling atheists aren't allowed in the Temple of Tolca."

"Suppose I went anyway?"

"I can't stop you," Tez would say, stopping him with the sanctity of her stance.

"I don't *disbelieve* in Tolca, Tez. Or Chimec. Or that other one."

"Iztac."

"In fact, I'm utterly *charmed* by the idea of pacifist deities. As a boy, I used to think: Murder is a horrid thing, no matter who does it and whom it's done to. If I made the rules, nobody who had killed, not even gods or saints or generals, would ever end up admired. So you see, I had Quetzalian notions even before I landed here. You should at least call me an agnostic."

"All right, fine," Tez would reply coolly. "Nearthling *agnostics* aren't allowed in the temple either."

The conversations went no further, and Francis's erection went unrelieved.

QUETZALIAN FLOWERS never ceased to amaze Francis. They faced a startling variety of hardships, from exotic blights to plunging temperatures to indifferent maintenance, and always emerged bright-hued and vital. Francis was in the Olo gardens performing some indifferent maintenance with a watering can when a mounted messenger appeared.

She was a robust child, not quite twelve, and her agility frightened Francis. "Where is Dr. Tez Yon?" she demanded, vaulting smoothly from her lipoca. "This is from the Hospital of Chimec." She waved a wax-sealed note.

"I'll give it to her," Francis replied, intercepting the note. Tez was in the house, doing transplants on marionettes.

The messenger remounted in one skillful jump. Before spurring out of the courtyard, she turned and studied Francis with eyes of sudden tenderness. By the time she spoke, the conceited snap was gone from her voice. "I believe the news is sad."

When Francis entered Tez's workroom, she was trying to attach a jester's head to its neckless body. She split the wax, saw the message, and let the head roll.

Francis took the page and read. "Tez: Teot Yon is comatose. Mool."

Together they went for their lipocas, saddling, mounting, galloping off. Halcyon Road ran straight into the city. Entering the great plaza, they met what seemed like Tepec's entire population sweeping toward the Library of Iztac. The lovers drove their lipocas into the mob, forcing it to part around them.

Dull with misgiving, Francis and Tez could not fully comprehend this outpouring, but the throng's ecstatic faces, its cries of "The Eater is dead!" and "Newman for governor!" made them realize that Burne was safe and triumphant. Reining up before the hospital steps, Francis looked down the causeway and saw that the Temple of Iztac swarmed top to bottom with citizens, Vaxcala presumably in the center of it all, and from this anthill, this stuttering mass of life, came hymns so happy they made him sick with jealousy. He dismounted.

Everyone who could walk had left the hospital. Tez and Francis drifted through frescoed corridors, past places emptied of all save the dying and paralyzed, until at last they stood in a sallow room that had no smells.

Mool was there, humiliation and defeat making unaccustomed appearances on his face. "It may be temporary," he began in a crippled voice. "But right now it is just as you said. Your words, as I recall them, were 'Testing an herb on an animal gives you that animal's reaction and nobody else's.' "

"Did you send your message to my brother?" was Tez's only reply. Mool managed to say yes in surprisingly few words.

Thanks to Tez, Francis knew all about Teot Yon. He knew about incessant energy and a private joke concerning an aunt and a fishing rod. He knew about ropy muscles that could make granite obey.

None of this knowledge could be guessed from the barely breathing form they now confronted. Teot's mouth was a sunken slit, his irises were locked wide open, and his skin felt like wet apples. Many times Francis had imagined meeting this man, first shaking his thick stonecutter's hand, then saying, "I just wanted to thank you for keeping your schedule straight the night you planned to father Tez," and now the whole warming fantasy flew to bits like a badly aimed gobletball.

"I had no reason to believe the counteractive would fail," Mool continued to prattle. "I was even planning to drink coyo myself, but—"

"I believe you," Tez responded mechanically. She touched him on the elbow. "You have my forgiveness, such as it is." The surgeons stood fast, commiserating through stares. Mool could feel Tez's great fear, and pity her for it; Tez could feel Mool's great guilt, and pity him as much.

Starting for the door, the elder surgeon decided to admit

that Francis was in the room. "Hello, Lostwax. I see your hair is back."

"Go to hell," Francis replied.

"As you wish. But don't think I *neglected* her father. I'm off to the celebrations now, but ask me to stay and I shall."

"Get out," said Francis evenly.

For the next hour they sat with the unconscious man.

Tez told Teot that she knew he could hear her, even though she didn't, and that she loved him, which she did. She attempted to say more, was blocked by misery. Francis held her tight, and her sobs were steady, like heartbeats. A cheer went up from the Temple of Iztac.

As they returned to the daylight and descended the jaguar-flanked steps, it occurred to Francis that he was furious. "Well, I really don't see how Mool learned any lessons from *that*!"

Tez was in no mood for words. "What did you want me to do, strangle him?"

"All of this happened to me once. A nurse killed my son and that's *exactly* what I did. There are times when you've *got* to be aggressive."

Tez mounted Mixtla. "I don't know about those times."

Evening arrived but not appetite. Tez and Francis entered the tapestried parlor and lost themselves amid wine and woven dragons. "It's peculiar," she said, "but I'm more upset by Huaca's failure to show than by this death that's going to happen."

"Maybe he came after we left."

"He didn't," said Tez knowingly. "Someday that man will be astonished to discover there's a whole world marching along outside his buzzing head."

Francis pressed his chitzal scar. "Your father's doomed?"

"I've seen this before. An unknown herb goes haywire, so they pour in keyta, but it's useless. The brain keeps shutting down, synapse by synapse." She gargled her wine. "This should be a happy time, Francis, with your friend victorious. Humans are a fickle species. My entire race is saved, yet I cry about. . . . What chitzal mourns its father's death?"

"Yes," said Francis quietly. He could think of nothing but to agree with her derangement. "We're fickle."

No MATTER HOW MUCH SADNESS it brought, family tragedy could never keep a Quetzalian from attending a Zolmec service. The next night found Tez gobbling dinner and dashing around the house in search of cap and gloves. She paused to say good-bye to Francis, who was backstroking across the indoor pool. "I'm off," she said.

"I have a better plan. Come in here and we'll play marine biology."

"No, it's *especially* important that I go tonight."

"Why?"

"Yesterday Mool's arrogance came to its climax, and I must see him in church."

"So you can officially forgive him?"

"Stop harassing me."

"I only want to cheer you up."

"Zolmec will cheer me up."

"How can you forgive such a villain?"

"Mool is not a villain," Tez said crisply, and exited toward the stables. Francis heard her preparing Mixtla. The water felt cold, cold like the air and the love of his life.

Francis surged out of the pool, dressed hurriedly. Seizing the handiest oil lantern, he reached the courtyard in time to watch Tez and Mixtla pass beneath an arch that sprouted wooden cutout letters. As one approached along the road, the sign read OLO SEMINAR CENTER; from where he stood, the sign read ʁƎⱢИƎƆ ʁⱯИІWƎꙄ OⱢO in the flipped-letter language of some forgotten race.

Screw this second life of hers, Francis thought as he rudely roused his lipoca from its nap, trotted it brusquely through the courtyard, and spurred it secretly into the night. Screw it, screw it.

12

THE NIGHT WAS STARRY with lanterns. White-robed, Francis blended with the pilgrims as effortlessly as a swamp aphid blends with bark. They trotted up Halcyon Road, across the edge of the city, and into the woods beyond, their numbers ever-growing. By the time the wall was in view, a river of lantern light stretched endlessly in both directions, radiant twin to the noctus moat on the other side.

A strident wind arose, grabbing the robes and billowing them like sails, so that the procession became a massive regatta coursing toward the wall. Howling *fortissimo*, the wind soon found its rival in a Zolmec song, weird as any in the galaxy, weird as the chirps of Nearth's gorgathon, but deeper and more *maestro*, weird as the threnodies of Kritonia's forsaken morgs—sad, noble seabeasts—only *con brio*.

SAAHHRREEEMMMMM sang the pilgrims in flawless unison, vibrating the earth. There were words, too, difficult to comprehend at first, being tuned to the ears of gods. Francis worked his mouth, pretending to join in.

> To Tolca's heart I give this song
> To Iztac's eyes
> And Chimec's brain
> To rip another's flesh is wrong
> Good souls despise
> The Eaters' reign.

It went on like that.

When the hymn was over, the worshipers dismounted, tethering their lipocas to bushes and roots. Francis let the crowd carry him to within five meters of the wall's dark foundation, where by lantern light a female figure climbed the stairs. She stood on the wall and faced her congregation, constellations arching over her head like a cowl.

"Peace!" boomed Vaxcala. Gold bands jangled about her swan's neck.

"Peace!" answered the congregation. A few centimeters in front of Francis, a gaunt woman turned to her pudgy son. "Tonight we're lucky. Our parish gets Vaxcala."

"Who?"

"The high priestess herself," replied the woman, thrilled. The kid didn't care. Scanning the top of the wall, Francis noticed that, every hundred meters, a priest or priestess stood as Vaxcala stood, erect and commanding, each the focus of eight hundred pious eyes.

"Come with me on a journey through time and space," Vaxcala began. "Come with me to the womb of our great-great-grandmothers, *Eden Three*. Come to the Level Nine Greenhouse, climb a tree, and watch Tellerist engage Brain Eater in ferocious battle. Next to you sits a little girl."

"Janet Vij!" shouted the parish.

Francis wondered what a Tellerist was.

"Suddenly the guns grow silent. And Janet Vij, ten years old, raises her little hand and speaks."

Instantly Vaxcala became Janet Vij raising her little hand and speaking. "Eaters and Tellerists!" she chimed. "Listen! Transcend your hatreds! Hand this battle down to history as the one where, right in the middle of the barbarity, every soldier said 'No!' "

Vaxcala resumed her accustomed voice. "Followers, what reply should the soldiers make?"

"I refuse to fight!" the parish chanted.

"But the soldiers do not refuse to fight!"

"They do not have Zolmec!"

"The Eaters aim at Janet Vij's raised hand."

"The Eaters shoot it off!"

"Who does have Zolmec?" asked Vaxcala.

"We do!"

"Who are you?"

"Quetzalians!"

"Where is Quetzalia?"

"Tell us!"

"Where flogging is a fiction!" shouted Vaxcala.

"Assassination a legend!" the parish fired back.

"Kidnapping a myth!"

"Torture a vanished nightmare!"

"Thieves are unknown!"

"Warriors unnamed!"

"Rapists unthinkable!"

"We are without prisons!"

"Penalties!"

"Weapons!"

"Revenge!" Now Vaxcala was dancing, throwing herself up and down in a practiced frenzy, screaming "Praised be Iztac! Praised be Tolca!"

And the crowd screamed back, "Praised be Tolca! Praised be Chimec!"

"Are you ready, followers?" She stopped dancing. "Are you ready to cast your sins, your biophotonic sins, into the river made of hate?"

"Yes!" said four hundred voices.

"Are you ready to tame your instincts and appease your teeth? Are you ready to show Chimec, god of the human brain, the black humming pitch that pastes your dreams together?"

"Yes!"

Until now Francis could believe the night was real. His faith evaporated the moment Vaxcala began pulling off the top of her head.

But it was truly happening. The high priestess was reaching up, was smoothing back glossy loops of hair, was pressing the sides of her skull between rigid fingers and tight palms.

She glided her hands upward, as if removing a helmet. The chitzal scar parted, revealing her rutted hemispheres.

Now, slowly, synchronously, each worshiper did likewise, and four hundred brains lay naked under the stars.

"To the temple!" Vaxcala exhorted.

Brainpans in hand, the crowd surged forward. As Francis rushed to join, old words emerged from his memory. "The Temple of Tolca is all around us." Now he knew what Mouzon Thu had meant. The temple was the wall!

In their rapture the pilgrims took no notice of the craniumed trespasser among them, even as he started up the hundred stone steps. Minutes later Francis walked where he had never walked before. The road atop the wall was dotted with intricately carved hatchways, and into these Vaxcala's flock now plunged. He thought: I've scored too many blasphemies to stop now. Firming his grip on the lantern, he followed the faithful down.

THE TEMPLE'S FIRST LEVEL was a network of corridors, winding around themselves and doubling back like the thwarting halls of a tomb. Without the boost of starlight, Francis's lantern grew suddenly impotent, and he advanced by groping. He was aware of shapes moving all about him, Quetzalians darting to secret destinations, and of something odder still. Sounds. Not human sounds, though there were many scurrying footsteps and paper-thin whispers in the air, but efficient drones, whirrs, buzzes, and hums. If sharks could purr, he thought, they would sound like the Temple of Tolca.

The floor was descending. Francis pursued tilted tunnels to blank walls, turning as his instincts bade, until at last he felt dirt under his feet.

A feeble light shone not more than ten meters ahead, enshrouding a man who faced sideways. The man's dress and deportment seemed unfitting for a Zolmec service, but Francis still guessed he was Quetzalian. Closer inspection proved otherwise. The stranger was not Quetzalian. He was not even a stranger.

Burne was back! Rushing to meet his friend, Francis instead met something hard and glassy that bruised his chin and bounced him to the ground. The lantern flew from his hand, contacting the wall with enough clout to explode the globe, spatter the oil, kill the flame, and further darken the corridor.

No way to greet a friend, Burne! Francis remained prone for a minute, nose to dirt, then rolled over and blinked back at the invisible wall and the phosphorescent image it contained.

Burne was behind glass. To be precise: he was behind transpervium, that muting substance Francis knew so well. Small wonder Burne could not see his friend or hear his shouts of "You bastard, it's me!" Nor was Francis surprised that Burne could not intuitively sense his presence, for the archeologist was understandably committing all his senses to the stunningly pretty and entirely naked Quetzalian woman who had just turned up at his feet.

Burne prefaced his passion by removing his robe. He dived on the woman. Her goosebumps grew.

Francis crouched in the darkness and played voyeur. This had to be a first for church.

Strange: the woman's face was a void. Logic said she could not be enjoying this moment, but she was not revolted either. Her mind was evidently elsewhere, probably on Burne's pack, toward which she rolled an eye, extended an arm. A searching hand moved through the pack until it found what it wanted, a vitreousteel cage.

Francis jumped with the ecstasy of a boy finding his lost spaniel at the pound. Knowing Ollie Cortexclavus was safe made him laugh, but then, shocked, he anticipated the purpose to which it would be put.

The woman pulled the cage across grass, across skin, bringing it to rest on Burne's lower back. She opened it and reached for the silent, hungry inhabitant. Legs rowing back and forth in the air, antennae working up and down, proboscis already swirling, the corkscrew beetle felt itself abducted by taut fingers, then freed on a scrumptious pudding of flesh.

A scream followed, barbed and bloody, enough to shatter the dead it woke. It is one thing, Francis thought, to be stabbed, and another to be drilled, to have your flesh augered out of you like wood out of a plank. The blood was a geyser.

He got to his feet, hoping somehow to rescue his friend. He banged upon ungiving glass. Looking to his left, then his right, he saw that the wall did not span the entire corridor but instead bent a full ninety degrees at each edge. The transpervium made not just a barrier but a structure, a—

And suddenly he knew where he was. Three opochs ago, burrowing through dirt, Francis and his friends had surfaced on the opposite sides of such slabs. The blind sides. Sides enclosing a vacant room. Sides enclosed by a wall so hollow that the magnecar's machscope had been deceived into proclaiming open ground above.

He raced to his left, turned, then squeezed himself between transpervium and stone. As he wiggled, heart thudding, face on the cold window, eyes on the dying man, he could hear the temple's hums grow louder. The transpervium turned again, Francis rounded the corner, and everything became clear.

First he noticed a machine, droning efficiently: here beside these sacred corridors, within this hidden chapel, the forbidden held sway. It was an obelisk of technology, the height of an upended magnecar, with twinkling lights and glowing wires. Francis had seen one before, not a real one but a picture in a Nearth volume called *Yesterday's Tomorrow*. It was an old-fashioned holovision projector.

The space arks, *Eden Two* and *Eden Three*, had been loaded to their gunwales with the things. They were a safeguard against boredom, a pillar against ennui, an escape from the neuroses that come so naturally to anyone who knows his fate is to mature and die in a big tin drum rolling through nothing.

Best of all, the images they produced were fictions of the purest sort, less actual than *Vicarious* or *Planet of the Interchangeable Genitalia*. Burne was not being slaughtered! The transpervium structure housed pictures—terribly believable, terribly dimensional pictures, but pictures just the same. Relief and gratitude jetted out of Francis like semen.

From a blue cone at the projector's top came a continuous beam of coherent light. The beam evidently carried not Burne's murder but the thought of Burne's murder, a thought neatly sorted into a billion biophotonic bits, tiny chunks of life traveling invisibly until they hit the transpervium screen and reassembled themselves into a vivid flow of images.

Where had the thought originated? No film, no tape, no software of any kind fed into the holojector.

Francis turned from the screen, which now displayed a man writhing in a lake of blood and a gleeful woman standing over him, getting dressed. He followed the beam to its source, looked down the twinkling lights, and saw for the first time a shape resting in shadows at the base of the holojector. It was a dazzlingly pretty woman: Burne's victim and murderer.

Ticoma sat on a fat red cushion, acknowledging the screen with a rapt stare, as if the image would vaporize the minute she abandoned concentration. The fantasy, clearly, came from her. It started in the naked brain, climbed to the electrode that jutted from the great cerebral commissure like a meat thermometer, then traveled along clear, rubbery wires to the projector. The noxious imaginings next materialized on the screen, where, entering the dreamer's eyes, they inspired new and even more noxious imaginings in turn. A perfect circle.

Francis resolved to let her be. He tiptoed across the floor, reached the far side of the machine, and slipped into a triangular doorway.

He was now in one corner of an architectural marvel, a room huge enough to breed morgs in, with a tripartite vaulted ceiling that apparently reached all the way to the top of the wall. The place was vacant but for the surly idols who gripped torches and stood guard along ten surfaces, and featureless but for the triangular doorways that opened from ten corners. He wondered: How many such rooms does the temple contain? Several thousand, if the wall runs all the way from the Ripsaw Mountains to the southern jungles.

Curiosity erect, Francis circled the decagon. At every doorway his furtive glance confirmed that a holojector and its companion screen occupied the chapel beyond. He circled again, this time slowly. He moved past scenes of horror and dread, past voyeurs eyeing their innermost evils and Toms Peeping at their own depravities, and every time he stopped to watch.

On one screen a man was caning his son for deliberately inverting an ashtray. In an adjacent chapel, a family argument that went as far as accusations of sexual infidelity quickly climaxed with the wife dropping her husband down a well. The next drama featured a dog who specialized in digging up flower gardens. Suddenly the animal struck a land mine. The air rained sections of dog.

The fantasies got grimmer as Francis advanced. In the fifth chapel, two speeding lipoca wagons collided on a stone bridge. Both drivers were equally guilty, but nothing could inhibit the older one, a pleasant-faced man, from first locating blame in the younger, a pimply teen-age girl, and next devising a punishment incongruent with the crime, a punishment that included raping her to death and flinging her body off the bridge into the brook below.

In the sixth chapel, a little boy shivered with envy as parental affection was heaped upon a recently delivered baby. When everyone had gone to bed, the boy entered the nursery, kidnapped his sister, and buried her alive in an unmarked grave behind the smokehouse.

In the seventh chapel, Francis saw the lipoca wagons crash again, only this time the teen-ager was writing the script. She spoke a throaty incantation over her lipoca, and the gentle creature became a spitting, rabid carnivore. It exploded from its harness, charged straight for the pleasant-faced man. Jumping free of his cart, he crossed the bridge and did not get ten meters down the road before he was gored to death by the long, serrated tusks that grew magically from the lipoca's nostrils.

The eighth chapel was empty.

The penultimate drama was set in an elementary-school classroom. By the time Francis arrived, the presiding instructor had grown weary of children who talked incessantly, wouldn't talk to her, failed to follow directions, followed directions to a fault, seemed unable to express themselves, expressed themselves too copiously, and picked their noses. She brightened her day by taking a drum of lantern oil, opening it, splashing the contents liberally, striking a match, and setting her responsibilities on fire.

Francis entered the last chapel. Somehow he knew what coincidence would bring. He arrived near the climax, just as Mool was telling Tez how wretched he felt about destroying her father and how he wouldn't do it again.

Tez's laugh jumped from the screen. "Yes, but there is only one way to *guarantee* you'll never do it again." She grabbed his sash. "Come with me."

The scene shifted to the funnel-shaped operating theater where Tez and Francis first met. On the table an anesthetized girl suffered from peritonitis. A balding surgeon with a fine obsidian scalpel was about to rid her of her appendix. Mool in tow, Tez entered, saw the scalpel, wrenched it away. Making a pathetic effort to break free, Mool tripped over his own panicked feet. He hit the floor and stopped moving. Tez followed him down.

The surgery that ensued was unorthodox and cruel, the messiest open-heart job Tez had ever done, but afterward she rose grinning. She had just performed a successful death.

The scene curdled. Its figures became a grotesque tableau. There was the surgeon, knife in hand, lips locked in a vile smirk. There was the sprawled patient, a nauseating crimson cave in his chest. And there was the heart, fine, perfect, undiseased, and sitting in the middle of the floor like a dog's dinner.

Francis was not surprised when a tarnish came, then total blackness as the image melted and seeped away. He had once seen the murder of an innocent boy transmute into this same gelatinous bile. At last he knew the river's source. The Quetzalians let their poisoned dreams go down into the earth, flow into the moat, and pass from their lives forever.

Throughout the fantasy Tez, the real Tez, sat still, never once altering the frozen stoniness of her face. She didn't notice when Francis stumbled over to one edge of the screen and squeezed himself behind it. She didn't even notice when he studied her for a moment with a look of betrayal and disgust.

Hypocrites! Francis thought as he started down the corridor. "Hypocrites!" he whispered as he weaved around corners and shot past great dull stones, his pounding legs carrying him higher, higher. "*Hypocrites!*" he screamed aloud as he reached the top of the wall, ran to its edge, and vomited into the river made of hate.

13

"HYPOCRITES?" SAID TEZ. "No, that's the wrong word entirely."

"You're angry," Francis informed her.

She seemed not to hear. "You violated our temple, and now you've taken on *obligations*."

"Obligations?"

"Such as trying to understand why Zolmec isn't hypocrisy."

"Then what *is* it?" His questions were hostile.

At least he's talking, Tez thought. That's a gain over the past two days.

After church Tez had come home to find Francis sitting in the tapestried parlor. He sat beside dark dragons, suffered under dark thoughts. Four wine bottles, two of them open and empty, formed a fence between the lovers.

"I visited your Black Mass in the wall tonight," Francis said in a wobbly voice. "Revolting."

Sarcasm was the only tone she could find. "Revolting? You mean like guzzling two bottles of wine?"

Whereupon Francis snatched an unopened bottle, thought twice, snatched its twin, and went and locked himself for thirty-two hours in his study, sulking without recess. He slept on the floor. Two mornings later, entering the sunny breakfast room, he decided to lower his pride and ask whether they had eggs. This caused a long conversation neither of them wanted to have about eggs, followed by a longer conversation they both wanted to have about religion.

It was in her court. "Hypocrisy, Francis, is saying one thing and doing another. What you saw in the temple were dreams, not behavior. At worst our race can be accused of believing one thing and imagining another."

He didn't know where to begin. Had he owned ten mouths, he would have said ten things at once. He settled on: "But what you imagine is so *horrible!*"

"Why not? Thoughts have no cutting edge. They leave the world as they found it." She began boiling water for tea.

"But surely there are *mental* effects. Thinking such things has got to be unhealthy, especially for the children."

"That's a plausible hypothesis, certainly. Maybe you and my brother would like to thrash it out in the Vij Memorial Arena sometime. But if *health* worries you, please recall that the human race was sick long before the Temple of Tolca went up. Zolmec is strong medicine, but sometimes you have to get worse before you get well. We are dealing with the species that *tortures*, so let's not pussyfoot around. Let's not worry about wrinkles or dinner parties or what the neighbors think."

The idea caught Francis by surprise. Its logic compelled him. "Another form of homeopathy," he mused.

"Shall we give the sickness a name? Some of us are epileptics and some hemophiliacs but all of us are carnivores. Touch your cuspid roots. Much too big—an evolutionary memory. When we had those fighting canines we probably used them as the jaguar does. Today we are Nature's great paradox, the predator with silly teeth." Her words gushed out with rapidity and precision, as if this speech had been building in her for opochs.

"We lost our weapons, but not the urge to use them. So we built fake ones—spears and guns. Zolmec fights fire with fire, technology with technology." She removed the kettle from the firemoss stove, lowered a bag of herbs into the misty water.

Francis touched his cuspid roots. "But a world without passion, Tez—you're heading toward sterility!"

"You think there's no passion here? We have our arts, and our loves, and we have hates, too."

"Still . . . there must be a change in your overall makeup."

"Indeed! After hundreds of services the average Quetzalian has a *very* special makeup: peaceable, vulnerable, incapable of doing harm. You might think we would expect such persons to attend the rites only infrequently, not every opoch. But if you miss once or twice, then why not twenty times, fifty times? And after that, what are you? An Earthling? A neurovore? That's why we must make Zolmec as glamorous as possible."

"And so you ban technology from everyday life."

She took the teapot, released an amber stream into her cup. "Exactly. Something forbidden is not forgotten, not thrown away. It takes up new residence in the parlors of imagination. It strikes awe. People *want* it."

"But the holojectors break down, of course. So you need a clergy."

"With a soldering iron for a crosier."

Francis took his knife and wounded a melon. "What if a Quetzalian hasn't bottled up any hostilities during a particular opoch?"

"That never happens. Look at your own life. There's always something. I'm riling you right now. Often our wildest dreams spring from *annoyances*. The Runner Bureau sends you a note saying they're going to deliver a large package, but you've got to be there to sign for it, so you waste a warm afternoon and they never come. I once bit a bureau administrator's thumb off."

"Yech."

"And ate it."

Again, cascades of silence from Francis. Finally, he swallowed a morsel of melon and spoke. "Aren't you going to be late for work?"

"I'd rather be late if I can get you to understand." She lifted her teacup and settled into a lipocawool chair. "I ought to tell you the whole story, beginning before the wall or Zolmec or anything."

"I *want* to understand," said Francis in the warmest voice he had used that day. "I'll listen."

He found an egg, fried it, put it on his plate. He forgot to eat it.

THE STORY TEZ TOLD began with a question. "If certain individuals were never born, would the world be something else?" Certainly *Eden Three*, the world of Tez's ancestors, would have been something else were The Teller never born.

He came into a civilization much like that on the sister ark, which is to say it was Earth in facsimile. *Eden Three* had barbershops and bowling alleys, taco stands and plastic parks, dried figs and cotton candy. It was a bland and tidy world—and it was just. Through three generations the commitment to tolerance never slipped. Relativism was the only creed in town. In the fourth generation The Teller appeared, fanatically preaching the divinity of the human brain, and nobody had any idea what to do about him.

According to myth, The Teller's mother, a fueler of reactors, bore him in an engine room, and several decades after his death pilgrims began visiting the defunct atomic furnace that tradition called his cradle. As a boy he learned from his parents the indispensable art of feeding the ark's engines. As an adolescent he had visions. By his thirtieth birthday he boasted political savvy sufficient to make his visions the state religion of *Eden Three*.

Like most visionaries, The Teller saw the distant future with optical-glass clarity, the intermediate future with beeswax clarity, and the immediate future with the clarity of dark glasses dipped in tar. In the distant future he saw a New Earth convulsed by riot, a New Earth where selfishness was the principal thing people believed in and where thousands suffered pointlessly from guns and hunger. And he saw that, to avoid an identical destiny, the *Eden Three* colony must make aggression as extinct as trilobites. What he could not see were the decades right after his death, when his ideas would be disfigured beyond recognition by a significant percentage of his followers, the insidious Cult of the Brain Eaters. Perhaps it was fortunate that these horrors were hidden from him. He might have capitulated to despair and never shown the world a way to peace.

The Teller taught that the human brain is a miracle, a sacred machine whose potential lies beyond its own comprehension. One doesn't use holy water to drown people or holy grails to bludgeon them, and when it comes to holy organs only benign actions are allowed.

He never bothered to get practical about any of this until he was dying. To his disciples he outlined his theory that the brain's inclinations toward evil might be periodically dampened through orgies of unrestrained but harmless violence. A holojector, rewired to accept neurological inputs and connected to a special transpervium screen, could give these fantasies an existence so tangible they would live outside the body—viable, pulsing, and able to be flushed away.

Foreseeing the vulnerability that the new machines would bring, The Teller declared that *Eden Three* must not land on the lushest planet, the fourth captive, the plum: that's where the sister ship would go. Instead they must enter the asteroid belt and find "a small blind sphere, sucking up the sun." They must orbit it until they saw the clouds part. "It is Luta. It is home."

The Teller died, and a hundred attempts to implement his dream followed. The common denominator was failure. Nobody could figure out how to get a holojector, which normally issued only light, to function in terms of biochemical bits. And since the electrodes were not implanted but merely pasted on the head—brain surgery was still a radical resort—the mental outputs remained too weak and undifferentiated to produce pictures that were viable, disposable, or even very entertaining.

Yet the Tellerists did not abandon the quest. They saw victory as a matter of more time, more luck.

Events took a particularly awful turn with the rise of the Brain Eaters. Probably their advent was inevitable. The Teller had been gone for fifty standard years, and in that time his teachings were interpreted and distorted by fifty lesser minds. The Brain Eaters represented an extreme, of course, a minority driven mad by the infinite claustrophobia of ark life. "So human brains are divine?" these twisted thugs reasoned. "Then eating them will make us gods!"

On the day *Eden Three* entered the UW Canis Majoris system, civil war broke out. Pitched battles were fought in the engine rooms and greenhouses. Janet Vij got her ten-year-old hand shot off. Tellerist murdered Brain Eater and Brain Eater murdered Tellerist while the eyes of science went bloodshot seeking a technology for beneficence.

There came a dark body, small for a planet, large for an asteroid, and when the Tellerists saw the gap in its clouds they knew this was Luta. *Eden Three* landed on scorching sand. Life in the promised land was evidently not going to be a picnic, and hostilities flared hotter than·ever.

Still in the majority, the Tellerists scattered their enemy to a huge eastern oasis. Then, suddenly, the Brain Eaters counterattacked, dealing Tez's ancestors a crushing defeat called the Battle of the Singing Rocks. During their long, meandering retreat the Tellerists returned to the ark, stripping it of everything they might need to continue their research: holojectors, transpervium, circuitry, hull plates. They took all the animals.

At last a river appeared. Crossed, it kept the Brain Eaters away long enough for the Tellerists to finish a crude timber defense wall. Behind the wall a great civilization grew. While the Brain Eaters went madder and madder, their devolution accelerated by a cruel, barbaric desert, the Tellerists practiced ecology. They irrigated and cultivated, forcing greenness from the sand. They found a quarry and founded a city. They named themselves Quetzalians—after Quetzalcoatl, the kind, cultured god of the Toltecs, an Earthian nation.

According to some histories, the Toltecs gave Earth one of its few antiviolence societies. According to other histories, that idea was bunk, and the Toltecs were as vicious as anybody else. The Quetzalians chose to embrace the bunk.

Further names were devised. Cuz, Aca, Iztac, Tolca, Zolmec.

Zolmec had become possible! First the rise of sophisticated surgical techniques made the human cerebral cortex as accessible as the human toenail. Then Janet Vij, recovered from her wound and grown to womanhood, resolved to try every conceivable synthesis of holovision circuitry, found that human knowledge was inadequate to the task, and invented her own private science, biophotonics.

Vij became Zolmec's first high priestess. She ordered the timbers ripped down and a great Temple of Tolca built in their place. She ordered the river drained; noctus would fill its bed. The work took years, but finally the world was ready to begin its cycle of, as Tez phrased it, "yearly harvests, opochly sublimations, and daily beatitudes."

THE WORD *beatitudes* lingered tangibly, waiting to be blown away by Francis's response. None came. He rose from the breakfast table, walked to the window. Autumn was crisping the air. He breathed on the isinglass, watching with satisfaction as the circles opened and closed like mouths.

He took his finger and defaced the condensation with a cartoon character.

"Naturally I'm impressed," he began on tiring of his game. "It would be dishonest of me to claim I'm not moved, awed even, by this heritage. You have proved our potential for nonviolence, and, as you said that day in the operating theater, what else is *worth* worshiping?"

A mammoth smile divided Tez's face. "You *do* understand."

Francis snorted. "However—and I'm afraid this is a *considerable* however—something gnaws at me terribly."

Tez crossed her arms, stuck out her chin. This had better be good, her body said.

"Tez, I'm always ready to embrace artificial solutions for biological problems. I didn't have to think twice about getting a plastic pancreas. But artificial solutions are not *desirable* solutions. What kidney patient would not prefer to drop his dialysistem down a grating? Nobody wants that kind of dependency. Circuits fizzle at the wrong time. Nature may not be benign, but she *is* reliable."

"Sweet Nearthling, it has been officially estimated by scientists much like yourself that every minute, somewhere in this universe of ours, an advanced civilization reduces itself to radioactive crud. When the stakes are that high, I'll take my chances on the circuits. *You* can throw in with Nature."

"The problem, I think, is that Zolmec . . ." He had trouble finding words. "I would say that it blunders into the psyche and confuses the proper order of things. You're not intervening in human affairs, you're intervening in the *soul*."

"Well, it's tedious waiting for *Heaven* to do it. When I think of innocent Tellerists cannibalized in the gardens of *Eden Three*, when I think of Planet Earth, where not a single day went by without a murder, when I think of cruelty—men who impaled other men on meathooks—then all your righteous ideas about Nature versus artifice start to

sound like low-grade primitivistic slop. Will you look me in
the eye and say you'd rather be natural than alive?"

"History isn't *all* fighting, Tez. The sloppy primitivists
get along pretty well."

"What *is* artifice, anyway? People build machines, bea-
vers build dams. Are beaver dams unnatural? Forgive me if
I'm confusing you with logic." Satisfied, she sipped tea.

"Very cute, Tez, but the fact remains that Zolmec siphons off juices that—"

"Zolmec siphons off *sludge*."

"It's perverse!"

"It's compassionate!"

"It's playing God!"

"It works!"

Francis returned to the breakfast table. His forsaken egg,
sunny-side-up and cold as a moon, glowered at him from
its plate. "Strange—all this past opoch I've been saying,
'Maybe I'll never get myself and my *Cortexclavus* back to
Nearth, and I don't really care.' Now I'm not so sure.
Quetzalia frightens me."

Tez finished her tea, left a tear's worth, plodded to the
door. "Our races have been separated for a long time. Perhaps the gap is . . ." She opened the door and watched a
stiff autumn leaf scuttle across the courtyard like a beetle.
"I'll be late tonight. If you have any trouble filling your day,
I suggest you meditate on War and Zolmec."

"Tell me something," said Francis. "Did you ever . . . do
it to me?"

"Do it?" She started toward the stables.

"You know: dream about me. Did you?"

"No," she called. "Until recently you had never done
anything that hurt me."

14

FOR THE NEXT TEN DAYS it rained. It rained cats and dogs, buckets and cisterns, testiness and discontent. Indoors, Francis and Tez strained to hold the climate somewhere between hostility and nonchalance, and at times it climbed as high as courtesy. They made love once.

Tez's puppets became their principal means of communication. Shag, a shy sea serpent with a droopy tongue and a horn, was Francis's mouthpiece. Tez used Mr. Nose, a clown. The four of them shared the bed. For minor grievances the game worked well. Criticism went down easily when sugared by a piping voice that issued from something small and cute. Francis agreed with Mr. Nose that he had a bad habit of letting his swimming pool acquire scum. Tez conceded Shag's point about not littering the house with half-drunk glasses of juice. When it came to the Zolmec rift, however, no amount of smallness, no quantity of cuteness, helped. Shag said that Quetzalians were bleeding their souls away, and Tez refused to answer. The closest they came to rapport was when Shag called the Zolmec fantasies "wet dreams" and Mr. Nose replied that they sprang from "holyjectors."

Outside the bedroom, silence ruled. At night Tez stayed in the library, writing a new play, *Laughing Matter*, about a planet whose scientists isolate a humor gene that multiplies rampantly and turns everybody into comedians. Jokes begin appearing in unlikely places, like road signs and theater tickets.

Francis, meanwhile, would walk the courtyard's graceful portico, rehearsing aloud a lecture on mites and studying the drizzly torch-lit gardens. Raindrops hit the puddles, made targets, always got bull's-eyes.

Each lover saw in the other an anger that was both just and indulgent. Francis knew that Tez felt violated and spied upon, but hadn't she invited it, with her refusal to tell him earlier how Zolmec worked? Tez knew Francis felt misled, but wasn't his repulsion proof she had been right to protect him? Like all good friends, they hated seeing their relationship lose its emotional innocence, its chastity of goodwill, and now that the thing was lost, now that searing statements had changed hands and left scars, neither looked forward to the future.

ONE OF LIFE'S SPICES for Quetzalians was the prerogative of clergy to declare national holidays at random. On the eleventh day of bad weather, Vaxcala concluded that everybody deserved to stay home and listen to the pleasant percussion of rain on windows. All over Quetzalia, workers who loathed their jobs and bosses who loathed their workers lit candles to the high priestess, while parents, stuck with their children, wished her warts.

The Hospital of Chimec continued to cure, of course, but inessentials were canceled, including the afternoon staff meeting. Reaching Olo before lunchtime, Tez found Francis bruising his fingers over a final longhand copy of a new encyclopedia article, "Locust Polymorphism," and she readily persuaded him to join her on the portico for soup and chess.

One hour later an irksome knight was forking Francis's black bishop and its neighboring rook. He stared toward the gardens, as if hope lay more in rain than in relocating the rook. The courtyard held something unexpected.

Out of the rain a mounted man loomed. He was a blur of

wetness, a trotting puddle, but Francis recognized him instantly. This time, Iztac willing, his friend was flesh and blood, not a vengeful projection.

"Burne!"

"Lostwax!" Burne reined up and slid from his lipoca as Francis vaulted the portico's railing. The Nearthlings dashed toward each other, met among flowers, shook hands, exchanged the sort of how-are-you-it's-good-you're-back-I-was-worried banalities where the meaning is in warmth of voice. Burne rattled around inside his saddlebag, drew out the vitreousteel cage. "This one's been anxious to see you, too."

Francis exuded gratitude, shielded Ollie Cortexclavus under his robe. Flushed with the happiness of this unexpected double reunion, he hustled his two friends out of the rain.

"Tez, this is Burne."

She glided across the portico, shook Burne's dripping hand. "The savior of Quetzalia," she said with imperceptible sarcasm.

Through the sop of his beard Burne smiled agreeably. "Dr. Mool told me that Francis was living in sin, but after seeing you I'd call it *style.*"

Noticing the chessboard, he indicated to Francis where the imperiled rook belonged. "I went to the hospital first, got the magnificent news that you were well again."

Francis parted his curls and pointed. "It left a scar." He explained that his diabetes was also cured, and then he put his rook where Burne had suggested: let Tez try to take the bishop now, just let her try.

BURNE CAME TO DINNER dry-robed and cheerful. On Francis's suggestion they abandoned the customary table and lazed by the fire roasting meat chunks and newly harvested corn. A wine bottle appeared. Outside, the rain was going slack.

Burne mentioned that Vaxcala had offered him a luxurious apartment in the city, whereupon Francis talked him into staying at Olo. "I think we could profit from each other's company until we've"—he was tempted to say "until we've left this nutty planet," but Tez was there—"er, decided about things. You know: recovering *Darwin*. You've given that some thought?"

The archeologist replied with a "maybe" that everybody knew had more to it. "Don't you want to hear how I slew the dragon?"

He proceeded to charm them with exploits, largely fabricated, spanning the eighty days from his hasty departure to his waterlogged return. At one point he had met a woolly mammoth in Big Ghost Bayou and won its tusks in a poker game. The actual dragon-slaying also acquired a supplemental sheen, for this time the beetle merely wounded the neurovore, forcing Burne into mortal hand-to-hand combat at the edge of quicksand, and only by a final, desperate sidestep was the him-or-me situation decided in favor of me.

He omitted Ticoma's rape entirely.

Burne's lies enjoyed the built-in absolution of his audience's knowledge that they were being fooled. Tez in particular seemed to have a good time, laughing in a way that reminded Francis how dear she was to him. Fear briefly knotted her when the Brain Eater came on stage, and upon its violent death she blanched with pity and shock. By the climax of the last yarn, in which Burne found a crashed space capsule containing the Holy Grail, the rain had stopped completely.

Tez excused herself from the company, explaining that surprise holidays were always a mixed blessing because duties still accumulated. "Quetzalians owe you their lives," she said to Burne. "We shall always be in your debt. I just hope it's never the other way around."

"WHAT DID SHE MEAN by *that*?" Burne asked when Tez was in the bedroom.

"She means we can't expect much help getting *Darwin* back."

Burne tipped his wineglass and gulped. "Do you love her?"

"She's the finest thing that's ever happened to me."

"Finer than *Cortexclavus*? Is this really Francis Lostwax I'm drinking with?"

"You're not seeing Tez at her best. Her father may die. And something's come between us."

"Something?"

"By which I mean nothing. The fifty million kilometers of nothing from Nearth to Luta. Love across planetary lines is folly, Burne."

At this point Francis could not resist startling his friend with some casual clairvoyance. "Speaking of love, what became of that pretty woman you raped?"

Burne gagged. "She didn't *fight* it!" He spat a tongueful of wine on the rug. "How in hell did you know?"

Slowly, and in great detail, Francis told how. He told about sneaking into the Temple of Tolca and seeing urges released in dreams. He repeated the history of Zolmec, from The Teller to the Brain Eaters to Janet Vij, the genius who invented her own private science.

Burne had visited too many planets, seen too many marvels, been appalled too many times to doubt a single word. When Francis was finished, his friend merely added, "It's all rather clever, don't you think?"

"Quetzalia is certainly *unique*," said Francis. "Every religion says war is evil, but one way or another they end up playing along. There were the Toltecs, of course."

"And the Quakers."

"But none of them had a systematic way to blow off steam. They had no *machines*." He said the word sneeringly. "Just ideals."

Burne replenished his wineglass. "How do you feel about all this, Lostwax? Have the Quetzalians sacrificed their humanity for the sake of absolute domestic tranquillity?"

"A good question. I wonder what they'd be like without Zolmec."

"Maybe we could find out." He dug a granite pegmatite from his robe, moved it toward Francis like a magician displaying a newly materialized dove. "Our ticket home. The southern jungles are lousy with pollucite ore."

"Burne, you're a certified deity!"

"The problem, of course, is transporting the stuff through neurovore country. We're going to need a small army."

"You've come to the wrong planet."

"True, but suppose, just suppose, that a few hundred of these pagans stayed away from the Temple of Tolca? After four or five opochs, wouldn't they be a little feisty? Hell, they'd be ready to *kill.*"

"How do we convince them to stop going?"

"How does a potter convince clay to become a vase? He pulls and pushes, and the message gets through."

A choking dread crept over Francis. "Burne, you *know* I want to get out of here and win that Poelsig Award. As for neurovores, they deserve whatever drubbings we can give them." Edging toward the fire, he studied the darting spikes of flame. "But what you're proposing is *ugly.* Zolmec goes back two centuries, and in that time no one has missed a service. We mustn't tamper with such a tradition. It could wreck their whole society."

"You sound like poor Kappie. But is there an alternative?"

Francis seized a poker, dueled the flames. Bold ideas did not normally come to him, but he could feel one growing. "Give me your indulgence while I plunge into unruly speculation. We've both studied cybernetics. As I see it, the Quetzalians are sentient computers grown weary of the knowledge of evil, so they're deprogramming themselves. But as every schoolboy knows, such loops are eminently reversible."

The theory Francis articulated presumed the possibility

of introducing discrete bits of violence back into the system, enough to make somebody a soldier but not a maniac, a Nearthling but not a Brain Eater. "What we're after is a *temporary* capacity. Yes, that's it. A mounted Quetzalian could get to the oasis and back in less than an opoch. He wouldn't have to forgo a single service!"

Burne, who treasured audacity wherever he could find it, took to the idea with glee. "But we need more than theory. We must know the chemistry of noctus. We must become biophotonics experts." He proposed an afternoon rendez-vous at the Library of Iztac.

"Why wait till the afternoon?"

Burne puffed up and announced in a blend of theatrical pomposity and authentic pride that, weather permitting, the clergy would tomorrow morning acknowledge his brav-ery with that most elaborate of honors, that most merry of spectacles, a parade.

THE PARADE TURNED OUT TO BE as elaborate as an overhand knot and as merry as a corpse sale. Its purpose was not to celebrate Burne's triumph but to lament the occurrence of violence within the country. The last such ritual, held ten opochs ago, marked the two hundred twenty-fifth anniver-sary of a key Tellerist victory. One of the floats, a sculptor's interpretation of the battle, showed how the neurovore bodies had been left in the sun quivering with maggots and pinned like memos on the sharp timbers that prefigured the Temple of Tolca. The children who watched the parade got no sleep that night.

The children who watched the current parade had trou-ble staying awake. Down the great causeway filed the black-robed priests and priestesses in thuddingly dull lockstep, their faces clothed in masks, their hands busy with stone gods and smoking censers. Vaxcala had situated Burnes in a place of high symbolism, the niche of a low wall encrusted with friezes depicting neurovores engaged in assorted abominations. Passing him, each cleric bestowed gratitude and sympathy—you saved Quetzalia, we're sorry you had to kill—and it was all Burne could do to keep from making one of his favorite irreverent remarks, which included not only "This looks like a beard but it's really transplanted pubic hair" but also "Wouldn't you agree that the average person likes the smell of his own farts far more than is commonly supposed?"

When the doleful parade had finally passed, Burne walked to the Library of Iztac and found Francis sitting on the north side reading a leatherbound copy of Janet Vij's *Biophotonics*. Scholars streamed up and down the jaguar-lined steps. Nobody noticed the Nearthian cabal that met in the bright sun near the entrance to the reptile museum.

Francis reported that *Biophotonics*, sadly, was little more than a repair manual, hardly the seminal treatise they had anticipated. Doubtless the clergy found it indispensable for servicing the holy machines, but when it came to the fantasies themselves Vij made only the most perfunctory and grudging references. The chemistry of noctus remained a mystery.

But there was good news. By lying through his teeth, Francis had convinced Loloc Haz, the handsome biologist-puppeteer to whom he owed his entomology lectureship, that Vaxcala wanted her Nearthling guests to know all about biophotonics, so that this wondrous technology could proliferate throughout the galaxy. Loloc responded by taking a crow quill from his desk and penning a letter that entitled its bearer to an extended peek at Janet Vij's unpublished notes. He surrendered it with a reluctance that was painful to watch.

"Whatever you learn, Francis, don't spread it around Quetzalia. If Zolmec loses its glamour, it also loses its followers."

The letter was addressed to one Loi Zeclan, whom Francis and Burne eventually located in the library's whimsically named Bird Wing. Loi proved to be a daffy old woman with a bouncy gait and dimples.

"Perhaps you've heard of us," said Francis, approaching. "Dr. Newman and Dr. Lostwax?"

She became pensive, then all winks and smiles. "The gentlemen from outer space! Your articles are superb, Dr. Lostwax, the *summit* of our encyclopedia." Burne, Loi knew, was the one who could kill, but she still found something nice to say. "And what a peerless honor it is to meet our deliverer!"

Her response to Loloc's letter made it clear that she was one of those people who could not discuss religion comfortably. Zolmec's mystique had become in her befuddled thoughts akin to taboos regarding intercourse and excrement. "Nobody looks at *those* notes anymore. They're full of talk about . . . *circuits*." You could tell she would have preferred to say "motherfucking."

"We realize that Loloc has given us a great trust," said Francis.

Extending her index finger, Loi Zeclan pressed the dimple on her chin. "Follow me."

She dribbled herself out of the Bird Wing, and Francis and Burne settled into the kind of unobservant somnambulism that typically afflicts persons being led through strange corridors. The journey ended at a door labeled UNBOUND. Loi opened it but refused to enter the same room with profanities.

"Number Twelve," she said. "It holds everything Dr. Vij ever wrote."

The room contained enough space for one marble table, two extraterrestrial scientists, and twenty large boxes luridly marked with numerals. Francis took Number 12 from its shelf. It was heavy. Lowering the box onto the table, he reached inside and removed a pile of loose, dusty pages, each coated with a spidery scrawl. With the side of his hand Burne sliced off the top half. "Here's *my* night's work," he said.

Midnight found them still inching their way through Vij's longhand. The lady was no duffer when it came to either brilliant complexity or self-important humorlessness, and the end of their search seemed remote.

Finally, just before dawn, Francis began grinning uncontrollably. He shoved a page under Burne's nose. There, in simple biology, clean chemistry, comprehensible physics, rudimentary information theory, and plain English, was a full disclosure of noctus.

Minutes later Burne had an even stronger card to play. "Try this," he said. Francis took the page and with a growing thrill read words of rarefied foresight.

In reviewing my work, several critics, Karnstein chief among them, have bemoaned the extreme vulnerability that the planned cartharses will impose. "It's a closed system," Karnstein writes (personal communication). "A hostile outsider could massacre us."

Thus I am obligated to consider the question, "What if our nation were invaded?"

For purposes of defense, I propose introducing diluted noctus into the bloodstreams of Quetzalian volunteers. Animal experiments could determine whether the saline solution must be swallowed or injected and, if injected, whether the shot must be intravenous, intramuscular, or subcutaneous. Naturally I have no hard data, but my computations suggest that, if the dose is kept to one cc per ten kilograms of body weight, a twenty percent solution delivered intramuscularly will render an organism capable of moderate, provoked aggression for six days, after which the drug will be either devoured by phages or neutralized through the normal processes of enzyme, gland, and duct.

If six days are insufficient for thoroughly vanquishing an invader, it should even be possible to maintain a standing army through carefully scheduled booster shots, the first coming after a six-day interval, the second after twelve days, the third after twenty-four, and so forth. In no event should the rites themselves be canceled, as such a precedent could destroy the entire harvest of these wearisome and bloody years.

In their minds Francis and Burne toasted Dr. Janet Vij. A hundred and seventy years after her death, she had given them a way to go home.

Now Burne began narrowing his eyes and twitching his cheeks in a manner that said it was time to get practical. "We'll need subjects. Animals . . . and humans."

"Quetzalia has rabbits, chitzals—whatever we want. Humans? Zamanta owes you a couple of favors, one for each child."

"We'll need moat fluid, liters of it."

"The markets have pots. Fired clay probably holds noctus for at least a minute, long enough to prepare a saltwater solution."

"Then, of course, Vij favors *injecting* the stuff."

"My needles are back at Olo, two five-cc syringes. Tez wanted me to burn them."

Burne's hands began writhing around each other. "Ah, Lostwax, this is going to be fun. I've been needing an adventure. Killing the neurovore was mostly work, but now I've got a whole goddam *war* to play with."

LEAVING THE LIBRARY, Burne at his side, the noctus formula in his pocket, Francis felt the elation of the night's accomplishment give way to embarrassment. In the mute simplicity of dawn, Tepec looked every inch a sacred city. This was a great civilization! What right had he, an obscure entomologist with a beanlouse theory, to tell them they must change their ways? Did he really expect pacifists to fight and die just so he could go home? He put it into words.

Burne, predictably, was unruffled. "Hell, these jellyfish have everything to gain by going to war. Do you think they *enjoy* having neurovores around? We're offering them nothing less than their freedom."

"Promise me one thing, Burne. *Offer* them their freedom,

don't force it on them. I don't want anybody injected against his will."

"You have my word." There was enough heart in Burne's answer to make Francis feel better. They continued down the steps, and the sun gave the city its first colors of the day.

"FRANCIS, WHAT IN IZTAC'S NAME is going *on* around here?" Tez was referring to the animals that for the past five days had been arriving at Olo sane and clear-eyed and frisky and leaving either crazed or comatose or dead.

"You don't want to know." As Francis continued down the hall, Tez at his heels, he drew a rude bronze key from his pocket. Burne in his romanticism had wanted to build their laboratory in the basement, mad-doctor style, a plan thwarted by their discovery that Olo had no basement; settling for the next best thing, they converted the villa's grandest room, the library. Its door, like all Quetzalian doors, had no lock, so Burne built one. Francis inserted the key, turned it, heard the homemade cylinders clunking into place. He slithered behind the door with the motion one uses to keep a puppy from following.

"Secrets are so juvenile," Tez called, thereby shaming him into leaving the door partially open.

"It's a Nearth religious ritual. Quetzalian atheists aren't allowed."

"You're doing something that you think will get your ship back."

"Yes," he confessed.

"I hope your experiments are going well," she said, her conviction that of a physicist consulting a Ouija board.

"Our experiments are going *very* well."

Their experiments were going wretchedly. Noctus was proving a cagey substance, resistant to forecast. Not that Janet Vij hadn't been right about most things. The drug indeed needed to be injected—gastric juices inactivated it— and the injection indeed needed to be intramuscular. But while Vij's recommended measure—a twenty percent solution, one cubic centimeter per ten kilograms of body weight—might have been mathematically rational, the newly created populations of chitzal-eating chitzals indicated that it was wrong.

The scientists cut the dosage to one cc per twenty kilograms, and the chitzals stopped being cannibals. They clawed each other's eyes out, including the ones on stalks.

The solution itself was reduced to fifteen percent, and the chitzals left each other's eyes alone. They went for the jugular.

Right now, however, Francis glowed with optimism. Today's experiment would be the most conservative yet: a ten percent solution, one cc per twenty-five kilograms.

"*Please* tell me," said Tez, almost moaning.

"All right. If we succeed you'll hear about it soon enough." He rooted himself behind the half-closed door. "The fact is, we're experimenting with the moat." Janet Vij's original notes, he explained, predicted that a diluted-noctus injection would render a Quetzalian temporarily capable of violence. He and Burne intended to raise a small volunteer army and rid the planet of Brain Eaters.

Tez's reaction was immediate and unmixed. "That's the stupidest idea I've ever heard. You must be out of your head."

"My head and I are in the same place." He started into the lab.

In a move that was as close as Quetzalians ever came to violence, Tez reached forward, found his arm, and grabbed it. "You must not do this." Her voice had an edge that could draw blood. "Do you understand? *Don't do this.*"

"Why not?" said Francis. "No avenue is forbidden to science."

"If the reason isn't perfectly evident, then I pity you and all your race."

He could hear Burne mixing a batch of noctus. "Excuse me."

"I have one more thing to say. If you dare go ahead with

your scheme, I shall walk out of your life for good. What is more, I shall fight you. Do you hear me? That's a strange word for a Quetzalian to use, but I'm going to *fight* you on this with every weapon I can think of."

All Francis said was, "I'd better get to work." Tez huffed off. He wondered: Was she serious? Didn't she realize he had a right to avenge his friends and regain his ship?

Burne sat amid a congestion of noctus pots. Stripped of their books, the library shelves held cages filled with pacing, edgy animals. The air reeked. Pigs whimpered, monkeys scolded, birds squawked, rabbits and chitzals sat dumb.

On the center table six cages, two animals to the cage, were stacked in a chitzal highrise. "It went into them five minutes ago," Burne said, running his hand across the top three cages.

Normally noctus reached a chitzal's brain in ten minutes. The five minutes that remained took about an hour apiece to crawl by.

Things looked good. Like their control-group cousins, the experimental chitzals showed not the slightest symptom of madness or mortality. But when Burne started banging them together like cymbals, thus convincing each it was being assaulted by the other, horrible fights broke out. This was the balance between civility and pluck they had been seeking. One cubic centimeter per twenty-five kilograms, a ten percent solution: magic numbers!

Six days later, Francis walked into the bedroom and saw that Mr. Nose, Shag the Sea Serpent, and Tez's clothes were gone. A note fluttered on the pillow. Its gist was that she had made good her promise to clear out. The last two sentences were particularly galling. "There is a difference between science and arrogance. I'm sorry to be the one who breaks this to you."

Francis felt tears in his eyes, tried unsuccessfully to stopper them with a wince. Damn you Tez, he thought, Quetzalia is not my home. He tore the note repeatedly, a piece for every word, and scattered it like confetti.

When Burne rushed into the bedroom, Francis lay transfixed, staring at a ceiling crack that looked like one of the constellations Tez had shown him, Janet's Dragon. "She moved out." Francis's voice was toneless.

"Are you surprised?"

"Moderately."

"I want to tell you about a nice little result from down the hall. Maybe it will cheer you up."

"I'm not really sure that I'm depressed." He almost meant it. "It had to end *sometime*."

Burne said, "I've been spending my morning banging chitzals together, and there hasn't been so much as a family quarrel. It's just as Vij predicted. In six days—poof!—the aggression is gone. Lostwax, buddy, I think we've got natural law where we want her."

"What next?"

"We sacrifice the chitzals, look for brain damage, liver damage, cancer."

"Suppose they're all right?"

"We go for results that *nobody* can dispute. We put it into chitzals again, ten times, twenty times. We put it into pigs, mice, monkeys, rabbits, the whole damn zoo."

"And if the animal trials fail?"

"We admit defeat."

"And if they succeed?"

"We put it into people."

15

GOVERNOR NAZRA installed his beefy rear in a lipocawool cushion and stared at the men below. So, he thought, these are the famous extraterrestrials who want to deliver us from neurovores—we'll see about that. Nazra, a great wadling pudding of a man, had a hard nose to offset his soft belly. It would take some awfully fancy arguments to convince him this army business was a good idea.

Of the two Nearthlings who occupied the Vij Memorial Arena, only Francis returned Nazra's gaze. Standing in the pit's red ring, the entomologist writhed with self-consciousness. He wanted to be anywhere but here—the festering swamps of Arete, the bleak moons of Kritonia, anywhere. Our governor looks intelligent, he thought. Not easy to please, but not hostile either. If Burne plays his cards right, Aca will swing over, and our war will happen.

Of course, Francis wasn't entirely convinced he *wanted* their war to happen. Could he really grab a sword and chop up neurovores? No, not even if he took a noctus dose himself. But without the war there would be no ship, and without the ship there would be no home, no *Cortexclavus* triumph, no Poelsig Award, and he would remain forever on this lunatic planet.

Nazra's arrival inspired the rest of the Aca power structure—the aides, the cabinet members, the legislators, the professional sycophants—to shut up and find seats. Cuz was also represented, in the person of an Antistasist named Minnix Cies. Francis guessed Cies must be the gaunt, straight-backed one who sat friendless in the front row, politicians spread around him like iron filings around a magnet.

The remaining invitations had gone to Tepec's great institutions: the library, the hospital, the church. Vaxcala was first to reply. She returned Burne's battle plan with three words scrawled across the top: "This is insane." Loloc Haz sent an angry note saying he was sorry to see Vij's speculations exploited in this way, sorry he had let Francis even *see* them. He would come to the council, but with the intention of asking as many unfriendly questions as possible. The Hospital of Chimec delegated Mool, who sat in uncharacteristic quietude behind folded arms.

"You have all read the proposal for this campaign," Burne began. "Some of you probably have reactions." Clearly an understatement, Francis concluded from the flood of grunts and nods. It subsided as Loloc stood and spoke.

"I shall not insult your cunning, Newman, by asking why you want exactly twenty-five days for this scheme and not twenty-six or twenty-seven. Obviously you know better than to disrupt the sacred cycle of Zolmec. But is such a time-table really workable? In twenty-five days can your hypothesized thousand reach the neurovore stronghold, wipe it out, and return to Quetzalia?"

"It would be unscientific of me to claim certainty in this matter," Burne began through a mouthful of humble pie. "Who can prove the future? Nevertheless, let me spell out several of our war's more impressive safety valves." He carried a wooden staff equal to his height, and he jabbed it into the ground whenever a sentence ended with an exclamation point.

"Before we were forced to abandon our magnecar inside your Temple of Tolca, its odometer gave the distance from the neurovore oasis to Quetzalia: nine hundred kilometers. Now, I think you will agree with me that a lipoca, even a last-legs, out-to-pasture, ready-for-the-rubber-cement-factory lipoca, can travel nine hundred kilometers in eight days. Our plan allows *eleven* days! The enemy numbers three hundred at most—fewer than a hundred and fifty attacked us at the oasis. Hence, I anticipate a one-day battle. But we can take *three* days! After that, Dr. Lostwax and I proceed alone to our spaceship, a day's ride, and the army returns to Quetzalia—another eleven-day trip that will in reality consume only eight. In short, we are assigning twenty-five days to a seventeen-day expedition!"

Approving noises rippled through the politicians. Loloc stayed on his feet. "I don't dispute your arithmetic, Newman, merely your premises. You are promising to obliterate the tribes in a single raid—which assumes they are all concentrated in one place. But suppose the small band that attacked you at the drawbridge still roams the desert? They might attempt an ambush. Suppose a neurovore escapes the battle? The desert cannot be ours so long as even one creature with killing capacity lives. Suppose there is a second oasis? Or a third?"

"I shall be honest," Burne replied. "My interests are not unselfish. Dr. Lostwax and I want *Darwin* back. But I hope you believe me when I say that I care deeply for this civilization and that, once I am home, my knowledge of Luta remains an imperishable secret. Nothing would pain me more than to see a Nearthian ship land here again. I owe you my life. You didn't have to lower your bridge to us, but you did. I tried to repay your heroism by stopping that renegade Brain Eater. But let me go even further. Let me cut the entire neurovorean worm from the Quetzalian apple!"

"That was a very pretty speech," said Loloc, "but if it contained an answer to even *one* of my questions then I did not hear it."

Burne left the blue ring and approached Loloc. His exclamation point went to work. "A thousand soldiers are not vulnerable to ambush, Dr. Haz, not on open desert. I hope we *are* ambushed! Every neurovore dispatched along the way is one less to worry about later. As for the main battle, it's true we may not kill them all. But we *shall* deal them a defeat from which they can never recover! If we eliminate only *half* the females, the whole race is on the road to extinction. Yes, there may be a second oasis, or even a third. I doubt it. But if Quetzalia can raise an army once, she can raise an army twice. Dr. Lostwax and I shall leave a syringe behind."

"Your shamelessness is a model for us all." In sitting, Loloc seemed to trigger Minnix Cies on the opposite side of the arena.

"I would like to speak in Dr. Newman's favor," Minnix began. He wore the flame-eyed, grim-lipped look of a man who had as little use for self-doubt as he had for other people's approval. "To me he is a civilized man. In the past this country taught its children that only Quetzalians are civilized. Yes, he can kill. But he can also *be* killed. His neurovore hunt entailed staggering risks. I think Dr. Newman is like the falcons that our ancestors brought on *Eden Three*. He has talons, but he does not use them capriciously."

"As long as things go his way," Loloc put in without rising.

"I give him more credit than that. Dr. Newman was not *forced* to hold this meeting. He could have rounded up a thousand of us. He could have dragged us onto the desert, injected us right before the neurovores struck. Outnumbered, they lose, and Dr. Newman regains his ship."

"Don't give him any ideas," said Loloc.

"All I can say is that the Antistasists find in this war the kind of boldness Quetzalia must embrace if she is to avoid stagnation and decay."

Now it was Mool's turn. He seemed not merely to stand

but to ascend. He hugged himself and addressed a cloudless autumn sky. "As many of you know, I am a man who *does* mince words. I mince, dice, and subdivide them. The Antistasist who just spoke assumes total victory as Quetzalia's destiny. I question this. In his proposal, Dr. Newman explains that the solution should be kept to ten percent, the dosage to one cc per twenty-five kilograms of body weight. Beyond these limits, the drug becomes a rabid weasel. As a scientist, I applaud his caution. But as a parent whose son may end up joining this bizarre adventure, I can't help fretting." Mool's gaze slithered from the sky to the pit. "Dr. Newman, you have proved—to my satisfaction, at least, through controlled studies destined to become classics in the annals of pharmacology—you have proved that diluted noctus can render a pacifist organism capable of the obscenity called battle, meaning that if attacked the organism will defend itself."

"Well put," said Burne.

"Then my question—I call it a question, but, as is common in such situations, I am not really asking a question so much as I am doling out an amalgam of fact, opinion, and challenge—my question is, when neurovores are the enemy, is mere defensiveness adequate, even when coupled with numerical advantage? You are dealing with one of the strongest and most vicious animals in the galaxy. You are not dealing with . . . Quetzalians." Mool looked around to confirm that he was drawing smiles.

"Finished?" asked Burne, regaining the blue ring.

"I am never finished. But you may speak."

"There is more to my strategy than numbers, Dr. Mool. My soldiers will have superior mobility. They will be a cavalry, our enemy a barefoot infantry. My soldiers will have superior intellect. Most Quetzalians are educated to levels that on Nearth would equal degrees in philosophy and medicine. Our enemy is educated to levels that on Nearth would equal degrees in soup dribbling and nose picking. Finally,

een sliver jammed between cannibals and sea. I think
ak for the overwhelming majority when I say this plan
rthy."

e arena broke into yesses and nodding heads. He *has*
t our arguments, Francis thought, shifting motives
s depression.

ra now focused on Burne. "I hope you realize that my
us beliefs would never allow me actually to condone
ar. Zolmec is evermore opposed to all forms of vio-
What I *shall* do is pressure my church to adopt an
y neutral stance. And with parliamentary support,
think I'll get, I can probably maneuver the clergy
tain dispensations regarding machines and war.
oops deserve to partake of hypodermic technol-
out guilty consciences. But first one thing must

?" asked Burne.
ven days I want you to bring me this woman. I
ee for myself that she has reverted to pacifism. If
a Nearthling, I shall encourage Vaxcala Coatl to
army as heretical and wicked."
rew radiant. "An informed and reasonable de-
ernor."

CLOSER THAN EVER. Yet Francis knew somehow
with the entire Aca bureaucracy tacitly behind it,
ould be less clean than recent speeches sug-
council, evidently, did not agree. They were
ttering, and otherwise communicating a con-
othing more needed to be said.
small female form stood up, face behind the
hood. "Wait!" the woman called in a husky
back the hood to reveal a flagrant familiar-
shock faded, became curiosity, became sex-

nvited here," Tez began. "I probably have no
eak."

---

my soldiers will have superior equipment. The neurovores
can fight only at close range, but Quetzalians can kill
at a distance." He made a sudden, checkmating move.
"Behold!"

Much as he disliked calling attention to himself, Francis
knew that he should now step into Burne's ring. Arriving,
he drew a lipocaskin thong from his robe. Burne, meanwhile, drove one tip of his staff into the dirt and bore down
on the other, causing a bend. He took the thong from Francis and secured the bend with a quick knot at each end.

And so it was that Burne Newman manufactured within
the walls of Quetzalia something that no citizen had ever
seen manufactured there before. A longbow: a weapon.

Francis fumbled inside his robe and procured a thin
dowel. One end, through radiating feathers, had been made
stable; the other, through a pointed rock, lethal. He retreated to the shadows by the north door.

Burne threaded the nock, drew back the thong. Aimed
high over the heads of the spectators, the arrow shot away
with dazzling straightness and velocity. It reached an apex
and, curving gracefully, passed beyond the eyesight of all
save the astronomers in the audience.

Mool sat down. "I am convinced," he said with a groan.

As THE MORNING SLOGGED ON, side conversations and feet
shufflings arose with increasing frequency. All of this became astoundingly evident the moment it stopped. Governor Nazra had lifted a finger.

"Each of you wonders what I think of this," he began in
an earthquake voice. "I shall tell you. I am impressed. Certainly we want the neurovorean curse lifted. And yet, one
question has not been asked." He slid his dumpling body
forward and addressed Burne. "What makes you think that
your results apply to *people*?"

"People do, Governor Nazra." Burne flung a finger
toward the north door. Taking the cue, Francis seized its

ring and yanked hard. Well-oiled, the door pivoted freely, revealing Zamanta and Momictla. Their accouterments were not customary. Each held a broadsword in one hand and a shield in the other.

Walking to the couple, Burne took Momictla's weapons, held them aloft. "Let me now prove the power of my science. Standing before you are two ordinary citizens. Seven days ago I took one of Dr. Lostwax's hypodermic syringes and injected Zamanta with three cc's, the right dosage for a human. I did not act against his will."

"That is true," said Zamanta, loud-voiced.

"Until yesterday he was capable of provoked aggression. Now the drug has worn off totally." Burne whirled around and charged. Zamanta sidestepped, not far enough to avoid Burne's thrust. Sword contacted shield with a crisp metallic peal.

"And now," said Burne, "permit me to amaze you."

Clutching his insulin kit, Francis quit the shadows and stepped back into the blue ring. He popped the kit open. Two five-cc syringes lay velvet-cradled like a pair of pistols. A black substance filled their bellies.

Resting sword and shield on the ground, Burne chose the topmost syringe, approached Momictla. She eyed the needle fearfully. In a coarse whisper that mingled reassurance with threat, Burne said, "Trust me. I saved your children."

Momictla stiffened. Burne slid back her sleeve and stuck her. He retreated the plunger: no blood. Confident that he had not hit a vein, he loaded her arm with three cubic centimeters. She did not wince or move, even when a green welt bloomed where the needle had entered.

"The drug takes effect in ten minutes," Burne explained.

Questions filled the time. A politician asked Zamanta if he had experienced any side effects, nasty or otherwise. No. In fact, he felt rather invigorated. Noctus had probably added "a good four hours to my life." The crowd broke into a collective chuckle. Momictla reported a slight headache

and a feeble twinge of nausea, but hast[e] she *always* got such symptoms when o[n]

"Prepare to defend yourself," Burn[e] ject, retrieving his own weapons fr[om] mictla took sword and shield from he[r]

Burne struck first, hitting Momictl[a] firmed her grip and returned the blo[w] shot up like a spew of lava. They co[uld] amazed had the woman turned int[o]

Momictla had never dueled befo[re] her feet and took well to novelty. [She] the kinesthetic side of violence, times in the Temple of Tolca. [blow] for blow.

It was not until they had circl[ed] gongs all the while getting sh[orter] them shorter, that Burne ca[ught] bashed the sword from her [hand] surrender, but grasped her sh[ield] ready to parry further attack[s]

But Burne had made his the dirt and held out his h[and] executed an acrobatic feat whether to cheer, gasp, or

The governor rose. "For locked behind stone wall His voice was building have a chance for free[dom] make a temporary and r tion. *Something in me*

He's against us! Fr into him, he experien cal depression woul[d] arguments.

"And yet," the g[overnor] the past. We must g

a g[reat]
I sp[eak]
is w[e]

Th[e]
boug[ht]
for h[i]

Na[me]
religi[on]
this w[ay]
lence.

official
which
into ce[rtain]
Your tr[e]
ogy wit[h]
happen.

"Wha[t]
"In se[arch]
want to s[ee]
she is sti[ll]
brand you

Burne g
mand, gov[ernment]

HOME WAS
that, even [when]
this war w[as]
gested. The[n]
shifting, mu[st]
viction that
But then a[s]
shadow of a
voice, flippin[g]
ness. Francis[']
ual longing.

"I was not i[n]
authority to sp[eak]

my soldiers will have superior equipment. The neurovores can fight only at close range, but Quetzalians can kill at a distance." He made a sudden, checkmating move. "Behold!"

Much as he disliked calling attention to himself, Francis knew that he should now step into Burne's ring. Arriving, he drew a lipocaskin thong from his robe. Burne, meanwhile, drove one tip of his staff into the dirt and bore down on the other, causing a bend. He took the thong from Francis and secured the bend with a quick knot at each end.

And so it was that Burne Newman manufactured within the walls of Quetzalia something that no citizen had ever seen manufactured there before. A longbow: a weapon.

Francis fumbled inside his robe and procured a thin dowel. One end, through radiating feathers, had been made stable; the other, through a pointed rock, lethal. He retreated to the shadows by the north door.

Burne threaded the nock, drew back the thong. Aimed high over the heads of the spectators, the arrow shot away with dazzling straightness and velocity. It reached an apex and, curving gracefully, passed beyond the eyesight of all save the astronomers in the audience.

Mool sat down. "I am convinced," he said with a groan.

As THE MORNING SLOGGED ON, side conversations and feet shufflings arose with increasing frequency. All of this became astoundingly evident the moment it stopped. Governor Nazra had lifted a finger.

"Each of you wonders what I think of this," he began in an earthquake voice. "I shall tell you. I am impressed. Certainly we want the neurovorean curse lifted. And yet, one question has not been asked." He slid his dumpling body forward and addressed Burne. "What makes you think that your results apply to *people*?"

"People do, Governor Nazra." Burne flung a finger toward the north door. Taking the cue, Francis seized its ring and yanked hard. Well-oiled, the door pivoted freely, revealing Zamanta and Momictla. Their accouterments were not customary. Each held a broadsword in one hand and a shield in the other.

Walking to the couple, Burne took Momictla's weapons, held them aloft. "Let me now prove the power of my science. Standing before you are two ordinary citizens. Seven days ago I took one of Dr. Lostwax's hypodermic syringes and injected Zamanta with three cc's, the right dosage for a human. I did not act against his will."

"That is true," said Zamanta, loud-voiced.

"Until yesterday he was capable of provoked aggression. Now the drug has worn off totally." Burne whirled around and charged. Zamanta sidestepped, not far enough to avoid Burne's thrust. Sword contacted shield with a crisp metallic peal.

"And now," said Burne, "permit me to amaze you."

Clutching his insulin kit, Francis quit the shadows and stepped back into the blue ring. He popped the kit open. Two five-cc syringes lay velvet-cradled like a pair of pistols. A black substance filled their bellies.

Resting sword and shield on the ground, Burne chose the topmost syringe, approached Momictla. She eyed the needle fearfully. In a coarse whisper that mingled reassurance with threat, Burne said, "Trust me. I saved your children."

Momictla stiffened. Burne slid back her sleeve and stuck her. He retreated the plunger: no blood. Confident that he had not hit a vein, he loaded her arm with three cubic centimeters. She did not wince or move, even when a green welt bloomed where the needle had entered.

"The drug takes effect in ten minutes," Burne explained.

Questions filled the time. A politician asked Zamanta if he had experienced any side effects, nasty or otherwise. No. In fact, he felt rather invigorated. Noctus had probably added "a good four hours to my life." The crowd broke into a collective chuckle. Momictla reported a slight headache and a feeble twinge of nausea, but hastened to explain that she *always* got such symptoms when on public view.

"Prepare to defend yourself," Burne instructed his subject, retrieving his own weapons from the ground. Momictla took sword and shield from her husband.

Burne struck first, hitting Momictla's wobbly sword. She firmed her grip and returned the blow. The entire audience shot up like a spew of lava. They could not have been more amazed had the woman turned into a toad.

Momictla had never dueled before, but she was quick on her feet and took well to novelty. She knew the visual if not the kinesthetic side of violence, having watched it many times in the Temple of Tolca. She matched Burne blow for blow.

It was not until they had circled the arena four times, the gongs all the while getting sharper, the intervals between them shorter, that Burne caught Momictla relaxing and bashed the sword from her hand. Even now she did not surrender, but grasped her shield in both hands and stood ready to parry further attacks.

But Burne had made his point. He drove his sword into the dirt and held out his hands, palms up, as if he'd just executed an acrobatic feat. The politicians did not know whether to cheer, gasp, or retch. They looked at Nazra.

The governor rose. "For two hundred years we have been locked behind stone walls, prisoners on our own planet." His voice was building to another shock wave. "Now we have a chance for freedom, and to take it we need only make a temporary and rather trivial break with an old tradition. *Something in me hesitates to do this!*"

He's against us! Francis thought. As depression bored into him, he experienced the curious feeling that an identical depression would have attended Nazra *buying* their arguments.

"And yet," the governor continued, "we cannot live in the past. We must give our descendants a whole planet, not a green sliver jammed between cannibals and sea. I think I speak for the overwhelming majority when I say this plan is worthy."

The arena broke into yesses and nodding heads. He *has* bought our arguments, Francis thought, shifting motives for his depression.

Nazra now focused on Burne. "I hope you realize that my religious beliefs would never allow me actually to condone this war. Zolmec is evermore opposed to all forms of violence. What I *shall* do is pressure my church to adopt an officially neutral stance. And with parliamentary support, which I think I'll get, I can probably maneuver the clergy into certain dispensations regarding machines and war. Your troops deserve to partake of hypodermic technology without guilty consciences. But first one thing must happen."

"What?" asked Burne.

"In seven days I want you to bring me this woman. I want to see for myself that she has reverted to pacifism. If she is still a Nearthling, I shall encourage Vaxcala Coatl to brand your army as heretical and wicked."

Burne grew radiant. "An informed and reasonable demand, governor."

HOME WAS CLOSER THAN EVER. Yet Francis knew somehow that, even with the entire Aca bureaucracy tacitly behind it, this war would be less clean than recent speeches suggested. The council, evidently, did not agree. They were shifting, muttering, and otherwise communicating a conviction that nothing more needed to be said.

But then a small female form stood up, face behind the shadow of a hood. "Wait!" the woman called in a husky voice, flipping back the hood to reveal a flagrant familiarness. Francis's shock faded, became curiosity, became sexual longing.

"I was not invited here," Tez began. "I probably have no authority to speak."

Correct, you sneaky little invertebrate, Burne's frown said.

"Who are you?" Nazra asked.

"I'll tell you who she is," said Mool in a lather. "She's Tez Yon, a resident surgeon. Dr. Yon, *I'm* representing Chimec here. I suggest you go back to work."

"I believe she has a minority report for us," said Nazra. "I, for one, would like to consider it."

Tez waited for dead silence, soon got it, began. "I sat here and heard it all, and I must confess to a bewilderment beyond words. I had always thought that Zolmec *stood* for something. Yes, nonviolence is certainly good business. It keeps people alive. It spares everyone the financial burden of courts and locks. But nonviolence is also *right*." She slid into the aisle. Reaching the edge of the pit, she turned to confront the whole council. "Are you really ready to forsake the noblest tradition in human history on the word of two carnival barkers from outer space? Are you ready to abandon our litanies because these conmen *say* you should? 'Thieves are unknown,' boasts Zolmec. 'Warriors unnamed.' Have you *forgotten*?"

Nazra watched Tez's face with pained, unvarying eyes. "You have done a brave thing in coming, Dr. Yon." He rumbled at the crowd: "We should all remember, in the impending days, that this woman may have spoken the truth!"

"Forgive me, governor," said Burne, "but this woman has spoken nothing but barf. An opoch ago Lostwax and she stopped loving each other. Dr. Yon is very *upset*."

Francis burst from the shadows. "No, that isn't fair. She has deep moral convictions!" His voice, louder than he expected, reached the farthest tier.

Tez spun toward the pit and offered Francis a grateful smile. "Thank you." Now she fixed on Burne. "I have no doubt that you are destined to get your criminal little war. But I shall not join it, nor will my brother, nor will anyone else I can influence, beguile, convince, or seduce."

"Zolmec," said Nazra, "has always taught that the greatest words are 'I could very well be wrong.' A world without neurovores seems to me a beautiful dream, one that will reap for Quetzalia far more loaves than stones. But I could very well be wrong."

Tez made her exit, charging for the nearest portal. As the dark tunnel closed around her, she cried out, in a voice that reached even to the pit, "And I have *not* stopped loving the Nearthling!"

The words bounced off granite and died. Francis thought: Nor I the Quetzalian.

16

SEVEN DAYS LATER Burne armed Momictla with a sword and brought her into Governor Nazra's private study, and no matter how many slaps, pokes, and pinpricks he heaped upon her she refused to strike back. Afterward, Burne apologized.

Momictla returned the sword, holding its hilt as she would the tail of a diseased rat. "In church I shall use this to behead you," she commented.

"I'd like to watch," said Burne. "I'd like to see me in your dreams."

Momictla's spontaneous recovery from her bout with violence so impressed Nazra that he offered to let his palace become an army barracks. Burne replied that palaces did not lend themselves to toughening up soldiers. Instead, he would establish a boot camp in the backyard. Nazra's backyard comprised ten grassy acres, flat and green as a billiard table.

Runners sent word that the adventure of the age was brewing at the governor's palace, and every population center from mighty Tepec to piddling Oaxa sent volunteers. Francis was easily convinced to pack up his beetle, move out of Olo, and come supervise the inductions.

Sitting behind a marble desk in the palace's main hall, he created soldiers at the rate of a hundred a day.

"Name?" He rarely looked up from the induction paper.

"Minnix Cies."

"Address?"

"The Cies family cottage, south of Cuz on Harmony Road."

"Now, repeat after me. The First Army of Aca hereby receives my strength . . ."

"This is silly," said Minnix. The previous inductees had expressed similar opinions.

"My will . . ."

"Of *course* it does."

"And my everlasting obedience."

"That sounds rather neurovorean."

Francis checked off the square indicating that Minnix had taken the loyalty oath. "We need to test your muscles."

The minute he handed Minnix the longbow, Francis realized this was the fiery Antistasist who had defended their war in the Vij Arena. "So it's *you*—our champion!"

"Bold ideas deserve nothing less. You are taking the dullness from our lives."

"Don't bother with the bow, soldier. We're in your debt."

But Minnix tried anyway, bringing the bow to maximum arc. Francis explained that new recruits must report to the brigadier general's tent behind the mansion, and Minnix fired off an uncertain impersonation of a salute.

In the brigadier general's tent, Burne gave pep talks about the new day that was dawning on Luta and how, throughout history, dying for your country had always been regarded as the chance of a lifetime. Most inductees, Antistasists included, replied that idiot patriotism was not for them. They were here to fight one war, one battle, after which they intended to become religious again. Often Burne found himself saying, "I don't think you would make a very good soldier," and with grating predictability he heard that *he* wouldn't make a very good pacifist. But he dared not shrivel his ranks by sending such upstarts home. He made them dig latrines.

ONE FINAL HOUR of recruiting, and the First Army of Aca would have its thousand. Eyes swimming with the day's succession of induction papers, Francis dragged his pencil up to the Name line. "Name?"

"Tez Yon."

Automatically he transcribed the words. "Address?" He read what he had written. "Tez!"

"I want to talk," she said wearily.

A dormant bitterness awoke. "*Talk?* Why not follow your custom and leave an insulting note on my pillow? The bedroom is upstairs." Tez merely glowered. "I thought perhaps you were joining the First Army." He meant this half-seriously. The crazed notion that Tez was reversing her scruples had come to him the instant he recognized her. Francis's weaknesses included jumping blithely past the absurdity of such a thesis and managing to perceive all subsequent words and deeds as fitting it perfectly.

"I would not join your army," said Tez in stately tones, "if you planted a barbary bush in my stomach."

"You, of course, are a virgin in such matters. You never thought about cutting Mool's heart out. You just *thought* you thought about it."

"I didn't come to quarrel, Francis!"

He rushed the remaining volunteers through induction, leaving out the loyalty oath and the longbow test. The First Army stood at one thousand exactly. "Let's go for a walk."

Traumatized by an incipient winter, the governor's garden looked blasted and grim. The snows were still two opochs away, but all the colors had gone south. Everywhere, fountains gurgled with incongruous jollity.

"I think about your father sometimes," said Francis.

"He's not suffering."

"That's good. I think about your brother, too."

"He's not suffering either. Just insufferable."

"And I think about you."

"I should thank you for defending me against Burne in

the arena. It must have been hard to go against a friend."

"It . . . happened."

"Then there's hope. Your intuitions say this war is wrong."

"I thought you didn't want a quarrel." Francis waved his thumb toward the boot camp. "You came to talk them into going home? I admire your determination."

"I'll say it straight out. I'm pregnant."

"What?"

"I am, to use an insipid expression, carrying your child."

"It's really mine?"

"And mine."

Joy possessed Francis. "Glory! Dwarf's foot is fallible!"

"On Nearthlings, at any rate."

"Obviously I was meant to be a father again. It's like *Barry's* coming back."

"Just remember the mother is different this time."

"That's the best part." He drew her near, half expecting rebuff, but their lips met comfortably.

"I missed you," she hummed.

"When you moved out I tried not to care, but I couldn't." Facing the nearest fountain, he moved his hand forward, rotating it until he felt the icy water pound his palm. "This baby won't get diabetes, either. We'll bring the pills when we leave."

"Leave?"

"For Nearth." He had spoken without plan, and it suddenly rushed upon him what he had said. *We.* Yes! He meant it.

"You want me to go back with you?"

He did not expect the idea to be automatically popular, and on the evidence of her collapsed face it was not. "I want him, her—the child—to be a Nearthling."

"Which can only be accomplished by making the mother one too?"

"If all goes well, we'll be launching *Darwin* in less than

forty days. The baby *can't* be born here if Nearth's to be his home. Oh, my planet has its humanities, you'll see. *Nobody* should grow up without riding a roller coaster." He smiled like Mr. Nose. "This child is going to be *happy*."

"*I* didn't ride a roller coaster, and *I* was happy."

"It's just that this is so *important* to me." He was practically jumping up and down.

Tez took one look and felt herself melting. God of the brain, I *do* love him. But—leave? No more marionette shows with Loloc? No more Legend Eves?

She broke the silence by announcing that she would seriously *consider* going to Nearth, "but only if two things happen."

"Yes?"

"First, we don't take off as long as my father is alive." Francis protested that Burne would want to leave the minute *Darwin* was in hand. "If my father is alive," Tez replied, "you will leave without me. The second condition is that you withdraw all your support for this war nonsense. I won't ask you to encourage desertions, but I expect you to leave Aca. Tell Burne you will stay behind when the army marches out. You once said the idea of genuinely pacifist deities charmed you. How could killers—generals and Joan of Arc—be thought great? Now *prove* your convictions!"

"Burne will think me spineless."

Her lips pressed together and vanished.

Francis withdrew his hand from the fountain, watched wet pearls fall from his fingertips. "There is also the matter of avenging Kappie and Luther."

"They will be avenged, and it won't matter one jot whether you're around or not. Look, if I'm going to change cultures, I want the goodwill of my friends. I want them to know that Burne Newman is not the paragon of Nearthlings. Some of them, like Francis Lostwax, have morals to match our own."

He pushed a sigh through his teeth. "Our foetus is already—what? An opoch old? He's been a fish—and an amphibian. Two billion years of evolution. It's time *I* grew up too." He explained that it would take him three or four days to settle his affairs, pack his belongings, and work up enough nerve to tell Burne his decision, after which he would join her at Olo.

"I appreciate your sacrifice," said Tez with no intended irony.

"*You're* making the sacrifice."

"Can Nearth use an experienced neurosurgeon?"

"And an experienced puppeteer. Oh, we're going to do splendidly, Tez. You can train our doctors in homeopathy, and they can teach you about robot limbs and dialysistems. We can fly kites in the spring and carve pumpkins in the autumn, and maybe, if you're very, very good, I'll teach you how to drive a magnecar."

WHEN FRANCIS FINALLY got around to revealing that his plans for the future included not only deserting the army but also bringing his pregnant lover back to Nearth, Burne predictably went up in smoke.

"Lostwax, what are you *doing* to me? How can I expect Quetzalians to fight for your ship when *you* won't?" The palace balcony overlooked a drill field, and Burne pointed down at his army. Officers watched helplessly as privates gavotted in outré patterns that fit precious few definitions of marching.

"I talked with Minnix Cies," said Francis. "He says he fights for Quetzalia's freedom, not for *Darwin*. The Antistasists understand my position."

"I wish I did."

Francis alternated between arguments stressing his frantic desire to raise a Nearthling child and arguments stressing his personal belief that mass murder was not a good thing to do, even when gilded by euphemisms like war and destiny. "I realize I'm being a crushing bother. Now you'll have to fly *Darwin* back here and pick us up. Still, I speak from deep convictions."

Burne went "hrumph," said that he should probably respect Francis's convictions, "even though they're wrong."

"Remember, I was the one who figured out we could reprogram these people. I've *made* my contribution to your war, Burne. One more volunteer can't win it for you, especially a marshmallow like me."

Burne suddenly brightened. "Actually, it's already won, as far as I'm concerned—and despite the quirks of my so-called soldiers."

"They march funny," Francis observed as he watched the army run into itself.

"They can't see the necessity of concerted action. Everybody's a goddam soloist."

Burne repeated a recent conversation with one of his more trustworthy lieutenants. "General, I've never been in a battle, but from what I've read it's a pretty individualist thing. You charge at your own speed toward the enemy, slashing your sword on your own initiative and at times selected by you, and by yourself you pick out a likely neurovore to kill, and if it throws a spear you don't wait for orders to duck, you just duck. I think you can see where I'm heading, sir. All this conformity you've been promoting— wearing liveries and walking in lockstep—it's useless. You should be training us in intuition and creativity."

Francis asked, "What did you tell him?"

"I told him he was a troublemaker."

"Hmmm . . . I'm not sure I disagree with him."

"Unfortunately, your lack of disagreement is shared by seven-eighths of this camp."

Burne began to prattle and whine. Two days ago he had issued uniforms, and everybody proceeded to restitch seams, add pockets, devise sleeves, and slap on designs until the First Army of Aca boasted a diversity rarely found outside the zoos. Every military custom since Troy was greeted with counterclaims and sneers. Burne would say, "We need bugles," and the volunteers would answer, "What for? We can hear you."

"We need banners."

"What for? We can see you."

"We need to group ourselves into regiments. The regiments into battalions, the battalions into companies, the companies into platoons, the platoons into squads. That's what we need around here—organization!"

"What for? We know who we are."

The more Francis heard, the more his puzzlement grew. "I don't understand. Your army is a shambles, yet you expect total victory."

"That's absolutely true. You see, these soldiers can do the one thing soldiers must be able to do—use weapons."

"You've seen them duel?"

"Of course not. Quetzalians won't cross swords, not for anything. It's their archery, Lostwax, *that's* where we've got the Brain Eater by the scrotum. Sure, we'll take armor into the desert, lots of it, but this war is going to be won from afar, I guarantee it."

"They can shoot well?"

"Come to target practice." Burne elaborated that every volunteer had made a longbow, and the bull's-eye got hit so often the rest of the target might as well not be there.

"Obviously they don't see it as aggression."

"They see it as a *game*. And they're mounted, too. From a charging lipoca they can shoot the tits off the queen of spades at fifty meters. Hell, they're the finest light cavalry in the solar system!"

"There, you see—everything will be great. I'd only get in the way."

"I suppose I should be furious, but who am *I* to stand between you and the love of your life?"

Nipped by the autumn air, Francis announced his intent to head for the nearest hearth. "But I have one last question. Why are you only a brigadier general? Why not a four-star general?"

"Because there must be a rank I can promote myself to for winning the war."

Francis shook his friend's hand, turned, and ambled toward Nazra's kitchen, a colossal smile on his face. Good old Burne.

THE NEXT TWENTY DAYS were the best Francis had ever known on Luta or any other planet. Once, twice, sometimes three times an afternoon a Tepecan would stop by, say hello, and thank the Nearthling for being more moral than Quetzalia's own Antistasists. In the sacred city an impassioned antiwar movement was fermenting, and Francis had become its avatar. For his afternoon visitors he symbolized the larger potential of humanity, the possibility that pacifism might be as natural as aggression. He glowed with self-respect.

Fantasy became his principal mode of thought. As he shuffled around his favorite places—Olo's gardens, Tepec's clean streets—mental images accompanied him like benevolent ghosts. He saw himself as a professor at the Galileo Institute, his office aswarm with prizes and several generations of corkscrew beetles. He saw Tez by his side, dazzling Nearth doctors with her uncanny knowledge of folk remedies that worked. And he saw a little boy—sometimes it was a girl—asking his father to take him to the circus. They went and had a grand old time.

Of course, all these dreams were predicated on Quetzalia winning the war. Every morning, incertitude knifed into him, and he had to remind himself that Burne Newman could do anything.

For Tez the days crackled with an expectation that was sometimes frightening but usually fun. She was not one for agonizing over decisions, even revocable decisions, and she knew how to squelch moping with busyness. Collecting her

tools from the Hospital of Chimec, selling off the con-
glomerated geegaws of her life, packing her puppets into
footlockers—all such tasks helped convince her that the emigration was going to happen, *had* to happen, and should be
viewed as an enviable adventure, not a loss.

Tez and Francis's hours together confirmed each as the
other's ideal mate. Through mental discipline and an herb
called motherweed, Tez eluded both the pesky nausea and
the sexual disinterest common to early pregnancy. Out of
bed, the lovers strolled through the city and rode their
lipocas far into the country. They collaborated on a puppet
play called *The Gestation Waltz*.

Not far from Olo a Quetzalian National Park was under
construction, and on opening day Tez and Francis rented a
canoe and explored a moody artificial swamp called Witch's
Fen. All around, reptiles imported from Big Ghost Bayou
dived, breached, hissed, and did their level best to amuse
every last visitor.

It was on this day that a formless apprehension grew in
Francis. He sat looking at his beautiful fiancée, her sensuous mouth, the roundness of her seeded uterus—sights
that normally brought only serenity—when some old words
of Burne's set upon him like a sudden fever. "Have the
Quetzalians sacrificed their humanity for the sake of absolute domestic tranquillity?"

Have the Quetzalians sacrificed their . . . ?

Tez's humanity was beyond question. He *knew* this. He
resolved to tear the notion from his mind.

It returned like a spring bird, again and again.

BRIGADIER GENERAL BURNE NEWMAN strutted to his tent
through a frigid twilight, oil lantern in his grip, arm swinging, flame arcing. He brushed back the tent flap and found
himself looking at the last thing he expected to see, a human face. It belonged to, of all people, Lostwax.

"What happened, another lovers' quarrel? Shall I cancel

her flight home?" Burne slid the lantern onto a table crowded with arrows, noctus pots, jerry-built compasses, and Francis's insulin kit.

"I need to talk."

"My schedule is tight."

"Just give me your opinion about something. How do you think Tez is going to fare back on Nearth?"

Burne sat on his cot, tugged his beard. "You mean, what happens when a pacifist is transplanted to a place where violence is an established way of doing business? I wouldn't worry."

But Francis had examples ready. Take your malfunctioning magnecar to a Nearth repair shop and half the time you walk away with a magnecar that has not been fixed but merely diddled with, or a magnecar that has been not only fixed but overfixed, so you get billed for repairs you neither requested nor required. At such times one must resort to total anger, complete with a stabbing finger and a pounding fist. Then, of course, there is overt violence—rare, perhaps, but still part of the deal. When a punk tries to grab your wallet or a rapist corners you in an alley, the situation demands toughness. It's a matter of survival.

Before Francis could offer yet another case, Burne shrugged and said, "As I remember my planet, one can expect to get through life without experiencing a single rape or even an intolerable number of phony repair bills. What's *really* bothering you?"

Francis confessed. The true root of his fear was the question Burne had asked the night they dreamed up the war. "Have the Quetzalians sacrificed their humanity for the sake of absolute domestic tranquillity?" For all her elegance and intellect, for all her ability to bear children and give love, Tez was to Francis not quite whole.

Burne said nothing to lighten his friend's anguish. He stood by his thesis that tranquillity was the inverse of humanness. "If I were you, I'd be wondering whether there's a way to make her a bit less placid. I'd probably want to find out before I bothered taking her all the way back to Nearth."

The conversation drifted to more innocuous matters. Nearth politics. The stunning incompetence of the Galileo Institute's administrators. Was Albert Thorne really on the verge of time travel?

Burne rose from the cot, moved toward the tent flap. "Like I said, my schedule is tight. Tonight we're making swords. In four days we ride across the drawbridge."

"I'll wave good-bye."

"Come at noon—Tolcaday. At the last minute I'll talk you into joining us."

"Let's not start on *that.*"

And then Burne said something neither of them expected. "If I get killed you'll *care*, won't you?"

Francis choked down his surprise. "God of the brain, of course I'll care. You're my friend." Was Burne stifling tears?

"I'm a tough old turd, Lostwax. But don't think for a minute that I *like* violence. I'm for mercy every time, and decency." His words, in their rareness, seemed ready to crack. "The human conscience—it's not just in Quetzalia, right?"

"I understand you perfectly." Rummaging uncomfortably among the table's oddities, Francis picked up his insulin kit. Burne had never moved him before, never shown his underbelly. Francis was befuddled.

As Burne started out of the tent, a sudden impulse made Francis thrust the insulin kit under his friend's nose. "I have a foolish fear. While you're out on the desert, I might have a relapse. Could one syringe stay in Quetzalia?"

"I'd like to have a spare."

"I'm nervous, Burne, and besides"—Francis forced a cough—"you'd prefer to bring nothing but *Nearthlings* back to Nearth, right?"

A knowing smile parted Burne's beard. "Leave me the crysanium box."

After Burne was gone, Francis removed one syringe and wrapped it in a green towel. Tucking the towel under his sash, he made a conscious decision to leave the insulin flask in its box. It was perfectly obvious, after all, both to Burne and to himself, that fear of recrudescent diabetes was not his reason for taking the syringe, so why pretend.

A squall of activity greeted Francis as he emerged from the tent. Steel cauldrons the size of kettledrums dotted the camp, their contents made bright and molten by fire-moss. Nothing seemed real. The world was ending. The sun had exploded and these glowing buckets served to catch the pieces.

Francis went to the palace's rear portico, untethered his lipoca, mounted.

Sparks made quick bright stitches in the air as metals were blasted from their ores, then fused into alloys of crysanium hardness and nyoplene flexibility. Before viscosity was lost the alloys were poured out, pounded, folded, pounded, folded, until the result had the form and strength of a sword.

Despite the fire and clamor, Francis soon spotted Burne. He sat in the middle of the camp, straddling a lipoca and looking like an equestrian statue. Attached to the lipoca was an iron vat, suspended on wheels and filled with something silver-black. The general addressed his troops.

"Soldiers! In thirteen days you will be fighting a lethal enemy. Are you ready to risk your lives for Quetzalia's freedom?"

"Yes!" said at least half the army in unison. Apparently Burne had finally managed to instill a mild jingoism.

"In thirteen days you will have conquered this planet and made it safe for your descendants. Are you ready to open frontiers and build cities?"

"Yes!" said the army, few holding back.

"Listen! This past opoch you have doubted the need for unanimous action. But today we are one, for all of us have fashioned swords, and now it is time to temper them."

Burne dismounted and from a sweaty woman took a trans-pervium cylinder where rested a blue-hot billet, shaped and pointed and folded twenty times. He raised its glow for all to see and walked to the vat. "Let the river made of hate now pour its secret powers into these crystals, so that we may slay our enemies on the desert as surely as we do in the Temple of Tolca!" In one decisive move he inverted the billet and submerged it point-first. Sizzling steam rushed up as the molecules were locked into place. He withdrew the billet, now tempered and whole.

Burne remounted. Slowly he weaved his lipoca through the camp, and as the vat got within reach each soldier came forward.

Francis did not wait for his friend to notice him, but left the camp at a gallop before even ten swords were quenched. Riding back to Olo, he realized that he had not seen so much noctus since the day Burne drew their experimental samples from the moat. It really wasn't such horrible stuff. He remembered once telling Luther about its holiness.

17

No CHEERING THRONGS, no flapping pennants, no show of any kind honored the First Army as it trooped through Quetzalia. A thousand lipocas carried as many soldiers plus packs gorged with everything from refried beans to sleeping bags, granite pegmatites to noctus ampules. The soldiers reached the wall and milled around, waiting for the bridge to drop. Sins sloshed as lipocas pawed the ground.

Hostile stares rained down from above. So profound was the ambivalence Quetzalians felt toward this expedition, and so meager the admiration, that the smiling sympathizers on the wall, a scant three dozen of the volunteers' friends and relatives, were outnumbered by the war protesters mixed among them.

Neckbands emblazoned with wolf heads marked the protesters. Centuries ago, Earthling ethologists had discovered that when a thrashed wolf admits defeat by exposing its neck, the conqueror wolf never, almost never, chomps. Wolves were one of Zolmec's few concessions to symbolism.

Francis, who wore neither a neckband nor a sympathetic smile, stood gawkily among the civilians, fingering his chitzal scar and shifting his weight from one foot to the other. "You shouldn't have bothered coming," he said to Tez. "The army can't see your silly wolves."

"I don't care, as long as they see my silly fiancé. I want them to know you aren't going."

"They already know. You think my presence will inspire last-minute desertions?"

"Only last-minute doubts. That's enough for me."

Detaching himself from the press of soldiers and animals, Burne galloped to the base of the wall, a caisson trailing behind his lipoca. His chest displayed a crude approximation of a Nearth Police Academy jacket, complete with blue sash and orange epaulets. "Good morning, Lostwax!" he called toward the elevated road.

Francis waved anemically.

"I'm John Philip Sousa," Burne persisted, "the great Earthling troubadour who wrote the soundtrack for World War I."

When Francis neglected to laugh, neglected, indeed, to do anything at all, Burne decided to try for a conversation with Tez. "What's that on your neck, lass?" She grimaced and stomped away. He tried shouting. "If we're going to be shipmates, we'd better act civil with each other." Tez folded her arms and stared toward Iztac.

Returning to Francis, Burne said, "Why so glum, Nearthling? *You're* not going into battle."

"It's my nature to be glum."

"Good for you, Lostwax. Sneer, frown, and be miserable, for tomorrow you live."

Finally Francis said, "Bring me a souvenir."

Burne gripped his sword, unsheathing it far enough to mirror the sun. "I'll bring you a nice shiny spaceship."

"Good luck. And don't get eaten or anything."

Burne released the sword, let it slide home. Wheeling his mount around, he rode into the gateway, where a morose female civilian glanced questioningly toward the windlass. Receiving Burne's nod, she began unreeling the cords.

This was the second time Burne and Francis had seen the portcullis climb skyward while the massive bridge creaked down to the far bank. The memory brought shudders. A kilometer from here, the moat scrubbed Luther's bones.

Burne rode onto the planks as soon as they came to rest. "Death to all Brain Eaters!" he shouted, hoping the soldiers would chorus back his cry. Instead they started somberly into enemy territory. The wall erupted with the sympathizers' waving hands. The protesters began to boo.

BY THE TIME FRANCIS spoke again, the last of the civilians had started home and the First Army had snaked far into the desert. "We're finished here."

"Nothing good will come of this," said Tez. "If the battle's lost, the neurovores will slaughter them all. If it's won, Zolmec acquires a permanent taint, and I become a Nearthling."

Suddenly Francis saw his chance to broach an impossible subject. "I understand your reluctance to leave. In fact, you may have more reasons for fearing Nearth than you know. You might not fit in."

"Fit in?"

He gulped audibly. It had to be done, *had* to. "I mean, don't you think that our plans for the future may be a shade too dreamy? You won't necessarily find happiness. Nearthlings are different from Quetzalians."

She massaged her baby, smiled. "You mean I might give birth to a grasshopper?"

"Suppose a Nearthling buys a bachbox and it doesn't work when she gets home. She takes it back and they won't refund her money because they say *she* broke it. At that point the customer screams and makes threats. But what could *you* do?"

"I could pay for the repair."

"A wasteful response."

"Can't bachboxes be repaired?"

"It could be *anything*. An electrostylus."

"Oh, birdturds, Francis. You needn't be Attila the Hun for somebody to exchange a crummy *pencil!*"

Francis blurted, "What if somebody tried to *rape* you?

You'd be helpless. Burne proved that long ago with one of your runners."

"Burne is neurovorean."

"What would you *do*?"

She gave the question a due measure of thoughtfulness. "I guess I would . . . try to survive it as best I could, the way I'd try to survive a flash flood or a fall down a mountain."

"People *die* from being raped."

"People die from flash floods."

"Tez, I have an idea. There's a way you could become aggressive enough to handle *all* the hazards of Nearth life."

She hooked a finger around her neckband, took the pressure off her jugular vein. "I hope not."

"You know what I'm talking about. Three cc's make a person capable of fighting back. You saw Zamanta and Momictla. It didn't hurt them a bit, not a bit."

"You want to pollute me with noctus?"

"Plus a booster shot after six days, another after twelve, then twenty-four—eventually no more whatsoever. It's all in Janet Vij's notes."

"Francis, I'm *pregnant*!"

"It won't pass the placental barrier. I've seen the formula."

"You're insane!" She banged her heel against the stone road, walked toward the nearest stairs. "I'll have none of this!"

He pursued her, pulling the green towel from his robe. "Don't make a snap judgment." As he unwrapped the syringe, a glint of Iztac exploded on its cold, immortal needle.

"God of the brain! Isn't it enough that I'm giving up my planet? Must I now give up my *personality*?"

"Your personality? The injections will only *add* to it. They'll make you more . . ."

"What?"

"Human."

Tez's eyes shrank to small molten beads, and the corners of her mouth plunged downward, as if grabbed by fish-

hooks. "I'll try to pretend you didn't say that, Francis Bastard Lostwax. You think aggression makes us human?" She
threw back her head to show her wolf. "*Wolves* are aggressive, and so are birds, and your damn roach. People are
unique only because they use the ability in consistently
pointless ways. Nearthlings flatter themselves when they
call their cruelties inhuman. They should call their re-
straints *animal.*"

"I'm only trying to help you survive a harsh world. Think
about it a few days, and—"

She moved a trembling finger toward the syringe. "Put
your penis away, Francis. I've already thought about it."
Suddenly she laughed. "Listen, this whole conversation is
ludicrous. On Nearth I can't practice the rites. That *alone*
will make me live up to your standards, whatever the hell
they are. I can't promise to beat our child or torture
the neighbors, but I imagine I shall become much more
like you."

"You're guessing. The moat is direct."

"Why do you think Zolmec requires us never to miss a
single service? Give me a year away from the Temple of
Tolca, and I'll be as . . . as goddam *human* as you want."

NOT UNTIL FRANCIS had met and tested the eyeless woman
at the going-away party did he start doubting that simple
abstinence from Zolmec would prompt Tez to repent her
pacifism.

Blind Umia looked fifty at least, thin as an electrostylus,
and for the first half of the evening she was the star attrac-
tion. Sitting on the floor in the middle of Olo's largest drawing room, she spun, for anyone who would listen, wondrous
tales of fantasy laced with dark humor. Yarns designed to
unravel your mind, she called them. There was one about a
villainous but seemingly whole man who turned out to be a
cripple at the end, another about a Dead Little Pig who
built his house of ectoplasm.

The party was Huaca's idea. Now that he and Tez verged

on a fifty-million-kilometer separation, he figured he should do something nice for her. His niceness, however, did not extend to donating his house for the party; instead he had everybody pop in and surprise her at Olo.

Overcoming her girlhood tendency to associate parties with terminal illness, Tez grew gayer with each arrival. Huaca's gesture made her know that despite his chronic aloofness, his constantly becoming wrapped up in himself like a turtle, he was still a lovable brother. Francis had never seen her laugh so many times in a single hour.

Midnight came, went, and the jam of guests around Umia began breaking apart and drifting to other rooms. For the next thirty minutes Francis had to clear up banal mysteries for Tez's friends. Do Nearthlings eat three meals a day? Keep pets? He expected to be asked whether he could sweat.

Of all the Quetzalians at the party, only Umia interested Francis. Eventually he worked his way to her knees. A meager audience heard her coyest yarn yet, about a scientist who one day discovered that the biblical story of God making the first woman from Adam's rib was literally true; through alchemy this genius converted his wife back to rib form, but then a dog buried her in the backyard.

God of the brain, Francis thought, an imagination like *that* in the room, and they would rather find out how many times I fold my toilet paper.

The story had a cryptic ending that Francis suspected of symbolism. No one stayed for the sequel. At last she was his alone.

Blindness, Francis learned, had not always been Umia's fate. Six years ago she was seeking a new anesthetic when a failed attempt exploded in her face, scorching her eyes beyond the reach of Quetzalian herbs. Francis made sympathetic noises, then said what was on his mind.

"I'm curious. Can a blind person practice the rites of Zolmec?"

"Not fruitfully," was the reply. "Without pictures the

cybernetic loop is impossible to maintain. In six years I haven't added a drop to the river made of hate."

"Aren't you afraid you might become a killer?"

"Hardly." Amusement curled the corners of her mouth.

Eight centimeters from Umia's head, a punch bowl loomed. He watched it. "But don't all those unrelieved urges make you more ready to do harm?"

"Zolmec doesn't merely help us to be gentle," said Umia. "It teaches that gentleness is *right.*"

The bowl—it just sat there. "Still, you must be more capable of violence than anyone in this room." Then he added, grinning, "Except myself."

She shrugged. "Perhaps."

The bowl—he must use it. "Want a glass of punch?" Umia declined. "Excuse me. I'm going to kill my thirst."

Francis rose and went to the bowl, spying in all directions. The guests seemed too busy with intoxicated chatter to notice what he was about, or, if they noticed, to care.

Satisfied, ready, frightened, resolved, he upended the bowl, flooding punch on the unsuspecting storyteller. The frigid stickiness made her shriek.

All senses at peak, Francis rushed to study his victim. He was hoping to be called a piece of shit or, better still, have his sleeve ripped in anger. "Sorry," he said as insincerely as possible, determined to do nothing that might salve her frustration.

"What happened?" asked a dripping, confused, but not-quite-bothered Umia.

"Chactol Eyes, I'm afraid you're a little punchy tonight." He was especially pleased at remembering about chactols, those sightless Lutan fish, and spontaneously inventing a corresponding epithet.

Yet—*damn her*—she laughed.

Before Francis could try further taunts, Huaca ran over. "Don't worry, Umia. Our Nearthling upset his own punch bowl."

"How amusing," she chirped.

Huaca faced Francis and said, "You can't hold your liquor?"

Umia licked punch from her lips. "I'm holding it for him!" She spoke loudly, so the bystanders could hear, and when she added a trilling giggle it didn't take long before everybody—everybody except the betrayed extraterrestrial—did the same. The room stank with laughter.

A drunken Tez arrived, squeezed the blind woman's hand. "Let's find you a dry robe."

"Do I look thoroughly ridiculous?" asked Umia.

"Thoroughly."

"Fabulous!" And the guests laughed again.

THE PUNCH-BOWL HILARITY marked the end of the party. Each guest in turn improvised his own exit line, from the predictable "It's getting late" to Umia's "I have to feed my dead cat." No one failed to hug the hosts or wish them well on their apparent marriage and impending child. The coming blasphemous voyage to Nearth, certain to be one of the major events of Tez's life, was alluded to with "Have a safe journey," but no one came out and mentioned the technology called space travel. Most Quetzalians still regarded rocket ships the way a Christian might regard a croquet set made of the True Cross.

Umia, cane in hand, was last to leave. The robe Tez had given her, all torn and coarse, inspired Umia to dub herself Cazloc, the god of mediocrity.

"I'm sorry I wrecked your clothes," said Francis, and by now he meant it.

Tez said, "Don't bother bringing the robe back. Where I'm going they aren't in fashion." Good-nights were exchanged, and Umia tapped her way into the gardens.

"How can she get home?" asked Francis.

Staggering from the doorway, Tez gave him a dopey smile. "She keeps a seeing-eye chitzal in her pocket." Francis snorted and marched back to the drawing room.

After drifting through the house for several minutes like an unmoored boat, Tez found the bedroom and collapsed. She snuggled into the sheets, shouted, "We could make love now, if you want!"

"I don't," he replied, appearing in the doorway.

"What's the matter?"

"Tez, you saw what happened tonight. I spilled a whole goddam punch bowl on her and she *enjoyed* it."

Tez's expression said, So what?

"Umia hasn't attended church in six years. Yet I couldn't make her mad. If abstinence didn't change her, there's no reason to suppose it will change *you*."

"God of the brain, Francis, don't start on that."

"Were you familiar with Umia's case all along?"

"It doesn't settle anything."

"Dammit, Tez, you lied to me. You *knew* Zolmec can be reversed only with a needle."

"I don't lie, Francis, to you or anybody else."

"But you'll admit it's disturbing?"

"Let me warn you about something, Nearthling. If I ever again hear you imply that Quetzalians are less than human, I'm going to take my pregnant body to some place where you'll never find it. Do you understand? It's the end of your fatherhood."

"Yes," said Francis, sneering.

"I'm going to sleep."

"Go to sleep." He faced the hall, saw the bedroom lamps die. Soon Tez snored. Returning to the parlor, he kicked a dormant fireplace. Outside, an animal wailed. He stared at the pile of logs, trying to ignite them with his eyes. Sad, angry thoughts churned in his brain.

Why is she so stubborn?

I must make sure she is a Nearthling *before* I take her home.

I love her too much to hesitate.

The laboratory née library had been under improvised

lock and jerry-built key ever since Francis and Burne performed the last of their noctus experiments. The key hung on a nail beside the door. He struck a match, touched it to the nearest lampwick. The globe glowed to life. Lifting the lantern, he let himself into the room.

Dust heaps lay everywhere like fresh snow. Francis held his breath to keep from coughing. The searching flame swept past mounds of notes and a ghost town of empty cages, settling at last on a far nook. Reaching into the wall, he drew out a ceramic pot, the unused deciliters of the same solution they had put into Zamanta.

Francis left the lab, locking the door and pocketing the key. He heard it clank against the noctus pot. Next he went to the kitchen, where, glistening in starlight, cushioned by its towel, the syringe lay on a windowsill. The stove was gorged with wood, and he had no trouble starting a fire and setting some water to boil. Feeble as Lutan germs were reputed to be, a sterilized needle still seemed proper.

Gloom commanded the bedroom. Francis entered softly, stomach aflutter. Easing the pot onto the nightstand, he began prying the stopper, which was jammed in hard and further glued by caked nightmares. After two minutes' effort, the noctus was free. The syringe drank deep.

Unlatching the window, Francis shot violence into the night until the barrel held the correct dosage for an adult human, not a drop more. On silent feet he approached Tez, peeled a crisp sheet from her thigh. She stirred but stayed asleep.

One day she'll thank me for this, Francis thought as he slid the hair-thin crysanium needle into her flesh. Slowly he retreated the plunger. No blood, good. The needle had missed her veins. He gulped for air, moved his thumb, and injected his lover with three cubic centimeters of hate.

18

IT WAS NIGHT, he was exhausted, and still Minnix Cies had excellent reasons not to be asleep. For example, the journey across the desert had been so amazingly free of hazard that the probability of ambush now seemed doubled. Also, squirting through his veins was an animate, biophotonic stimulant called noctus.

Also, tomorrow he might be murdered.

Lying beneath the warm consolation of a thick, twice-folded lipocaskin, eyes wide open, Minnix stared toward the stones that paralleled his face and smelled their brisk mossy wetness. The shelf he had bedded himself under shot deep into a cliff, far beyond the reach of his lantern. Bored, he turned on his side and faced the desert, watching the place where the stars became campfires. First the fires had heated dinners, now soldiers, but how many of those soldiers were asleep? Only a few, he guessed, a very few.

Even in this modest light the desert was stunning. Like the other volunteers, though, Minnix had crossed it in fear, his senses blunted by expectancy. Whenever he had scanned the horizon, it was not to notice the shifting colors of the dunes or the wind-sculpted wonder of the cliffs, but to learn if any Brain Eaters were about. Whenever he had cocked an ear toward the night, it was not to hear the breezy songs of rocks or the soothing hiss of desert lizards, but to intercept the bipedal crunchings of neurovores crossing sand.

Day followed day, and their luck held. A case of exhaustion here, a delaying caisson repair there, but so far not a single authentic setback. Was Catastrophe waiting for the battle itself? Minnix shuddered. The burden of proof is on Newman, he thought, but no small measure of responsibility lies with my party, at whose urging dozens joined up. If we fail, there's egg on our faces and blood on our hands.

Suppose the moat betrayed them? In the case of two people named Zamanta and Momictla, of course, Janet Vij's forecasts had held. For six days these citizens had remained in the grip of instinct, then on schedule became lambs. But what about people who weren't named Zamanta and Momictla? What about people named Minnix Cies? In another person's brain, might noctus fade sooner? What if it lasted *three* days? Or three hours? What if he were about to skewer a prone neurovore when suddenly . . . he can't! Paralysis. The monster's claws puncture its attacker's throat. . . .

Grotesque fantasies came easily to Minnix Cies. He was Quetzalian.

The injections had been meted out with typical Burne Newman efficiency. He arranged his thousand in a grid of forty ranks and twenty-five files. "Ampules!"

Packs were swung to the ground, and, after an interval of unmilitary fumbling, each Quetzalian held a ceramic sphere containing one noctus dose.

"Soldiers!" Burne continued, brandishing the syringe and his own ampule. "Tomorrow we attack the Brain Eaters. All signs foretell a total victory. You have only to aim your arrows and shoot. But first you must drink the moat!"

The soldier at square one was Minnix Cies.

"Do as I do," said Burne, approaching, filling the syringe. On his own arm he demonstrated how to insert the needle and prove that it was not in a vein, but he did not advance the plunger. Burne Newman had so far in his life killed dozens of wild animals, a young crysanium mine striker, and a rampaging neurovore. Ersatz instinct was something Burne Newman did not need.

"Watch what he does," Burne commanded, rudely tapping the soldier at square two and ascertaining that he was ready to study his neighbor's ordeal and learn from any blunders that might happen. Before handing the syringe to Minnix, Burne emptied its contents on the ground and sanitized its needle with a thermalstone.

Minnix made no blunders. With a confidence he couldn't account for, he drained his army-issue ampule and pushed the refilled syringe into his deltoid muscle. He injected himself slowly, blotting the needle's sting by thinking about his little brothers, the twins, back home.

"Pass it on," said Burne, and Minnix handed syringe and thermalstone to the soldier at square two. "Dismissed."

Minnix walked to his lipoca, gave it some sugar, and waited to change. His arm, aching softly, bore a green welt. Soon he would feel evil—whatever that meant. Would he want to strangle his brothers? Thumb out the eyes of desert rats?

No such urges appeared. Like Quetzalian herb tea, noctus was arousing, exhilarating even. It made him feel good, nothing more.

The soldiers kept passing the needle. By midnight, the entire army was possessed of its secret weapon.

There was no doubting that the stuff worked. All during dinner, scuffles erupted over portions. As darkness appeared, the excuses for roughhouse ranged from "You stole my campsite!" to "That's *my* blanket!" Two women realized they had an old score to settle. It concerned a lover. They walked to the edge of the camp and beat each other up.

But now, sprawled sleepless under the cliff, Minnix worried that his aggressiveness was waning. The thought passed as a soldier approached. From where he lay, Minnix could see only the feet, one of which swung back and rammed itself obnoxiously into his knee. He groaned.

"Sorry," said a cheery female voice. "I had to know that I could still do it."

"Yes . . . I understand." And if *you* can do it, he thought, *I* can do it. Soon the wrenching pain in Minnix's knee was helping him to fall asleep.

LIKE AN INFLAMED EYE, Iztac rode the cold morning sky. Before Burne's army the desert sprawled uninvitingly. Burne studied the distant oasis for two minutes, made nothing of it, and summoned Ras, a balding astronomer whose visual acuity was legend. Ras studied the distant oasis for fifteen seconds.

"They haven't spotted us," he said, nervously rubbing his lipoca's neck. "Business as usual."

"How many?"

This time Ras took thirty seconds. "Five—no, six are stalking wild chitzals at the periphery, ten are in the nearest trees."

Attack now, Burne thought. The tribes will become enraged and rush into our arrows, or else panic and retreat: I don't especially care which.

The First Army of Aca was deployed in a huge circle around the oasis, rendering the enemy, as Burne put it, "outflanked, outfronted, and outassed." At a prearranged signal from their general, a loud "Advance!" passed from officer to officer, the soldiers trotted forward, and the circle collapsed, dooming its center.

"Stop us at fifty meters!" Burne shouted to Ras, fifty meters being the effective range of a Quetzalian longbow.

"All right," he called back, and in fascination watched the approaching oasis. The facelike flowers and silvery waterfalls astounded him to the point of hypnosis. At the last moment he remembered his orders. "Now!"

"Halt!" Burne cried.

"Halt!" answered his officers, and the army halted.

Ras's fabulous eyes were no longer needed, for at this distance everyone could see that the oasis throbbed with action. The chitzal hunters had retreated toward the center, screeching warnings as they went. At first the camp reacted with the confusion of a termite colony whose nest is knocked open by a gorilla's probing twig. Then, slowly, the scurrying became a concert. Enmities between tribes were hastily dissolved, alliances hastily forged. Dozens of neurovores poured forward from deep within the oasis, where scant seconds before they had been calmly bathing their children and quietly searching out rivals to eat. Dozens more abandoned their naps and leaped from the trees. Within minutes of the first warning-cry, every able-bodied Brain Eater, spear and ax in hand, was busily dispensing itself around the edge of the oasis.

"They've seen us!" Ras sounded more thrilled than afraid.

Burne studied the amassing enemy. "Arrows!"

"Arrows!" came the echo. A thousand arrows slid from their quivers.

"Load!" cried Burne.

"Load!" came the echo. A thousand bowstrings snuggled into nocks.

"Pull!" cried Burne.

"Pull!" came the echo.

"Mark your targets!"

"Marked!" A thousand arrowheads were aligned with stomachs, hearts, brains.

"Fire!"

"Fire!" But for the moment not one arrow was fired.

Burne waited for the neurovores to die, and after twenty seconds his patience decayed into fury. "Fire, I said! Open your fingers! Kill your enemies!" The bowstrings remained taut. "Cowards! Slime molds!" Nothing. He presented his helpless face to Ras. "What's happening, astronomer?"

Ras relaxed, restoring his bow to erect impotence. "I'm sorry, general, but the neurovores have done nothing to merit my killing them."

"The neurovores have devoured your countrymen and

robbed your world of its rightful peace of mind!"

"Peace of mind is relative."

"You eggheads, this is a battle, not a seminar!"

"The enemy deserves another chance."

"If these monsters decide to rush us, it won't take two minutes before we're in range of their spears. Two minutes after that we're in range of their axes."

"Then we'll wait. We're a *defensive* army."

"You're a *dead* army! Come here!" Animated by a sudden scheme, Burne took the reins of Ras's lipoca and burst away at full gallop. The slack vanished with a jerk that caused the astronomer to drop his longbow. Stubby as it was, the lipoca's neck became something to grip for dear life.

Ras in tow, Burne rode straight for the nearest path, a broad stream of earth lined with tufted organic parasols and fat blue fruit. At the path's end, Burne knew, sanctuary awaited—momentary sanctuary, to be sure, but a moment was all he needed. Only three neurovores guarded the start of the path, only four more thought to reinforce them. The defenders released their spears simultaneously. Burne veered, whiplashing the astronomer, and the sharp stone points flew harmlessly into a dune. The neurovores readied their axes.

"Jump!" Burne screamed, returning Ras's reins to him.

If other choices existed, the astronomer did not notice them. Reaching the path, he nudged his frightened lipoca in the manner that meant "Jump!" Ahead of him, Burne was already off the ground, sailing smoothly over the neurovores, whose axes whizzed forward but cut only air. Ras followed, stealing a glance at the hairiness below. He had never before seen a neurovore close up, never been face-to-face with devolution's crowning calamity. It was fascinating. Hooves hit sand, and he was off.

Blue blurs jumped by as twenty, eighty, a thousand meters grew between the soldiers and their pursuers. Suddenly Burne screamed, "Dismount!" The blurs stopped, and Ras beheld a bright placid pool whose surrounding trees were weirdly silent, save for an occasional bird-squawk.

Ras dismounted. "Why are we here?"

Burne unsheathed his sword. "I need a place where my army can't see us."

"You're going to kill me?"

"No . . . your lipoca."

"He's my pet."

"We need blood. I want you to play possum."

"That's deceitful."

"That's an order."

"An *evil* order."

"Here's a virtuous one." Burne removed his jacket, epaulets fluttering. "Tie this around its head."

The astronomer took the jacket, held it listlessly. "Can't you kill *your* lipoca, sir?"

"Look, soldier, I'm at the end of my wistar rod. I want this victory. So either I slit this animal's throat or . . . *yours!*"

Persuaded, Ras glided the jacket across the lipoca's face, tying the sleeves like bonnet strings.

"Stand back!" said Burne, readying his sword, and the astronomer kissed his friend good-bye.

Ten minutes after Burne and his captive disappeared into the oasis, a rider burst forth, outrunning the spears that followed. The nearest soldiers, leaning forward on their mounts, soon recognized their general—and more. Sprawled across the lipoca's shoulders, the naked body of a Quetzalian astronomer dripped blood-puddles onto the sand.

Burne charged for Minnix Cies, reined up. The nude victim showed more blood than skin. More blood than skin! For Minnix the thought became an inner call for vengeance. He started to itch. The noctus was in command now, spitting its demands into every cell of his body. His arousal peaked and spontaneously he drew back his bow.

Burne galloped around the circle, one hand waving his sword, the other steadying Ras, who continued to act a corpse. "The enemy has struck!" Burne bellowed repeatedly, watching in satisfaction as arrows were again nocked. Completing his journey, he lowered the astronomer to the ground, gently, though not so gently as to reveal the ruse, and screamed "Fire!"

"Fire!" echoed the officers. A swarm of arrows took off. For five seconds the neurovores watched in dull-headed contemplation, wondering why these intruders would use such small spears and why they would release them from such a hopeless distance. The seconds ended, the arrows arrived, and the neurovores wondered no more. Even as dozens fell—pierced, bleeding, shrieking—a second volley was in the air. Ignoring the throes of the dying, the chiefs dashed onto the sand. Each took command through yelps that in the protolanguage of neurovores said, "Get them in range of your spears!"

The neurovores charged in an ever-widening wave. More arrows arrived; the wave left bodies behind. By the time their tormentors were in range, the tribes had lost half their numbers.

"Shields!" shouted Burne as the tribes halted and, at the growls of the chiefs, drew back their spears. From his lipoca's shoulder every other soldier snatched a huge oval shell that had once guarded the back of a Lutan tortoise. Like hailstones the onrushing points slammed into the raised carapaces, and the shafts rattled to the ground.

But something was wrong. Instead of shouting triumphantly, the First Army found itself gasping in bewilderment as gravity went every which way. Surprised by the spear attack, the lipocas, normally phlegmatic creatures, were running in berserk circles.

What *else* can go to hell? The question almost managed to amuse Burne as he dismounted, pulling the insulin kit from his shirt and an ampule from his saddlebag. Very well, he thought as he filled the syringe, if that's how Mother Nature wants to play the game, then we'll turn these goddam *lipocas* into soldiers.

Taking advantage of the animals' madness, the neurovores scuttled forward, retrieved their spears, threw them toward the turned backs. Dozens of Quetzalians, run through and screaming horribly, fell. Burne responded by ramming the syringe into the flank of the first lipoca that happened along.

"What in Tolca's name are you *doing?*" the rider called down.

"Giving you a mount worthy of yourself!" But before Burne could push the plunger, the already crazed creature bolted away, taking the syringe with it.

Even now Burne refused to accept the possibility that his army was on the brink of retreat. He ran around the battlefield, exhorting everyone to "Dismount and fight!"

Minnix dismounted but he did not fight. Reluctantly he drew his sword. Neurovores, Quetzalians, and riderless lipocas whirled around his body, anesthetizing his mind. In vain he tried to think. Have I killed today? For answer he had only muddled memories—aiming his arrows at neurovore organs, releasing his bowstring, closing his eyes before he could see what happened.

Staggering forward, Minnix beheld dozens of his fellows prone on the sand, spears in their backs. Many were still flailing, like a gigantic insect collection come horribly to life. The sight rekindled his sense of purpose. "Revenge!" Minnix cried, rushing into the thick of it, his sword oscillating fiercely. Soon he found a life to end. The neurovore's weapon, a clumsy slice of stone roped to wood, was no equal of First Army alloys. Neither was the neurovore's skull. Decerebrated, the thing fell forward.

"Eat your *own* brain, you—" Minnix cawed, stopping short on recognizing the Quetzalian who fought beside him.

It was Ras, glistening head to toe with blood. Minnix gasped. "Back from the dead!"

"I never went!" Ras shouted, burying his sword in a liver.

The battle raged on like a slowly dying animal. The sand was cemented by blood, excrement, urine, and vomit. Cries vibrated the reeking air. It was a day disconnected from all decency and humor.

Minnix reveled in his potency. Never before had he been the equal of a Brain Eater, much less its master. Seize the opportunity, he thought. Give yourself a war story to tell, something that will spellbind your little brothers.

He slashed his sword and an arm came off, sailing by on a comet tail of blood. In its agonized unwholeness, the resulting neurovore was sickening to behold. Minnix, having one of his few rational thoughts of the day, decided that the mind's need for bilateral symmetry ran deep. He wanted to throw up.

A second slash ended the monster's misery. So, he thought, *this* is how my Earthling ancestors ran their affairs. This is how lands were won, empires expanded, insurrections resisted, prisoners taken, slaves kept, heretics converted, captives made loquacious. For the first time in his life, Minnix felt himself a part of history.

History, he decided, was a terrible idea.

BY EARLY AFTERNOON 957 Quetzalians and one neurovore stood. The one neurovore stood because his own spear had been rammed through his stomach and into the ground below. The day belonged to Burne.

Cautiously the First Army entered the oasis and, following orders, marched to the largest pool. Burne, posing on a high rock, awaited them, as did his mirror image, reflected in the liquid below. With exultant sweeps of their sword arms, the twin generals spoke in lofty tones.

"Soldiers! Today you have won a great victory. Quetzalia

is free!" Abruptly the gestures stopped, the tones descended. "But let me remind you that the vilest work is still to come. Scattered throughout this oasis are the final remnants of the neurovore race, the ones who could not join the battle. I speak of the sick, the old—and, yes, the infants that the sick and old are watching over."

"Must we kill infants, sir?" asked a pale lieutenant.

"In a few days you'll be practicing Zolmec again, and your weapons will be of no use to you. Meanwhile, the children grow to malignance. It's that simple."

"We could inject ourselves when the time comes," the lieutenant persisted.

"You won't be any more anxious to kill them in fifteen years than you are now. Draw your swords!"

THE MASSACRE LASTED through a blood-red sunset. So unspeakable was this final violence that when it ended the soldiers ran pell-mell from the oasis, making their camp in the desert. Again the pools belonged to the neurovores, to their slain corpses and angry ghosts.

The desert bloomed with flames. Campfires cooked dinners, bonfires consumed dead Quetzalians. Wakeful, Burne wandered among the pyres. Their heat warmed but did not cheer him. Winter's air was more easily defeated than the ice he felt inside.

Come on, Newman, he told himself, feel victorious. That's an order. God's sacred tax return! The neurovores didn't produce *children*! They produced hairy little *things*!

A brusque voice broke out of the darkness, ending Burne's torment. "Who's *that*?"

"General Newman."

Teakettle in hand, a private stepped into the light of a pyre. His puppy face and hesitant manner suggested that the brusqueness was forced. "I thought you were a neurovore."

"There are no more neurovores. What's your name?"

"Petla, sir." He rested his kettle on the ground.

"Walk with me, Private Petla."

The pyres made a well-lighted avenue. Burne attempted conversation. "Did you know any of these people?" he asked with an inarticulate wave of the hand. Petla nodded. "You probably feel like crying."

"That will come. In front of us, Ras is burning, my old tutor. Behind us is Mochi Shappa, a cousin."

"Ras the astronomer?

"Yes. The one who was killed right away."

"No, he wasn't really dead, not then. I guess he lived a few hours longer."

Petla said, "I wonder if those hours mattered to him?"

They continued in silence, making only left turns. In a few minutes they were back at Petla's kettle. He put it in the pyre, pulled from his jacket a ceramic mug decorated with a subtle visual pun, a glazed eye. "Want some tea?"

Burne did not answer but said, "I saw lipocas burning. Did we lose many?"

"I've counted eight. Seven fell to neurovores and the other you know about."

"I do?"

"Yes—it belonged to my best friend. He says you tried to dose it with noctus." Petla explained that, as the battle was winding down, he came upon a supine, exhausted lipoca that had a syringe protruding from its flank. Recognizing the animal as his friend's, he started to approach, when suddenly it rolled over, simultaneously injecting itself and crushing the syringe. A few seconds later the lipoca went mad, and Petla had to slaughter it.

"I suppose they're an unusually sensitive species," said Petla, "unable to handle noctus in any amount."

"Was it absolutely necessary to kill the animal?"

By way of answering, Petla stretched a bare arm toward the firelight. Plunging four millimeters into his flesh was a serrated valley. "Can you believe that, general? My best friend's pet tried to eat me!"

WHEN IZTAC'S FIRST RAYS groped across the battlefield and struck the heaped, unburied corpses of three hundred neurovores, it became horribly evident to Burne's soldiers that they had done murder. Of course, one could claim that the enemy deserved it, that neurovores were murderers of a far less redeemable sort than a Quetzalian would ever be. But without the corpses of slain compatriots on view, this point was easy to forget. Some soldiers grew nauseated, some catatonic. All wanted to leave the desert without delay.

The general had no objections. Within two hours the well soldiers were mounted, the wounded lashed to caissons. Nothing was done about the neurovore corpses. To bury them would be to admit that they existed.

Burne arranged his army in three concentric circles. Riding to the center, he sadly noted a block of riderless lipocas. "Soldiers!" he began. "Today I leave you." He reached a hand toward the sun, stretching the index finger until it curled upward. "That way lies my ship. I can ride there in one day, fuel it in two." Here he smiled. "I'm going to beat you home." His hand made a one-hundred-and-eighty-degree sweep. "That way lies Quetzalia. Return to it as civilians. There is no more business between us. Here and now I renounce my command."

From the outermost circle a reedy voice arose. "Wait, Dr. Newman. There *is* further business between us!" The tone, resentful, stirred in Burne a seething memory, as if a dread disease once thought cured were suddenly back.

All eyes on her, the speaker trotted through the middle circle, then the inner circle, soon reining up before Burne. The former general forced his smile to return. The pretty woman he had raped grinned back.

"Draw your weapon, doctor"—Ticoma's words mixed sound and spit—"before my power deserts me."

From a belted sheath Ticoma slid her blood-stained sword. Urging her lipoca forward, she brought two thrusts hard upon the tortoise shell at Burne's knee. The halves hit the ground together.

"Defend yourself, doctor. It's a better chance than you gave me." Staring past Burne, she pivoted her mount and addressed the First Army. "He raped me!"

"We should *discuss* this," said Burne.

In reply Ticoma shot forward, her weapon poised for slaughter. Burne raised his sword, checked a fierce blow. He spurred after his attacker. Twice Ticoma circled the lipocaflesh arena. Turning suddenly, she advanced her sword with the full fury of all her muscles, all her loathing. The swing was at its strongest when Burne's weapon arrived, and the shock unseated him. The waiting sand, soft, was not soft enough to muffle his headfirst fall.

Ticoma dismounted, noting with a sly laugh that Burne's weapon sat in a dune. She rested her blade gently on his crotch.

Straining to steady his dazed thoughts and spinning vision, Burne examined the crowd. Their faces showed curiosity, plus the smugness that typifies bystanders to melodrama and anger, but none seemed ready to help.

"Soldiers!" was all he said.

"They aren't soldiers anymore," Ticoma reminded him gleefully. Burne groaned. "You mustered them out. But don't fret, Nearthling. I won't kill you, much as I'd like to. And I won't geld you, much as you deserve it. I'll merely even the score between us. At my hands you will know humiliation and pain. The humiliation comes from losing a fair swordfight to a lifelong pacifist! And the pain—that can only come from the ancient act in which you have tutored us so well!"

Someone called, "Ticoma, don't!" Too late. The runner had already pushed her sword deep into Burne's left thigh. She drew it out, and there was much blood.

19

TEOT YON WAS DEAD. It happened by degrees, without melodrama, during the same hours that Tez reveled in farewell wine and Francis listened to Umia tell tales, but the lovers did not learn of it until late the following afternoon. Francis's mental agenda for the day originally read: observe effects of noctus injection. He had planned to be a relentless bother. With luck he would inspire Tez to curse him out, threaten his life, or at least throw crockery across the kitchen. With luck he would *prove* the wisdom of his treachery.

Now, clearly, such experiments would not only border on cruelty, they would probably fail. Whatever furies the moat aroused, they were certain to be this day neutralized by grief.

Dinnertime came, and Tez ate nothing. Between bites of chactol Francis said, "Perhaps we should go to Witch's Fen tomorrow."

"Why not?" Tez mumbled. She retired to the courtyard and watched the stars and wondered which of them had died before its light reached Quetzalia.

Appetite lost, Francis rose and joined her. "A year from now it won't seem so bad," he said, immediately wishing he hadn't. He added a non sequitur—"Perhaps you'd like privacy now"—as if this would cause his remark to become unuttered.

"No." She turned and pushed herself into the softness of his robed shoulder. His hands swung up behind her like doors.

"Mool deserves whatever you give him," said Francis. Her living belly felt warm and right.

"When Father was a hauler, money was scarce. And I saw this bear. A big stuffed panda. Real pandas don't occur on Luta. The ark brought four real Kodiaks. Huaca once saw a Kodiak in the mountains. That was . . . last year, I think."

"You wanted the stuffed panda?" Francis eased his grip, and she slid away.

"The vendor said twenty cortas. My sixth birthday came and there on the breakfast table was a bear, only it wasn't the right one. It wasn't the bear the vendor had."

"Where did it come from?"

"It's amazing, isn't it? The man hauled rocks, and he sewed this thing together from . . . things. The horrible part is, I let him know I was disappointed. Children can be so . . . I mean, he hauled *rocks*. . . ." Weeping, she grabbed clumsily at the stars. "There's our Toy Queen."

"Did the bear have a name?"

"His name was Fropie," Tez replied, and Francis was weeping too.

A SHARP BREEZE etched its way through the Quetzalian National Park. The lovers glided into Witch's Fen knowing full well they wouldn't stay long enough to justify the four-corta canoe rental they had paid to a goofy, good-hearted kid named Popet. The canoe was disreputable—peeling paint and no seats—but it rode high in the rumpled water and kept its passengers dry. Francis paddled from the stern while his lover leaned over the bow, dragging a twig and meditating on eddies. Muscles knotted with cold, the swamp's imported reptiles did not move.

She was steadier today. Grief had become to her something peculiarly worth experiencing. It must not be resisted or denied, she decided, nor even rushed through, but accepted as inevitable, natural, like giving birth or retching or rain. Speech came easily. "I wonder how the First Army's doing?" she asked, casual as beer. "The battle was scheduled for yesterday."

"The day before," Francis corrected, surprised by her taste in conversation. "My intuitions place Burne at the ship now. He's busy rendering your Quetzalian pollucite down for its cesium."

" 'There are no necessary evils.' Janet Vij used to say that. Was she wrong, friend? Is Burne's war all to the good?"

"I am irrational on the subject," he said, staring heavenward. Thin bronze clouds were scrawled across the sky.

"Now I remember. Ever since the neurovores ate your friends' brains out you've had this grudge."

"Tez!" Francis's anger outstripped his amazement. "That's no way to talk!"

She was giddy now. "How would you like me to talk? With a twig between my teeth?" She put a twig between her teeth. "Very clever, the way Burne killed that neurovore. Skewered fore to aft! Did he have to train it first—the bug, I mean?" The twig fell in two as she bit down.

Francis stopped paddling. "No, once a *Cortexclavus* starts drilling it just keeps going. It stops for nothing."

"The ideal soldier," she said without irony. "Burne should have raised an army of corkscrew beetles."

"You don't usually mention such things."

"I still think about them, Iztac knows." Her smile looked like a wound. "Only today I'm thinking about them in a new way. I ask myself, Could Burne be a hero? Could a certain *kind* of killing be right, if the aim is to foster civilization and if the enemy is . . . ? But there I go, pigeonholing again."

For some reason, these unpacifist jabberings brought

Francis no joy. Unease crept over him. "I think we'd better leave now," he said, eyeing the bottom of the canoe. It held puddles. "And besides, it's wet down there."

Tez pitched the twig-halves into the swamp and followed Francis's stare. "God of the brain!" she screamed. "We've sprung a leak!"

"A first-rate reason to go home," said Francis dully.

"Doesn't he ever check these things ahead of time?" she pouted. "Doesn't he *care*?"

They paddled with a frenzy that brought further puddles into the boat. The water slapped their clothes and woke their skin, sensations Francis might have enjoyed were he not preoccupied.

Shore was reached quickly, hours before the silly leak would have endangered them, but they still felt rescued. Tez was first to jump out and sally up to Popet. "Excuse me," she commanded. "That tub you gave us is wormy!"

Popet stared unhappily at the beached canoe. "Just your luck, huh? I'll find you another."

Francis arrived in time to hear Tez say, "No, it's cold out there. Give us our money back."

"All of it?" Popet hammered his heel into the sand.

"All of it," said Tez stiffly.

"I'll have to ask my father."

"You'll have to ask no such person" was her immediate reply. "We want our money now."

Bewildered by this small woman's unpleasantness, Popet detached a lipocaskin bag from his wrist. He spread it open and shook four cortas into his palm. "I see your point," he said, meaning that he didn't.

Tez snatched the money. "We were practically *drowned!*" Wheeling around, she started off. Francis followed for a few meters, then turned toward Popet and spoke his feeble explanation.

"Her father died two days ago."

"I'm sorry," Popet replied. "We don't usually leak."

Sprinting away, Francis pondered the change he had so deftly wrought in Tez and drew a deep orgasmic satisfaction. Never before had he seen her quite so feisty, quite so Nearthian. He liked it.

"You really got your way that time," he said, pulling alongside her.

"I guess you're having some sort of influence on me after all." Confusion hobbled her voice. "I didn't traumatize the boy, did I?"

"He'll recover."

"That's the sort of forcefulness you have to use all the time on Nearth," she asserted.

"Yes. All the time."

"It's not so bad. I rather enjoyed it."

Without explaining why, Francis kissed her. Good for you, Tez. "Enjoyed"! Your word, not mine. Now it will be easy telling you about the injection. I'll confess before the first booster falls due. Your father's funeral will be a three-day-old memory by then. No more secrets between us, Tez. No sneakiness. Hell, you probably won't even get mad.

MR. NOSE WAS BEING EVIL. With obvious deliberateness he had tangled his strings and left them on the workbench in a Gordian knot. Seeing the deviltry in his porcelain eyes, Tez decided to teach the puppet a lesson. She picked up her hammer and went at him with the claw end, chopping deeply into his forehead. Shards of skull exploded across the workbench.

The noise lured Francis into the room. The mess startled him. "God of the sun!"

"Poor Mr. Nose." Tez's contriteness was somehow sinister. "He tried to make me angry."

"Zolmec permits revenge on puppets?"

She did not respond. Slowly she closed her hand around the largest fragment, offered it to Francis with a morbid playfulness. Her smile was ugly.

"Want a bite?" she asked.

Francis noted that she was simultaneously parodying neurovorean depravity and her own childlike qualities. He thrust his hands into his robe and left, shaking his head. Outside Olo, darkness descended.

IT WAS SAID that Teot Yon talked to his stones. He cajoled them, told them that, if they fell into neat blocks instead of splintering, they would go to Aca and become great public buildings. How poetic, Francis thought, that this pyre rests beside an eastern quarry, from which place the wind will lift Teot's ashes and scatter them among the rocks he loved.

The people Teot loved stood in a stodgy fog and waited for the cremation. Huaca, typically, was the holdup. The day's debate should have ended hours ago, but he had no doubt worked himself into a fit of discourse, and his thought-stream could not be diverted by anything so ordinary as a family tragedy.

Tez's angry eyes probed the crowd. "Eat his brain," she proclaimed in a husky whisper.

Francis heard her. "My vote exactly."

Surrounded by the authentically mournful, Francis felt phony and small. He did not belong at this funeral. A symbolic wreath of leaves from the frail ipu tree, whose lifespan was the same as a human's, ringed everyone's head but his.

Many of these people, most of them, had been at the party. Today they wore new identities: gray faces and black clothes. Francis found himself constantly nodding in recognition—blind Umia, the emaciated fish catcher, *et alii*—and rattling off "Good to see you," and each time he was struck with the peculiar dissatisfying continuity, the awkward mix of familiarity and mystery, that accompanies meeting a person for the second time.

A sour-looking young priestess approached, lighted torch in hand. The fog spat on the flame and made it writhe. "I don't like eulogizing when wet," she said coarsely.

Tez got a precarious grip on her composure. "We'll start without my brother."

Moving in a solemn, solitary procession, the priestess brought the torch near the pyre, which rose tapering from the fog like the ghost of a pyramid. Francis had assumed that the torch would be applied immediately, before the logs got soaked. Instead, the priestess faced the mourners and rattled off a short but considered summation of Teot's life.

"As a race of scientists and thinkers," she concluded, "we cannot claim with absolute certainty that Teot Yon's personality is now beyond Heaven's gates or inside Satan's stewpot or about to enter the embryo of a bull. Some of us subscribe to the Afterworld Hypothesis, some to less cheerful views. We *all* know that as an empirical event Teot Yon's existence is over, and it is time for his molecules to become air and ash and after that—where will his drifting pieces go and what new things will they help to form? Let the transformation begin!"

The priestess jabbed the pyre repeatedly with her torch. Francis noted the gratification he always experienced at seeing a fire take hold. He gripped Tez. She watched dizzily and murmured, over and over, "Eat his brain."

Thickening suddenly, the fog shut the fire from view. Sizzles resounded as the logs dried. Licks of bloody flame burst defiantly forth, sank back, died.

"Eat his brain."

WHEN NOTHING OF THE PYRE remained but gray glowing lumps, when most of the sun was behind the bellying foothills that formed the eastern horizon, when all of the mourners had gone save a half-dozen with little better to do than mill and speak of things unrelated to the funeral, Huaca finally showed. He marched straight for his sister. The stragglers stopped milling and gaped. Francis backed off.

"Don't forgive me," the professional arguer began, "but

realize that I am probably no less furious at Huaca Yon right now than you are." He had meant to sound contrite, but it came out glib.

Tez tucked her moist hands inside her robe. Saying nothing, she faced him with feral eyes.

"Is my peccadillo really beyond words?" Huaca looked at the ashes. Already the wind was bearing them into the quarry. "God of the brain, Tez, I loved him too—perhaps as much as you. If I thought a funeral would do him any good, I'd have dropped everything. But I was on to something, a new theory of art. I owed it to epistemology to stay in the ring. Now please, let's part amicably."

Half from anger, half from icy fog, Tez shivered. "You . . . are . . . correct, brother. This . . . time . . . your thoughtlessness . . . has . . . gone . . . beyond words, and so . . . my response . . . must also . . . go . . . beyond words."

From her robe Tez pulled a weapon: five fingers and a palm. She drew it back and sent it hard across Huaca's mouth. His head pivoted with the blow.

All around, a hundred eyes swelled.

Gasping, Tez took two steps backward. She examined her hand as if it were a grafted lump of alien flesh, screamed "God of peace!" Huaca's face was upright again and, but for an amorphous redness, bore no sign of her vengeance. "I'm sorry, Huaca!"

His anger dropped away before he could shout it. The same happened to his fear. Only pity and perplexity remained. "Are you sick, Tez? Do you think you're in church?"

"I don't know what's happening!"

I must tell her, Francis concluded. But before he could move he made the mistake of thinking.

This is the wrong time, he thought. She's upset. She'll miss the point.

Finally courage came. He walked toward her, but the space between them did not narrow. She retreated quickly, turned, and ran to where the fog was deepest. Again she screamed, "I don't know what's happening!"

"Tez!"

"Later!" Her words dissolved into snorts from a fog-bound lipoca. Mixtla's saddle creaked as she mounted.

"Tez!"

But the only reply was six drumming hooves.

20

VAXCALA COATL, high priestess of the Temple of Iztac and spiritual adviser to the Quetzalian race, had a bellyache. She was in no disposition to receive further visitors. Hour after hour the troubled citizens had come with their burning, tiresome questions. Vaxcala, is it all right to give my little girl candy for telling the truth? (Yes, but only if she knows you are rewarding honesty and not mere obedience to your wishes.) Vaxcala, is the tiger sinful because it kills? (No, because the tiger does not hate.) Vaxcala, what should I tell my children about Burne Newman's war? (I don't know.)

Outside the pyramid, Iztac descended in coppery pomp. "Who else is waiting?" Vaxcala asked.

Mouzon Thu waddled out of the shadows. "Three. A wall mender, a chess master, and a young surgeon."

"I'll heal them tomorrow."

Mouzon left the nave. Vaxcala rose from her divan and began blowing on the candles. They hovered between life and death until she found the precise intensity that would put them out: a childish experiment, but it kept her mind off her stomach.

Mouzon returned, his warty face twitching with annoyance. "The surgeon won't leave!"

Vaxcala burped. "The name?"

"Tez Yon."

"A cutter named Teot Yon was cremated this morning."

"Your visitor is his daughter."

"I'll see her." Vaxcala relit the candles.

Tez's timid footsteps echoed down the passageway, past the flames, up to the dais. She doused her lantern and eased it self-consciously to the floor.

Leaning forward, Vaxcala offered her most reassuring smile, but the visitor remained rigid and sad. "Your father was famous for his kindness and his accomplishments. His death starves us all."

"I've just come from the funeral. No, that isn't true. I've just come from Olo." Then she added, cautiously, "I live with Francis Lostwax."

"Not without consequence, I see."

"You can tell I'm pregnant?"

"Nobody on a surgeon's schedule looks *that* healthy without reason. What's the matter, won't he marry you?"

"He wants our child to be raised a Nearthling."

"And you seek my opinion on whether you should go?"

"I've already decided to go. My emotions are mixed, naturally. I love Quetzalia, its science. But my ties are dissolving. My brother dislikes me, my father is dead. Nearthlings have science too. One day I'm going to dethrone Charles Darwin for them."

"Is Francis a good person?"

"Good, gentle—not brash like Dr. Newman."

"From my own perspective I'm glad. You will be a constant reminder that they pledged to keep Luta a secret."

"And, of course, there is the glamour of travel—*adventure*! Francis has given me an enviable opportunity."

"Then why are you here?" asked Vaxcala sarcastically.

Tez chided herself with a smile. "Twelve days ago Francis told me that a Quetzalian's happiness on Nearth would be guaranteed only if she were capable of aggression. He wanted to inject me with noctus—practically on the spot."

"God of the sun! You could destroy your baby!"

"Not according to Janet Vij's notes. Francis read them all."

Vaxcala continued protesting: "The capacity for violence vanishes in six days."

"There would be booster shots. Naturally I found the whole idea repulsive. In recent hours, though, my feelings have changed."

Vaxcala frowned. "Why?"

"I'm not sure. The influence of Francis? Anyway, I've become—this sounds coy—I've become less hostile toward aggression."

The high priestess laughed unspontaneously.

"Yesterday," Tez continued, "I yelled at a boy for renting us a leaky canoe."

"Hardly a heresy."

"The *strange* part happened this afternoon, at the funeral. My brother showed up late. Didn't *care*. I was boiling. I wanted to kill him."

"Still normal. Not average, but normal."

"Yes, only this time I didn't wait for Zolmec. I didn't hold it in."

Tez explained how she assaulted her brother. Never before had Vaxcala's ears recorded such a confession. She swallowed a sphere of air.

"You *slapped* him?"

"Hard. On the cheek."

The high priestess's fingers snaked forward and coiled around the front edge of the divan. Her voice went brittle. "I suppose . . . you . . . were overwrought. Have you been missing services? Perhaps you should try something *especially* depraved next time. An ax murder."

"There won't be a next time. *Darwin* is due this week."

Raw anxiety was unfamiliar to Vaxcala. "Dr. Yon, what is it *like* to slap somebody?"

"That's the bewildering part. It doesn't feel sinful at all. It's not very different from slapping somebody during a service."

"And so now you've started to favor Francis's proposal?"

Tez's answer was long in coming. "Yes, but I want your blessing, Vaxcala. You sanctioned injections for Burne's army."

"I did it under pressure."

"I'm trying to pressure you."

Vaxcala rose, cast dead eyes on Tez. Their light went inward, searching for an answer. "These are wearying, unsettled times, Dr. Yon. The Antistasists press upon us with new ideas. Who is to say these ideas are wrong? And now this whole war business. Change frightens me." Turning away, she began again to torment the candles. "Tez, you are poised between two cultures. For reasons still murky to me, you have already behaved in a manner wholly opposed to Quetzalian conviction. Whether you know it or not, you are converting to extraterrestrial ways. I suggest that you now complete the process and—with my blessing—become a total Nearthling." She whirled and attacked Tez with her sternest face. "Only don't expect to find yourself welcome in Quetzalia ever again."

Despite the harshness of this last remark, Tez felt comforted. "Francis will be so happy! I'm going to the wall right now!" She pulled a green towel from her robe, flashed a syringe.

"Does Francis know you have that thing?"

"No."

"It sounds as if your scruples are decaying *without* help from noctus."

"I didn't steal it. I'll return it."

"You stole it," Vaxcala explained.

"I stole it for the greater good—a surprise. The injection will be my wedding present to him."

Vaxcala sagged onto the divan. "We're finished now, Nearthling. I need to nurse my stomach." She gestured Tez away. "Go. Drink the moat."

Tez lifted her lantern. This time her sandals clacked confidently across the nave. Reaching the outside steps, she saw that the drizzly fog had risen, leaving the night dry and starless. Despite the suffocating dark it took her only a minute to plunge down the side of the pyramid, untether Mixtla, and strike out for the Temple of Tolca.

DURING OFF-HOURS public buildings grow haunted and weird. Children feel this when they return by night for pageants in their dark-halled schools. Minus the rush of lanterns and the accustomed clamor of worshipers, the Temple of Tolca seemed to Tez forbiddingly unfamiliar, even though she had walked these passageways five hundred times before. This was the temple's time to be alone.

Reaching one of the great vaulted decagons, she entered the nearest chapel on tiptoes. The hollow screen awaited, potential with hate. Its face was dead to the touch.

A quick tug and her cranium was off. She nested it behind the fat red cushion, sat down.

Eyes locked on the screen, she stretched her fingers high over her head until they brushed the electrode. She yanked it forward, pressing it deep into her unfeeling cerebrum. The screen began flooding with green haze.

Her eyes closed briefly, then sprang open and grew to their fullest. Her teeth met and crunched. Her thoughts gathered potency.

On the screen the haze transmuted. Green became yellow, yellow became orange. Amorphous orange took shape. It was a fire, a flaming pyre.

Consumed, the pyre collapsed and jumped into the background. Huaca Yon rushed on screen. He had no legs. Tez concentrated. He got his legs.

"Is my peccadillo really beyond words?" Huaca said from the screen. "God of the brain, Tez, I loved him too—perhaps as much as you."

A stray orange swirl lingered before Huaca's image. She went to work, inventing herself from it. The projected Tez stomped up to her brother, who was still repeating the morning's speech. Seeing the obsidian scalpel in her hand, he departed sharply from the script.

"But I was on to something, a new . . . way to . . . paint pictures of lipoca dung. Just pour the pigment into your nose and sneeze. A masterpiece. . . ." He eyed the knife nervously.

Tez fell upon him, slashing, shredding, making ribbons of his robe, then ripping it from his body entirely. She aimed low, and the blade flew smoothly into Huaca's unathletic gut. A ghastly mass of entrail popped out. It dripped and vanished.

Vanished? She was losing concentration. This service seemed to her profoundly different from its predecessors. How? She could not decide. Then the obvious became apparent.

She was having a good time.

Like any worshiper, Tez used the pictures to maintain a vivid dreamflow and wring every drop of violence from her pent-up frustrations. But where other Quetzalians would have addressed the screen with humorless, hypnotized attention, Tez addressed it with glee, laughing until her eyes swam.

"Go to it, doctor!"

The intestine returned. As the bogus Tez squeezed it a transformation occurred, and she found herself hauling foot upon foot of masterfully woven rope from Huaca's abdomen. He tried to escape, but Tez moved faster, dashing in wide, then moderate, then narrow circles around her prisoner, until he was a bundle of rope.

The real Tez kept laughing. Her fantasy wobbled, began to fade. She cursed herself: Pay attention, damn you!

The scene regained its luster. Now she was lifting her bundled brother high into the air. She carried him to the edge of the quarry, tossed him over. Through the magic of thought, Huaca's projection became a six-foot egg. Screaming hideously, the egg hurtled two hundred meters toward undebatable oblivion.

Tez switched to a subjective viewpoint, grabbing the corners of her cushion as the ground zoomed up. Her stomach went into free fall, and she cackled. Then, at the moment of impact, she spirited herself high above, watching with rapture as her oval brother hit the rocks and splattered himself into a snotty glob of yoke and white and shell. The show was over.

GRADUALLY SHE SOBERED UP. Her laughter became peeps, then smiles. Plucking the electrode out, she blinked toward the screen. Within its walls nothing remained but a broad puddle of gall.

One hand replaced the electrode while the other pushed an adjacent lever. Squeals of friction testified that the device had been little used over the years. Looking behind her, she worked the lever to its apex. Silently the screen glided upward, drawn on strings of magnetism. It coupled with the chapel ceiling.

Stepping forward, she squatted by the silver-black leavings of her latest fantasy. They gurgled and stank and oozed into the floor. In minutes they would be gone forever, random molecules of the communal nightmare.

Tez had never been so close to noctus. The smell was adamant but not sickening. Cautiously she broke the surface with her index finger, brought finger to tongue, tasted the sweetness. Sweetness! Sweet dreams! Sight, sound, smell, touch, taste—she had performed all available tests.

Pain drilled into her tongue and finger where the caustic candy had been. She was ready for it. Patiently she waited while the pain became a pleasantly endurable throb.

Her robe held a jar of salt water, nine-tenths full. She unscrewed the lid and used it as a noctus ladle. Two scoops gave her a ten percent solution. She shook the jar.

In its crisp symmetry the needle looked far crueler than

Tez had remembered. Perhaps I should let Francis stick me, she thought. No. This must remain a gift. Find your courage, surgeon.

Setting the solution on the floor, she let the syringe drink deep, then pushed the plunger till it spat away all but three cubic centimeters. Three. The safe, perfect, magic number.

There was, of course, a final hesitation. Tez had expected it. During this time she played at injecting herself, massaging her deltoid, tickling it with the needle. Then, like a timid, chattering swimmer up to her navel in an icy lake, she managed to stop her mind and let her matter take over.

Came the submersion.

The needle was under her skin. The plunger was active, was moving back—no blood—was moving forward, was forcing lurid imaginings into her body.

"For love!"

Tez did not expect instantaneous effects—this was only three cc's, after all—nor did she get them. She removed the needle, returned it to the green towel. I must cover my tracks, she thought, lowering the screen, recapping her brain.

Came the effects.

They came with a fury. Her digestion was struck first. The bony fingers of ten thousand rat skeletons clawed at the imprisoning walls of her stomach. She toppled, howling. As the moat squirted into her brain, pain dissolved into shivering frivolity. Her face, she could tell, was alternating between contorted grins and grotesque frowns. Her eyeballs spun in their sockets. A psychotic rainbow entered the chapel. It danced around, and when it exploded a hundred octaves of the invisible spectrum were revealed. From the air, shrill, loathsome chimes arose, assumed unnamed geometric shapes, became chimes again. The chapel walls groaned and pulsed like heart muscles.

Tez dreamed that she had reinserted the electrode. No fantasy happened. Instead, a geyser of noctus shot from her brain and began filling the screen. Capacity was reached, surpassed. The screen shattered, but the bile did not gush; it slithered, a dark sheeny monster. Quivering tentacles reached into Tez, and suddenly the thing had her baby. It was a boy.

Her own choked cry woke her. Her body was wound in a tight, pale, pregnant ball. Mercifully, the hallucination stopped.

Came the darkness.

THREE

The Apostle

21

ACROSS THE MOUNTAINS, through the valley, into the cities, winter ate its way. Life in Tepec became cold to the touch. Citizens fondled their coats, looking for holes to mend. Gardens decayed into formless brown. Chitzals headed for the southern orchards and sustained themselves on frozen, nearly impregnable opos. On the river made of hate, ragged shelves of ice formed and grew toward the middle. Like a healing wound, the moat began to close.

The opoch called Lamux was famous for sudden snows. Made of purple vapor, lit by a jade sun, the flakes were the luxurious blue of unoxygenated blood. Twice already they had lightly burst upon Quetzalia like seeds from a farmer's palm, and both times Iztac had burned them away. But now it was snowing with conviction, in such quantities that the citizens decided to stay by their hearths. If *Darwin* arrives today, they told themselves, the news will spread soon enough, and, besides, this tea is warm and sweet.

Alone on the wall, Francis paced, shivered, and waited for the overdue ship. Drumrolls poured from the bones of his mouth. Am I crazy to be here?

He was of two minds. If I go home, said the first mind, I'll start thinking of Tez. I'll brood and masturbate.

You're thinking of Tez *now*, said the second mind. And you're brooding, too. You're not masturbating because the weather's wrong.

Ever since the slap, Tez had been a missing person. Her colleagues at the hospital assumed she was vacationing without notice. Her brother, still shocked by the assault and guilty over its aptness, could offer no theories. Depressed by his inadvertent role in the exploitation of Janet Vij's notes, Loloc Haz shrugged at Francis's inquiry and reminded him that Tez was too resourceful, Quetzalia too benign, for her to be in any physical danger. "This isn't Nearth, you know, although it might be by the time you and Newman get through with it."

Pained by the emptiness in his bed, Francis took first to sleeping in a guest room, then on a couch, then to not sleeping. He moped: if Tez's system went another ten hours without a noctus booster, her newfound humanness would devolve into Quetzalian pacifism. But that was not the worst of it.

Nor was the worst of it that she might be lost. As Loloc had suggested, Tez could surely rescue herself.

The worst of it was that she was hiding from him, tacitly rejecting his plans for her emigration. She didn't really love him.

At twilight the snow began to wane. Like the farmer closing his barn door behind his escaped cows, Francis buttoned up. Following local custom, he had recently fattened his robe with a wool overcoat. His wool cap was shaped like a gourd. The ensemble performed so impressively that on Nearth it would have claimed the undivided attention of a hundred entrepreneurs, who, depending on whether its design might be revised to include some sort of impermanence, could readily shape it into either a dazzling fortune or a handy tax write-off.

Francis studied the Quetzalian side of the wall, trailing his eyes across the heterogeneous geometry—square stones, round stones, smooth stones, chunky stones—until he saw two figures talking solemnly and indecipherably near the base of the nearer drawbridge tower. Today's gatekeeper was a frisky middle-aged woman whose head appeared taped on by scarves. Her companion, a runner, likewise middle-aged, but male and lethargic with cold, was obviously no casual acquaintance. Once he advanced and kissed her, but she pulled away suddenly like a gull realizing it was on the wrong nest. Good, Francis thought. He's not for you.

The second mind had won. Go home now, it said, and he approached the steps. A snowflake settled meanly into his eye. Facing the forest, he saw his lipoca tethered to a bush that looked like a large fleshless hand. Carbon dioxide steamed from the animal's nostrils.

He was about to go down when, unmistakable and insistent, a metallic scream rushed out of the clouds. Like a great actor entering, reducing his audience to an expectant hush, *Darwin* broke upon the dusk.

Seeing a spaceship for the first time in their lives, the Quetzalians grew agog.

Recovering, the runner shot away. The gatekeeper went for her windlass. Fifty meters from the river, *Darwin* halted and hovered while the bridge began a raspy descent.

Francis felt like a patient learning that he wasn't going to die after all. The war had worked! Noctus solution was predictable and tame. The injection could not have harmed her.

Realizing where Burne intended to land, Francis experienced unbounded admiration for his friend's sense of diplomacy. *Darwin* was not headed for the desert. Appreciably smaller than the average dune, it would there have been a pathetic answer to all the blood it cost. Nor was *Darwin* headed beyond the wall. Brimming with circuits, it would there have stood as a palpable affront to the Quetzalian ban on technology.

The moment the windlass was unreeled, *Darwin* spun toward the gate and settled directly onto the drawbridge.

Groaning under unaccustomed metric tons, the timbers stayed miraculously whole as Francis crossed the narrow lip of bridge that jutted between ship and moat. He unlooped the key from his neck, then felt his smile collapse as, prepared for nothing less than Burne Newman's thick figure and shaggy face, he unlocked the hatch and pivoted it away from an empty frame. Rehanging the key, shuddering as its coldness cut through his robe, he entered and raced past the organic-looking oxygen tubes that led to the control deck.

Hearing footfalls, Burne rotated his chair and pulled his face into a grin. "Sorry I wasn't at the door," he said weakly, pointing downward. A bandage engulfed his left thigh, the white linen yielding to a gruesome yellow stain.

Francis gasped. He couldn't stand being around pain, would rather be hurt himself. "We should get you to Dr. Mool."

"No," said Burne with a macabre wink. "It's only as bad as it looks."

Francis shucked his coat. Good God, the bastard *wanted* to get wounded. "It happened while you were saving somebody's life, right?"

Burne concurred with a grunt. He didn't feel like admitting that his misfortune was wholly unrelated to the war.

Francis shook Burne's hand hesitantly, as if he thought war wounds could be transmitted like diseases, but he spoke with affection. "I looked up and saw old *Darwin* and it was the prettiest sight this side of Ollie Cortexclavus."

"You doubted I'd win?"

"I don't see survivors."

Burne explained that the First Army of Aca, dirty and happy, was two days behind him. "They ought to be *five* days behind, but in my fevered state it took forever to coax a tank's worth of cesium out of the damn pollucite."

"Wouldn't the Quetzalians help you?"

"My lieutenants carried me to the ship, but their bughouse religious convictions kept them on the desert side of the hatchway. They wouldn't even put their casualties on board."

"How *many* casualties?"

"Forty-three Quetzalians are dead. Thirty are wounded."
Burne scratched his thumb on the longbow that rested incongruously by the L-17 terminal.

"And the neurovores?"

This time Burne grinned for real. "*What* neurovores?" he crowed.

Francis danced. "Dr. N, you're a miracle."

BURNE SUGGESTED DINNER. Francis went to the galley, returned carrying two cans of distasteful meatballs. He heated them with kelvinsleeves. And to think—some poor animal had given its life for this stuff.

Francis expected war stories, but Burne was too miserable. They talked idly, of entomology, archeology, time travel, Nearth, with Francis supplying most of the words. Rolling the last meatball into his mouth, he went to the holovision monitor and pushed Power On.

"You did it, Burne. You brought it off. Of all the audacious bastards in the galaxy—"

A sharp groan cut him short. Turning, he saw Burne pitch forward like a buoy. The monitor sang with current.

Francis advanced, hands outstretched, but the hero rallied and refused charity. "Can't move my damn toes." Burne spoke through locked teeth. "I won't say 'wiggle' because I never *could* wiggle the little warthogs."

"Go to the hospital, Burne." He tried for maximum petulance.

Seizing Francis's sleeve, Burne reeled him to within whispering distance. "Under no circumstances will I leave this boat." His voice was somewhere between a faint mumble and a strong thought. "Not if my leg starts to rot. Not if God farts in the air ducts. Understood?"

"Your fever could return."

"Then *you'll* fly the ship."

Oh sure, Burne. But for some reason Francis smiled. "There's a rumor around that you want to go home soon."

"I hate this place, Lostwax. I didn't think I'd get my leg

half cut off, but I did. Before something *else* goes haywire, you scoot to Olo and find your toothbrush and your beetle and your pretty little fiancée—what's-her-name, the pacifist—and be back at sunrise."

"Tez has been missing for two days."

"There's one thing my life doesn't need right now, chum, and that's *complications*."

"Look, Burne, I don't like to bicker with a wounded man, but if not for me you wouldn't have *thought* about using noctus as a weapon."

"All right—noon tomorrow, no later." He placed his mouth over the meat can so the words would echo. "If you're not here then, count yourself among the marooned."

Francis nodded. This is fair, he thought. If she doesn't show tonight, it will absolutely *prove* that Quetzalia is the only home she wants. Maybe it's just as well, Tez. Maybe Nearth is unworthy of you.

Burne was at the control panel. The monitor glowed yellow as the running-lights came on. Outside, a cone-shaped crowd was building. It began at the far end of the gateway and fanned outward toward the forest. The fat ones, Governor Nazra and Mouzon Thu, stood at the apex, swinging their lanterns and catching snow on their tongues.

Burne looked at the scene, snorted. "I don't want any curious bystanders wandering in here."

"You owe them a victory speech." Francis grappled with his coat, orienting it.

"You make it, Lostwax. I'm giving this leg the sleep it needs." Rising, he grasped the longbow and poled his way uncertainly across the deck.

Francis stepped forward, pushing buttons into buttonholes. He became Burne's second crutch. Enmeshed, they tottered toward the cabins.

THE SNOW WAS NOT QUITE OVER when Francis moved into *Darwin*'s wan glow, locked the hatch, and edged to the prow. Meeting the lights, the blue flakes became a storm of green peas. Nazra and Mouzon rushed up greedily. Francis reported the news, fending them off with his woolly arm, and smiles flourished all around.

Nazra waddled triumphantly into the crowd, eager to advance this latest argument for his reelection.

Mouzon clawed at Francis's collar. "It's horrible and obscene." Then he added, after some thought, "But the planet is ours now. I should go thank him."

"No visitors. He's sick." On cue from a line in Nazra's speech, the crowd became a cheering throng. The noise buffeted the snow. Francis grew cautious. "Stay with me, Mouzon. I'll need you if I'm going to reach my lipoca."

The cheering had ended by the time they passed the portcullis. As the throng descended, Mouzon's holy authority, radiating outward in all directions, kept Francis safely inside an invisible two-meter bubble. Names fell upon him with the snow.

"Kitu Pon! Is Kitu Pon alive?"

"My daughter was Quilo Loir!"

"Topi Hazpec!"

"Mochi Shappa!"

Each time he could offer only an agonized look and eight words. "No casualty list! Survivors return in two nights!" He said it thirty times.

Without breaking stride they reached the lipoca, still tied to its bony bush. "You'll be taking off soon?" Mouzon asked. Blue flakes clung to his coat, giving him a snowman's belly.

Francis displayed a bumpy cylinder. "This opens *Darwin*. Tonight I want you to find Tixo Mool and let him in."

"The spaceship is a forbidden place, Dr. Lostwax."

He fought to keep his voice strong. "It won't be after you've blessed it." His success surprised him.

Reluctantly, Mouzon accepted the key. "What should he do?"

"Examine my friend—cabin number two."

"Dr. Mool may have other plans for the evening."

"Look, cleric, you want to get rid of us, right? You won't unless Burne recovers."

"Is it really so very important?"

"Important," Francis echoed, stretching the word into ragged syllables. Then, in an equally unsettling voice, "I think his leg is dead."

22

THEY NEVER DID SOLVE the public lighting problem in this town, Francis thought as he steered his lipoca through the blunt, oily glow of the streetlamps. In this frantic time of year, all but the heartiest citizens left the northern population centers and escaped to Tepec, Aca, and Oaxa, where winter was traditionally a few degrees easier to take. Even after dark the immigration continued, and Francis rode amid thousands of Quetzalians rushing to install themselves in the sundry hotels and relatives' houses they had arranged to occupy until the ordeal of aphelion was past.

"Say, did you come from the spaceship?" The voice was soft but perky. Its owner, a small boy, stood in the dim valley between Francis's lipoca and a book-filled cart. The boy was unloading the books. That made sense; winter would go faster with books.

At first Francis thought he'd been spotted for the extraterrestrial that he was. "Yes," he said tentatively, reining up.

"The Nearthlings will be leaving soon, won't they?"

"Yes. Did you know anyone in the army?"

Despite the dark, pride swept visibly across the boy's face. "My family, my friends, we were all against it. Everyone. Father says don't kill your principles just because the government is paying for the funeral."

"But now the planet is ours."

"Father says it won't help anything."

Francis stammered, turned the noises into a forced cough. Just my luck, he thought, to run into a goddam budding priest. Lipocawool, thick and splendid with winter, oozed up around his thighs as he settled into his mount and sped away.

AT OLO EVERYTHING WAS SNOW-BLUE, quiet, normal. But then he got closer. Dismounting, walking through the gardens, he saw that the main door stood as glaringly open as an ax wound. Its source invisible, a yellow light spilled through the jamb. In this chummy country, where the people never heard of locks, only latches, anybody who felt like it could barge into your life, and somebody obviously had. His first thought was to arm himself against a mugging, but then he remembered with a chuckle that the planet under his feet was not Nearth. Probably he'd been invaded by some Cuzians who, like bugs, knew where the warmth was. No need to turn them out. If Mool revived that sorry leg tonight, Francis would have no further need of rooms.

Entering the house, he soon located the light in the banquet hall, a vast cheerless cavity he normally visited only because it contained the door to the wine cellar. The table, in scale with the room, was sliced from a mammoth tree that antedated *Eden Three*. At the far end, starglow pierced a window to reveal three raw lambchops encircling a wine bottle, almost spent, that rose from the center of a ceramic plate. A small woman hunched over the meal, face wrapped in shadows.

"Tez?" He hated this moment, hated it for expecting him to dash forward like a kinepic hero and take her in his arms. Realizing he couldn't do it, he was attacked by embarrassment, and he approached with a sluggishness suggestive of *Darwin*'s bogus gravity.

She raised her head, bringing her sculpted features into

the starglow. Sagging eyes broadcast decay and dissipation.

"Your face looks like you slept in it," said Francis, still moving.

"I'm *sick*." The words came with a spite sufficient to stop his advance. "Sit down!"

Without quite knowing why, Francis sat down. An entire table kept him from his lover. "Shouldn't you be in the hospital?"

"It begins with an *A*."

"Alcoholism?"

"No." Her mood leaped without transition from melancholy to joy. "Francis, dear, I have a sweet, most wonderful, entirely *premeditated* surprise for you! Well, don't just *stare*. Can you no longer register pleasure with that crooked mouth and tinny voice?"

"A pregnant woman shouldn't drink so much."

This inspired her to grab the bottle and upend it over a nearby champagne glass. The wine ran dry just in time to prevent a flood. "A toast!" she said, lifting the glass and conducting a presumed orchestra with it. The wine sloshed. "A toast to . . . toast. Here's to you, toast, you smug cosmetizer of stale bread." Bringing the glass to her lips, she sent a rippling wind across the surface.

"What's my surprise?" asked Francis.

"Your surprise is . . . I don't remember. Give me a hint. Come on, is it digestible?"

Francis munched his lower lip. "Tez, where have you been? The hospital?"

"The Temple of Tolca. Six orphan chitzals and I. They all have names now. I got hungry. Have you ever tried eating fur, Lostwax? It can't be done. So I came back."

She went for the champagne glass, sucked up a mouthful, and Francis saw his chance. The speech came out in a jumble, words tripping over themselves, but the gist was clear even to Tez's fogbound comprehension: the neurovores had been vanquished, Burne was wounded, they were scheduled to depart tomorrow, assuming he recovered. Did she still want to go?

"Of course I want to go. I think I'd make a good blaster-ball player, don't you? Spiked kneecaps, how witty."

"Why did you run away?"

"God of the brain, we won! I should have enlisted. It must have been a picnic, squeezing their rancid eyes out like pus."

"Tez, dammit—!"

"Burne makes a reasonable enough hero, doesn't he? Truth to tell, there's a part of me that always wanted to screw with him. I could say *which* part, but I'll leave that to—"

Francis jerked up from the table. "For the last time: Why did you run away?!"

"I don't know!" she fired back without skipping a beat.

"*I* know, Tez. Four days ago you chewed out a boy for renting us a bad canoe."

"I should have chopped his family jewels off."

"And then you slapped Huaca at your father's funeral."

"Father made me this *bear*, Lostwax."

"You've been feeling strange lately."

"A panda of some kind."

"There's something I must confess. You owe this change to something I did."

"I love confessions."

Francis cavorted internally. This was going smoother than he had dared imagine. "I *knew* you'd understand. Sometimes you love somebody sǒ much, you have to do what's *best* for them."

She grew suddenly sedate. Her latest guzzling was not yet in her brain. "And so, you did what was . . ."

"Best."

"For me?"

"Best for *you*."

"I was asleep?"

"You'd had a lot to drink. Like tonight."

"Three cubic centimeters?" She was breathing hard now, catching on.

"Of a ten percent solution. The right and proper dose."

"With a hypodermic?"

"How else?"

"With *this* hypodermic?" She rose, trembling, to full height. Despite the cold, a robe was all she wore. From it she yanked Francis's syringe and plunked it on the plate, splashing lamb blood.

He nearly strangled on his amazement. "Why do you have *that*? It's a *machine*."

She poured her wine onto the table, slapped the puddle like a child playing with food. "You call yourself a scientist. And yet you break its laws the way you'd break a—" She seized the empty champagne glass, and when she'd finished there was only the stem.

"You're right," he said. "I was rash."

"You were *rash*. A rash on the ass! Snot sucker!"

"I deserve those names."

"Brain Eater! In my sleep? I suppose you raped me while you were at it."

"It was only three cubic centimeters."

"Three cubic centimeters! You've no *idea* what you've done!" Her ears thundered with blood. "I thought it was all a dream! Thought I'd made it up!"

"Made it up?"

"I can't face this, not without—" Before he could repeat his question, she had picked up the syringe and plunged, robe billowing, into the wine cellar. He decided not to follow.

SOUVENIRS DID NOT HOLD much status in Francis's life. When he had gone to Nearth's famous Natwick Desert, everybody was appalled that he'd returned devoid of singing cacti; he'd come back from Orchard City without a sin-

gle graven image of the famous Cathedral Bridge. And so it
was natural for him to leave Quetzalia empty-handed. The
half-full, ready-to-go knapsack he placed by the parlor's
smoldering hearth contained only his Nearth clothes and,
on top, the vitreousteel cage.

He went to the kitchen and returned with a greasy pile of
sausages. *Cortexclavus* sat silent and inverted, feet gripping
the barred lid. In the insect mind, Francis decided, upside
down must be remarkably like rightside up. He inserted the
sausages between the bars, and the beetle scrambled after
the scent.

"Ollie," he said, "I could pin your wings, sever your antennae, file your nose into a spoon, and you'd *still* be happier than I." The beetle drove its mandibles through the
meat. "Burne is half-dead, Tez half-crazy. Do you hear me,
bug? I *love* her, no less now than opochs ago when she
brought me—"

A crescendo of glass cut him short. He jumped to his feet,
and there were more brittle reports as he followed his ears
through the banquet hall and into the wine cellar. Realizing
he would have to deal with Tez again, he said aloud,
quickly, "I want to cry."

She sat on a moldy cask, back propped against a champagne rack. Over her shoulder the wall degenerated into its
constituent bricks, which she was freeing and heaving one
by one at her designated target, a façade of claret. Even
drunk she could not miss.

A carpet of glass and wine spread before Francis, and he
crunched forward. Loathing and fear mutilated Tez's face.
The bursts of wine on her robe looked like wounds.

"Tez, you should go to bed."

"I remember what your surprise is," she said droningly.
"I remember what your surprise is."

"Yes?"

"Your surprise is . . . three."

"Three," he repeated.

"Three and three make six."

"Six what?"

"Cubic centimeters. I wanted to be *human*, Francis."

"You injected yourself?" He was touched, also terrified. "When?"

"The night of the funeral."

Francis fought to master his dread. At least there was a three-day interval. "If the overdose were dangerous," he stuttered, "you'd have known by now."

As if mimicking the floor, her eyes became red and glassy. "But I *do* know. Noctus has made me *angry*."

"I deserve your anger."

"Angry at Huaca."

"So does Huaca."

"At Mool."

"Mool gave your father coyo root."

Suddenly Tez's face opened into a huge horrid grin. "At *our baby*."

This was unexpected, and Francis took a moment to collect his thoughts. "He should be angry at *you*, the way you've been drinking."

Tez had held the grin so long that it was no longer a grin but something far less natural. "He kicked me. Not now. I ate an herb." She pointed to the mess on the floor. "What do you suppose it's like to make love on that? Does life hold thrills we don't know about?"

"What herb?"

"Azti. My illness begins with an *A*, remember? I just walked into the hospital and grabbed a jar. When you're a thief, everything is free."

"Azti lulls a foetus?"

"Lull, lull, lullaby," she said autistically.

A foreign, tingling fear weaved through Francis. "Tez, open your robe."

Casually she undid the cord and pulled the halves apart. Her stomach was starkly flat. "It's gone," she gurgled. "The loathsome thing that leased my body kicks no more. *A* is for azti, *A* is for aborticide."

Francis screamed until he felt his throat would rip.

Tez hugged herself, closing the robe. Four terse strides brought her to the steps, which she ascended until reaching Francis's height. "I'm no longer a Quetzalian," she said, an infinite exhaustion in her voice, and left him with his tears.

PARAGON OF WINTER CONSTELLATIONS, Lamux's Teapot lit the room. Francis moved woozily toward the bed, wishing for a miracle. He wished that it were six days ago, that he were approaching Tez with a polluted syringe—not this champagne bottle—that he were changing his mind, that he were throwing the syringe out the window.

He shoved the bottle into his mouth and swilled. A meter away, Tez's unpregnant form rested beneath a bulky blanket. "Lover?" he slurred.

She moved. "Yes?"

"Tez, I've thought this out, and if we leave for Nearth tomorrow and try to forgive each other and simply realize that, hell, we can have another child, I think everything, all the splinters, will still fit together, as long as we feel hope. . . ."

Tez's reply was a warm, wanting hand that rose from the bundled wool and in one motion undid the knot at Francis's waist. Closing around the sash, the hand hauled him to bed. The moment the two bodies touched there was a flurry of movement that left him feeling slightly molested but nevertheless satisfied.

Spurred by the winey blood in his brain, sleep came to Francis in one unbroken wave. He dreamed that he and Tez were painting a huge rainbow bird on an outside wall of the Galileo Institute. A small male child with Tez-brown hair mixed the colors.

23

OTHER DREAMS DEBUTED that night, none of them odd enough to be remembered, but daybreak found him getting his stolen insects back from Robert Poogley. The two enemies were adrift on an acid sea, a circumstance that plainly argued for reconciliation. Poogley reached behind his back, ready to draw forth the glass cigar box, when an insistent banging arose, capsizing the boat. Francis hit the acid and surfaced into consciousness, the bedroom swirling around him. In an instant he took stock. Reality was now. There would be no baby. Tez had been overdosed with noctus.

"Tez!" Ears still numb with sleep, he was practically screaming. "Answer the door!"

No movement on the left, her usual place. Groaning, he performed a sit-up. The banging continued to punch its way into the room.

He studied the bed. Empty. His patience hit rock bottom. So you're out of my life again! This time please just stay there!

He launched his bare feet over the side of the bed. The floor shot coldness through his body, rousing him so completely that, after throwing on a robe, he found the front hall without a single wrong turn. He opened the door cautiously, as if it led to a possibly-occupied toilet, then shuddered to see a frightening, familiar face.

Huaca Yon looked mauled. His murm suture was fissured

and awry. Gore bubbled from his bruised nose and divided lower lip. His left eye was split and running. He appeared to be crying blood.

"God of the brain!" said Francis.

The debater lurched into the hall. "Good morning," he said, torturing himself with a smile.

"You should be in the hospital."

"No, there's no protection."

"From Tez?"

"She's gone crazy."

"I think she's just gone . . . a bit plucky."

"Plucky." In Huaca's mouth the word sounded unbelievably dumb.

"I gave her noctus. Three cc's, same as the army." He guided Huaca toward the bedroom.

"You gave her *what?*" The silence meant: You heard me. "In Iztac's name—*why*?"

"So she'd survive on Nearth."

"I expect she'll *kill* me next time." He followed Francis through the doorway. A large chair, gorged with wool, cushioned his hurting limbs.

Francis left, returning shortly with a water-beaded kettle. He sent cool rivulets down Huaca's face.

"Well, Lostwax, what's the root of this evil? Tez? Science?"

"The problem is that she went and injected herself before the dose I administered had worn off."

"And you didn't bother to tell her she was already contaminated?"

"I intended to, naturally. I didn't know I should be quick about it."

"Then *you're* the one to blame. The irony is, you're also the one I must cling to. At least until she—" His look would freeze wine. "*Will* she recover?"

Francis started to swallow, got halfway there. "I wish I knew." In the closet he found a spongy length of linen.

"A queer time to start hedging your bets, don't you think?"

"I *believe* she'll be all right." His gawky fingers began bandaging Huaca's face. "She attacked you at home?"

"The sun wasn't up yet. She used a fire poker, all the time screaming about Father."

"Where did she go afterward?"

"Out the door. God of peace, I wish I'd brought him flowers every day!"

"Once would have been smart."

"Lostwax, at this point aren't you just about the last person in our galaxy who has any right to *criticize*?"

"I won't argue with you." He spiraled the bandage downward.

"No, please, *do* argue with me. I'm good at it. What I'm not good at is beating people up. I must leave that sort of thing to you and the people you poison."

"I didn't want this!"

"And you haven't yet agreed to be my bodyguard."

"I have plans, Huaca. Nearth plans."

"Look, Lostwax, we don't know each other very well, and if we did I have a feeling we wouldn't want to. But you owe me something after the puking shambles you've made of the art and science of biophotonics."

"You don't seem to understand. This is my last morning in Quetzalia."

"Gather around, children. Get your genuine, official Scientist's Kit, just like the one Francis Lostwax fools around with. Now you, too, can conduct secret and atrocious experiments on your loved ones." His face was a linen ball. "You don't care what happens to me, do you?"

Francis surprised himself by getting annoyed. "Huaca, *you* have no more to fear." His voice held firm. "She's *had* her revenge."

"I don't believe you."

"Burne blasts off at noon," said Francis decisively, slipping out of the room. "The trains don't run after that." His clothing and his vitreousteel cage, Ollie scuffling inside, were still by the hearth.

Huaca called into the parlor. "Don't you like it here? Is it the food? What's so special about Nearth, anyway?"

Francis reappeared, bent by his knapsack. "I'm off. There's food—apples, at least—in the kitchen. Use the banquet table to barricade yourself in."

Huaca got to his feet, every centimeter an agony. "I'm coming with you," he said. "You can shield me from here to the ship. After that I don't know *what* I'll do. Take noctus myself."

"You can't."

"Why?"

"Tez has the syringe."

EVEN AT THIS EARLY HOUR Halcyon Road was a torrent of migration. Encumbered by a lipoca wagon, Francis had no choice but to plow through the Oaxa-bound crowds, kilometer after tedious kilometer. Occasionally he would twist in his seat and try to make conversation, but Huaca, supine and sullen in the back, confined his replies to the perfunctory. All right, Huaca, you win. I feel guilty as hell.

The suburbs finally came, went, and they veered west onto an open Kinship Road. Francis swatted the lipoca. The wagon sailed away, wheels meeting road with the sound of a marble crossing a table. Forest, then sand, rolled by, and the recumbent drawbridge was before them. *Darwin* sat spangled with noon sun.

Something was wrong. All panting and eyes, the gatekeeper's face showed it. "You're Francis Lostwax, aren't you?"

"Yes." He remembered her, remembered her would-be lover and taped-on head.

"They've taken Dr. Newman to the hospital."

"He's very sick?"

"They needed a stretcher."

Francis ordered the portcullis raised. He dismounted, ready to scream, then ran forward, shoes thumping oak.

Mouzon Thu had left the key in the lock. But of course. Shed the unholiness as soon as possible. Francis ripped open the hatch, kept the key.

"Burne!" There was no Burne, naturally, not on the control deck, not in the cabins, not by the . . .

Eventually he started whimpering like his boyhood collie. He wasn't going home today.

BUILT BY A GERM-FREE CIVILIZATION, the Chimec pyramid lacked the fierce, nostril-drilling smells that Nearthlings associate with hospitals. No disinfectants, *that's* why this place has never seemed quite real, Francis thought as he moved down the clean, frescoed corridors, Huaca puffing behind. It was the sort of foolish, out-of-context thought that typically came to him when, as now, he was delirious with gloom.

Outside the operating room, Tixo Mool studied a mural. An artist who hadn't fought in it offered a brutal, blood-spurting impression of the recent Neurovorean War. The Quetzalians were dry, the Brain Eaters still wet.

"My son was in that," said Mool as Francis approached.

"He's probably alive. Only forty-three died."

"Forty-three," Mool repeated dully. He seemed to be in a trance. "Forty-four if we lose the Nearthling. How did it happen?"

"War wound. Is it infected?"

"I remember what a war wound is. *You* had one, Lost-wax, the first day we met. That was on the whole a better day than today—before all this army business." He spun away from the mural, found himself staring at a wad of bandages. "Who's *this*?"

Huaca said his famous name.

"Clever idea you've got there, Mr. Yon, mummifying your

brilliant brain." Mool's vacant gaze returned to the mural. "It's *worse* than infected."

"I know the word," said Francis. "Gangrene."

"Where was *Darwin* coming from?"

"Arete."

"The planet must favor *Clostridium welchii*."

"And we brought them into the ship?"

Mool grimaced. "There they stayed, waiting. We don't see much gangrene here, Nearthling. What do you know?"

"Keep the wound clean. Trim the granulation tissue."

"We're doing that. The germs will still get to the blood."

"Cut the leg off," said Francis stiffly.

"That's what we've decided." Mool swung through the archway. Francis followed, bristling with the memory of that amazing day when he was carted here and Tez went into his brain.

The gallery was empty. Near the farthest door a flutist, this time a woman, arched her fingers and made music. Trying to look indispensable and productive, but obviously waiting for cues from Mool, the rangy young man who had assisted in Francis's ablation walked in circles around the padded table.

Francis approached, and the sight of his friend lying unconscious tore from him a brief, involuntary moan. This was not the real Burne, the juicy man of action, but a wasted shape in which the real Burne had once lived. At the moment drugged sleep spared him the pain of his infection. Protruding from the swollen depths of his thigh, a catheter poured cleansing fluids into a ferocious battle with necrosis.

"We're going to ablate the wound," said Mool, more compassionate than clinical. The nurse jumped and left, returning shortly with a cart of brilliant tools: scalpels, saws, icesticks.

"I can't watch this," Huaca announced from the archway.

Francis sighed. "Do your best, Mool. Quetzalia owes its freedom to this man."

"I'll do my best, but I hope you know we're on a desperate course. I also hope you know Burne Newman will not become our national hero."

"In the Vij Arena you said our studies were . . . Now I remember, you called them classics. You were right. Burne knew what he was doing."

"I'm afraid I've started to see the world Tez's way. Zolmec and backward tradition are not the same thing. There will be no statues to Burne Newman, not if I can help it."

"Hypocrite," said Francis, almost inaudibly.

"Yes," answered Mool with a wry smile. "But a harmless hypocrite—and less dogmatic than in earlier days."

"Not even a *small* statue?" a husky voice called from the gallery. Tez sauntered down an aisle, her left hand bouncing along a column of seats, her right clenching a bright invention. "I think he should be a doorstop, at least. Or a paperweight." With a cat's competence she vaulted the railing and dropped two meters to the stage. "He was quite a genius, really, when he pumped our best citizens full of bile and sent them off to war." She lifted her right hand. The blatant syringe, dark with noctus, made Francis choke.

"Throw that thing away!" he screamed.

"Soon, lover." Her lips parted, unsheathing her teeth. "I've been to the Temple of Tolca, and it would be scandalous to waste such a luscious dream." She pointed to the barrel. "*You're* in here, Francis. Look hard, and you'll see yourself confessing to a secret injection. This time you don't survive my wrath."

She tore at her sleeve, and it fell away like meat from bone. The men stared incredulous and immobile while the needle made its descent. "Going in is the best!"

"No!"

But the plunger was already traveling, bringing the moat

to her flesh. Finished, she slipped the syringe out, licked the needle. "Don't ever touch that stuff. It feels too good and it answers to no one." She displayed her deltoid, which was multiply perforated, like a shower nozzle. As she touched the newest hole, a welt began to bloom.

Mool retreated, trembling, toward Francis. "What is she going to do?"

"I believe she intends to kill you," he said, sucking air through his teeth. "You'd best leave."

But already Tez was at the instrument cart. She chose a fine obsidian scalpel. Francis shuddered. He had seen this particular knife before, the night he sneaked into the temple. He had seen her use it—on Mool.

Tez charged. There was a slash, an astonished shout, and Mool staggered away. The incision in his side was shallow and as yet painless.

"Lostwax, can't you control her?"

I'll try, he thought, and ran for the flutist, a reckless plan firing his brain. He saw that Tez had circled back to the instrument cart.

"Why don't you defend yourself?" she screeched at Mool. "A saw is worth plenty against a knife."

She sprang forward, guiding scalpel toward neck, when the corner of the ablation table caught her robe. The inertia pulled the syringe from her hand—*smash*, it was a hundred glassy shards—while the now off-target knife burrowed deep into Mool's left shoulder, staying in her hand as, bleeding, moaning, he lost hope and balance.

She kneeled, both palms wrapped around the handle: the sacrificial position. Mool writhed like a smashed worm. The blade arced toward the glass ceiling.

There was a thud.

The blade went down—not swiftly, not intelligently, but in a pathetic little jag that ended on the stone floor. Tez toppled forward and stayed still. Francis lifted the bent flute away. Blood encircled the mouthpiece.

"I'm taking her to the ship," said Francis, crestfallen.

"Help me, Huaca." He scanned the archway, then the whole room. Huaca had vanished.

The flutist and the rangy nurse swarmed over Mool, dressing his wounds. He motioned them away and regained his feet. "Will this be the end of it?"

"It's an unusual case," said Francis.

Tez was groaning her way awake. On Francis's orders the flutist poured a liquid sedative down her throat. Instantly she was seized by a sleep that the bottle label claimed would last ten hours. Skeptical that the sedative would be so soporific for a noctus addict, Francis tied her hands and feet with bandages.

"I owe you my life," said Mool.

"And nearly your death. It was my idea to . . . humanize her."

Mool touched his wet shoulder. "We'll have Zoco finish the ablation."

"When will Burne be fit to travel?"

"He shouldn't go piloting spaceships for an opoch at least."

"Suppose *I* flew us home?"

"We'd be willing to release him in two days, no sooner. He'll need absolute rest. You must change his dressings constantly."

"Yes," said Francis slowly. He picked the bloody scalpel off the floor and put it in his coat pocket.

"Why do you want that?" asked Mool.

"I feel a sudden need of weapons."

SHE WOULD HAVE KILLED HIM! The fact was as indisputable as it was unthinkable. Hunched beneath Tez, Francis descended the steps of the pyramid. To prying bystanders he feebly dismissed her unconsciousness as a fainting spell. Her bound hands and feet received no explanation at all. She fit snugly into the wagon, where, blankets shaped around her, she became just another load traveling down from Cuz or Uxco. There were no more questions. The crowds bustled across the plaza, trying to get some-place warm.

Would have killed him! Mounting the wagon, Francis pointed his lipoca toward Kinship Road. Hooves rattled on frozen stone. The road ran east, to Aca, and west, to the forest and the wall. Killed him! He went west.

The road undulated, the trees moved up and down like flotsam, and Francis brooded. He saw himself as the con-victed sorcerer in one of his favorite kinepix, *Mind Things*. He was lying in the dirt, each of his four limbs roped to a different horse, each horse pointed in a different direction.

The quarter of him that loved Tez wanted to fly her to Nearth right away, leaving Burne behind. The quarter of him that pitied Tez wanted to return to Olo and hold her in his arms while she raged. The quarter that feared Tez wanted to abandon the wagon and disappear before she could wake up and attack. The quarter that understood Tez realized how his presence only aggravated her disease, so that the best course might be simply to lock her up like the werewolf in *Mind Things* until the noctus passed from her brain.

Assuming the noctus *would* pass from her brain.

Reining up before the Temple of Tolca, he jumped from the wagon and hoisted Tez over his shoulder. The snow corrupted his balance. Stumbling, he carried his curi-ous burden toward the bridge, and the gatekeeper asked, "Who's that?"

"The last neurovore," Francis replied. "Raise your portcullis."

His habitat had not changed: bunk, desk, pantry, moni-tor, porthole, insects on the walls. He eased her toward the bunk. She looked miraculously innocent, and as his lips moved into hers he felt he was kissing a child.

From the galley he commandeered a shiny assortment of cans, carrying them back to his pantry. They comprised half a dozen square meals, enough to imprison Tez for two days. After two days of abstinence, he hoped, she would be rid of her addiction, and the overdoses would start becoming subject to the appetites of phages and what Vij's notes had called "the normal processes of enzyme, gland, and duct."

By way of convincing himself that optimism was proper, he decided to place his beetle and his clothing on board. He returned to the wagon, shouldered the knapsack, and noticed that the gatekeeper was approaching, suspicion and anti-Nearthling sentiments printed on her face.

"Why are you still here?" Francis asked. "Quetzalia has no more need of guards."

"Habits aren't like people, Dr. Lostwax. They can't be killed instantly." Oh, the layers of sarcasm. "I have a feeling that after this fat machine of yours is gone, I'll be told to raise the bridge."

"You'll just have to lower it again. One day Quetzalia will have *colonies* out there."

"Possibly," she grunted.

Once back in his cabin, Francis went to the desk and, locating electrostylus and flimsy, began to write. He smoothed out the note, pinning it in place with the scalpel on one side, the electrostylus on the other—a construction she could not fail to notice upon rousing.

I have brought you to *Darwin*, the one place in Quetzalia with a lock. The cabin is sealed beyond even your capacity to wreck things. Expect me back exactly thirty-five hours after you awake. Burne will be recovered by then, and we can go home. The pantry holds meat. Feed yourself and the *Cortexclavus*. It is summer on Nearth now, and the roller coasters are rolling.

Love,
Francis

A bit of dried Mool blood fell from the scalpel, dotting the *i* in "Francis."

I should never have left the bug with her, Francis thought as his lipoca wagon bounced into the sun-flecked forest. Once she cuts her bonds, she'll put the scalpel to Ollie. What better way to inaugurate vengeance on the man who depraved her?

He was about to turn around when a rival theory suggested itself. Yes, she'll knife the bug. But might such an action—her one actual kill—might it be enough to drain the last of her anger? Might the corkscrew beetle be the sacrificial lamb that will save Quetzalia? If restoring Tez means losing Ollie, I've struck a generous bargain with the moat.

Or am I grasping at straws?

He decided to continue toward Tepec, and, as Iztac seeped through the leaf-sieve above his head, he found himself saying, aloud: God of the sun, don't let her torture him. Use your surgeon's skills, Tez. Burst his beetle's heart and be done with it.

24

PALMS DOWN, then up, then down, Minnix Cies warmed his hands over the steamy ghost rising from his tea. His father, Aras, crossed the kitchen, the cottage's one grand room, and spoke yet another variation on it's-good-to-have-you-back-son. This time it was "Lix and Lapca will go out of their minds when they see you."

"I bought them a present," said Minnix, "a desert gem that hums." He never did figure out why his parents, normally quite reliable in their unpredictability, had capitulated to convention and given his twin brothers alliterative names. Right now the boys were in Tepec, helping a decrepit aunt begin her hibernation.

"Lapca beat me for the first time last week. A Queen's Indian Defense."

"They'll be back for Legend Eve?"

"Yes. We're hoping to make it a real *family* time." Aras pressed his ancient nose against the kitchen's solitary window. Outside, an early morning sun hopped across the sharp mountains.

They were a tough breed, Aras and his wife, and without doubt the oldest Quetzalians to merit the prestigious epithet of "Cuz year-rounder." While the majority fled south, the Cieses stayed behind and plied their trade—cutting and selling the long-burning fuel called firemoss, the only thing that made a Cuzian winter survivable.

Minnix tested his tea—too hot. "I don't *want* to miss it, Father. I love to see the Light City, and the twins' eyes." Suddenly he jumped. "Here's the solution! You can all come with me to Aca."

"You *know* that's unreasonable." He placed a great spindly hand on the isinglass. "Cuz is counting on us."

"Let them find their own goddam fuel."

"Maybe next year we'll retire." There was no conviction in Aras's voice. "Meanwhile, it keeps us on our feet, and we're rather fond of snow."

"One day those feet will collapse, and we won't find you till spring thaw."

"Maybe next year," Aras repeated, same voice.

"Then it's a stalemate. The first debates will be the most important. If I'm not in Aca by next week, Nazra won't know Minnix Cies from the man in the moon. Where does that come from? 'The man in the moon.' "

"Earth had a moon, I think. I don't know who the man was. Luta should have one. After you've got Nazra in your palm, tell him to arrange a moon."

"It's no joke. Aca's postwar policies are unbelievably important—the most pivotal Nazra will ever formulate. If we don't start claiming the desert right away, building a city, a road, *something*—a hotel—the psychological consequences will be dire."

"Always the Antistasist, aren't you? I should have raised a firemoss cutter. *Then* we'd get you home for Legend Eve."

Minnix struck a debater's pose. "The priests will say: Let's pretend it never happened. Raise the bridges. Ban all commemoration of this war. But what that really says is: Forty-three Quetzalians died for no reason. A tradition of peace was ended for no reason. Then, in fifty or thirty or only fifteen years some visionary country boy, my own child perhaps, will say: Listen to me. This time I've *found a reason* to eat noctus. If we can bring ourselves to bury this hoary religion and build spaceships and forge hypodermic needles, why, there's a whole goddam *galaxy* to conquer."

"Practice your speeches if you want, Mannix, but it's certainly not politics we're disagreeing about, not today. To tell you the truth, we were afraid you'd come back convinced that Zolmec is obsolete."

Minnix dropped into the chair and sipped tea. "No," he said wearily, "Zolmec is strong. If I had it to do over again, I'm not sure I'd go."

"What was it like?" Aras said slowly, easing away from the window.

Minnix sniffed down steam. "I murdered four at least, maybe five or six—I didn't watch where my arrows went. I saw people fall and scream. And it's not enough that they hit the ground. You must *make* them die. I had a sword for that. More efficient than an ax. It's especially good with children—like a dog." He laughed, stopped abruptly. "You don't *want* me home for Legend Eve, Father." He was almost sobbing.

Aras rushed forward and threw both arms around his son, as if holding a pile of firemoss together. "Nonsense. We civilians are tarnished too. In the Temple of Tolca *everyone* is a soldier. I've beaten your brothers to *death*." He released his grip and headed for the stove. "The point is, how do you feel *now*?"

"I feel . . . human. As if I'd never been dosed."

"Good." He slopped tea into a ceramic mug. "Evidence?"

"Coming home my lipoca lost a shoe. The blacksmith kept me waiting. Not only that—I'm sure the bill was too high. I took him to the tavern and bought him a drink."

"Good. Everything is as usual."

"Yes. In seven days the opoch changes."

"You'll go to the temple again."

"And take him to the tavern again. I'll drown him in beer. After that I leave for Aca."

Whistling across his tea, Aras retraced his steps to the window. "What about the other soldiers? Has the noctus worn off completely?"

"No evidence for believing otherwise."

"I'm asking because your mother, who as you know is something of a witch, had a dream last night. To be blunt, she thinks there's to be more violence—murder. Minnix, could a neurovore have escaped the massacre?"

"Possibly. But we're still a fortified nation. I was one of the last to cross the Northern Drawbridge, and I saw them raise it again."

"It's probably nothing. But promise me you'll be wary on the road to Aca."

"I'll avoid all strangers who say they intend to kill me."

Aras took a big swallow of tea. "It might be wise, son, to avoid your own kind as well."

FOUR HAD ENTERED. That much he could tell. One, a tall female, was almost certainly Vaxcala. Beyond, a second visitor stood muted by shadows. The sad heap in the chair hinted of Huaca Yon. Near the window a round man waited.

Francis stirred. An empty bottle sprouted in silhouette from the windowsill. The gray pounding in his head told where the wine had recently been; the pressure in his bladder told where it was. Forcing an arm up through the blanket, he beheld his coat sleeve. At least I'll greet them dressed, he thought.

The fatness at the window moved. "Would you object to some sun?"

Francis recognized Nazra's earthquake voice. "Bring it on," he said, yawning.

The governor drew back the curtain, and Iztac's jade rays soared into the bedroom. Mid-morning, Francis decided. I must go to Tez. "Is that Mool back there?"

Vaxcala stepped aside. "Your friend woke up three hours ago," said Mool, a sling-cradled arm bulging beneath his robe. "He alternates severe depression with brave talk about prosthetics."

Francis's memory got to work. Happy pictures flooded

back. Spending the previous day at the Hospital of Chimec, hearing from Dr. Zoco that the ablation had gone perfectly, seeing Burne in peaceful one-legged sleep, returning to Olo and its wine cellar.

"On Nearth it's an advanced art."

"Depression?"

"Prosthetics. Depression, too."

"We're not here to discuss *Burne*," said Huaca huffily. The bandage was off. Scabs swarmed like insects upon his face.

"I didn't think so. An impressive delegation. Science, politics, religion . . . and talk."

"Philosophy," Huaca corrected.

Vaxcala approached, entwining her beetle-leg fingers. She spoke in low, getting-to-the-point tones. "Last night two people were murdered. One of my own priests. Then, at the Oltac farm, a little girl. I notified the governor."

As Francis sat up in bed, the most terrifying of Vaxcala's words took on a monstrous tangibility, so that *people* and *murdered* were now crawling, rapacious, worm-furrowed life-forms, set free in the room, seeking him out . . . *people* . . . God of the sun, my name will be for Quetzalians the darkest of profanities. *To Lostwax someone* will mean to ablate his colon without anesthesia . . . *murdered!*

His tongue thickened and sagged forward, and he wondered whether he would succumb first to nausea or to fainting, but somehow he worked his way back into awareness.

Nazra was saying, "We entered your cabin at sunrise."

"It was locked," Francis protested feebly.

"We used the porthole. The viewbubble was cut away."

"How did this happen, Francis Lostwax?" asked Vaxcala.

For Francis there was no mystery. "The *Cortexclavus* can drill through solid rock. Solid macroplastic too, evidently."

"Tez is smarter than you, Nearthling," Huaca sneered. "She got out of your stupid jail. What will you do *now?*"

"I assume from this visit that the four of you have an

answer to that question." He peeled back the blankets and stumbled toward the center of the room.

Vaxcala resumed in a raspy voice. "This morning on Tranquillity Road a zookeeper was found crushed by his own lipoca wagon."

"Is this sinking in, doctor?" asked Mool. "She has become a germ to which we have no resistance. All Quetzalia is at her mercy."

"Tez is not a *germ*."

A sulfurous glow encircled Mool's eyes. "She is a germ—a loathsome plague that could obliterate this world."

Nazra cut in: "You're the only one who can save us."

"I'll go find her," said Francis, wincing. "It's the damn drug. You understand that, right? It's not Tez."

"Ride north," said Nazra. "It won't be hard to track her, except for the cold. Tonight she'll be in the suburbs. In four days, Hostya. In fifteen—Cuz. Cuz is a *city*."

"I'll recapture her. I'll take her back to Nearth. She's still . . . everything." The words came surely, spontaneously, and despite his despair he experienced great satisfaction in speaking his heart.

"I doubt that she'll go willingly," said Huaca. "You may have to hurt her."

"Hurt her? I *love* her."

Huaca placed his delicate hands on an oil lantern. "Damn it, Nearthling, so do I!" With an angry flourish he hurled the lantern through the window, spraying isinglass into the morning.

Silence shrouded the room. Eventually Francis made a wild, incomprehensible gesture and spoke. "Why don't we simply inject a Quetzalian volunteer with noctus?"

"How?" asked Mool. "*You* saw the syringe get smashed."

"Yes, but there's a second, the one Burne took into the desert."

Vaxcala sighed. "This is a foul business. The injections were supposed to end with the war." Her sorry eyes fell on Nazra. "What do *you* suggest?"

The governor lifted the wine bottle and crunched it into the isinglass fragments on the windowsill. "I want Dr. Lost-wax to get us that syringe," he said hoarsely.

"THERE IS NO SYRINGE." Burne's voice suggested a *Cortex-clavus* drilling through slate. "Is the diabetes back?"

"No, it's not for insulin." The window lured Francis's eye away from his friend. Outside, the hospital gardens slept under gathering snowdrifts.

"It got destroyed."

"Totally?"

Burne said nothing.

Destroyed! Moaning in disappointment, Francis walked past walls that contained no paintings. The whole room, in fact, was notably unadorned, like a crown pitted of its jewels. By putting Burne here, was the staff expressing its contempt? "I wanted to inject someone with noctus."

"Your girl friend?"

A lie would be best now. "Yes." For an instant he looked straight at where the bedsheet should have swelled but didn't.

"I thought she was missing," said Burne, likewise eyeing his asymmetry.

"She was found."

"Any other news? What do the locals think of my campaign?"

Yes—lies were best. "Burne, you're the hero of Quetzalia. There's talk of a statue."

"A statue, that's perfect. I wonder if they'll—"

Francis cut him off. "Burne, how did it get destroyed?"

"It was in a lipoca. The poor jackass fell over and crushed it."

"I don't suppose anyone saved the needle?"

"There was a *war* on, Lostwax."

Francis poked at his chitzal scar. The matter was settled, then, horribly settled. "I'll be traveling for a few weeks, north, perhaps as far as Cuz. When I get back you'll be well enough to fly us home."

"Will she be coming?"

"I hope so."

"Your relationship is not exactly *simple*, is it?"

"Maybe I'd be happier with a Nearthling."

Burne groped for a pot of cuiclo tea. "Why this trip to Cuz?"

Francis explained that "a predator" was headed there.

"A neurovore?"

"That's one way to put it."

"But the massacre was total." Resentment glared from Burne's face.

Francis kept allowing his gaze to wander furtively across the bedsheet. "Must be a vagabond."

"I wish I could help you. If only my erections went south instead of north, I'd have a leg to stand on."

"You're taking your loss very well."

Burne filled his mug in awesome silence. "You'll need a weapon, Lostwax. When I had your job, I used *Cortexclavus*."

"He escaped."

"My sword is back at the ship."

"No, I don't want a sword."

"What will you use?"

Francis shuffled sheepishly. "Promise me you won't laugh?"

The tea soured Burne's face. He nodded.

"I'm going to use love."

Burne was still laughing when Francis left the room.

25

NORTH OF HOSTYA a great granite spire, chiseled with the names of four population centers, rises from the earth like a tombstone. The positions of the names tell the traveler which road will take him to the fishing village of Uxco, which to the mountain metropolis of Cuz, which to the seacoast capital of Aca, and which to the sacred place called Tepec. In the opoch of Timlath the spire is particularly purposeful, for the roads themselves vanish completely under snow, though often as not the spire also vanishes, and the traveler must pause and rub it like a magic lamp until his destination appears.

Alone and cold, Francis stretched forth a gloved hand. Cakes of snow dropped away like scabs, revealing Tepec. Cuz, he remembered, was north-northwest, so he kicked his way to a likely spot where his rubbing brought forth a C— the C in Cuz, not Aca, unless, of course, he were lost. The proof lay in further rubbing.

A human eye appeared, staring from beneath a stuck lid. Francis fell over and lay gasping in his snow-mold. God of peace, it's true! I'm tracking a murderer!

Throwing a hand over his eyes, he raised his boot and flailed at the corpse. Blue chunks struck his foreleg. He pulled his hand away and abused himself with a glance.

The glance told that the corpse was young, male, and lashed to the spire by Tez's wool scarf. It told worse. The top of the head had been plundered like a nutshell. Snow collected in the hideous cavity.

He glanced again. Above the ragged murm, the letters *u* and *z* lay varnished by frozen blood.

Nauseated, he trampled toward his lipoca, mounting on the third try. He started for where the dead eyes looked— the awesome Ripsaw Mountains. As the peaks grew closer, his mind hopped crazily from thoughts of Tez to thoughts of Burne to thoughts of how the next visitor to the spire would find at its base an icy mound of undigested breakfast.

BLUE. BLUE ON BLUE. Blue that reached maddeningly in all directions. Glistening blue that caught the far, paltry sun and flung it squarely into Francis's pinpoint eyes. The lipoca loathed the blue, refused to walk at a productive clip until Francis blinded it with a double-wrapped scarf. The blue kilometers trotted by.

At night Francis would pound the blue until it became a hard platform on which to spread his groundcloth and pitch his tent. Whether in Arete's cozy swamps or Luta's feverish deserts, camping had never been for him anything but a festival of inconvenience. But now he found himself admitting its romance, and he could even understand how Burne managed to perceive the collateral discomforts as fun.

Francis did not doubt that Nazra was correct in naming Cuz as Tez's goal. But where the governor had used the same crude connect-the-dots logic that opochs ago brought Burne to his neurovore, Francis had tried entering Tez's disordered brain and reconstructing her reasons. Above everything towered her guilt. Flee, it said. Carry your drives to a place of such peerless desolation—the southern jungles, the eastern oceans, the northern mountains—that you can do your race no further harm. Yet the drives would remain. Tez knew this. Building insidiously, they would one day fall upon her like rabid dogs. She would need people then—not a lone jungle ecologist or even a few Uxco fish catchers. She would need Cuz. Francis promised himself she would never get there.

After nine days they were among mountains. The self-pitying lipoca strained audibly as it ascended the crags. Nights proved equally unsatisfactory to the creature. The campsite was inevitably a cave, and the lipoca quaked as the animate night poured arcane scuttlings from the dark recesses into one ear and wolf howls from the outside forest into the other.

Aided by his lantern, Francis one night discovered that the scuttlers were some sort of mutant chitzal, their bodies bristled with venomous quills. Luckily, the light sent them into full retreat, leaving him to meditate on a range of incandescent stalagmites. The stalagmites evoked memories of poor Luther, then poor Kappie, whom he had loved unrequitedly, then poor Tez, whom he still loved in spite of everything. At this very moment Tez was alive somewhere, sleeping or, more likely, awake and thinking. Always thinking. If you want to understand people, Francis mused, you must realize that they never stop thinking.

And then he pushed deeper into the cave, half believing that he need turn just one more corner, slither under just one more slab, and there she would be, ready to talk and make glorious love.

CUSPID-LIKE, the tall mountain erupted from the forest. The lipoca balked at crossing the timberline. Francis dismounted, tethering the beleaguered animal to a tree. He stuffed some firemoss chunks in his coat and for balance hung a lantern from the opposite pocket. He found a dead branch, called it a staff, and began, step by step, to narrow the distance between himself and the sun.

Late afternoon found him on the mountaintop, calves throbbing, lungs feeling scraped. In the distance lay his reward, a sun-boggled glimpse of Cuz's pyramids. Spanned by a footbridge, a chasm yawned in fierce prologue to the snowbound metropolis. A footbridge—perfect! There he would wait.

He stacked his firemoss on the ground, brought a lit match near. Iztac-green flames shot high, then settled into a pulsating glow. He looked west. Peeking between each pair of mountains, the Temple of Tolca weaved along its sacred river. Snow crowned the gateway of the Northern Drawbridge.

Francis lay down. The thought of having come so far warmed him no less than the firemoss. He had earned his nap twice over.

THICK SHADOWS CLUTCHED the mountains when Francis awoke. A northern aura spoke of abundant fuel in Cuz. He looked toward the low sun, saw another, more compacted aura near the timberline. Tez's campfire? He blinked. No, it was too large. He blinked again. A cottage.

Squalls of snow followed him down the mountain. His oil lantern forged a clear bright path to the lipoca's tree. But there was no lipoca. Wrong tree? Blue drifts rushed toward him like lava.

Holding the lantern aloft, he inspected the trunk. Stiff with frozen saliva, a length of tether shot forward, ending in a mass of teethmarks.

The storm laughed howlingly at Francis. Setting down the lantern, he used both palms to push his collar tight against his hurting ears. Gradually they got warm. Food gone, pack gone, it would be madness to head straight for Cuz. Where was that damn cottage? Northwest? He marched into the screaming night.

For two hours Francis fought the lashing, tentacled blue. His teeth chattered beyond his capacity to stop them. The wind carved him up.

Suddenly, wonderfully, the cottage was there, beaming through the storm like a huge friendly jack-o'-lantern. Heedless of the wind, Francis began to run, kicking the drifts apart before they could suck him down. He reached a squat oak door and slammed it with his palm.

The plump woman who answered was exactly what Francis needed, all smiles and cheer and you're-just-in-time-for-tea. She was well past forty and didn't seem to mind.

"I'm going to Cuz," said Francis.

"Not tonight you aren't. It'll be a blizzard before it's done." She led him through a negligible parlor to a kitchen boasting roominess and a firemoss stove. "Have a seat. Tea?"

"Yes." Francis killed his lantern and flopped into a leather chair. On the table, an open, handbound copy of *Tales from the Id* prompted him to assume that the woman had been reading when he knocked.

"There's also hot chocolate."

"Tea is fine." As soon as he said this, he knew his preference was hot chocolate. But he also knew that, had he requested hot chocolate, he would have wanted tea. He laughed at himself. It was good to be here.

She pranced to the stove and unhooked two cups. "Going home for the holidays?"

"I'm Francis Lostwax. Does that mean anything to you?"

"It means they made fun of you at school." Steam hissed out of her little kettle. She plopped two tea bags into their respective cups, flooded one bag with hot water.

"I went to school on Nearth."

"Nearth! God of the brain—the spaceman! That name gives you away. Why don't you call yourself Talo Cies like *I* do? It's a privilege to serve you tea, Dr. Lostwax. Are you sick of answering questions about your planet? The twins will pester you."

"I'm tracking a neurovore."

Talo froze while filling the second cup, and the water went all over. "Sorry," she said, recovering. "That word . . ."

"Ummm," said Francis knowingly.

"Many days ago I dreamed of violence. A murder in Tepec."

"There have been others since then. I believe she—it—is headed for Cuz."

Still unnerved, Talo piloted the steaming teacup over to Francis. She gestured broadly. "We'll put you here in the kitchen. The bedroll snuggles right between the stove and the wall. Warmest spot on the planet."

"You're very kind."

"God of the sun, I've *got* to take care of you. . . . I mean, you're the only one who . . . That Brain Eater could eventually kill us all."

"That's something of an exaggeration."

"This happened once before. You saved us then, too." She was back at the stove, replenishing the kettle from a cistern.

"No, it was Burne Newman. And please don't assume I'm going to save you. I'm merely . . . looking into the matter."

"Oh, but you *must* save us," she said, mingling sweetness and urgency. "If not you, then Dr. Newman."

"Burne's in the Hospital of Chimec."

"A war wound?"

"Yes. He'll recover." The wind pounded brutally on the door. It seemed to be at this cottage and no place else.

"Our son was in the war."

"How did he like it?" The minute the words were out, Francis felt inept.

"Actually it made him vomit," said Talo matter-of-factly. "Minnix has gone to Aca. Plans to tell the governor a thing or two."

Without warning, an icy rod of fear pushed into Francis. He thought: Think fast, Lostwax. "I . . . I believe I may have seen your son in Aca." He had to know, had to. "What does he look like?"

Across the room drawers rattled, and Talo was soon displaying a small portrait. Francis's hand closed around it.

The brainless corpse at the crossroads had a large, un-
gainly nose. Minnix's was stately and thin. The corpse had
ballooning cheeks. Minnix's plunged. Still, the face seemed
familiar. Then he remembered: Minnix Cies was the fiery
Antistasist who had encouraged his party to join the war.
Reality, evidently, had altered his views.

Francis reported that he hadn't seen Minnix after all.
"You mentioned twins."

"They're hibernating upstairs with Father Cies. Everybody had a gruesome day delivering firemoss in Cuz." She
pointed to an opowood ladder affixed beside the doorframe,
then swung suddenly into the parlor.

Francis's tea-warmed voice followed her. "Any trouble in
the city?"

She called: "If there were do you think we'd be so tran-
quil now? And a lucky thing we are, because tomorrow
night Iztac visits and *nobody* gets much sleep."

"Iztac?"

Talo returned, a large bedroll bulking before her like a
pregnancy. "That's what the children believe. It's a *tradition*. You don't have Legend Eve on Nearth?"

Francis made an *O* of his mouth, drew up tea. "No. We
have Halloween. This sounds better."

"Iztac—that is, Father Cies and I—Iztac builds a Light
City in the parlor. Too bad you can't stay." She unfurled the
bedding. It was voluptuously inviting.

"Will you wake me at dawn?" asked Francis. Talo
nodded. "And one more thing. If anybody else knocks on
your door tonight, let *me* answer it."

FRANCIS STAYED AFTER ALL. He awoke to find the blizzard at
a peak of rage, rattling the cottage to its core. In Talo's
words, "If you leave now and the wind hurls you over a
cliff, the neurovore wins by default."

Seeing Talo with her husband, Francis thought of book-
ends. Aras Cies's fat places, like his wife's, did not strike

the observer as unconsidered superfluities: they were necessary components of a design. He sang while he made breakfast, Talo providing the choruses.

The eminent odor of cured meat on flame brought Lix
and Lapca down the ladder and across the kitchen. On
Nearth the holovision industry would have instantly seized
upon these two charmers and used them to sell something.
Not quite nine years old, whirling toward adolescence like
bright sturdy tops, the boys reminded Francis of his own
Barry. Surely Barry would have become like Lix and Lapca,
all smart and eager, even with that damn disease. Francis
struggled to change his thoughts, decided to ponder the
usual questions about twins. Which was the more talented?
Which the more assertive? Which the more envied?

As the morning wore cozily on, it became clear that these
problems resisted one-word answers. Lix was garrulous and
engaging enough, but when Lapca spoke a touch of profun-
dity hung delicately in the air. Lix played the flute and
knew five epic poems by heart, but Lapca could think six
chess moves ahead. Lix was prone to a precocious cynicism
and had difficulty speaking his true mind. Lapca was always losing things around the cottage and grew forlorn
without good reasons.

The afternoon found Francis trying to answer the twins'
questions about Nearth and the rest of the solar system. He
kept wishing he were a salty raconteur, not so much because his ego needed a spellbound audience but because it
would be a nice treat for these kids, whose lives were so
totally barren of kinepix and holovision and other slick
diversions. He spoke of Halloween and roller coasters,
blasterball trading cards and cloying robot toys—the whole
mountain of Fudge—and of bigger things. Planet Arete.
Planet Kritonia, with its morgs churning through silent
seas. As the session ended, Lapca said, "That was very entertaining, Dr. Lostwax." He said it with such guileless enthusiasm that Francis wanted to hug him and cry.

During dinner the twins announced that in their recent and unanimous opinion Iztac would *not* be descending from the sky this night. In fact, the whole holiday was an illusion, all right for *little* children but not for them. This particular Legend Eve, Lix and Lapca fully intended to assist their parents in the construction of the Light City. They'd even drawn up plans.

Aras leaned back from his porkchops, carrying a teacup with him. "Talo, it would appear that our sons are growing up."

She tut-tutted in mock solemnity. "And we always said, 'It can't happen here.' "

"We don't *reject* the legend," said Lix. "It's still . . . how did you put it last night, Lapca?"

Lapca smiled an elf's smile. "It's still of profound allegorical significance."

"I don't understand anything I've heard for the last twenty minutes," said Francis, spearing a potato.

Lix began to explain, his family supplying details and digressions.

The boy told of a bygone age when Planet Luta harbored Light People, beings of pure energy, greatest and grandest of whom was Iztac. For the Light People, pure matter was as abstract and elusive a reality as pure consciousness would be for humans. But gradually, under Iztac's spell, the Light People exercised their science and achieved a tentative hold on the tangible. They wrought a vast soaring city upon Luta, a city half of thought and half of substance, half of particles and half of waves. A City of Light.

One day Luta spoke to Iztac, warning her of an imminent destiny. The present age was ending. Matter was the dawning truth. Soon the Light People would be frozen in time and banished to the sky, there to become stars, while rocks, then animals, then sentient animals claimed the planet.

Iztac grew despondent at the thought of losing her city.

"I can offer you one consolation," said Luta. "When you

are thrown outward, I shall try to catch you and hold you near. Then, once a year, while the humans sleep, you can return, rebuild your city, and invite your people in. Once again pure energy will walk your milky avenues and lodge in your glass palaces. But by the following night your city must be gone, and you must all return to the sky."

Iztac agreed, and ever since then, on Legend Eve . . .

As RECONSTRUCTED in the parlors of Quetzalia, Light Cities owed their existence to a sweet-smelling, transparent substance called zarc, a distillation from the hearts of eels. When heated to two hundred degrees Celsius, zarc acquired a host of uncanny properties. Francis watched in awe as Talo, Aras, and the children stabbed the steaming pots with hollow reeds, then dueled the air to make the gossamer batter splash outward in great dripping sheets. Solidifying as it cooled, zarc assumed whatever strange geometry the reeds had traced.

Aras erected the city's walls while Lix, following his blueprints, poured the principal highways. Lapca blew into his reed and out flew a smooth conical tower. Talo tried a circular motion, spinning a fat castle. She handed the reed to her guest. Delighted, eager to experiment, Francis jammed the northwest quarter with an approximation of a Nearth roller coaster. By midnight the city had grown clear to the ceiling and taken over most of the parlor.

Now the Light People came out, fifty candles stuck behind windows and strung along avenues. The oil lamps were extinguished, and the city's crystalline luminosity suffused the cottage. Most wonderful were the shadows, intricate patterns flicking across ceilings, spiderwebbing down walls, changing as the tiny flames winked.

Everybody just watched.

In the gathering quiet Francis realized that the once hysterical blizzard had fallen to a low, intermittent moan. Opening the door, he was momentarily surprised to see that the Light People had not really abandoned the sky. Below the stars a great rolling blueness stretched into the frigid dark. The snow no longer fell.

"I should go," Francis said somberly.

"Rotten idea." Talo was at his side. "With those drifts—you take a wrong step and it's just like quicksand. Wait for morning."

Francis lingered by the door, petting the nailed-up fur that served as insulation. "All right, I'll leave at sunup. An hour *before* sunup."

With these words the Cies family scattered to assorted nooks around the cottage, returning behind piles of happily ribboned packages. Like pilgrims seeking entrance, gifts accumulated before the city's waxy gates.

Aras reached forward, drew out a red cylinder, passed it smilingly to Francis. "This one's for you."

"May I open it now?" The package was heavy.

"Open it!" said Lix.

"We want to see!" said Lapca.

Francis pulled at the paper and a blade appeared, shiny and perfect even by candlelight. "It's a firemoss knife," Aras explained. "It cuts fuel."

"Tomorrow night you'll have a splendid fire," said Lapca.

Francis balanced the knife on his index finger. The handle, alive with intricate and fantastic animals, brought a sad memory of Tez's obsidian scalpel. "I don't have anything for you," he said, distressed.

"Just deliver us from neurovores," said Talo.

At midnight Aras went to the kitchen and returned with two tureens, a white broth sloshing over their rims. Mugs were distributed, and everybody dipped in and drank. Francis learned the broth's name—rizka—and it was hot and thick and sinfully sugared.

Lix brought out his flute, and soon the family was happily bleating madrigals of some sort. For the first time in his life, Francis experienced no self-consciousness about holding back from a songfest. He sat listening to the music, enjoying it, feeling fine except when the thought of Tez would suddenly drill into him and he had to spend a minute getting it out. The rizka helped—not because it was intoxicating but because it wasn't intoxicating. Rizka was so damn agreeable in its lack of alcohol that it made you drunk. He thought perhaps he would lift his ban on souvenirs and take the recipe back to Nearth.

BEFORE FALLING ASLEEP that night, Francis flipped over on his stomach and peered through the open kitchen doorway toward the radiant metropolis. He stared fixedly at its fragile towers, its high yolky walls, its brilliant tapered citizens. The candles were not noticeably lower and the gift-mound retained its gay spectrum. There is a bewildering goodness, here, he thought, a goodness that must survive. Quetzalians share tea with perfect strangers and through kind surprises send them off feeling not a little loved.

He had no belief that the Cies family envisioned him stabbing flesh as well as firemoss. For Francis the knife was nothing more nor less than his very first Legend Eve present.

26

ALWAYS HER DREAM was the same. In a vast tide the river made of hate surged from its bed and spilled across the land, leaving a trail of demolished cities and immaculate bones. Millions fled before the juggernaut—but not Tez. She stood her ground, shaking angry fists as a quicksilver wave leaped toward her. Then, suddenly, in midair the noctus froze solid as a mountain of coal.

From within came a tap-tapping. Something was pecking its way into the world.

Instantly an enormous human foetus, tall as a rearing lipoca, stood wet and round amid the chips of gall. Great blue eyes darted beneath a forehead bulging with infinite neurons. The mouth was moving. "*Father* killed me," said the foetus in a dull rasp. It raised a glistening finger. "It wasn't you."

Here the dream would end. Of Tez's five victims, only the aborted foetus returned at night. The others—the surly priest, the sniveling little scritch, the ugly wagon driver near Hostya, the vain troubador at the crossroads—waited for day, and when their memory came Tez stood screaming across the snowdrifts.

On Legend Eve the dream attacked twice, after which she awoke to find an early sun, uncommonly warm for Timlath, splashing across the cave floor. An odd appetite rose within her. It was not an appetite for food—not quite. Last night she had gorged herself on a stray lipoca. This appetite, seemingly unnameable, somehow concerned . . . a city? Yes! She was hungry for Cuz. Even in winter, Cuz harbored ten thousand lives.

Outside the cave, pack crooking her back, she got ready to resume her prowlings. Sniffing the frail gases that at these heights passed for atmosphere, she marched forward and sank to her waist in the soft remains of last night's blizzard. She cursed, conjectured: With luck I shall reach Cuz before sunset.

As morning became noon, Iztac's power grew. Everywhere the snowdrifts dissolved into bright rushing creeks. The trees, thick with icicles, drizzled steadily as any rainstorm. Another hour of this, Tez mused, and I may even see mud.

She saw no mud that day, only the monotonous grandeur of ice-glazed timber. The branches looked sealed in glass. Repeatedly she pondered the essential absurdity of weather. Very well, if crystalline flakes can fall from above, paralyzing all human commerce, then why doesn't the earth spit stones into the air? It occurred to her that she was no longer functioning as a scientist.

SPANNING THE CHASM like a huge grin, the footbridge to Cuz swayed in the winter wind. Forty meters below, a stream of melted snow shone and gurgled as it poured its way toward the Temple of Tolca. With raindrop delicacy a tracery of cord rose from the deck, securing the planks to bowed cables anchored at each end by stone towers. Beyond, the mountain city pushed its untempled pyramids into the sun.

Seeing the bridge for the first time in her life, Tez gave no thought to its lacy beauty. In her eye it was merely practical—it would take her to the ten thousand brains of Cuz. Even from here she sensed the throbbing meat.

Breaking into a run, she got nearly to the deck when a tower door creaked open. "Hello, Tez." Francis's voice ripped into her like a repulsive odor. He stepped forward, the last of the sun catching his tiny eyes. "I've been waiting for you."

She faced him without chagrin. In her small dark features Francis saw what he wanted to see. Not the lunatic who had almost killed Mool and had surely butchered the young man at the crossroads—and others—but the distinguished human he loved.

Francis said, "I'll give you a choice." He raked his palm down a jutting tower stone. "It's warm as tea in here. I've got some firemoss burning." Stepping forward, he touched the puffy front of her coat. "Let's get out of the cold. I'll show you how to be loving again."

"I don't want to be loving." She looked down at the defiling hand, and, coughing a fat wad of mucus into her mouth, spat with precision. "I want to be Nearthian."

"Very cute," said Francis, drawing the humiliated hand away.

"What's my other choice?"

"You can cross the bridge to Cuz. Do that, and I guarantee you'll—"

"Regret it?"

"Yes."

"Naturally you expect the moral thing from me. But I've learned something, friend. Morals don't count for a hell of a lot in this galaxy. I rank them somewhere between straight teeth and the ability to carry a tune. Mool killed my father and he goddam *deserves* whatever—"

"Did the man at the crossroads deserve to die too?"

"I can't have reasons for *everything* I do, Francis Bastard Lostwax. People die anyway." The words spewed through drooling lips. "Next time I'll pry open Mool's rib cage like I'm eating a hen."

Francis clutched his abdomen. The voice mouthing these grotesqueries came from some sick parody of Tez. Tez herself was already dead.

"Then the hell with you! Go to Cuz, stinking cannibal!"

She whirled around and approached the bridge with short crippled hops. Something—a premonition—made her stop.

"You've doctored that thing," she said, spitting onto the deck. "I *know* it."

Francis said nothing.

"Do you think it makes you any less a murderer if you don't touch me—if I just *fall* to my death?"

Silence.

She jerked a thumb toward her pack. "You have more reasons to warn me than you know. Once I carried your child, now I carry your beetle."

"A yarn worthy of Blind Umia."

"When I hit bottom, *Cortexclavus* does too. We both get crushed."

I've seen that evil look before, he thought, that snide bug-plundering look Robert Poogley used to wear. Suddenly Francis's hands were inside his coat, seeking the fire-moss knife.

Eyeing the cold erect blade, Tez felt her initial fear yield to a peculiar mix of anger and relish. "God, but I *hate* you!" At last she had found not just another victim, but a bona fide enemy.

The shadow of a cloud rolled across Francis's face. "Give me your pack." She merely grinned. Slowly he advanced, knife poised. "I'll *throw* this, Tez. God of the brain, I'll *throw* it."

Tez pondered his threat, judged it sincere. She hunched and wriggled until the pack swung freely on her forearm. Released, it thudded into the snow, turned over once, lay still.

"I just saved your roach's life, Lostwax. You *owe* me something." Her insistent foot thumped the nearest plank, as if in time to a dirge.

Francis stopped moving. Was that an Ollie noise he heard

coming from Tez's pack? He could not be certain, but in any event he was grateful for this excuse to postpone her murder. He spoke without hesitation. "Don't use the bridge. I sawed through the cables."

A smooth sphere of ice, large as an opotree stump and obviously as heavy, brushed Tez's calf. With a furious tug she uprooted it, raised it aloft in her strong surgeon's hands, heaved it like a shot put. Ice met wood, and the cables above her head joined the deck in a violent, audible swoop. Like a shutter in a hurricane, the bridge slammed the chasm and flew to pieces.

A foul laugh, escorted by spittle, leaped from Tez's throat. Francis heard her mutter something about a crafty bastard, and the next thing he knew she had turned and bolted west.

HE LOOKED AT HIS KNIFE HAND. It was shaking uncontrollably, as if connected to a badly injured brain. Would I have stabbed her? he wondered. Cut the flesh I used to love?

It came to him that if his next action did not consist of retrieving Tez's pack and giving chase, it might very well consist of walking toward Cuz and jumping into the chasm.

As he lifted the pack, its shape and heft convinced him that the vitreousteel cage was indeed his again. Entering the warm tower, he freed the cage and found himself staring into Ollie's right compound eye. The bug fluttered its antennae.

"Friend," he said, kicking the fire to death, "this is the worst day of my life."

Outside, Francis took a deep swallow of wind. The coldness pained his teeth. Decisively he rejected the gorge and ran to where the hulking drifts and onrushing dark had borne her away.

HE PASSED THE NEXT HOUR watching Tez's footprints, shallow pits made bottomless by the expiring light. Proceeding stealthily, imagining her ready to pounce behind every drift, he eventually reached the Temple of Tolca. Here he stopped, shivering forlornly as Iztac touched the earth and vanished.

Why the temple? Could it be that Tez was reformed, was returning to the Zolmec fold? The notion prospered for an instant, dying when he saw that she had not ascended the wall. Two meters from the nearest stairway her footprints veered sharply and followed the foundation to a huge indiscernible shape.

The temperature was dropping now. In the sky, The Toy Queen blazed forth. Francis stomped the ground, anything to keep warm, then, wrapping himself in his arms, each rubbing its mate, he resumed the hunt.

Why the temple? The answer became clear when he arrived at the dark shape—the gateway of the Northern Drawbridge—and saw at its base a male, human body. Below a copious beard the throat was open, slit in gross facsimile of a laughing mouth, blood vomiting through parted, pulpy lips. And, of course, there was the usual scooped-out cranium, adrift on red starlit puddles. This time Francis could not rise to nausea. Whether actual or holojected, the gaudy violence of Quetzalians no longer shocked him. He felt only a renewed purpose in his mission. Tez must die. That was all. Every other truth dropped away.

It was the easiest decision he had ever made.

The portcullis was raised, its long fangs reduced by the night to a black cutout. Beyond, the lowered bridge reached across a wide ribbon of frozen noctus. Francis advanced, booting snowchunks off the planks and watching them explode on the ice below. Here and there the day's thaw had penetrated the snow completely, dotting the river with great round pools that seemed to suck the light from the stars, leaving behind only the blind sheen of polished obsidian.

In the distance a green light burned. Francis kicked at the nearest snow until a patch of oak lay ready to receive his body. He sprawled chest-down, sliding his legs over the edge of the bridge and easing himself by degrees toward the ice. At the point of no return he pushed away and, without losing his balance, dropped two meters into a slushy mound of snow. His senses collected, he forced his heel through the slush and in slow motion began hammering, ready to run for the wall at the first hint of frailty.

But the river was hard as a fossil. Satisfied, he struck out for Tez's campfire.

Crossing the first ice pool, he recalled his initial impressions of noctus. The moat harbored evil—you could feel it—but not the crude mindless evil that sickens good souls. Noctus was creative evil.

It was evil made tame and holy.

"Who's there?" Tez's voice drifted feebly on the nightwind. "Don't come any closer. That gatekeeper had a firemoss knife. I'll split your head."

He stopped abruptly near the third ice pool. She was probably telling the truth. What chance had he against an armed, practiced killer? To advance was suicide.

Studying the wan plain that stretched between himself and Tez's campfire, Francis realized that he knew this place—not from direct observation but from his map studies in the Library of Iztac. He knew, for example, that while she probably thought her camp lay on the far bank, the river grew so wide here that she was practically . . . in its center!

And suddenly Francis saw exactly how he would do it.

"I'm in pain," Tez called. "I wrecked my hand on the bastard's jaw."

"I wish I could see you," said Francis, letting Tez's pack slide from his shoulders.

"Yes," said Tez, meaning, I wish I could see you too. "I love you."

"Yes." He was on his knees now, chopping into the ice with his firemoss knife. In seconds the blade touched noctus. He sawed in a circle.

"You're going to kill me, aren't you?"

Francis lifted the ice disk away. Pinpoints of starlight settled into the flowing gall. Of the knife blade nothing remained but charred and twisted junk.

Tez was babbling now. "We named our own constellation. The Shit Queen!"

Shedding his gloves, Francis opened the vitreousteel cage and grasped Ollie by the thorax. He stroked the bug affectionately, then lowered it into the hole, stopping at mid-thickness and aligning it with the campfire. "Perhaps we'll meet again," he whispered as he jammed Ollie's proboscis hard against the inside surface of the hole.

The beetle responded reliably, behaving as its kind had always behaved and always would behave until extinction knocked on the door: it drilled and shot forward, tunneling through whatever matter blocked its way.

Like tissue under a surgeon's knife, the ice began to part. The incision bled onto blue snow.

Tez kept ranting. "You called me a cannibal! You think I can *control* this?"

Francis backed away from the treacherous rivulet, kicking the cage as he went. It scudded across the ice and burrowed into a snowdrift. "There's an old cannibal joke!" he shouted, hoping to distract her. "A missionary says to the native chieftain, 'I know a horrible rumor. I've heard that you kill people and eat them.' And the chieftain replies, 'Yes, it's true. But I know a rumor that's even more horrible. I've heard that you kill people and *don't* eat them.' "

Too late, Tez saw it coming. Ever-advancing, a hissing geyser steamed upward from the beetle's swirling proboscis. A terrible ripping sound, the ripping of a giant's bedsheet, spread through the frigid night.

Suddenly the creature was past her, and she found herself facing an ugly silver-black crack. On the other side, spurting noctus attacked her campfire. She turned dizzily and broke for the shore, but the way was fissured. The shelf beneath her feet snapped off. Her weight upended it.

She went down soundlessly, surrendering to the current, and the glutinous sins of Quetzalia rolled over her like an ebony coffin lid.

BENUMBED, FRANCIS DID NOT STIR from the opening to the *Cortexclavus* tunnel. He wept as children do, with discharges from his nose as well as his eyes, the mucus making stiff waxy stains on his face. He was trying to find some way out, a door—perhaps he should gulp the noctus, let it carve open his throat, boil the fat of his heart—but there was no door, only the grotesque eminence of his boots, the snow piles, The Toy Queen, everything his stare touched. Unlike his past experiences with violence, this particular one, Francis knew, would never, never end.

27

Darwin, AIRBORNE, gyrated like a wet dog. Snow hurtled outward in all directions until the hull was clear. On the control deck, Burne smiled to see his plan work so well. The shakedown flight completed, he dropped below the clouds and roared across the barren sleeping blueness that showed on the monitor.

Its ice gone, the river made of hate zoomed up, a running sore on the land: though far from over, winter was clearly in remission.

Considering that she had been so long encased in snow, *Darwin* performed miraculously. She needed no major repairs, save a new viewbubble to replace the one eaten by the damn bug. But Burne's thoughts were not on *Darwin*. They were on his stump.

The healing had taken a full opoch. He passed these days in planning rejoinders to anyone who might ever call him crippled. Galileo Institute intellectuals he would threaten with physical harm. Crippled? You want to see crippled? Wait till I tie a sheepshank in your spinal cord. (He makes a sudden move, and the intellectual runs fearfully away.) In the case of his Nearth Police Academy buddies, satisfaction would lie only in baffling them. Crippled? Just remember: behind closed doors, laughter sounds like crying. (The buddy smiles weakly.)

Once out of bed, Burne set about mastering his crutches. The vile appendages at first made him feel like some mutant that Nature kept around only to remind herself never to try three legs again. Phantom-limb pain, from which he suffered acutely, complicated his rehabilitation. But then one afternoon he found himself oscillating around the hospital corridors, happily convinced that crutches made him a wilder character than ever.

On this same day, Tepec hummed with a rumor. The last neurovore had been hunted down and killed by Francis Lostwax.

But close behind came a second rumor, muzzling all cheers. The mass murderer was not a neurovore but a Chimec Hospital surgeon driven mad by a noctus overdose. When Francis himself, stumbling into Tepec with a thirty-day beard, confessed to the swarming crowds that his victim was Dr. Tez Yon, Burne became so disturbed that his missing leg began immediately to ache.

Burne had reasons to be furious at Francis. Francis had lied—not only about the Quetzalians regarding their general as a savior (hell, they'd sooner erect a statue to a child molester) but the real purpose of his trip to Cuz (how did he ever bring himself to kill her?). Yet Burne was not furious at Francis. He was in awe. After all, he mused, a Hero of Quetzalia fantasy was exactly what my one-legged ego needed at the time. And Lostwax *could* have blamed me for that whole Tez Yon disaster. I'm the one who decided that Quetzalians aren't human.

And so, as *Darwin* chewed a broad furrow in the snows lining the moat banks, Burne found himself looking forward to the imminent homeward voyage. In the coming weeks he would try to get to know, really know, this sad, peculiar entomologist. He had obviously underestimated the man.

IN A SNUG SANCTUM in the Temple of Iztac, by a hearth that projected its audience as massive shadows on the plastered walls, Francis Lostwax and Vaxcala Coatl took afternoon tea.

"I understand that you got your insect back," said Vaxcala, trying to rescue a foundering conversation.

"A wallmender spotted the cage, and *Cortexclavus* was
only a few meters away." Francis's voice ached with
an unfathomable weariness. "My guess is that the specimen surfaced soon after reaching the shore, then turned
around."

The reunion with *Cortexclavus* had been notably joyless.
For Francis the thing was now permanently tainted.

He no longer called it Ollie.

Still, he did not intend to let the specimen's newfound
connotations keep him from a Poelsig Award.

Vaxcala said, "Are you depressed?"

"Not exactly. I feel . . . contaminated."

"Con-tam-i-na-ted." Vaxcala rolled the word around,
found it to her liking. "Yes, good. You'd never harmed anyone before?"

"On Nearth they give you a yeastgun for your thirteenth
birthday," said Francis coldly, "and if you bag a school-
teacher you're considered an adult. I thought you knew
that." A sudden shame whipped through him. "I'm sorry. I
get bored with hating myself, so I try hating Quetzalia."

"Do you?"

"What?" Francis's shadow grew as he went to the fire.

"Hate Quetzalia?"

"No." He turned and watched his huge twin on the wall.
"If Nearth ever learns about this planet, it won't be from
me or Burne."

Vaxcala gulped tea, left a tear's worth. "Good. But that's
not why I invited you here."

Francis frowned, not at Vaxcala but at Vaxcala's shadow.

"It occurred to me, Dr. Lostwax, that somebody from
Tepec ought to say good-bye to you. You went through hell
for us. So . . ." She approached, smiled, and gently slipped
her hand into his.

Francis was moved, a condition he proceeded to conceal
under bitterness. "You owe me no gratitude, Vaxcala, only

blame." He shook her hand with the same detached efficiency he might have used to steal the ring off a corpse. "I'm the *real* mass murderer."

"I'll make that clear at her funeral."

"Do all surgeons rate an oration from their high priestess?"

"No. Tez is special."

"Because she died violently?"

"Because her tragedy teaches us that noctus is . . . noctus. It's not the answer to anything."

"But she was overdosed by mistake."

"Yes, and until we find a cure for the common mistake, I think we'll go back to total pacifism around here. We'll leave our river in its bed."

"Along with Tez's bones. The cremation will be a flop, Vaxcala. You haven't got a body."

"We could burn her tools, perhaps—her scalpels."

"Why don't you burn me?" said Francis, almost meaning it.

"No. That would be . . . violent." Her smile was sly.

"Tez's victims, they all had friends, families."

"Yes. But you misunderstand Quetzalians if you think they'd relish any actual suffering on your part."

"So instead they'll rip my flesh in the Temple of Tolca. That won't end their sorrow either. The irony is, Tez *believed* in nonviolence. She didn't even *need* Zolmec."

"It may surprise you to learn that quite a few of us around here believe in nonviolence."

"What I meant is—"

"You meant that Tez was an exquisite person. She is the Heroine of Quetzalia."

Suddenly the weariness lifted. "I'm glad you know," said Francis slowly.

As she often did, Vaxcala measured the sanctum with her stride. Nine paces: it never changed. "What do you want out of life, Francis Lostwax?"

Francis smiled. "To never hurt anybody again." His lack

of hesitation surprised him. "To feel clean."

"What do you know, Nearthling—I've decided to bar you from Zolmec no longer. You may, if you wish, attend the next service."

"We're taking off tomorrow afternoon."

"Yes. Just the same—you are now an honorary Quetzalian."

"I feel like I'm receiving a posthumous award."

"You aren't dead, Francis Lostwax."

SOON THEY PARTED, and Francis descended the eastern steps of the great pyramidal library, his thoughts confined to a mild envy of the Quetzalians who tomorrow and the next day and the day after could explore this massive convoluted brain where all knowledge lay stored in countless cells of rolled parchment and bound paper. He looked over his shoulder and saw how Iztac loved her temple. Setting, she kissed it till it went all gold. Back on Nearth, they ought to erect a temple to UW Canis Majoris. He would see to it.

In the plaza below, Quetzalians scurried with apparent happiness and purpose. It hadn't snowed for half an opoch, and the remaining drifts, pushed aside, had long since ceased to slow the public pulse. In Francis's imagination spring bloomed. He saw bright flowers array the causeway with reds and purples. Beyond, a hundred agricultural terraces offered their green succulence to the world. Lagoons shimmered in a rejuvenated sun. Francis smiled. It was an honor to be an honorary Quetzalian.

ON *Darwin*'s CONTROL DECK, the corkscrew beetle sat silently in its cage, thinking cryptic insect thoughts. Having fed his specimen, Francis turned to the holovision monitor and played with the buttons. The screen glowed white, then yellow as Burne switched on the running-lights.

"Damn, but it's good to be near coffee again." Although belted firmly into the pilot's chair, Burne could still reach

Darwin's urn. He pressed the lever and it responded like a squeezed teat, his mamula-shaped mug catching the stream. "At the hospital we drank tea till we pissed it. You could serve our urine samples at a ladies' lunch, and if you had a lemon nobody would know." He emptied the mug in three slurps.

Francis said nothing.

"This phantom-limb pain is the damnedest thing," Burne continued, refilling his mug. "I wonder if eunuchs have phantom testicles."

"That's where the ghosts come from," said Francis dully.

"You'd better go strap down, chum."

Francis hammered his boot against the metal floor. I'm ready to say it now, he thought. My mind is rooted.

"Burne, there's something you should know about this trip."

"What?"

"I'm not going on it."

Burne spat coffee. "God's holy fastball!"

"I thought you'd say something like that."

"You're pulling my phantom limb."

"I want to make Quetzalia my home."

"For what *conceivable* reason?"

"I like the weather."

Burne pointed to the vitreousteel cage. "What about your Poelsig Award?"

"I don't sacrifice it with ease—be assured of that. But there are insects on Luta, too. Experiments to do. The next time you visit Arete—you're certain to get financed—release the beetle. There's no life for it here."

"*She* converted you, didn't she?"

"Tez was a person, not a pronoun."

"Tez converted you."

"You were always envious of me and Tez. That's why you never use her name." In a sudden hara-kiri move, Francis unzipped his pressure suit.

"Let's not *quarrel*, Francis."

"All right, yes. She *did* convert me." He moved to the cage, lifted the lid. "She converted me from the first day I met her."

"I thought you were an atheist."

"I am. But I believe in what they're trying to do here." He stroked *Cortexclavus* with his index finger.

Burne pried a splinter from one of his crutches. "It won't be easy keeping this place a secret."

"You can do it."

"There might be an investigation."

"You're a capital liar." Peeling the last of his suit away, Francis walked toward Burne.

"People will want to know why you didn't come back."

"You'll think of something."

"How Kappie and Luther died."

"Place the savages on Arete. Nobody goes there." Francis brushed Burne's crutch. Burne put it aside.

The men pressed together in awkward affection.

"I'll miss you, friend," said Francis, drawing away.

"Yes." Burne went back to his coffee. "I'll forward your mail."

MINUTES LATER Francis stood on the far bank of the river made of hate, watching *Darwin*'s lights rise like moons and glide across the night. A halo of ions encircled the chem-thruster's exhaust. Knowing he was too dim to show on the monitor, Francis waved without enthusiasm.

The gatekeeper of the moment, a blowzy man in his thirties, trudged across the drawbridge and drew up next to Francis. "You'll have to come inside. I'm raising the bridge."

Francis kept watching the ship. "I'm Dr. Lostwax, the Nearthling."

The gatekeeper imitated Francis's gaze. *Darwin*'s lights congealed into a solitary, shrinking dot. "Was he your friend?"

"Not a *good* friend. Not like—"

"That's quite a machine." He tracked the dot with his finger.

"Why are you raising the bridge?"

"I have to go to church tonight."

Francis followed his companion to the windlass, then continued alone through the gateway. He gave himself X-ray vision, imagining the wired chapels that surrounded him. As he stepped onto the sand, the squeal of the windlass announced the bridge's ascent. A hollow bong: it was raised. Hoisting his collar against the nightwind, Francis began the long walk back to Tepec.

When he reached the forest, his ears caught the low wail of a Zolmec hymn. Now the night lost its blackness. Four hundred shimmering robes waltzed the wind. Sleeves and hems moved in ghostly undulation. Slowly the parish advanced through the trees, lanterns sparkling like the faces of Light People.

Francis stopped near a bush, waiting for the white tide to sweep over him. When it came he allowed it to control him, turn him, bear him back to the sands.

The parish got no sermons that night, no tales of Janet Vij, only a short improvised speech by Mouzon Thu. He waddled back and forth atop the temple, exclaiming in his musical voice how grand it was to see the bridge up again. He hoped that it would remain up.

A young woman at Francis's shoulder shuffled in discontent. "We aren't here for *politics*, Mouzon," she growled softly. Francis turned and beheld a face that by lantern light looked staggeringly strong and smooth, as if shaped from bronze. He had seen this comeliness before, but he couldn't place it.

"Cut his leg off, Ticoma," whispered a clinging young man, probably her husband.

Ticoma chuckled. Francis's memory still failed. "I'd do it," she said.

"Really?" asked her husband.

"In my dreams—but tonight I've got bigger fish to fry. I need to get back at you about that freeloader remark."

"Fry away," said the husband amiably.

Mouzon began the benediction. "Are you ready, followers? Are you ready to cast your sins, your biophotonic sins, into the river made of hate?"

"Yes!"

"Are you ready to tame your instincts and appease your teeth? Are you ready to show Chimec, god of the human brain, the black humming pitch that pastes your dreams together?"

"Yes!"

Francis was readiest of all. When Mouzon removed his cranium, Francis was the first to do likewise. Braced for a chill, he felt nothing, recalling in time that the human brain is nerveless as a brick.

All along the wall, cortices rose from heads like eggs from eggcups.

"To the temple!" screamed Mouzon.

As the pilgrims mounted the stairs and filed into the hatchways, Francis kept his glance on Ticoma, determined that this time he would not get lost. Around corners, through corridors, down, down, he followed the bob of her lantern.

At last a vaulted decagon yawned before him. Nine pilgrims, Ticoma included, distributed themselves about the room. Each vanished through the handiest door. The tenth chapel is mine, Francis thought.

Once inside, he rested his cranium near the red cushion and plucked the electrode from its cradle. The chapel groaned to life. Lifting the electrode, he pushed it deep into his cerebral commissure, where it stayed erect, like a spoon in pudding.

He turned his eyes, his kinepic-addict's eyes, to the screen. Within its walls green haze swirled and bubbled in languid revolution. Francis molded the haze, pressing it with his thoughts, slapping it with his passions.

A swamp emerged. He recognized it. Half a kilometer from this place he had gone to elementary school.

Francis concentrated.

A small-eyed, curly-haired boy squished across the screen, briefcase in tow. Suddenly a shadow unfurled, blocking his path. "They in there?" asked the shadow's owner, an especially farty incarnation of Robert Poogley.

"My best insects," the boy assured him. Robert Poogley snatched the briefcase, clawed at the latches, flipped back the lid . . .

When it was over Francis lingered in the chapel, watching his hostility ebb. A small contribution, not the monument Tez deserved, but a beginning at least. He felt sleepy and bathed—also clever.

Just before it jumped, he had figured out how to make the corkscrew beetle smile.